THE IMPAVIDUS CYCLE BOOK ONE

BIRTHRIGHT

M.A. VICE

This is a work of fiction. Names, characters, places, and incidents either are the product of the author's imagination or are used fictitiously. Any resemblance to actual persons, living or dead, events, or locales is entirely coincidental.

Special thanks to everyone who listened to me go on and on about this book for the last decade, who encouraged me, and helped me see this thing through to the end.

To my awesome friends: Mimi, Syd, James, Jon, and anyone else who has indulged me, helped me brainstorm, let me learn about my characters through your own amazing stories. Thank you for nurturing and cultivating a creative atmosphere that helped me make my story the best it could be.

Thank you to Mom and Dad, who always have my back.

CHAPTER I

All was quiet and still as the sun set on the woods, the heavy chill of autumn settling down to the forest floor. Distantly, the sounds of the nearby village faded as its denizens finished the last of their daily tasks, glad to shut themselves into the comfort of warm cabins and glowing hearths and forget the encroaching dark that surrounded them.

Up the mountain far beyond the village walls, beneath a great tree, a child slept. He had been there for some time, nestled into the deadfall, unnoticed by the hunters as they returned from their day's work and the children that played in the deep woods. The light sharpness of the cold air cut through the thin clothes he wore, rousing him from his deep slumber.

Eyes the color of flames, set in a thin, angular face, opened slowly, focusing to take in dimly lit surroundings. His pale skin, dashed with freckles, stood out against the blackness that surrounded him.

The child blinked several times, peering around at the dim forest curiously without moving. He curled deeper into the shallow hollow in the earth, breathing in the old musk of soil and long-dead leaves.

Long, tangled tresses of crimson hair spilled over his shoulders and into his eyes as he sat up slowly. He brushed the locks away as he carefully stood, using a tree for support. His legs were weak, they nearly buckled beneath him, but he steadied himself enough to remain standing. A shiver wracked his slender frame.

After a few long moments of observation, he moved slowly, weakly pushing himself to a sitting position. Bits of dirt and grass clung to the loose clothing he wore, and he carefully tried to brush them away, finding his movements sluggish and clumsy.

Welcome to the world of humans, child. I have led you here from our own world.

A voice spoke into his mind, mingling with his own thoughts. It was warm and powerful, startling him from his daze. He turned around in place, trying to place its source, but found nothing but darkness and empty air.

The voice gave a soft laugh. *You can search for me, but it will prove difficult, as I am housed within your being.*

He staggered back and fell against the tree, having lost his footing after the small fright the voice in his mind had given him. The roughness of the bark as it scraped his back drew an audible wince, and his breath fogged before him.

Careful now, my child, the voice crooned. *Your legs have little strength as of yet. Even with my help, walking here from the dark world on them proved difficult...*

The boy's understanding of the words spoken by the presence within him was vague at best. The presence communicated with images, feelings... fragments of the boy's own memory. The feeling of companionship, a consciousness separate from his own, was comforting, and he clung to it as he struggled to make sense of his surroundings. Everything was unfamiliar. The musty scent of decaying foliage on the forest floor, the chill of the early autumn air, the sound of the wind through the trees.

He had no memory before he had awakened. Everything in his mind was black and empty, everything but the voice that was not his own. Looking down at himself, the boy felt an odd sense of detachment as he examined his own body, turning his hands over, clenching them in fists. He wore a loose tunic and trousers, made of earthen-colored canvas. His eyes slowly adjusted to the darkness beyond him, and he shuddered again at the cold that surrounded him.

My name is Lucifurius, the voice said carefully, making sure the boy understood. *I have no body of my own, so I entrust myself to you to carry me. In turn, I hope you will entrust yourself to me... So that I may guide us both on a path of success.*

This voice was his only companion, the only thing there to offer him any guidance. He embraced it without reservation, feeling safe within its gentle grasp on his thoughts.

The boy moved forward slowly, watching his own feet. He was barefoot, and his steps were shaky and hesitant as he moved cautiously across the ground that pricked at the delicate soles of his feet.

Before I found you, you had never moved, nearly your whole life has been spent in slumber, Lucifurius explained, with a hint of understanding patience. *You will find it difficult at first, but I will assist you in becoming stronger. Now, we need sustenance. There is a human settlement close. I will lead you there, and then, we hunt.*

Hunger. Drained and in need of energy. He associated the feeling with the hunt the voice spoke of.

You learn most quickly, my child.

The detritus of the forest floor crackled beneath the boy's feet. He looked past the trees down the mountain to the faint lights of the village below, drawn to the newness of the sight, quickly forgetting the things that laid behind him. He climbed over the obstacles in his path, carefully balancing himself as he made his way down the steep mountain. His hair fluttered around his face in the wind.

Something cold dropped on his face from above, and he looked up at the dark expanse of the sky above him, flinching as a drop of rain fell into his open eye. He rubbed at his face in his alarm, wavering unsteadily where he stood.

You are alright. Merely a drop of water, certainly no match for such a powerful force as we are, Lucifurius said with a dash of amusement. The boy felt calmed by his voice and the feeling of safety that enveloped him as he heard it.

He continued on forward through the thick forests, watching the lights in the distance shimmer and twinkle in the dark. His curiosity slowly turned inward, and within his mind he reached for Lucifurius. Like a newborn child, puzzled and inquisitive.

Lucifurius seemed to sense his wordless questions, and proceeded to offer explanation. *I am the ruler of a world beyond the one in which we stand now. You are my vessel... and my child. Together we will gain strength, and return to our home when I have amassed the power to create for myself a physical form.*

The boy felt his understanding growing, and the meaning of the words more clear as time passed. There was much more he wished to learn, he was hungry for more knowledge.

He stumbled and fell, crying out, the sharpness of his own voice startling him. Pain flared from his knee and he rolled over to find a shallow gash, a steady trickle of blood flowing from it. He watched the trickle uneasily for a moment until the pain faded and the flow came to a steady stop, his chest stinging with cold air as he drew sharp breaths.

I will help you to heal your wounds. It is essential that this body be protected... It houses the both of us, after all.

The boy slowly pushed himself up to his feet, trying to remain steady. The shallow gash quickly faded, leaving only the faintest smear of blood as the pain evaporated.

His body gained strength as he continued his path down the mountain. The first few hours of his trek had been spent tripping, stumbling, struggling to remain on his feet. But in time he walked with a steady, even gait. Though his bare feet had taken a beating, scraped up by the rough ground beneath him, they had begun to toughen, and he had learned to tread more carefully.

There are humans near to us, in the settlement ahead. You are not one of them, no... But you appear as one, which will allow you to move among them more freely. Still, child, you must be careful.

The boy silently accepted the instruction, continuing along in the direction Lucifurius had sent him. By this point, his need for nourishment had grown to an uncomfortable level, and though he was strong enough to walk, his body ached with fatigue and famine.

When he got close enough to the village walls, he slowed to a stop and hid himself in the edge of the brush, observing carefully. He could see that there were humans moving around within. There were all sorts, some as small as himself, darting around the streets, shrieking with laughter. The elder and larger among them yelling in sharp voices for them to hush. A few carried strange tools, food, and firewood, weaving in and out of the rows of small huts they resided in.

They are preparing for the approaching winter. Humans are beholden to the whims of nature, but we will not face such hindrances.

The boy was aware of a strange essence lingering in the air around him, similar to the presence of Lucifurius within his mind, but much weaker.

Life. This is the force you feel around you.

The boy carefully crawled closer to watch the humans move, awaiting more explanation from Lucifurius.

You are slowly growing strong, but your body is not invincible, as you have seen... And I can heal you only so much before the wounds become too grievous for us both. You require some form of protection. A weapon will provide you a means to defend yourself as well. There is a place to obtain both. Enter the building on the wall, and I will help you to take what you need.

It was as if some force moved his eyes to the direction he had been instructed to go, and the boy made his way through the gate and along the edge of the wall to a humble stone structure with smoke rising from the chimney. He opened the door slowly, the old wooden floor creaking as he stepped in. A fire burned bright in the hearth, casting a warm light through the room, and he looked in awe at the collection of weapons before him. Blades of varying length, fashioned of glinting steel. He ran his fingers over the cold metal, enjoying the smoothness beneath his fingertips.

He settled on the sword that shone brightest in the firelight and lifted the blade from its mounts. Taken by surprise by its weight, he let it fall, the tip sinking into the wood of the floor.

“Careful, there, boy,” a low voice rumbled behind him. “Those there are sharp.”

The boy gasped and whirled around to face the source of the voice, finding himself facing a man. His heavy boots clomped noisily across the hollow floor as he approached. He was large, well-muscled, nearly twice the boy's size.

“Looking for a weapon, boy? That one looks a bit big for you, and it isn't cheap either. I doubt you could pay for it, from the look of you. I could help you find something better suited to you.”

The boy looked at the man, hearing his words but unable to form his own in response. After a long moment of silence, confusion overtook the man's expression.

“Can't speak, can you? Well, let's put that blade back and we'll find you another. Plain to see you’ll have trouble lifting it, much less wielding it.”

The child felt Lucifurius’ presence clutch around him protectively. *Pay no heed to this man. He does not know your strength. If this is the blade you wish for, my child, then this is the blade you shall have. I will help you to carry it.*

A surge of strength coursed through the boy’s body, and he found himself lifting the sword with surprising ease. The movement felt odd and unnatural as Lucifurius guided his body into position from within, pointing the end of the blade at the man’s head.

Realizing his mistake, the man backed away slowly, eyes widening.

“C-careful with that, boy. If you really want it, then fine, I'll sell it to you. But – let's be reasonable, it's expensive. I can't sell it to you for anything less than full price.”

Now, I will teach you how to hunt, my son. This one will be our first prey.

The boy took another step forward as Lucifurius urged him on, and the look in the man's eyes became more fearful as he was backed against the wall.

“I'll give you another one. Don't fool around like this. Put it down.”

The boy studied the man curiously, finding it difficult to comprehend this display of emotion. His hands were raised, fingers splayed, his posture tense. It made the boy uncomfortable, and he drew back slightly.

Go on, now. Use the weapon...

“Stay back!” the man cried, grabbing another sword from the wall and swinging in the boy’s direction.

The boy felt Lucifurius deftly move his arms into position to parry the incoming strike. The man staggered back – Lucifurius was quick to see the moment of weakness.

Now, boy! Strike!

With all the force he could muster, the boy followed his instinct and brought the sword down in a strong arc into the man's neck. The blade tore diagonally down through his chest, rending through flesh and bone with a wet crunching sound. Blood sprayed from the wound, and a bewildered look crossed the man's eyes before he collapsed. A weak groan escaped him, but quickly faded to a muffled gurgling of blood as the life left him.

A swell of pride from Lucifurius. *Well done! You will be a force to be feared, indeed.*

The boy stared down at the pool of blood as it seeped across the floor, soaking into the old wood. He felt uneasy... But before he could reach out to Lucifurius for guidance, a wave of power overtook him. It was dizzying... euphoric. His body was poised with alien strength.

The wave of raw energy faded after a moment, but the emptiness of starvation was filled. The exhaustion and weakness that had plagued him was gone.

The force of life sustains us. We must harvest it from other sources... adding it to our own power. In time, once we have gathered enough, I will be able to create a body for myself.

This is the power we seek. And that was only one weakling, my child.

Only one... it was only one! If just one held this much strength, this much substance... What would more be?

What would this whole village be...?

That thought was staggering. The thought that so much power existed, his for the taking, was almost incomprehensible.

But before you move on, that wall behind you... On that wall is armor. It will protect you from injuries you cannot sustain.

He stepped over the corpse of the man, examining the armor and clothing that hung on the wall. Lucifurius urged him away from a bulkier suit of shining plate, from a leather coat with a woolen lining – *Too heavy, you will lose all ability to move quickly... Too light, and you are vulnerable. You will need shoes as well.*

Lucifurius guided him to a rack of boots in the corner, told him how to wind the cloth wraps around his feet before he slipped them on. He laced up the boots, his fingers clumsy, and stood, feeling awkward, separated from the ground by the thick sole of the shoe. He took a few careful steps around the room, noting that his footsteps now made sound on the hollow wood floor, where before his movements had been all but silent.

He looked over the armor on the walls, selecting pieces Lucifurius guided him to. Between leather and metal plate, his selections would keep him well protected. The boy encountered some difficulty, wrestling with the leather straps that fastened each piece until the armor was securely in place.

It was then that his attention was drawn to an odd sight on the wall – the skull of a beast.

A symbol of death. This suits us.

Attached to the skull were short antlers – they clearly did not belong to whatever manner of beast this has been in life, and made its appearance unsettling.

The boy took the skull from where it was mounted on the wall and turned it around in his grasp, curiously examining it before placing it over his head. It had been carved and fashioned to be worn as a mask.

A perfect visage for us to don.

Pleased with Lucifurius' approval, the boy found he liked the mask, and the way it veiled his face from view. Hidden in its shadow, he was less exposed.

He stepped out of the shop, feeling more comfortable moving across the cold ground now that his feet were protected. He held the bloodied sword at his side and rounded the side of the building. The humans in the distance did not look his way, and he watched them curiously for a moment.

The boy jumped, startled, instinctively raising the sword to defend himself, as a young man approached the doorway. He carried a bucket of water, and slowed to a cautious stop as he looked over the boy standing there, bloody sword in hand.

As the man seemed to realize what had just transpired in the smithy, he dropped the bucket and reached for a hatchet on his belt. The boy watched with detached curiosity as he lunged forward, and Lucifurius jolted him to action once more, bringing him to parry as he had before.

Kill him.

The young man was much smaller than the man inside had been, closer to the boy's own size, and the boy overtook him easily, pushing back against him and knocking the hatchet from his hands with an upward sweep of the sword. His movements were clumsy, but Lucifurius was able to augment his strength enough, just for the moment, that a second sweep of the sword removed the top half of the man's head. The boy stepped back as the corpse fell forward, soaking the ground in blood.

He was again staggered by the rush that followed. The surge of strength from the first kill had been nearly overwhelming, and this one left him momentarily paralyzed, unsure of how to process the raw energy that followed. It seemed entirely too much.

This will not sate us long. We need more.

He moved forward to the village itself. Sounds echoed across the streets – footsteps, voices. The cobbled stones he moved across felt strange beneath his feet, too hard and too smooth.

Ahead of him, a group of humans was moving down the other side of the street, coming toward him. He could sense their life force through

Lucifurius – weaker than the two he'd just killed, but Lucifurius urged him to confront them just the same.

They took note of him and slowed to a stop. The man held out a hand to signal to the woman and two children that trailed him to wait, and he cautiously approached the boy. The boy waited patiently as the man, weathered-looking but tall and strong, approached him. There was no hostility in his expression yet, but he seemed suspicious.

"I haven't seen you here before, sir." The boy took a single step back, fighting between instincts that urged him to flee and his desire for more of the power this prey had to offer. "Who are you?"

The boy looked him up and down, and stepped back again.

"Can you not speak? Is something wrong--?"

The boy ran him through with the sword, then, planted a foot in the man's gut, and pushed him off the end of his blade. He fell to the ground, features frozen in bewilderment.

As the rush of life force emboldened the boy, Lucifurius urged him in the direction of the woman, still standing frozen in fear at the other side of the street. She tried to move to defend herself, but the boy cut her down easily, slashing her arms out of the way before thrusting the blade through her throat.

The two children looked on in wide-eyed, unmoving horror as he stared them down. They whimpered.

He recoiled – there was some odd familiarity in the sound, the smell of blood... Their fear seeped its way into him, he could feel it in the very air.

It dawned on him that he was the cause of this fear, and he froze where he stood.

The children bolted, wailing in terror, before he could pursue them.

Every nerve in his body was buzzing and alive, and he felt breathless and overstimulated. He studied the blood flecked across his gauntlets, watching it drip onto the cobbles beneath his feet.

You do well, but we will need far more than that.

The boy heard more humans nearing him, and he started, his body tense with fear. He turned and rushed for the gate, where he'd entered. His movements were clumsy and awkward, restricted by the newness of his armor and the unfamiliar strength that surged through him.

He could hear the humans close behind him in pursuit, and he moved more swiftly, dashing through the village gate and out into the forests, weaving through the trees, his heavy boots crunching on the ruins of the forest floor.

Fatigue had begun to slow his movements by the time the boy stopped to rest beneath the canopy of trees. He panted, peering through his mask of bone as he looked back over his shoulder, listening carefully for signs of his pursuers.

Their voices were sharp, but distant. With mild relief, he moved deeper into the safety of the darkness.

They will not follow you this far, my child. They fear what lurks in the dark more than they fear you.

The boy looked over himself as he finally stopped, leaning against a tree. Blood covered everything. The shining steel blade of the sword he had taken was splattered crimson up to the hilt. Rivulets of it dripped over the surface of the armor he wore, soaked his underclothes at the armor's open joints. The smell and warmth of it made him uneasy.

Lucifurius took great pleasure in these sensations, and the child found himself pulled into the joy of the praise and joviality that Lucifurius showered upon him.

My pride for you, my child, knows no bounds. I have decided I must bestow you with a designation... a name. The world must have something to call you by as they cower at your feet.

Your name will be Albtraum.

The boy's heart fluttered in an abundance of joy at the name. The feeling of his own existence, his identity, had begun to solidify. He was eager to engage his next foe, eager to please his caretaker.

It is a word used by some humans to name the dreams that make them fear sleep... Dreams of the dark, dreams of the monsters within it. Together we are the essence of the dark, the embodiment of fear itself. Humans have known such fear before only in the darkness of their most sinister dreams, but this time there will be no awakening. Nowhere the dark will not reach. And so, there is truly no name better.

Albtraum... The nightmare from which there is no awakening and no escape.

CHAPTER II

High atop a mountain, hidden away in the crags, a newly built temple stood. The white stones were clean and unblemished in the piercing sunlight that filtered from the newly set windows above, casting the hall in a burst of many colors.

A young woman garbed in white perused the room slowly, watching the last few workers pace the floors as they completed the last of their work. The building of these temples marked a new beginning for the organization she belonged to – and thoughts of where this new path might lead them made her somewhat uneasy.

She turned to the entrance when she heard footsteps approaching, her golden hair falling over her shoulders.

"Good day, Ishtar."

She nodded and smiled slightly in greeting to the approaching scholar, her oldest and closest friend. Though they belonged to the same developing Order, the rigid separation interposed between them in recent years by their chosen paths often made it difficult to remember they were meant to be allies and not rivals.

"Good day to you as well, Septimus. What brings you here?" she asked, her tone made uncomfortably formal and proper by the fact that they were not alone and free to speak as affectionately as they normally would.

Septimus smiled, stopping in front of her. He, in contrast to her, wore the deep indigo and black robes of the members of the Order who had chosen the path of darkness. His hair, which fell to his shoulders, was silver, and his eyes were a dark shade of slate-gray. The color of the lake in the autumn, she thought. "I thought to see how the construction was progressing, and to pay you a visit."

"But... Shouldn't you be—" She stopped.

"At the lower temple down the mountain, with the rest of my lot?" His smile faded, just barely, and he seemed the slightest bit hurt. He clearly knew that Ishtar had not entirely avoided the prejudices of her position – the leaders and organizers of the Order. Though her thoughts of superiority were largely unconscious, she did her best to quell them when they arose.

Ishtar shook her head, internally chiding herself for thinking herself above him, even for a moment. "Forgive me. I meant no offense. Rather, it seems odd that you'd come, there really is nothing here for someone in your position. I thought you might have more to gain from time spent with your fellow scholars, not us peacekeepers... I'm afraid you'll find this visit to be a waste of time."

Septimus shook his head. "Not at all, I believe our coexistence is vital to the survival of this Order. I believe we should spend time in each other's respective domains. I was hoping I would find you here, actually..."

"Oh? And why, pray tell?"

"I find your views on the world fascinating, Ishtar. I can never fathom them for the life of me, no matter how many of the peacekeepers explain them, but still... I love to talk of them." He looked wistfully at her, his

expression softened. "As much as we talk, our ideologies never come into conversation, I'm afraid."

Ishtar smiled slightly at him, carefully watching the people milling around them to deter eavesdroppers. "And what would you like to speak about?"

"You who follow the light find your power in faith. You believe in that which is intangible, that which you cannot see, cannot hear, cannot feel. That which may not exist. Your view lies entirely in perception. Your duty is to carry out the will of our superiors without question, and ensure others do the same."

Ishtar stepped forward. "Do you mock our way of life, Septimus?"

"Of course not, Ishtar. Allow me to continue." He began to pace, slowly, but his gaze never left her eyes. "We of the dark draw strength from knowledge, from understanding. We seek enlightenment on everything, and do not believe in that which we cannot observe."

Ishtar blinked. "What, then?"

"I want to learn, Ishtar. I want to learn this world's secrets, I want to know its origin. I seek knowledge, knowledge that I cannot possibly hope to gain from human teachings. And I cannot obtain that on tangibility and observations alone."

She felt her heartbeat quicken. He wouldn't. Septimus... She had always known he had far-fetched ideas, ever since they were children, but this seemed especially mad. She'd had her suspicions in the past about Septimus's dealings with the dark beings whose names none dared to speak, worshipped but feared, and largely left alone, but he could not possibly be seeking out the absolute knowledge forbidden to any human...

He could not be that foolish.

Still, she felt she had to ask him. She had to hear it from him to reassure herself.

"...What are you planning, Septimus?"

"A symposium with the dark. I want to know it all, Ishtar. I want to know everything." He smiled, the same gentle smile he always gave her. The smile that had swayed her to his side on so many matters, and threatened to do the same now. "You see, I believe that as powerful as our lifestyles are on their own, they can become almighty when united... I am going to attempt communication with the beings of the dark world... I will put faith in that darkness... In order to achieve absolute knowledge."

"You do realize what this would mean?" she asked him, an edge entering her voice. "You will upset our careful balance... you could destroy everything, Septimus!"

He couldn't do this, she knew, if anyone else of the order learned what he was planning, he would be executed. But he sounded so reasonable about it. He truly believed he could gain something from this.

He shook his head, turning slowly. "I will be in control of the knowledge I gain. Think of it, Ishtar, think of what I could do for the world, if I knew that much." His voice was softer now, the words a promise. "I...I had hoped you would be more accepting. But alas, I hoped in vain. In time, you will come to understand..."

Ishtar stood frozen in place, helpless to do anything but watch as he turned and slowly exited the room, his footsteps fading eerily into the hallways.

She could not call out to him, clinging to a weak hope that he would abandon this folly on his own.

Albtraum travelled slowly as days passed, reaching the foot of the mountains and lingering in the quiet safety of the forests there.

He was huddled under a rocky outcropping as storm clouds rolled in, finding himself too exhausted to sleep. There was a chill to the air, but it was somewhat warmer where it was dry. His hands wandered over the smooth stone behind him, and he dug the toes of his boots into the soft earth beneath him.

As the rain began to fall more heavily, he removed his mask, setting it aside, and curled in on himself to lay down in the small indent in the earth he'd sat in. He looked up at the grey skies above, watching curiously as the clouds rolled and swirled into themselves, glimpses of sunlight shining through as they did. The ground was high enough here that the rain did not seep into the outcropping, and he watched with sleepy interest as small streams of rainwater formed around him, running over the ground and pooling in the dips and indents at it streamed down the face of the mountain.

Even with Lucifurius' guidance, Albtraum still found the world was vast and overwhelming, and for the time, he was happy to huddle beneath the rocks as the gentle storm poured over the woods.

I suppose it is time I taught you more of our purpose, my child.

Intrigued, Albtraum fidgeted with his mask as he waited somewhat impatiently for Lucifurius to go on. Lucifurius' lessons were a point of great interest for him, and he craved more information about the world and his place in it.

So eager for knowledge... Strange, my child, but you sometimes call to me the memory of someone I knew long ago. The first body to host me.

Ah, but that is a story for another time.

You know that we must hunt to gain power, and that we are not of this world. We will return home someday, when I have gathered power enough to take physical form. I will reassert my place as the ruler of our world.

Albtraum hadn't known that Lucifurius held such status, but it did not surprise him. He was so awed by Lucifurius' majesty, it seemed only natural that he should hold a position of great importance.

But the thought that Lucifurius may one day have a body of his own... What would become of Albtraum then? He could not imagine existing separately from Lucifurius, and the thought frightened him.

Fear not, child. Though I will one day take form in this world on my own, you may always remain at my side. I have kept many hosts over my many centuries... but none have served me as well as you have.

Men's hearts are tainted by their own desires—justice, vengeance, power, curiosity.

Power-hungry warlords leading charges into battle, invigorated by the strength I offered them. Pious men who thought they might be able to master me and use me for their own purposes. Men who sought the allure of forbidden knowledge.

I find human desires so tiresome and trivial... They have only served to slow my progress. Many hundreds of years have proved that humans will always be the same, even as the world changes and grows around them. The power hungry eventually grow fat and lazy. The pious are quick to abandon their faith and give in to despair. Those who lust after knowledge soon learn that their minds are not fit to hold it.

No... A child of my own was the only host who could have ever served me properly.

Albtraum felt great pride in knowing that he was of Lucifurius' bloodline. Serving Lucifurius gave him purpose in a world where otherwise none existed.

He sat in silence for quite some time, listening carefully to the sounds around him. His mind wandered as he waited for Lucifurius to go on, lingering over his curiosity for the other world they had come from. Try as he might, his memories did not reach that place... and so, he reached out to Lucifurius for answers, though his own questions were nebulous and ill-formed.

I am the progenitor of our kind, the daemons.

Ours is a noble blood, and I have spread my seed among the humans so that I might have more children... And humans, in their insolence, discard my children as though they were nothing but rubbish. From the time a daemon is born, the thing he has most to fear is the mother whose womb he was birthed from.

To carry a child of mine is a great honor, but they spit upon it. It hurts me so, my child... There are so few of you, but there could be many more.

Faint images passed through Albtraum's thoughts—of squalling infants with bony nubs on their skulls, of screaming women snuffing the lives of their newborns.

He was drawn into the well of deep sorrow that rose up from Lucifurius, bewildered as to how violent and cold this world now seemed.

Those they do not kill are mutilated, formed to the image of the humans themselves...

Visions of older children, with longer horns, crying out for mercy as the pieces of them that marked their daemon heritage were sawed from their heads.

Such was done to you, dear child... Your mother took away your beautiful horns.

Albtraum's hand wandered, as if guided, to his scalp – where he could feel the hard protrusions of his severed horns, just as Lucifurius had described. Three on each side. His scalp had long since healed over them, but they were there.

Astonishment shot through him, and hurt and anguish tightened his chest. From what Lucifurius had taught him, humans were obviously beneath them, but he had never thought that they had been responsible for such horrors.

That is why we must hunt, my child. We must see that these humans are punished for scorning and murdering the sons and daughters I have gifted them with. Your brothers, your sisters... and you.

We must see that justice is done.

Albtraum tugged his cloak tight around his body, and shivered at the chill of the air. Tears welled at the corners of his eyes, and his breaths became quick and strained.

Do not despair, dear child. I will remain with you until every last one of them kneels before us. My children will know peace again.

A month passed.

Albtraum walked, guided by the call of human life, killing any who crossed his path with Lucifurius' careful guidance. Though still inexperienced, his comprehension of the world was increasing, helped along by Lucifurius steadily teaching him more every day.

Lucifurius taught Albtraum about the ways of humans, so that they might better hunt them. He augmented the boy's strength, enabling him to stand against any foe they may face. He whispered praise and instruction, and the bond between the two of them grew strong.

Albtraum observed, he listened to the voice that guided him, he learned. He learned the laws of the world, he learned to read the written word, he learned to interpret the behaviors of humans. Even so, he remained only a transient wanderer in their world, knowing that his home was waiting in another. One day, when the time was right, he would return there.

As Lucifurius had taught him more about the humans and their world, he had come to look on them with hatred and disdain, the images of the slaughter of his kind always burning behind his eyes. The peace of his kin depended upon the downfall in his wake.

He traveled slowly onward, and as he did, rumors traveled ahead of him. Superstitious mutterings of a daemon beast who slaughtered entire villages without mercy gradually became widespread – in some villages, inhabitants found themselves afraid to even step outside the safety of their homes.

As he trudged on through the forests, his path faintly illuminated by the weak light of the rising sun, he could feel it—though it was miles away, he could sense a mass of human souls, the strongest he had ever encountered. He had followed the call well. He wrapped his tattered cloak more tightly around his shoulders as he exited the thick of the woods and entered a clearing. A soft rain was falling, casting a haze over the sights in the distance.

This was to be their next hunting ground, their next harvest of power. Albtraum had come to enjoy hunting – at first, he had found himself unsettled by the terror with which his prey reacted to him, but over time Lucifurius' praise and affection, as well as his hatred for their enemies, had become a strong motivator.

Warriors were the strongest humans of all, and the only humans Albtraum now sought out. Unskilled humans posed no challenge, no threat, and Albtraum tended to avoid them. Though Lucifurius was perplexed by this aversion, he did not oppose it – after all, warriors held a much more enticing strength.

We have never encountered humans in these numbers before. Though your strength far surpasses that of any individual, they vastly outnumber you. It poses a threat... Take care you are not caught off guard.

Albtraum eventually came to the edge of the cliffs and looked out over the place of this human gathering. They were all clad in armor, armed with fine weapons and marching across the field at one another. Watching them all move around in the valley before him made Albtraum anxious to rush into the fray. Where to start? Which one to kill first? But there were so many, and Lucifurius had just warned him that they were quite capable of causing him injury if they wished it.

Albtraum quietly made his way down into the valley, careful to keep himself hidden in the shadows. He watched the clashing groups of humans before him, the cacophony of battle sending a flutter of excitement through his chest.

A smaller group of warriors moved about on the outskirts. Five, perhaps six. He would start with them.

Albtraum closed in on them quickly, as they had stopped to rest. He hid in the thin border of trees at the foot of the cliffs, where he would not be seen, and waited for an opportunity to strike.

One man constantly glanced into the shadows, no doubt trying to source the faint sounds he had heard when Albtraum approached. As the young warrior gathered the attention of his comrades, Albtraum dared not breathe. Any movement would attract attention to his position.

After a few moments, the humans had written off the young man's concerns, and they all turned their attention back to the battle before them.

Albtraum rushed forward.

He drew the sword at his belt and ran through the man closest to him, thrusting it through his back. As the man fell forward, grasping at the blade that stuck out from between his ribs, the rest of the men took notice and quickly turned to face Albtraum, bewildered.

As Albtraum pulled his blade from the man he'd attacked, another human ran at him with a hatchet, catching him across the arm. Albtraum yelped and drew back as blood flowed and the sharp chill of the air stung the edges of the wound. He returned the injury by slashing across the man's chest as the small group of humans erupted into shouts, charging at him. He ducked and weaved to avoid them. They were armed only with rudimentary weapons, a far cry from the men on the battlefield. Perhaps they had not been a part of the battle after all.

He felt Lucifurius take control as he hesitated, his body moving effortlessly outside his control. Albtraum watched as his body moved to fell the rest of the men, easily avoiding their attacks and returning them.

A cry of outrage from another one of the young men. "You son of a *bitch*, you killed my brother! *I'll rip you to shreds!"*

The man picked up the dagger that had moments earlier been in the hands of his now-dead brother and charged, swinging the blade out ahead of him. Albtraum caught it in a parry, breaking the hold their weapons had established on each other, and thrust the sword forward, through the boy's chest. He slammed a booted foot into his stomach and ripped the sword away. More blood soaked the damp earth.

He cut them down to the last man, who faced Albtraum with blade drawn and eyes blazing.

"N-no... My sons, y-you killed them... *You killed them!* You bastard, you murderer! *Who the hell are you?"*

Albtraum stepped forward, flammeous eyes glinting from beneath the shadow of his bone mask.

"I am... That which will remind you humans why you fear the dark."

He had not meant to speak, Lucifurius had spoken through him. It was the first time he had heard his own voice. He liked the way it sounded. His own voice...

"Fear, why is there anything to fear now? My sons are dead, you've taken everything from me! *I'll kill you!*"

The man snatched up a hatchet and lunged, but Albtraum managed to lean out of the way and slashed across the man's throat, leaving him gurgling on his own blood as the life left him.

"Thomas... run..." the man groaned as the last breath escaped him.

A whimper sounded from the bushes, and Albtraum turned in place quickly to place the source – a boy crouched near the bushes, eyes wide with fear, a small hunting knife clutched in his hand. He was a good deal younger than Albtraum himself, clearly not an experienced warrior by any measure.

Albtraum approached the child, weapon raised. The boy was young, perhaps a few years younger than Albtraum himself. He seldom encountered children – they were the first to flee. He had never hunted them down, as they offered little strength.

But this boy had not fled. From the knife clutched in his hand, it seemed he was intent on fighting. He had made his choice. He would die here.

Albtraum readied his blade to cut the boy down.

But hesitation stopped his sword arm as the boy looked up at him, terror twisting his expression. The same terror daemon children must have felt as they died at the hands of their own mothers...

He lowered his blade. His kind was above such barbarism. This boy would be a reminder of that.

Albtraum knelt down to eye level with the boy, peering through the eye sockets of his mask of bone. "You will run from this place," he whispered, slow and deliberate as he struggled to form spoken words on his own. "You will tell your kind that their transgressions against the children of the dark will not go unpunished. You will live knowing that the only reason is because we allow it."

Albtraum stood again, taking a single step back. The boy stared back at him, shuddering with fear, before stumbling to his feet and bolting into the woods behind him.

Silence, once more.

And then the far-off sounds of combat faded back into his focus. Albtraum examined the remains of the battle around him, but his attention was soon drawn to the battlefield. There was great power laying in wait, and Lucifurius urged him to it.

Yes, good. More. We need more...

As the armies were enraptured in battling one another, they did not immediately take notice of the vagabond killer. But word slowly began to spread among the soldiers as Albtraum struck and disappeared again and again.

"Sir, I've brought a report," a young soldier stated nervously to his commanding officer as he skittishly rushed into the man's tent.

"Well, what is it, boy? Don't stand there looking like you're facing down death. Speak!" the commander ordered.

"Our attack on the enemy is all but over," the soldier stated, composing himself. "Lord d'Auvergne's forces are severely weakened and are proving to be no trouble to eliminate."

The commander gave a hearty laugh. "Then why, pray tell, did you come in here white as a sheet? I understand I can be a frightening man when I so choose, Bleiys, but that is no reason to act as though I am the Devil himself-"

"Sir..." The boy interrupted with a frown. "Some of the men on the battlefield have reported seeing the daemon that is rumored to be slaughtering masses, on both sides of the field. Apparently he is responsible for a great many seemingly inexplicable deaths behind the lines of the battle."

The commander went silent.

He was not a superstitious man, and when the stories of the uncannily strong daemon knight who razed whole villages and slaughtered any who crossed his path had first reached him, he had dismissed it as no more than a fairy-tale told by bored soldiers as they sat around their campfires.

The commander stood, shaking his head, and stepped forward to give the young man an encouraging clap on the back. "My boy, frightened soldiers will believe almost anything they think they have seen. I have heard quite a few ridiculous stories in my day. I get the feeling that this is no exception. Now, if you would, head back and tell the men that it is most likely an enemy mercenary and they should continue on with the fight as planned, remaining vigilant. Do not allow the enemy to unsettle our victory with fear."

The soldier hesitantly nodded and exited the tent to carry out his orders.

The old commander shook his head once more and left the tent himself for a breath of fresh air.

The rain was still falling, and it made the battlefield seem oddly serene. The sounds of battle were muffled, seeming far off... He watched as the armies advanced further, and a triumphant smile came across his face. Here was one more victory he would add to a long list of them since the day he had first taken the position of commander. The scent of the rain on the air was crisp and clean, as if to signal that this was a new and better start for this kingdom.

Then, he smelled something else, and a cold feeling of dread flooded his veins.

Blood. And the rank, musty scent of death.

He turned slowly to try and place its source, and came face-to-face with a young man wielding a battered, bloodstained blade. His clothes were ragged and stained with blood. A mask fashioned of the skull of a wolf and antlers of a stag shadowed his face, hiding all but a tangled mess of crimson hair and the daemon's glowing orange eyes, piercing through the mask's shadow like firelight.

Eyes that burned with a sort of malevolent longing.

Hunger.

The second his mind had begun to work again, the old man quickly drew the blade at his belt—he was an expert at combat, few had ever beaten him—and made a slash for the daemon's head, which he ducked to avoid. The daemon rose to his feet again and slashed at the man's legs, succeeding in taking one off just below the knee. The man let out a cry of pain and fell forward, catching himself before he hit the ground. The sword was still gripped in his hand, and he tried to use it to push himself back up as he watched the monster that was slowly closing in on him.

The tip of the sword met the underside of his chin, lifting his head so that he was forced to look into his opponent's eyes.

"You have a strong essence, human..."

"What?" Even here, with a leg missing and death clearly looming ahead, the man managed an annoyed tone. "Who are you?”

"I am the servant of he who rules the dark. It is my duty to reap the essence of your lives so that he may manifest in his true form.”

The commander only stared. What was he speaking of? Ruler? True form?

"If there is any god you feel has not forsaken you... I suggest you pray."

These words had scarcely reached the man's ears when the blade met where his neck connected with his shoulder and sliced diagonally downward, splitting his body in half with an uncanny strength.

The man’s last vision was of blood, his blood, running from the blade to the ground, as the boy turned his back on him.

Our time draws ever closer, my child.

Soon only we shall remain.

CHAPTER III

The dark was stifling as Septimus waited on the Rift. It was little more than set of stairs around a pit in the temple floor that led down into seeming nothingness, and only a few of the Order's scholars knew of its existence. The temple had been built to contain and protect it, but the scholars were to remain in the rooms above ground and never descend to the lower levels, they had been told by the elders.

Septimus found himself wondering why they had bothered to build a corridor leading to it if it was truly meant to be locked away and forgotten about.

There was an odd sense of decadence about the air around the place – the air was cold, but thick and hazy, the darkness too drunk on its own overflowing. Something about the lingering haze in the room seemed conscious, and Septimus knew this could only be the presence of the ruler of the dark.

A soul this far-reaching was unnatural, a sign of deep corruption and instability. This was an opportunistic venture on his part, he knew, but if he could take something as disastrous as this and turn it into something good, then it would be of far more benefit than hiding the withering god's rot away as if that would make it disappear.

I should think that your superiors would be displeased to know that you have approached the Rift without their permission.

Septimus was not quite as startled as perhaps he should have been that something in the darkness had spoken. He did not hear the voice - rather, it was as though it spoke directly inside his mind.

"I see this as better than leaving it untouched and not utilized."

Your want for knowledge is so apparent it precedes you like a stench, human.

Septimus was taken aback, but again stepped closer. "I don't suppose you can blame me, not when I've been in such close proximity to it for so long and never been allowed to see any of it for myself."

The voice almost seemed to laugh. You think your frail mind can contain such vast reserves of knowledge?

"I believe that it can."

Then you will be my vessel. I will not give freely, no, but I will reward you for cooperation with my will.

Septimus stepped down into the darkness. It enveloped him like water, freezing and boiling at once, sending his skin prickling with goosebumps, the hairs on the back of his neck standing up. His footing beneath him felt uneven, as though standing on rippling waves.

The feeling of burning cold seeped into him, sending an ache that reached all the way through to his bones. His senses dulled, his sight growing hazy and the sound of his own breathing quieting to a distant hush.

And then the essence of the dark overtook him.

No longer did the voice speak into his mind, it now seemed to be completely a part of it, holding his mind in a vice grip. Unfamiliar memories flashed through his mind, sights he'd never seen and moments he'd never lived burrowing their way into the gaps of his own thoughts. It was a terrifying presence, powerful enough to make him feel like an intruder in his own body and mind. Septimus blinked, his body trembling from the chill of the room around him. He hauled himself from the pit of darkness and collapsed onto the stone floor, feeling battered and exhausted.

Until I have a physical form of my own, you will carry me through the world. You will kill anyone who stands in our way, that I might gather enough strength to create a body for myself.

Septimus heaved up from the floor and staggered his way back up to his quarters, not wanting to be caught in the base level of the temple. He had known his quest for knowledge would come at a price, but he had not anticipated his benefactor being so bloodthirsty.

Still, he thought, he could choose his sacrifices carefully, and surely the lives of a few who perhaps deserved death was a small price to pay for the things he could do, for his own Order and those beyond it, when he knew and understood more.

He repeated this to himself over and over that night, and for many nights on into the years to come.

Albtraum's infamy grew as months became years. He had ascended to legend – soldiers muttered tales of his rampages, parents used accounts of the wild daemon to frighten children into behaving. Lucifurius guided Albtraum cautiously, taking care to ensure that they left just enough rumors to sow fear, but not so many that they would be tracked and hunted down by overzealous vigilantes.

Albtraum grew tall, but remained narrow-framed and thin, his lithe build belying the inhuman strength Lucifurius channeled through him. He picked up weapons and armor, spoils from the battles he fought, producing a strangely mismatched conglomerate of different pieces. Only his mask of bone remained, a lingering symbol of the terror left in his wake. He went through blades quickly, he scavenged other weapons, he learned to use what was available to him.

Albtraum and Lucifurius had learned to work together so seamlessly that at times they seemed to be one being. Albtraum's mind had been tempered with Lucifurius' ire toward humanity. They were united in their solitude.

They were between hunts today, moving through the mountains. Albtraum trudged through persistent, drizzling rain, little specks of rust flaking off his armor as he moved. Both his hodgepodge armor and his old sword were worn-down and rusting, and he was wrapped in thick, tattered cloaks. It made his appearance somehow more fearsome, as though he were an ancient monstrosity, ages older than he really was, and he delighted at the thought of how he must have appeared to his foes.

His trek this day had been uneventful thus far. He reached for Lucifurius in his mind, as a child reaching to a parent for attention. Lucifurius obliged, and Albtraum was happy to receive his affections.

Let me tell you more of our home.

I was a proud god once. I created our world... A small, dark thing, but mine all the same. I created things from the dark to inhabit it, my servants of shadow-dust and moonlight, beasts of the earth and the skies. But my children were the most precious to me.

There are so few of you left...

As Albtraum recalled their discussion long ago about the other daemons, Lucifurius was jarred from his reverie, alerting Albtraum to the presence of a follower.

It would seem we are not alone, child.

Albtraum slowed his pace and looked around carefully, focusing his senses to attempt to pick up on signs of his pursuer. The rain made this difficult, drowning out any sounds and limiting his vision to a short distance ahead.

He could sense the presence of the one following him before he heard the footsteps. This was a strong one.

You will have to fight carefully, Lucifurius warned, and Albtraum was baffled at the somewhat *uneasy* tone he spoke with. *This one seems... unusually powerful.*

As the human trailing him neared, he slowed to a stop and turned around. It was a young woman, wearing a heavy black overcoat that was hemmed with fine embellishments, and a cloak to shield her from the rain – dressed well for a hunter. She was tall, and her stocky build was apparent even under her coat.

Albtraum tensed, a hand resting on the hilt of the sword at this belt. Lucifurius' uneasiness had invoked some apprehension in him, and he was the slightest bit hesitant to fight the woman. He was strong, and he was confident, but he was not a fool. He had exercised caution in battles before, but for Lucifurius to have expressed doubts... Albtraum knew he was potentially outmatched.

The woman chuckled as she neared him, staring him down as she readied her weapon, a bladed staff. A shock of short vermilion hair fell into her violet eyes. “Finally caught you up, devil. You must be the one they've been talking about... You've been making your way across as many towns and villages as you can, killing anyone in your path. I'd be remiss if I didn't put a stop to that.”

Albtraum scoffed. “You are not the first headhunter to challenge me, nor will you be the first to fall to me.”

“We’ll see.”

She dashed forward and thrust the staff blade forward, and Albtraum drew his weapon and deflected her attack. Ducking to the side, he slashed at the woman's legs, but she leapt out of the way and countered with a jab at Albtraum’s neck, which he only barely managed to avoid.

They both stepped back, circling each other, each contemplating their next attack. Albtraum moved first this time, hefting the sword over his shoulder and bringing it down towards the woman's head. She parried the strike with the handle of the staff, knocking him off balance, and caught Albtraum across the throat with the handle of the staff.

He coughed and wheezed. She had winded him, and he had to dart to the side to avoid being run through when she lunged again. The blade of the staff caught his side, leaving a shallow wound.

The woman was quick, light on her feet, and she was proving difficult to kill.

Clenching his jaw, Albtraum lunged to the side and made a stab at the woman's torso. Leaning away with almost ridiculous ease, she drew a knife and hurled it at Albtraum's head, aiming under his mask. He moved to avoid it and it glanced off his shoulder guard.

To Albtraum it seemed a foolish move until he realized its purpose – to distract him, so that the woman could attack again from the side, this time hitting his leg, slashing into the side of his knee left unprotected by the joint of the armor.

Albtraum managed to move back before the strike damaged his ability to move, and the woman breathed a curse.

This is proving to be a bothersome foe...

Albtraum growled as he backed away from her, his shallow wounds stinging. The woman opposed Albtraum's own combat ability in every way, though she was not exceptionally skilled. She had agility and speed where Albtraum moved slowly. Finesse where Albtraum lacked it. A strategy, where Albtraum had only the plan to kill and kill again.

Still, nothing about her seemed particularly extraordinary... which lead Albtraum to wonder what power Lucifurius had sensed in her that had put him so ill at ease.

“You aren't even an interesting opponent, boy!” The woman taunted, tossing her head and readying herself to attack again. “Always the same, you brutish thugs... I'm surprised no one's beaten me to you, especially with how much your head's worth.”

By a sheer stroke of luck, when the woman lunged again, Albtraum managed to run his blade through her gut, at the cost of catching the blade of her staff in his shoulder. The wound was fairly deep, and the pain gave him pause, but it would not hinder the movement of his arm.

Albtraum breathed a sigh of relief, gripping the hilt of the sword as he began to pull back.

But the woman remained standing, and seemed unaffected by the injury, the likes of which Albtraum had come to understand to be fatal to most. The blood flowed freely, and the woman cried out, wrenching the blade out of herself as Albtraum backed away. A surprising reaction, as he'd thought such a wound would cause her a great deal of pain.

And more surprising still, the woman lunged forward again. Albtraum ducked to the side, dropping to one knee and narrowly avoiding catching her blade to his eye.

Dumbfounded, he looked at the woman's abdomen. Any trace of the wound save for the hole in her coat was gone.

She smirked at him as he stared.

Rage from Lucifurius burned at the back of his neck. *This is one who will not die! Child, as this stands, we cannot kill her. She is immortal... You must run.*

Albtraum snarled, the sound hurting the tenderness from where he'd been hit in the throat, and rose to his feet again.

I promise you, my child, when you are yet stronger, we will track down this human again and we will repay her for daring to spill our blood.

He moved slowly, stepping back, his weapon still raised. He did not expect to be allowed to flee easily.

The woman thrust forward at him again, and again he ducked away, his pace quickening as he moved for the cover of the trees. He had never before had to run from a battle, so escape would prove difficult. Minutes dragged on, and eventually he stopped trying to counter the attacks and put all of his focus on parrying and evasion. The woman was too quick, and impervious to injury beyond that, so any attempts to deal damage to her would be in vain. Frustration rose up from the tightness in Albtraum's chest.

The screech of metal on metal, once a thrill that drove him on, had become a grating sound, an annoyance. The fatigue of battle, usually satisfied immediately by the intake of life force from those he had defeated, now weighed heavily on him, a hindrance.

Finally, feigning an attack, he rushed forward, and the woman dodged as expected. Instead of turning to face her after he rushed past, he kept going, running into the cover of the forest. Realizing Albtraum was trying to run, the woman rushed after him.

“And a coward, along with everything else! Surely you can handle one girl after felling entire armies... No? Then you can't possibly be worth enough for me to waste my time killing you. Go on then, run from me!” she called after him, mocking amusement dripping from every word. “And don't think running will save you from anything – *I will kill you if it’s the last thing I do!*”

Albtraum looked over his shoulder and noticed the woman come to an abrupt stop, whirling around on her heel.

His pace slowed to a stop and he watched her carefully. He heard distant voices echoing through the forest, calling after her. A large group of uniformed soldiers was moving toward her. Albtraum ordinarily would have attempted to engage them, but given his current state and the woman’s apparent invincibility, he decided that it would be prudent to flee.

The gash in his shoulder stung as he moved, but he gritted his teeth through the pain. He ducked and wove through the trees, and after a while, glancing over his shoulder, he saw that the woman was no longer chasing after him, and the group that had come after her did not seem to be interested in following him.

When he finally came to a halt, shoulders heaving as he panted heavily, he began to process what has just happened. He rarely had to turn tail and flee a fight, and against a single assailant... It was shameful, to say the least. What was the strange power this woman possessed, which made her immune to death? His own wounds healed quickly with the help of Lucifurius, but Lucifurius had always been very clear that death was a possibility if he sustained too great a wound. The idea of power that exceeded their own disturbed him.

This was no fault of yours, Lucifurius assured him. *That woman was a wandering immortal. As it stands now, we cannot hope to kill any of them. Just a little longer, my child, a little longer, and you will be strong enough to face them. The more you entrust yourself to me, the stronger you will become.*

Feeling unsettled, Albtraum bit down hard on his tongue to draw himself back into reality. He could not allow this to hinder him or set him back, not when there was so much left yet to accomplish.

He and Lucifurius grew ever more starved of energy, increasingly eager to fell the next mass of humans, to move closer to the day when only darkness would remain. One human, even if she had outmatched him, mattered little when there were so many more to be added to his strength.

That was what he would have liked to believe, anyhow.

Something like a festering illness gripped Albtraum in the days that followed his first real defeat. It was a shame that boiled deep, deep down, a sudden doubt that made him want to bury himself beneath the earth, to fade from being. He was not fit to serve Lucifurius... If he lacked the power to defeat a single foe, how would he carry them to a full conquest? How was he to lead Lucifurius back to his throne, and protect their kind?

He felt frantic to gather more power for their cause, to fell any humans he could. He had never hunted with such fervor before, and this both surprised and delighted Lucifurius.

Oh, my sweet child, do not let these dregs shame you so. The woman only outmatches us for the moment...This is what all humans are at their core, arrogant, foolish, thinking themselves superior to us... They will always believe it, they will believe it until the moment they lay dying at your feet.

Albtraum clenched his jaw, feeling bones click into place and muscles tighten. His surroundings were a blur as he moved forward, in a state of dazed half-awareness, searching for any hint of life. The forests went by unnoticed, his own footsteps soon followed the cadence of the blood pounding in his ears, and he heard nothing but that steady rhythm.

Then the sound of human voices penetrated the veil. He had entered a village. A visceral disgust rose in his gut, twisting it in two.

Their very existence was an insult. This, he could not allow.

Albtraum attacked with renewed violence, refueled monstrosity. He left nothing in his path alive. He had to prove himself worthy to Lucifurius, he had to ensure that their path remained open. In mere minutes all that remained of the small vagabond settlement he had happened across was a pile of corpses and smashed pieces of the tents that had been set up there.

It's the most beautiful thing, isn't it...? Silence... Nothingness. The dark is a beautiful thing.

The slaughter had acted as a sort of catharsis. Calmer, now, Albtraum sheathed his blade in the hilt strapped to his back. He thought of the woman he'd had to run from and felt a twinge of wrath, but quelled it with the resolution that the next time they met, he would possess the strength to properly eliminate her.

Albtraum turned back to the forests. Free of distractions now, he realized that despite the essences he'd consumed, he felt exhausted, as if he'd gained nothing from the hunt. In fact, it felt as though his energy had been drained – he felt heavy, sluggish, and it was difficult to move. The memory of his rage was hazy now that it had faded... Everything within his mind became a cloud of confusion.

It had been a long time since his last successful hunt, longer than he normally allowed. Or perhaps these humans had been too weak. Lucifurius needed more, as always. More and more. Someday, they would be enough.

But as the hours progressed, Albtraum became even weaker than he had been long ago, in the first days of his awakening. As he trudged on, he felt his knees start to buckle, his head begin to swim. He grew so faint that he had to stagger to a stop against a tree to rest, if only for a brief moment. What was the cause of this? Regardless of how long it had been since his last hunt, any ill effects should have faded by now...

Forgive me, child, but my hunger grows as yours does. I may have taken too much...

Albtraum had always had the understanding that whatever sustenance he obtained was primarily for Lucifurius, but some of the life force had always been given to him to sustain him. He had never been left this starved.

He felt almost hurt that Lucifurius, who had been his only guide through these first few months of his life, albeit only as a presence within his psyche, had done this to him. It felt faintly like a betrayal, but as he struggled to keep himself conscious, feelings of betrayal lost pertinence.

I cannot return what I have taken, as it is completely a part of my essence now. Find another gathering of humans... Replenish yourself. You have my apologies.

Slowly, Albtraum pushed away from the tree and moved on. He devoted no more thought to the occurrence and fought now through fatigue rather than fury. He nearly collapsed several times, but prevented himself from falling – he knew if he fell, he would be unable to get back up again. He placed each step carefully, deliberately. He ached of exhaustion.

Quickly, Lucifurius urged. *If this goes on, you could be in danger of death.*

Albtraum hastened as much as he could onward. He had no sense of direction, knowing only that he was moving, until his own rapidly starving essence caught the trail of another. His head snapped up, he saw two young men ahead, dressed in threadbare fabrics and furs, laden with game. Most likely, they were returning from a hunt to the small settlement he had just destroyed.

Shaking, weak, he drew his broadsword and waited for them to approach, partially obscuring himself behind a tree.

As they neared, one of the men slowed, having noticed him. He murmured to his companion, and they each set down their game and drew their knives, slowly closing in.

“Who's there?”

Albtraum staggered out to face them. They watched, cautious, finally determining by the lack of any response from him, the drawn weapon, and the fresh bloodstains splattered across his hunched form, that he was no ally.

The first dashed forward and avoided Albtraum's initial attack, leaving a long knife wound along the bottom of Albtraum’s ribcage where his plate armor ended. The pain came as a dull, barely comprehensible ache, and Albtraum swung again, by a sheer stroke of luck managing to hit the man's chest. The rusty, dulled blade left a ragged wound, blood flowed, and Albtraum felt a spark of life return to him.

While he had been absorbed in killing the first, the second man came from behind and tried to put the knife in his back – he turned, gripping the man's weapon arm, grappling with him for a moment as the man managed to stab the knife into his shoulder with a cry of rage. The pain came stronger this time, exacerbating the injury that was already there, and with a hiss, Albtraum dropped his own weapon to wrench the knife away and grabbed the man's neck, pressing his thumbs into the man's windpipe.

He struggled, hard to hold, for a moment, before his choking gasps became more desperate, his clawing at Albtraum's arms became weaker, as Albtraum steadily tightened his grasp. Finally, with a satisfying *crack,* he felt the neck break, the man's eyes rolled back into his head, and he went limp.

Tossing the corpse aside, Albtraum retrieved his sword and stood motionless for a moment, allowing the newly acquired power to sink in. It wasn't much, but he felt revived now, their life force would hold him over until the next hunt.

Though they shouldn't have had to, he realized. He had just completed a hunt, a fairly well-sized group at that. He should have been brimming with vitality for weeks.

Lucifurius had siphoned away nearly every last bit of not only his acquired power, but Albtraum's own life force.

Albtraum's feelings of hurt and betrayal returned, and he extended inquiries to Lucifurius, his wounded psyche pleading for comfort.

What he received was a sharp admonishment.

Senseless fool... You know not the true consequence of our toils, else you would see that, in this crusade, your own existence is of little importance. If you gave one moment of thought to the future we fight for, you would die happily for it.

Albtraum froze. The harshness of Lucifurius' words struck him like a blade.

Lucifurius had guided his every step, watching over him with all the care and concern of the most loving of fathers, and now told him his life was worthless, a thing to be cast aside for the good of the cause. He had been obedient to Lucifurius' orders, he had taken human souls as he was instructed. He had done everything he could to be a good and loyal host. An obedient child.

And he was just something to be discarded... just as humans discarded their daemon children? The thought hurt to hold, burning his chest as if made of fire.

You pathetic little imbecile. How dare you compare me to the filthy dregs who scorn our blood. I have led you to where you now stand, boy, you'd best remember that, ere you question my will ever again.

Or would you rather face this world on your own?

Albtraum's hurt faded into growing shame. Lucifurius was all Albtraum had in the world, the only thing that had shown him any path to follow. He had to give not only his trust, but the entirety of his being to his master.

As much as he feared death, if he had to face it to further their objectives, then face death he must.

Forgive me my harshness, child. I grow impatient for the time of our rule. We must not tarry any longer – our prey calls for destruction. The change in Lucifurius' tone was so sudden, Albtraum wondered if he had merely imagined his rage.

Albtraum silently accepted his master's apologies.

But somewhere, deep down within, something faltered in him. He did not move forward with the same purpose as he had before... There was hesitation in his steps, so slight that perhaps even he could not feel it.

Albtraum, the perfect puppet, had been tainted by doubt.

Chapter IV

"Septimus?"

Ishtar's voice rang out high and clear through the room, echoing over the high stone ceilings.

Broken from his reverie, Septimus looked over to the doorway of the study he had sequestered himself away in. Some of his fellow scholars milled about among the records, paying him no notice. Their ignorance had been strangely comforting.

Ishtar stepped inside, a look of concern written across her fair features. Septimus tried to smile in greeting, but he knew he could not hide his exhaustion from her.

Nevertheless, she did seem relieved enough upon seeing him. "I apologize if I am intruding, but you have not paid me a visit in some time..." Her tone was strained, made careful as it often was in the presence of others. She frowned, motioning for him to follow her. "Come, let us converse elsewhere."

When they had passed the doorway, Ishtar gently took hold of his hand, leading him to a dark and secluded corner in the halls.

"Have you...?" Ishtar spoke in a hushed voice as she looked over him carefully.

Oh, this is the one you have kept me from...

She is powerful indeed. Perhaps you should add her essence to our own before she learns of me... She will never look upon you in the same way again.

Septimus bit down on his tongue, fighting back Lucifurius' influence. He could not lie to Ishtar. If only for her own safety.

"Yes," he answered, his voice hardly above a whisper. "I have made contact with the dark. I house a piece of his soul within myself."

Ishtar drew in a breath, hard and sharp, but took Septimus' hand into hers. "Septimus..."

He gave a humorless laugh. "I have already arrived at the conclusion that you were right... His intentions are not benevolent. The knowledge he has paid to me of late has been far beyond my ken."

Ishtar pressed closer to him, concerned and protective. "What has he requested in return?"

"Life." Septimus could not meet her eyes. "As much as I can gather... more and more all the time. He is insatiable. Ishtar... I..." He bit his lip, his grip tightening on her hand in his. "I have tried to visit death only upon those who might be deserving of it. But my will is slipping..."

His voice broke, and he wrenched his eyes shut as they misted over with tears. "Ishtar, I have killed innocents. I have awoken far from where I went to sleep, standing over those I have slaughtered. For months, I was convinced I could use this for my own benefit, that I could control him... what a fool I was."

He expected Ishtar to pull away, to run from him, to leave him there and never look upon him again. He wanted her to. He willed her to, silently.

But she only swept him into her arms and held tightly to him. "You will not fight him alone, love. I will stand with you."

All will only rot from here... you know this.

Kill her, now, and you may live within this moment forever... I can make it so.

Septimus held to Ishtar as if she were the only thing that anchored him to the world.

"We have to leave, Ishtar. We must run far from this place, and we cannot look back."

Albtraum woke with a start, his gaze darting around in the dim light of the dawn to see what had broken through the haze of sleep. He found nothing but a gentle wind, and dead leaves rustling across the snow-dusted ground.

You still dream of my first host... how curious. I wonder if my own memories have passed to you...

As Albtraum considered this, he slowly stood, gathering his scant belongings and putting on his mask. He was on the trail of a large source of power, as he had been for days. Lucifurius told him it was a kingdom, a far cry from the small villages they had hunted before. Anticipation fluttered in Albtraum's chest. He was eager to prove himself to Lucifurius, to demonstrate his loyalty and his strength after the mistakes he had made before.

He climbed over the snowy path, the frozen ground crunching beneath his worn leather boots as his mind wandered to thoughts of what lay in wait for them. He felt the chill of the air, and his toes were somewhat numb in his boots as he moved. His breath fogged before him, barely visible in the dim light of the early dawn.

He slowed to a halt as he began to sense another essence mingling with the distant essence of the kingdom at the top of the mountains. It was a great power, but a familiar one... It did not feel the same as prey.

Ah, of course... We are close to a Rift.

Albtraum tilted up his mask to peer into the dense woods – just beyond the trees, in a small clearing, stood a small stone structure. He moved toward it, placing his footsteps carefully as he came upon the stone archway was built into the side of a small hill. Ruins of a structure that had once stood above ground littered the forests around it, great blocks of stone crumbling from age and covered over with moss. He stepped closer to the archway, it was too dark to see much inside, but as his eyes adjusted he could make out a faint glow deep inside the structure.

This was the first of my Rifts... Places where I have reached from our world into this one, feeding on the life of this place to strengthen my own. They have attempted to contain me... But it will take more than stone walls to do so, now that I have you. The Rift is within this temple. We will return here soon... these are the only paths we have back to our home, and this is where I must complete the body.

This, then, was a path to his home. This was hallowed ground, thus why he had sensed such a great power. His hand carefully extended into the heavy darkness beyond the archway, his fingers stretching out as though reaching for something. The air felt warm, as though a fire burned somewhere deep within, out of sight.

Half formed questions danced in Albtraum's mind for a few moments, and Lucifurius offered back equally half-formed answers. Home... What lay in wait at the top of the mountain? The body?

Up the mountain may be the last place we must travel before I can gain physical form.

It seemed baffling to Albtraum that they were here – he had always known that to exist in a body of his own was Lucifurius' ultimate goal, but he was suddenly uneasy at the thought of what would happen once his guidance was separated from him. Albtraum could not imagine himself existing independently, and the idea of being alone was terrifying.

My child, you have nothing to fear. You will remain at my side when I crush this world beneath my heel.

Albtraum still stood at the small archway, trembling. He tugged at his gauntlets as he struggled to steady himself.

He had to prove himself worthy of being kept.

He drew back from the warm darkness of the temple and advanced up the narrow path that lead to the top of the mountain, determined to reap whatever power lay in wait for Lucifurius. The trek up the mountain was long and arduous, but with Lucifurius' strength, Albtraum did not tire. The morning sun had fully risen when the path led him above the trees, and he looked forward to their newest hunting ground – the city, nestled into the mountaintop, surrounded by sizable escarpments and a great wall. Impassable for an army, but for a single assailant, the natural defense amounted to little.

Albtraum scaled the steep path to the city gates with ease. He could hear the bustling of activity as he neared, and the life force contained within the city walls was indeed great... A veritable feast for his master.

He moved quietly into the city as instructed. He found it difficult not to be in awe of the towering walls surrounding it, the intricately elegant architecture of the buildings within the city. It was built on a mountainside, leveled like a staircase, with ledges leading up to the magnificent estate at the city's center. Ramps and stairs were built between levels, plazas and marketplaces on each. Clearly, this was a prosperous kingdom, filled to the brim with powerful essences to be obtained.

Hiding himself in the shadows, Albtraum slipped past the idling guards towards the mass of energy at the city's center, weaving in and out of the cover provided by the buildings as he scaled the levels of the city. There were many humans milling about in the streets, idle chatter filling the cold morning air. He wanted to lurch into the crowds, to begin his attack – but Lucifurius urged hesitation.

Take care, child. There are many men who stand ready to defend this place. To have you struck down when we are so close to our objective would be problematic, to say the least.

Albtraum was somewhat apprehensive as he emerged into the streets, unnoticed as of yet as he struggled to decide where to begin.

He realized through his mounting tension that he was walking among the townspeople. He had never walked alongside humans in such a manner before, he had always been hunting them. It was strange, almost surreal. There were so many of them. He had never seen this many humans in such a state of calm.

For a moment, he stood almost mesmerized.

There were merchant stands in the streets, people dressed in furs milling about talking to one another, gathered around fire pits that burned along the sides of the streets for warmth. It seemed odd to Albtraum that there would be so much activity with the weather that was moving in, but none of the people seemed deterred.

The soldiers in particular caught his attention – they were watching their city vigilantly, weapons at the ready. They were attired in uniforms of gray and green, light armor over the coats. They carried spears and swords. With such numbers they could overpower him quickly, so if he were to engage them, he would have to be wary – he would have to kill efficiently.

It was not long before Albtraum was noticed by the townspeople surrounding him. They eyed him suspiciously, whispering to each other. The guards walking along the road glanced at him and muttered to their partners, reaching for weapons.

The calm had faded. He had been noticed.

The humans scattered, the quiet of the open air splitting into shouts of alarm as Albtraum drew his own sword. The guards rushed at him.

There were two of them – more would come, he knew – and he lunged forward, sweeping his blade out in front of him. The men moved back, and he saw that he had only grazed one across the arm. He darted away from them, backing towards the overhang into the lower level of the city.

The two guards shouted, calling for assistance, knowing this to be no minor threat – they were not fools. They may have even recognized him.

Perhaps it is unwise to continue, Lucifurius mused, uneasiness edging into his tone. *There are so many of them, and you find yourself in a disadvantageous position...*

Albtraum held the guards off at the ledge's end, trading blows that accomplished little, and Lucifurius' apprehension grew as the fight continued. Albtraum would soon be outnumbered, outmatched, and defeat was a looming possibility.

Still, he could not back down here. He could not give in to his weakness. For all the humans had done, they had to be punished.

The guards, though, seemed to be holding back. Albtraum gave them a wide berth, knowing he would leave his back open to attack no matter which one he chose to attack.

Albtraum was jolted out of thought when someone dashed past the standing guards, approaching quickly enough that he only had time to catch his attacker's weapon in a sloppy parry, and was knocked onto his back.

He quickly rolled over, climbing to his feet again to face his attacker -

A rush of rage shot through him as he came face-to-face with the immortal woman he'd fled from in the forests.

This time, *this time...*

The woman reeled back, looking just as surprised as himself, and her face twisted into a snarl. "What a surprise," she greeted him. "You're still at it – well I'll tell you this, boy, you're ever more the fool for coming after *these* people in *this* city. *My* home. You won't walk away this time."

One of the guards rushed over, grabbing her by the arm.

"Uemytlach!" he shouted at her. "The queen wants him alive!"

"I find that very hard to believe," the woman snapped back, pushing the messy fringe of her short hair out of her face. "He's a well-known murderer, you're just afraid to fight him."

Albtraum pondered what the guards had said, his thoughts tangling in confusion. He was wanted alive by the ruler of the city? How had they known he would be here?

The other guard lunged to restrain the woman, but she was faster, breaking away and rushing Albtraum, sweeping her weapon out in front of her. He sidestepped to avoid her, irritated that she was faster than he was. More guards had started to gather at the head of the street, watching them. She lashed out again, and he blocked the strike with the flat of his blade, but she kept moving, forcing him backwards.

Albtraum quickly surveyed his battleground. He was backed against the very edge of this level of the city, and thus, as Lucifurius had warned, in a disadvantageous position. He glanced behind him, and then quickly turned and made a leap to the roof of a building just below him, landing squarely on his feet. The woman did not hesitate to follow.

"Look what a coward you are, running away." She grinned, following after him.

She irritated him. There was a lofty, arrogant confidence in the way she spoke, the way she moved.

"Your words are empty air. Let your blade speak for you if you truly believe you can kill me." Lucifurius spoke through Albtraum, and Albtraum's fist clenched around the handle of his weapon.

The woman smirked, readying her own weapon. "Can't wait to die? All the same to me."

Albtraum's eyes narrowed, his jaw clenched. He lunged, slashing at her—the woman parried expertly, hooking the blade of his sword with the end of her own weapon. He wrenched free, the scream of metal against metal piercing the damp air.

"Terrible form! Just awful!" she laughed, ramming into his chest with her shoulder, knocking him onto his back once again. As he fell, he kicked one foot out from under her, sending her tripping and falling onto her backside.

As they both climbed to their feet to face each other again, he swiped at her again, slicing shallowly across her knuckles as she tried to move away.

She yelled out and then hissed, holding her injured hand at her side, though her pain quickly faded into a mocking smirk as the wound healed instantly. Albtraum's eyes darted to the guards behind her – a large gathering had formed, and they seemed to be hesitant to enter the fray.

"You can't kill me," she taunted, shaking her hand a few times before returning it to its grip on her staff. "You fight like a buffoon."

Albtraum answered with a sudden swing at her head that she ducked to avoid. Lucifurius spoke again, maintaining an air of calm in Albtraum's voice even around his own breath, heavy with exertion. "You'd do well not to insult the future ruler of your world, human."

She nimbly darted back, still laughing. It was perhaps the most irritating sound he'd ever heard. "I suppose you think that's you? You must have forgotten to factor in the unfortunate fact that I'll have killed you by the end of this fight."

You are wasting time with this one, Lucifurius spoke directly to Albtraum. *We are not yet powerful enough... I had thought we might be stronger by this time...*

There were guards at his back, now, carefully circling the two like they were a pair of wild animals.

We should take this opportunity to flee. The guards may pursue you, but you can easily outmaneuver them.

Albtraum stood fast. He refused to flee again, he would not be made the fool again. He was frantic with anger and fear. Fleeing again would mean utter defeat. It would mean admitting, to himself and Lucifurius, that he was not worthy of the task.

He would be calling for his own demise.

He moved to strike again, and the woman evaded the attack easily – so damn quick, and Albtraum's irritation was none the less for it.

They circled each other, traded blows. A dull ache radiated behind Albtraum's eyes as Lucifurius continued to urge him to flee.

The dance of battle continued – attack, parry, counter, avoid. The smirk in the woman's eyes spurred him on, his attacks became more violent, his swings less controlled. Exhaustion had begun to slow his movements, but he could not afford to give in.

Enraged, panting hard, Albtraum advanced once more. She only dodged and countered with small nicks to his unarmored joints.

"You're not terribly good at this, boy. Where'd you learn to fight?" the woman asked, smug and scornful.

Albtraum snarled at her. "You humans are all the same! You think yourselves superior to us, but you kill and mutilate our kind because you fear the power we hold!" The words were born of Albtraum's frustration, but tempered and spoken by Lucifurius. "To birth our race is a gift you have foolishly cast aside, and you are all too damned foolish to see the truth until the *moment you lay dying at my feet!*"

The woman's smug smile only widened. “Deep issues, hmm? Temper, temper... You'll never get anywhere, swinging that sword around like a dolt – Don't worry, I'll put you out of your misery, whelp.”

Almost before Albtraum could react, she jabbed toward him with the blade of her staff, catching him in the gut, cutting down *deep,* past where he could feel it. Dark blood seeped through the tattered black tunic he wore beneath his armor when the blade was pulled out of him.

He inhaled sharply, pushing the pain away. He could still continue.

But as he took an instinctive step back, his foot found no purchase. He caught sight of his opponent’s face, twisted into a triumphant smirk – and then fell.

He realized the woman had pushed him back to the edge of the roof... there was nothing behind him but empty air.

A moment of regret pierced his consciousness – such a foolish, insignificant mistake, and it had cost him his victory...

The shock of hitting the ground jarred him, and then he went numb, crumpled in a heap on the stone street, a small pool of blood glistening on the damp stones beside him. Blood coated his tongue and he tried to draw in a breath, but it was as if all the air had gone and there was simply nothing left to breathe.

He thought he managed one feeble gasp before his vision blurred and went black.

Chapter V

Sleep felt like death, awakening like birth.

Albtraum became aware of his existence from the ache that spread through his body as he slowly gained consciousness. He groaned, shifting one muscle at a time, carefully rolling onto his side, feeling sharp pain stab into him as he did. His body had become little more than a net of aches, some dull and some sharp as knives.

As he gradually remembered where he was and how he'd gotten there, he let out an involuntary growl of frustration. He had failed once again. Slowly, he pushed himself up to a sitting position, and the gash in his torso protested. He winced. His blood on the stone street around him was dark and congealed, and a light dusting of snow had begun covering the ground. He had been unconscious for a while.

On your feet, child. We are not alone.

Albtraum's hand clumsily grasped for his sword until his fingers brushed the hilt, he gripped it and carefully craned his neck to observe his surroundings. He had fallen into an alleyway, far from the activity of the city. His mask of bone lay in scattered splinters on the ground around him. And most surprisingly... his wound had been dressed.

His hand unconsciously moved to the bandages. The blood had seeped through them, but they held fast. He could not say for certain, but... the dressings might have saved his life.

As consciousness slowly returned to him, he became sharply aware of a great power near to him... more power than he had sensed in the whole of the city. His eyes focused ahead.

He jumped back, crouched on his knees and holding the sword defensively in front of him as he saw the line of soldiers facing him down. They had weapons at the ready, but did not seem intent on attacking. Albtraum groaned as the sudden movement sent bursts of pain through his body. He was at a distinct disadvantage... his mind raced as he tried to formulate a plan to escape.

“I'll thank you not to undo my work, sir.”

A voice, high and sharp, echoed across the alley. Albtraum’s eyes darted to the source, a young woman dressed in lavish finery, a wine colored dress embellished with gold threads and tiny jewels, a thick-furred white cloak draped around her shoulders. She stood at the center of the group of soldiers, the men rallied around her. She was clearly no commoner.

Waves of dark chestnut hair framed a soft-featured face, cascading over her shoulders and down her back. She was thin, delicately boned, almost reminding Albtraum of a bird, but there was something undeniably powerful and authoritative about the way she carried herself. Albtraum looked her in the eyes – jade green, and something almost disturbing about them... They were out of place, ages older than their owner looked to be.

He could sense that she was the source of the immense power he had noticed. Albtraum prepared himself to lunge. She was his chance to prove himself...

She would be last necessary sacrifice on Lucifurius’ altar.

No, you fool! You are wounded, and she holds more power than you can even comprehend! She can end your life with but a word.

Albtraum considered this. Indeed, this woman held a massive strength, matched only by Lucifurius. She had the means to kill him... but she had not. Every moment that passed was another chance to snuff him out, yet she and her soldiers stood fast. She had tended his injuries, saving him from death. Why?

No one moved, the only sounds were of tense breaths and the distant clamor of the city above them.

There had to be some reason she had kept him alive... Curiosity, more than anything, had overpowered Albtraum's thoughts. He turned to Lucifurius, questions dancing between them. His arm was slowly lowering to place his sword on the ground.

You are too gravely wounded to escape, and I lack the strength to heal you... I fear we have no choice but to surrender ourselves, and hope for a chance to break free.

Lay down your weapon... Do not resist.

"I do hope you are not planning to engage in combat," The woman called, breaking the silence. As Albtraum looked closer, he could see that her hand rested on the hilt of a sword at her belt, half-covered by her cloak. "You are in poor shape and will end up none the better for it."

Albtraum dropped the sword to the ground with a sharp clatter, slowly rising to his feet. The soldiers rushed him, but he remained where he stood, unmoving, as one on each side roughly took hold of his arms to restrain him. It was painful, and he struggled not to wince.

"Do be careful," the woman instructed the guards. "It would not do to injure him further."

Albtraum remembered his missing mask, feeling uncomfortably exposed without it. As the guards silently led him up to the gate of the castle, he shook his head, allowing his tangled crimson tresses to fall in front of his face, obscuring it from view. Still, he peered past the strands in front of his face to get a better look at his surroundings.

Inquisitiveness cut its way through his tension and fear as he saw the city around him. The architecture was magnificent, unlike anything he had ever seen. The towering levels, built into the mountainside, were filled with large, ornate structures, and the streets and stair steps were cobbled with smooth and even stones.

The people in the streets spoke in hushed voices as Albtraum was led through, bowing their heads as the woman passed. It seemed she was their queen.

She is one of them. One of our enemies.

Before Albtraum could ask Lucifurius to tell him more, they had reached the castle gate. Though not as large and assuming as some of the fortresses he and Lucifurius had seen, it was certainly impressive. He had never been this close to such a structure before, much less inside one.

The warmth of the air beyond the doors of the castle enveloped him as he was led inside. The soldiers' grip on his arm tightened slightly as they stepped passed into the halls, and he squirmed slightly, uncomfortable in their grasp. He turned his head to stare at them as they moved, fascinated to see a human in such close quarters. Battle was different, in the chaos of combat he had never been able to closely examine a human face before.

Shallow lines crossed the man's face, hinting at encroaching age, and a faint haze of stubble covered the lower half of his face.

The man turned and looked back at him pointedly, scowling. Albtraum frowned and turned his gaze forward again.

The inside of the castle was well-lit, abundant candlelight casting a warm glow throughout the halls. Guards stood at attention at each doorway they passed, greeting the woman at the head of the group with a brief nod.

The hall they traveled had grown slightly dimmer by the time they reached its end, a large, thick wooden door, slightly open. The woman stood aside as the guards made their way in first, guiding Albtraum past the doorway into the large room ahead of them.

A line of beds stood against the wall, some with dozing occupants, some empty. A row of large cupboards and shelves stood against the back wall, filled with glass bottles in many sizes and colors, along with neatly folded sheets and piles of hastily crumpled up linens.

A stocky-framed young woman with mousy brown hair twisted into a messy braid was looking through one of the cupboards. When she heard the group approaching, she turned, bowing.

"Your Majesty. What can I do for you?" She raised an eyebrow in Albtraum's direction.

"This young man is injured. I did what I could to tend to him, but I believe he has need of further treatment, and your expertise exceeds my own," the queen answered.

The guards pulled Albtraum over to a table, forcing him down to sitting on it. The queen gave a curt wave of her hand, carefully approaching

Albtraum as the men released him and stepped back, awaiting further orders.

"I must say, I am surprised to have seen you give yourself up with so little resistance," she said slowly, crossing her arms as she circled the table and came to a halt directly in front of Albtraum. Her cloak was pushed back, giving him a clear view of the small sword that hung on a belt at her waist. It was well maintained, but the wear of use showed beneath the shine. It was not simply for show.

Albtraum peered up at her from behind the tangled mass of his hair. In this state of tension, he could not find his voice – Lucifurius spoke for him instead. "Clearly, it would have been a fool's errand to resist."

She eyed him carefully. "Do you know where you are?"

Lucifurius began to answer, but Albtraum caught his words before they were spoken. Lucifurius knew this place, and if he said as much, Albtraum risked not receiving an explanation.

"No. I do not."

A den of enemies. That is all you need to know.

"What is your name?" she asked him, leaning against the table behind her.

Albtraum hesitated before responding. Declining held the risk of making him appear fearful, and he did not wish to show any weakness. But to give his name to another...

"...Albtraum," he answered quietly after a long silence.

“Albtraum,” she repeated, and it sounded odd, spoken in another’s voice. “Welcome to Sylva, Albtraum. My name is Mianna, and I am the queen of this kingdom. We have much to discuss, but your injuries must first be seen to.”

The queen, who had introduced herself as Mianna, stepped aside as the medicine woman approached, arms laden with bandages, bottles, and a knife. Albtraum tensed, his hands gripping the edge of the table he was sitting on. Surely they would not have led him all the way here simply to kill him...

The woman gripped a fistful of Albtraum’s clothes and cut through them with the knife with a labored ripping sound, and he flinched away from her as she pulled the musty layers of clothing away from his body. When she’d cut through the coats, she began pulling off his ragged undershirt and tunic, catching them on his unwilling arms. The clothes were stiff with months of unwashed blood and grime, reeking of the scent of death. The air was a shock against his skin, which had not been exposed in weeks. His body was covered in dark bruises and blood from the wound in his gut.

The medicine woman stepped back to look him over once he wore nothing but his boots and tattered smallclothes. She huffed. “What happened to him?”

“A clash with Ismaire, I’m afraid,” Mianna answered.

“Oh ho,” she chuckled, “That certainly explains it.”

Her touch on his skin was alien, and he pulled away from her slowly, frowning as she felt along his side, prodding the tender bruises. He winced audibly, squirming in place.

"Treating you will be a mite difficult if you don't sit still there, boy." She jabbed his side, and he grunted.

"Aleksandra, please do be gentle," Mianna interjected firmly.

"'Course, Your Majesty." The woman, evidently named Aleksandra, sighed. She carefully tipped his head up by his chin and looked at his head, poking and prodding and pulling his hair aside a bit – which *hurt* – before stopping just above his ears, frowning slightly as she rubbed his head on each side, feeling the remnants of his horns. "Odd," she commented. "Protrusions from the skull..."

Albtraum jerked away. *"Don't,"* he snarled.

The doctor drew in sharp breath to retaliate, but Mianna stepped forward. "Tend his injuries, Aleksandra, nothing more."

Albtraum's attention turned to Mianna, and he found himself overwhelmed with uncertainty. He turned to Lucifurius for answers.

She is one of the Order who have tried to contain me... We once worked together, but she opposes us now. She seeks to end my reign... To destroy my children. The whole of this kingdom kneels to her...

I believe she knows you are my vessel... She intends to hold us as prisoners.

Aleksandra retrieved an amber bottle filled with a dark liquid from the table. She opened it and poured some onto a rag, then scrubbed at the wound. Whatever was on the rag, it brought on a fresh sensation of stabbing pain. Albtraum hissed. He turned his gaze back to the queen, expecting to find her watching with amusement at his pain, instead met with a carefully expressionless countenance.

“I wouldn't complain, boy, this will stop the rot,” Aleksandra muttered. She tossed the rag aside and reached for clean linen bandages, binding them tightly around Albtraum’s abdomen. As she was checking her work, Mianna said something Albtraum could not hear to a guard standing near her.

“As I said,” she said clearly, turning back to Albtraum. “There is much we still must discuss. But given the severity of your injuries, you require time to heal before we begin our talks... At least until the morning.”

A guard handed Albtraum a threadbare, but clean and soft set of clothes. He cautiously accepted them, removing his boots and then pulling the clothes on over his aching and broken body, suddenly uncomfortably aware of all the eyes on him as he dressed himself. The clothes felt better against his bruised skin than his rough old coats had, though they were ill-fitting and hung too loosely on his thin frame while still being too short.

“Nothing too serious,” Aleksandra informed Mianna. “Won’t want to knock him about any more than he has been, though. Bit fragile, this one.”

“Thank you, Aleksandra, you are dismissed.”

Aleksandra gave another quick bow and returned to her work elsewhere, gathering the supplies she had used to put away.

“I do hope you will not require us to restrain you again,” Mianna said to Albtraum as he stood from the table again. Her posture was relaxed, but Albtraum’s gaze was quickly directed to her hand – faintly resting on the hilt of her blade once again.

“...No,” Albtraum said simply, as the guards came to stand on either side of him once more.

A faint smile quirked across Mianna's lips. "Very good. Do get some rest, Albtraum."

One of the guards motioned for Albtraum to move toward the door, and he did so obediently, watching carefully for a means of escape. He was unarmed, defenseless... He had little chance of success in this state, and Lucifurius silently agreed, urging him to remain cautious.

Albtraum was led through the hallways once again, his bare feet making no sound as he moved across the cold stone floors, the guards' metal-clad boots clanking rhythmically as they walked close alongside him. Although they had not touched him, their hands firmly gripped the weapons at their belts. They came to a stop at a door, the guards opening it and motioning for Albtraum to step inside.

He hesitated, looking each guard in the eye before stepping into the doorway. They returned his gaze with unease – they were afraid of him.

The door was quickly shut behind him and he heard the gentle clicking of the lock shifting into place. Albtraum looked around the room – it was beautifully ornate, with a large window that looked out over the city. He frowned as he looked down – the window was far too high to consider escaping from, but if death was required of him to prevent them from falling into the grasp of the enemy-

We have no need of such thoughts just yet, child.

Albtraum turned to examine the large bed in the center of the room, covered with an intricately embroidered velvet duvet. Everything about the room was drenched in opulence – to Albtraum, it seemed a very odd place to house a prisoner.

As thoughts of escape became more and more faraway, beyond his reach, Albtraum began to consider another course of action.

For the first time in his life, he addressed Lucifurius directly.

They want something from us.

Lucifurius chuckled. *You are most observant.*

Albtraum sat upon the bed, running his hand upon the duvet. It was the softest material his fingers had ever touched.

We are very close to them... And they are very powerful enemies.

Lucifurius' amusement turned slightly exasperated. *Yes...*

We have a chance to learn their weaknesses. To infiltrate their organization. To learn.

Lucifurius was silent for a very long time.

This is what has made you the favorite among my children, he crooned. *What a magnificent idea. We will remain... Dancing the steps they require of us, holding a blade behind our backs. They will be the instrument of their own destruction.*

Warmed by the praise, Albtraum eased back to lie down on the bed, curling under the soft layers of blankets. It was the most comfortable place he had ever laid down to sleep in the whole of his life, and he could not stop a slight sigh from escaping him as he found the pain of his wounds slightly eased.

He began to consider how to proceed – how he would execute his deception, how he would learn his enemies' weaknesses – but the moment he had settled into the bed, his eyes slid closed, and the weight of exhaustion dragged him into sleep.

Chapter VI

The sun was high in the sky when Albtraum awoke, bright light shining through the tall window and glinting off the gilded surfaces inside the bedroom. He remained nestled under the duvet, finding the soft warmth of the bed impossible to part with just yet.

Slowly, he opened his eyes, squinting in the bright morning light as he looked around the bedroom. He pushed himself up to sitting, the aching of his body reminding him of the injuries he'd sustained. He examined his surroundings, his eyes drawn to a pair of leather shoes that had been left next to the door.

Albtraum frowned as he climbed out of the bed and made his way to the door to pick them up. Someone had come into the room without alerting him... A realization that made him somewhat uneasy.

I would not advise giving yourself over to sleep so deeply in the future.

Albtraum grimaced at Lucifurius' subtle admonishment, guilt rising up in him at the thought that he had placed Lucifurius in jeopardy. He examined the boots carefully before pulling them on. They were made of soft leather, lined with some kind of fur. They were far more comfortable than anything he had worn on his feet before.

We have much to do.

Lucifurius' tone was curt and somewhat impatient, urging Albtraum on. He reached out and carefully tested the knob of the door, surprised to find it give way and open. Either someone had forgotten to lock him in again, or...

"Plan to sleep the day away, do you?"

Albtraum jumped, his eyes darting to find the source of the gruff voice that had addressed him, finding himself facing one of the guards through the half-open door. The man was dressed differently from the others, more embellishment in the gray coat of his uniform, a dark green cloak draped around his broad shoulders. He was older, but brawny and well-built, with reddish brown hair graying at the temples, and stern green eyes. A thick beard, also peppered with gray hairs, covered the lower half of his face—but a scar running from the side of his mouth was clearly visible.

Albtraum straightened to look the man in the eyes, somewhat surprised to find that he stood a few inches taller than Albtraum himself. Albtraum had always been quite tall, and was used to standing above most people he encountered.

The guard regarded Albtraum coldly, suspicion heavy and piercing in his gaze. "You are due an audience with the queen."

Albtraum rubbed the sleep from his eyes, rolling his shoulders back and waiting for the man to offer further instruction. Like the queen, the man exuded an aura of great power – was he perhaps immortal as well? That would explain why he did not seem at all uneasy as the other guards had been.

"I feel you should be informed that royal guests do not usually sleep until midday," the man grumbled.

"Well, I seem to be rather more a prisoner than a guest," Albtraum mumbled sourly, a frown wrinkling his brow.

Tread carefully, child.

The man replied with a heavy sigh. “Do you have a name, boy?”

“Albtraum,” he answered reluctantly, barely audible.

“Well, Albtraum, I would advise you speak more respectfully when you meet with the queen.”

Albtraum glared at the guard's back as he turned to lead him down the hall. He detested being talked down to so. Who did this man think he was?

You must be cooperative if we are to gain their trust.

Albtraum huffed quietly, continuing along after the guard as they walked from the narrow hallway of guest rooms to the wider halls of the large estate. The skies outside were still gray, and light snow was falling. But the light of day was still filtering in through tall windows, and the beauty of the hallways was even more apparent – the stones were immaculately polished, the walls draped with fine tapestries, and the shadows where the light from the windows could not reach were gently illuminated by ornate candelabras.

Albtraum looked around the halls carefully as they moved, familiarizing himself with the tangled web of hallways, ignoring the stares from the young guards pacing around the doors. They watched him like they would a wild animal, ready to strike if he moved wrong.

Their alertness reminded him only of his own weakened state... Injured, imprisoned, and unarmed. There was little he could do.

They came to an abrupt stop upon reaching an open door, and the guard Albtraum had been following motioned for him to step inside. A large desk sat at the center of the room with a large armchair behind it – where the queen, Mianna, sat waiting for him.

She gave a pleasant smile as she saw him, motioning to the smaller armchair in front of the desk, across from herself. “Please, sit.”

Albtraum glanced behind him at the guard as he stepped inside and shut the door, standing like a wall between Albtraum and the path to the outside. Frowning, he eased himself down into the armchair, trying not to wince the pain of his broken body flared sharply.

“I see you have met Brunhart, our Captain of the Guard,” Mianna commented, nodding to the guard. “How are your injuries?”

“...Well enough,” Albtraum answered quietly, grasping for Lucifurius’ guidance and finding himself met with silence.

“It is good you are able to move, but the doctor has informed me that you should still be resting whenever possible. You have made no attempts to resist me or my guards, so I am hoping this means you may be willing to hear what I have to say.”

Albtraum straightened, regarding her coldly. “As your prisoner, I do not seem to have much choice in the matter.”

From what Albtraum understood from Lucifurius’ teachings, royalty were generally thin-skinned and easily offended. But Mianna seemed more amused at his brusqueness than anything. With a smile that was just condescending enough to irritate him, she said, “Well, you are not required to stay, if you do not wish to. But I can do nothing to stop my guards from killing you if you choose to leave. Besides, I believe we can both be of assistance to each other.”

"Really? And how, pray tell, do you suppose you might assist me?" he mumbled, eyes narrowed suspiciously.

She leaned back in her seat, eyeing him carefully. "You are the host of another being, are you not?"

To attempt deception will only make you harder to trust. She knows.

"Yes," Albtraum replied.

"I am sure you must want independence. Control over your own mind and body."

Albtraum's brow furrowed – though he understood her words, he could not fathom why she thought this might be something he wanted. His first instinct was to agree... but a need to understand overpowered it.

"Why should I desire such a thing?"

"I am sure it is no secret to you that your master..." Mianna paused, looking pointedly at him. He stared blankly back.

My name. She wishes to know my name.

"Lucifurius." Speaking that name was even more uncomfortable than speaking his own had been.

"Lucifurius," Mianna replied with a nod. "Surely you must have realized by this point that you are nothing but a pawn to him."

Albtraum had never questioned this fact, but Mianna spoke of it as though it were something he should not be satisfied with. "I suppose," he answered, guarded, wondering what she might say next.

Mianna seemed to consider how to proceed for a moment. She held Albtraum's gaze for a time before letting out a soft sigh and turning toward the window.

"There is more that we can offer you, if you are willing to provide us your support." She looked back over to him. "I am sure he has told you something of us... We are the Order of Azoth, an organization dedicated to preserving the balance of power in this world and the world of your birth."

And to meddling in affairs they have no business in, Lucifurius hissed.

"You provide us with a uniquely valuable insight – a deeper understanding of the being you are host to. In return, we can offer you a chance at independence... We can help you to separate yourself from him."

Albtraum recalled that for Lucifurius to exist without the need of a host had been their goal from the beginning. This arrangement would surely be beneficial to them... along with the chance to give Lucifurius greater access to the weaknesses of those who would stand against him.

Mianna cleared her throat, breaking the long silence that had gone on between them. "I am sure you must be quite overwhelmed by all that has happened. We can discuss matters further at a later time... perhaps after you have had more time to rest, and a meal in your belly."

"I will consider it," Albtraum replied, trying to sound somewhat disinterested, but finding it difficult.

She smiled at him. "Good. I look forward to discussing our plans further. I will have servants tend to your needs – but I must warn you, should you harm any of them, my offer will be rescinded, and you truly will be a prisoner here. Do we have an understanding?"

Albtraum shifted, uneasy. "Yes."

“Wonderful.” Mianna stood, and looked to Brunhart, the guard. “Please see our guest to the kitchens, I believe he must be quite famished.”

Albtraum’s nose wrinkled slightly at the idea of consuming human sustenance, but he did not have any other options at present if he wished to remain in Mianna’s good graces, and his strength was beginning to wane as he had not had a successful hunt in quite some time.

Brunhart nodded in response to Mianna’s order, opening the door for Albtraum and waiting for him to step into the hall before following after him.

The hallways were bustling with of guards and servants, and Albtraum found the flurry of activity dizzying to watch. It was so different from the chaos of battle – alien and wholly unfamiliar. Although Albtraum was accustomed to battle, he had no desire to return to those routines now – the newness of this experience excited and intrigued him. In fact, his self-appointed mission to gather information for Lucifurius was far from his mind as his curiosity grew around the new experience before him.

He glanced over to Brunhart, who walked beside him. Although the man’s posture feigned relaxation, Albtraum could see in the careful way he placed his steps and the way he frequently glanced over that he was ready for the possibility of combat.

The silence between them felt odd after the conversation he had just had. Perhaps there was information Albtraum could glean from him.

“You are an immortal,” he commented.

“Yes,” Brunhart answered gruffly, with no hesitation. “I suppose the daemon in your head told you as much.”

Albtraum was taken aback – he had been hoping to unsettle Brunhart, but instead was unsettled himself by Brunhart's response. He fell silent, avoiding Brunhart's gaze as they continued forward.

"There's not likely to be much food left from the guards' and servants' mealtime, so I suppose you'll have your choice of what the kitchens will prepare for you," Brunhart added.

"I have no preferences. I have never consumed human food," Albtraum answered abruptly.

Brunhart looked to him with a raised eyebrow. "Ah. I will choose something for you, then."

Albtraum could smell the scents of food lingering in the halls as they reached the tall archway to the dining hall and stepped inside.

The ceiling was high and there were no windows, casting dim, murky lighting over the hall. There was so much chatter Albtraum couldn't discern any particular words or conversations, and the sounds blended into one another as a collective, constant roar that hung in the air. He didn't think he'd ever been in a place so alive. The air smelled of wood smoke and cooking food.

"I will go and have something prepared for you. I trust you to behave yourself if I leave you here," Brunhart said to Albtraum as he stepped around him to go to the kitchens. The subtle threat in his voice was readily apparent.

Albtraum stood in the middle of the room as Brunhart left him. He drew many stares from the guards and servants milling about, causing tension to rise in his shoulders. He sat down at the bench of one of the emptier wooden tables, watching the commotion carefully. Gradually, the lingering stares faded as the crowds returned to their activities.

Albtraum's mind had started to wander when suddenly, something sharply caught him in the back of the head.

His face smashed into the edge of the table—his vision went white and he felt himself fall back, cracking the back of his head against the hard stone of the floor. As he furiously blinked his vision back, he tried to maneuver himself to stand and face whatever had attacked him, but his legs were caught between the bench and the table.

Someone forcefully planted a knee into the center of his chest and yanked his head up by a fistful of his hair. He snarled and tried to push himself up, blood running into his mouth from his nose.

"I bet you pissed yourself over how clever you thought you were, getting new clothes as if it should make you any less of a monster," an oddly familiar voice hissed at him. He found himself face-to-face with the woman from the roof, a knife at his throat.

He swung his arm at her, trying to bat her off, but she intercepted him by jabbing the knife in his forearm, using his own movement to make a deep gash across his arm.

She drew back and stabbed at his neck again. He felt the knife point just break his skin before someone forcefully hauled her away from him.

"*Brunhart!*" she shrilled, flailing against Brunhart's grasp. He had lifted her off her feet. "I *had* him! Let me go!"

Lucifurius was raging, suddenly protective, adding to the already potent pain throbbing through Albtraum's head as he sat up, fading adrenaline leaving him groggy. *Damnable whelp! She will be first to die when we have the necessary strength...*

Brunhart pinned the young woman against the wall as easily as if she were a child. "You are endangering your welcome here, Ismaire, attacking a guest of the queen."

"A *guest?!*" the woman, evidently called Ismaire, thrashed more, scrambling for her knife as it fell from her hand and clattered to the floor. "While we're at it, why not let the children play with the forest bears and invite bandits for tea!"

He scowled at her, setting her back on her feet before pointing to the door. "Get out. We will discuss this with the queen later."

She glared fiercely at him, stooped to retrieve her weapon, and briefly turned her angry gaze on Albtraum before storming out of the hall, several guards following behind her to escort her away.

Albtraum noted how silent it had gone. Everyone was staring. Brunhart waved them off and they slowly regained their earlier volume, turning back to what they had been doing before.

Blood gushed from his nose and the deep gash across his forearm. His head thrummed with ache.

Through the watering of his eyes, he saw Brunhart approach him with a hand extended, which he ignored as he shakily tried to get back on his feet. The older man grumbled and hauled Albtraum up by his uninjured arm.

He stood stiffly as Brunhart looked him over, sighing. "We won't have time for anything else, if we have to keep delivering you to Aleksandra like this. Let us have you seen to, then..."

Brunhart led Albtraum out of the dining hall, keeping a gentle grip on his arm as they walked. Although Albtraum was unnerved by the touch, he found himself leaning into it more than he would like – he was unsteady on his feet, and his head was swimming.

He had been used to combat and injury his whole life, but he suddenly found himself entirely exhausted by it. Though Lucifurius was able to quell some of Albtraum's pain, he lacked the strength to do anything more.

We may need to do something about that woman. As much as it would serve us well to gather information here, she clearly cannot be controlled.

Feeling himself trembling slightly, Albtraum all but collapsed on one of the benches in the infirmary as soon as they stepped inside. He felt unsteady on his feet. Brunhart waved the doctor over from where she was handing off a bowl of soup to a recovering patient. Her mouth was screwed to the side, her expression annoyed.

“Can't stay away, can you? It's barely been a day and already you've gotten yourself into a fight.”

“Ismaire again,” Brunhart informed her curtly.

She sighed and shook her head. “Well, I suppose Her Majesty will need to take extra measures to ensure this does not happen again.”

Albtraum audibly winced when Aleksandra touched his nose. He was ashamed with himself, showing such weakness, but the pain had overtaken his stoic facade.

“Broken, I'd wager.” She dabbed at the area around his nose with a damp cloth, cleaning away the blood. “That could leave quite a nasty scar. Not a bad thing, necessarily. The captain here's had his face sliced up pretty good and he's still tolerable to look at.”

Brunhart sighed heavily. “I did not come here for unsolicited pleasantries, Aleksandra.”

“Suit yourself.” She finished wiping away the blood on Albtraum's face, then suddenly took his nose between her hands and jerked it to the side.

The sharp sensation that followed was far worse than the initial pain of having his nose broken. Dizziness overtook him, such that he felt himself start to slip backwards off the bench. Brunhart caught him and pushed him forward again, and he groaned weakly. His ears were ringing. The sounds in the room sounded far away.

“There, I've set it,” Aleksandra chirped as though it were a simple, painless task. Albtraum’s resentment for her cut through the agony. He was vaguely aware that she had pushed up his sleeve and started to bandage his arm. “Has he had anything to eat?”

“Not that I know of,” Brunhart replied, still holding Albtraum upright.

“Because, generally, I don't have them go this green on me. Glen!”

A soldier who had been guarding the door stepped in. He was tall and broad-shouldered, with messy, mousy brown hair and a slightly uneven beard. “Yes?”

“Get us a plate of food from the kitchen, would you?”

The guard nodded, quickly moving to do as he was told.

“I'm fine, let me go.” Albtraum tried to push Brunhart's arm away, but the captain stood like a statue.

“I don’t believe you’re in any position to judge for yourself, boy,” he sighed in response, sounding more exasperated than angry.

“Good god, and a bleeder to boot.” Aleksandra caught the heavy stream of blood still running from Albtraum’s nose with the damp cloth in her hand. “Hold that there.”

Too dazed to argue, Albtraum did as he was told. She finished the bandages around his arm and lifted the hem of his shirt to check the ones she'd applied the day before to the wound in his gut.

“Bandages need changed.” She stood and retrieved a knife from the table near the door. Lucifurius’ presence bristled with alarm, but Albtraum was far past caring whether someone else was moving to attack him. She cut away the old bandages, and they stung as they peeled from the wound.

Humming an off-key tune, Aleksandra cleaned up the wound and repeated her bandage work. She was not especially gentle, and Albtraum could not help but flinch as she pulled the bandages tight around his waist.

“There, should be good now, eh?” She looked to Brunhart. “Keep him out of trouble this time, will you?”

Brunhart nodded. “Of course.”

The captain finally seemed to trust Albtraum to hold himself upright, and sat down at the bench across from him.

“I don't need you to watch me,” Albtraum huffed, leaning forward and pressing his forehead against his palm, still holding the rag to his nose. Pain bloomed behind his eyes.

Brunhart simply sighed. “I know it must not seem the truth at present, but we are not your enemies, boy.”

Before Albtraum could reply, the guard from the door returned, carrying a platter of food and utensils which he handed off to Brunhart.

"Here you are, Captain. They had some lamb and peas left in the kitchens." He cast Albtraum a sidelong glance before returning to his post at the door.

Brunhart handed over the plate and utensils to Albtraum. "I apologize for Ismaire. We will take steps to ensure she does not have the opportunity to harm you again. You should eat, you don't look well."

Albtraum looked at him warily. "Why?"'

"The food will help you get back some strength, and—"

"No, I..." Albtraum shook his head, cutting into the slice of meat on the plate. "Why are you *apologizing* to me?"

Brunhart shifted slightly, leaning back into his seat. "Because someone in our charge did you harm."

Albtraum looked back at him with suspicion, remaining silent.

"You don't seem an unintelligent boy, surely you must know something of common courtesy," Brunhart added with the raise of an eyebrow.

"I don't see how someone like you affords such a thing to someone like me," Albtraum muttered, poking at the peas with his fork. They were bright and round, and didn't entirely look like food.

"I'm aware of your reputation, as are the queen and most everyone here. We offer you another chance at a different life than the one you know."

Albtraum found Brunhart's presence somewhat intimidating, as though he were looking right through him. He found himself once again missing his mask – having his face exposed still made him feel all too vulnerable.

He'd never considered that another life outside what he knew was possible for one such as himself. He'd never truly considered that there was any other way to live than traveling through the wilderness from village to village, battlefield to battlefield, following Lucifurius' orders. Alone. Only the two of them, and the world standing against them.

The life they offer is a lie. A beautiful lie, perhaps, but a lie all the same. Take care not to be lured in by what they offer... They are but empty words, my child. We will always be monsters to them.

Albtraum avoided Brunhart's gaze for the moment, examining the hunk of meat he'd cut away to eat. He'd been given enough knowledge of human practices from Lucifurius that he knew how humans typically ate, but going through the motions himself felt awkward and unnatural, and Brunhart's attention to him did nothing to help.

He bit the meat from the fork, and chewed, surprised to find that the ravenous emptiness that had overtaken him in the days since he'd last made a kill went away even more quickly in the presence of human food. He cut another piece from the meat, and before he could think much further he was devouring everything he could from the plate, barely bothering to cut it into pieces anymore.

The rich taste of the food and the warmth in his belly was somehow more satisfying than any essence he had obtained from a hunt. Life force from hunting was pure, raw energy, but this seemed oddly less... hollow.

"Careful, now, you'll choke yourself," Brunhart muttered with the slightest smirk of amusement.

Poor child. So long without a hunt that you find this inferior human sustenance desirable... We shall need to remedy this soon.

When he'd eaten everything and sat wondering if he should lick the plate clean, Brunhart took it from him. “Have you eaten before?”

“Never,” he replied flatly. His hunger had been sated, but he was still debating on whether or not to ask for another plate.

“Well, you must have been hungry, then.” Brunhart’s tone had softened. “I’ll inform the queen of what’s happened. You should take the remainder of the day to rest. I have other duties, but there will be other guards and servants nearby to assist you with anything you should need.”

As Albtraum was led back to his room, he could not help but withdraw from Lucifurius, his mind lingering over what Brunhart had said. He had been here but a short day... And he’d been looked after, fed, made comfortable, and treated as an equal by the queen. Lucifurius’ conquest, once a close and attainable goal, now seemed far-off, too much a fantasy to consider with any degree of seriousness.

Albtraum was conflicted.

Mostly, he decided, he really only wanted something more to eat.

Chapter VII

Ismaire Uemytlach had never been accustomed to following orders.

And Mianna had been ordering her around like a child lately, this latest occurrence being no exception. What the hell did Mianna think she was doing? When she had showed up after Ismaire knocked the wanted murderer off the roof, telling her she would take care of it, Ismaire certainly hadn't expected she'd meant she was going to *keep him alive.* Even less so that she was going to take him in and treat him as an honored guest, guarded escort and all.

Her hands clenched and unclenched, and she fiddled with her sleeves and pulled at her hair, sitting down at the desk. After attacking the daemon in the dining hall, she'd been sent to her quarters, forbidden to leave. That morning, she had awoken to a summons to see Mianna in her office. She'd been waiting there for quite some time for Mianna to arrive. She was anxious, and having a murdering madman in her house did not sit well with her.

The door of the office opened and Mianna stepped in, irritation barely showing through her poise. Ismaire sat back in the chair, trying to straighten herself out.

"You mind telling me what the hell possessed you to take a murderer into your home, Mianna?" she snapped before Mianna could say anything.

Mianna shut the door and stepped in, staring her down, hard and dangerous. "I'll thank you not to take that tone with me, Ismaire. I have chosen to allow you to be my ward and work alongside the guard force rather than locking you away, but you are still in my charge and my debt."

"And as someone in your charge I'd like to know why you expect me to stand idly by as you allow someone like *him* into--"

"Unbelievable as you might find it, Ismaire, we've actually spent a great deal of time looking for him, trying to follow the rumors, hoping they would lead us to him. It's nothing short of miraculous that he's turned up on our doorstep."

Ismaire scoffed. "Miraculous... Right."

Mianna stood straighter, eyes narrowing. She was a good deal shorter than Ismaire, but that hadn't ever stopped her presence from being intimidating. "I do not expect you to understand, Ismaire. We are not equals and I do not discuss my business matters with you."

"Mianna, are you not aware of what he's done, exactly? He's killed hundreds, and that's only the ones we're aware of. Hundreds of innocents, Mianna. Probably thousands."

"You think I do not follow the events happening in our world, Ismaire?" Mianna's posture had slightly relaxed, and she regarded Ismaire haughtily.

"I'm saying it seems rather odd you'd actually seek out a vicious murderer, Mianna. Someone who's killed innocents and children, in our ranks."

"He is not the picture of morality, no. But the stories say he's never killed a child, Ismaire. The rumors had to come from somewhere, you know... And what do you consider worse? Killing a child? Orphaning them? Or taking them from their families in the dead of night and loading them onto a boat to be shipped far away from their homes and sold into a life of torturous slavery? Personally, I find them equally distasteful."

Ismaire opened her mouth to respond, but snapped it shut, feeling her chest tighten. "That was not necessary, Mianna."

Mianna raised an eyebrow at her. "I believe it was. If you lay a hand on him again, I will rescind my previous generosity, and you will be imprisoned." She turned back to the door. "I gave you a chance to better yourself with us, Ismaire. And I have been feeling more and more that you take that for granted."

Ismaire huffed as Mianna stepped out, shutting the door behind her. Feeling incensed, Ismaire sat fuming for a moment until Mianna's footsteps faded from earshot and then stood, storming out the door and making her way to the staircase to the second floor. Really, what could Mianna be thinking? Ismaire had never known her to do anything this foolish. She had always been a very smart woman, and for the most part all of the decisions Ismaire had seen her make only served to further prove that. But this... This was madness.

If Mianna wasn't going to do anything about this, Ismaire would have to take matters into her own hands.

She rounded the corner and rushed up the stairs to the guest quarters. She figured Mianna must be keeping the daemon there, if she wanted him safe. Perhaps there was something she could do to break whatever spell he'd put on Mianna...

Only one guard stood in the hall of guest rooms, and he was a trainee. Ismaire could tell from the way he stood. Nervous, timid. His face still held the chubbiness of youth and his hair flopped across his forehead in messy curls.

"Hey!"

He glanced over at her, eyes wide.

"Is the murdering bastard in here?" She leaned against the door, causing his eyes to widen even more and his grip to tighten on his sword.

"Miss, I've been given orders not to..." He mumbled meekly, but Ismaire held up a hand to silence him.

"Oh, it's fine. I'm not going to hurt him." She removed her weapon belt, laden with throwing knives, and thrust it into the guard's hands before stepping into the room. There was the daemon, nestled into the downy bed and buried beneath a velvet duvet.

He was sleeping. Sleeping! She scoffed, kicking the bedpost nearest to his head. "Bonehead! Wake up, I need to have a chat with you."

He groaned, peeking out from under the duvet. She hadn't gotten a good look at him until now – even with the ugly gash across his nose from where she'd smashed it into the table, he was a looker. She knew something about this had seemed odd. Manipulating Mianna with his pretty face, more than likely. He blinked at her, looking confused.

"You sure sleep soundly for a murderer, you know that?" She leaned in closer. "I don't know what your game is. This doesn't seem like your style. You're more the sort to kill without a thought, I didn't think you were smart enough for something like this – but you're in my city now, and if you step out of line at all – I mean if you *breathe* in the wrong direction..."

The daemon glared at her, the sharpness of the expression slightly blunted by the way he winced at the pain from his nose. "I don't know what you're talking about."

"Oh, like you don't--"

"*Ismaire!*"

She turned, finding Brunhart standing at the door, staring her down with steel in his gaze. The squirrelly young guard stood behind him, still holding Ismaire's weapon belt. She growled.

"Look, I didn't touch him! All Mianna said was that I couldn't touch him. And I didn't!"

"This is not what she meant and you know that, Ismaire."

"Does he have his claws in you too, Brunhart? I feel like I'm going mad, here, when a murderer has protected status and everyone is acting like nothing is wrong."

"You are not involved in Mianna's political business, you are her ward, which means you also answer to me. Out."

She huffed and rolled her eyes. "Fine. Fine! Let him in! You'll all wake up with knives in your backs!" She grabbed her belt from the guard and stormed back out to the staircase, grumbling curses under her breath.

She reached the end of the hallway, away from where anyone could see or hear her, and let out a stifled cry, falling back against the wall and gripping her head tightly in her hands.

She would not let him harm this place. She could not.

She would stop him whether Mianna believed her or not.

Albtraum rose from the bed, still reeling from his sudden and startling awakening. Tension from Lucifurius wound itself deep into his chest – there had been far too many close encounters in such a short span of time.

I am only glad the others seem not to take her words to heart... She clearly will never believe our deception.

“Once again, I apologize. I will ensure we have a more adequate guard force set up at your door.” Brunhart sighed, directing Albtraum’s attention back to him. He was carrying something at his side – something covered in fur.

Albtraum watched the fuzzy, writhing thing in the crook of Brunhart's arm warily. It was burrowed against him tightly enough that Albtraum wasn't entirely sure what it was – vermin, maybe, perhaps this was some bizarre part of human meals...

But Brunhart moved to hand it to him, and he stared.

“What is this?” Albtraum asked flatly, raising an eyebrow.

“The dog the servants keep in the kitchen had a litter of pups,” he replied matter-of-factly. “The children have all had their pick of them, but they passed this one over. He's got a mean streak, evidently. I thought you two would get along.”

Brunhart passed the tiny animal over into Albtraum’s open arms, and Albtraum was left suddenly unsure of what to do with the squirming, growling thing in his hands. Growling, of course, was a generous way to describe it – the pup was so tiny every sound it made was a squeak, laughable rather than intimidating.

Albtraum looked back up to Brunhart for an explanation, and he nodded to the pup. "I thought you might like something to occupy your time while you settle in. It will probably be some time before the queen trusts you enough to move forward, you'll need something to amuse you and keep you company."

A small and weak life force such as this will be all but worthless to us, Lucifurius informed Albtraum with disappointment. *Still, such a helpless waste of breath. Crush it as soon as you have the chance.*

Albtraum hesitated at Lucifurius' suggestion, feeling that perhaps this was some sort of test, a trial of his humanity. He knew that humans often kept dogs as pets, and if he were to kill it, he would likely only further perpetuate his reputation as a monster.

The pup was warm and soft, with a fat belly and a coat of patchwork colors – rust red and brown and white – like fallen leaves, late in the autumn, when the snow had just begun to cover the deadfall.

Albtraum hissed and sharply drew back one hand as the pup clamped down on his finger with needle-sharp teeth. He grumbled at it, but found his ire hard to hold as it whimpered and wiggled into the crook of his arm.

Brunhart chuckled. "I did warn you about the mean streak."

Lucifurius seemed conflicted, pleased that they were gaining the trust of their enemies, yet finding the lengths they were made to go to detestable. A slight shame prickled at the back of Albtraum's neck as he considered his own feelings toward their predicament – he was not as eager to escape as he perhaps should have been, enticed by the promise of more new experiences to slake his growing curiosity about the world of humans.

"I'd like something to eat," Albtraum interjected suddenly as he was struck by his own hunger.

What? You should have told me if you were this starved... I am sure there is something I can do to arrange a hunt for us, so you will not be forced to stoop to the indignity of human sustenance.

Brunhart seemed to be taken aback by the sudden nature of Albtraum's statement, but turned back to face him. "Well, it has been some time since your last meal. I'll take you now, if you like."

Albtraum held the pup at his side and hurried to pull on his boots, trying to ignore Lucifurius' frustrations. Though he insisted on going hunting, Albtraum feared it would be too much of a risk with so many eyes on them. The guard captain seemed accepting enough, but Albtraum was not fool enough to wonder why the man had spent so much time hovering around him – he was keeping careful eyes on him.

Lucifurius settled into quiet displeasure as Albtraum followed along behind Brunhart towards the kitchen. *Admirable as it is that you wish to ensure the success of our task, you must hunt soon, lest your strength fades any further.*

By the time they reached the kitchens, the pup was all too happy to be let down to the floor. It flopped on its belly, sniffing at Albtraum's boots as he looked around the kitchens. They were wide and bright, clean countertops of light wood and marble shining in the sunlight that poured in from the tall windows. The room was warmed by the heat of the stoves, and the smell of cooking food permeated the air. The attention of the servants was directed to the doorway as Brunhart entered.

One young woman quickly scurried over, curtsying before Brunhart, her gaze darting to Albtraum for the briefest moment. “Lord Captain, what can I do for you?”

“I'm aware that we are between mealtimes, but this young man is rather a bit behind on a reasonable meal schedule and needs something to eat. Do you have anything?”

The woman nodded. “We have some pierogi and onions in the pan right now he can have, if that is suitable.”

“I believe that should suffice.”

Albtraum watched the pup crawl around his ankles, gnawing at the toe of one of his boots. It was a strange little creature, but Albtraum could not help but find it somewhat amusing.

The kitchen servant chuckled. “I see the mean pup has met his match,” she said lightly, and her smile only burst forth into a chuckle as Albtraum frowned at her.

Brunhart moved to sit at one of the counters, watching Albtraum as he gazed around the kitchen. The smell of the food in the air was enticing, and hunger had twisted his stomach into knots.

Someone had left something on the table, a vegetable of some sort, round and cut in half. It was white and shiny, almost iridescent. Albtraum’s hunger was so great that without lending much thought to it, he picked it up and bit into it.

The pungent taste was strong enough to burn, so much that Albtraum felt his eyes tear up and his nose burn with pain all over again. It hurt to eat, but he was so hungry he couldn't stop, he kept eating in spite of the searing pain.

When he glanced up, Brunhart was staring at him. “You don't need to eat that, boy. They'll have real food out in a moment. An onion is not exactly edible until it's been cooked in some way. You'll see when they've finished the pierogi.”

Albtraum stared at the onion with vitriol for a moment, and set it on the table with a defeated sigh.

All the more reason we must hunt. Human sustenance is needlessly complex.

Although Albtraum knew Lucifurius spoke the truth, the plate the kitchen workers set in front of him was infinitely more attractive than a killing spree at the present moment. A pile of small dough pockets was piled on the plate and drizzled with what looked to be cream and butter, surrounded by crisped bits of what he assumed was the onion he'd taken a bite from. On the floor, they placed a bowl of meat trimmings, which the pup quickly took note of and began eating.

He took the fork they handed him and started eating, more than a little surprised at how good the mysterious pockets of dough tasted, browned in butter and filled with some sort of soft, crumbled cheese. He'd scarcely had time to notice himself devouring them before half the plate was gone.

“You eat like you've never seen food,” Brunhart observed, “and sleep like you've never had a moment to rest.”

Albtraum shook his head. “I haven't,” he huffed between bites. He was beginning to feel self-conscious, everyone here looked at him and questioned him as though he were some infinitely rare and interesting specimen of fauna, and he feared his ruse may not last under such intense scrutiny.

He stopped eating abruptly, spitting out the bite he'd taken, somewhat surprised at the unpleasant taste he'd encountered. This particular pierogi had not been filled with the mild, savory cheese but with something starchy and slightly bitter. He examined it and then looked to Brunhart for an explanation.

"Something wrong?" Brunhart asked.

"This one tastes..." He grimaced. "Terrible."

Brunhart raised an eyebrow and leaned forward to look when Albtraum pushed the plate towards him. "Ah, that's potato. Often times they'll run out of cheese to use and have to fill them with something else.

Albtraum sighed and pulled the plate back to finish off the last few left, though he had found his appetite had dissipated and he continued mostly out of obligation.

When he'd eaten everything, he returned his attention to the pup at his feet, licking at the last bits of food in the bowl that had been set out for it. It looked up at him, tiny tail wagging slightly as their eyes met. Albtraum sighed, unable to muster any contempt for the tiny thing.

If you truly find the creature so amusing, perhaps I might take exception...

Albtraum was quietly pleased to receive allowance from Lucifurius, and knelt down from his seat to sit with the pup on the floor. It waddled into his lap, yawning and resting its head on his knee.

"What will you name him?" Brunhart's voice sounded behind Albtraum, startling him.

Albtraum floundered for an answer. “I...” He was unsure what names one might even give to a dog, and toyed with words in his head for a moment.

“...Renegade,” he finally answered, hoping the answer would be enough to free him from the question.

Brunhart nodded. “Good name. Be sure you use it when you speak to him, so he learns.”

Albtraum stood, lifting the newly-named Renegade in his arms. He knew he would soon be taken back to his room – a comfortable prison, but a prison all the same. If he was to find a way to hunt, finding some way to escape those bonds was paramount.

“Surely this creature is not the only thing I am expected to amuse myself with,” he said, his voice low but firm.

The slight smile of Brunhart’s expression hardened back into a stoic and inexpressive scowl. “For the time being, yes. But if you find boredom that unbearable, we will try to have the queen arrange something more for you to do.”

Albtraum was almost glad for Brunhart’s immediate shift in tone – back to suspicion and steeliness, rather than cautious patience. As much as Albtraum wanted to delve into this world, familiarity would leave him more exposed. He could not afford any interactions to move beyond that veil.

Intriguing as their offerings may be, you can never be a part of this world. They will not allow it. The only world you will ever belong to is a world with you and I, and nothing more.

For what may have been the first time in his life, Albtraum no longer found this thought particularly comforting.

Chapter VIII

As Mianna opened the heavy wooden door of her office, she could not help but frown at the glittering cloud of dust that greeted her, lit up by the rays of sun that filtered in through the windows. Her office had fallen into a state of neglect of late, but she could not abide the servants disrupting the careful arrangement of her documents and books, and so, the dust was left to accumulate.

She brushed a few escaped curls of hair from her face and stepped around the desk, thumbing through some of the papers she had left out to be attended to. Her mind had been flooded with nebulous planning, and now that more pieces had begun to fall into place, her usual daily work had fallen by the wayside. There was a part of her that relished the chaos and the newness of it all – more than a hundred years in power certainly made for plenty of chances for boredom to fester.

Still, the state of her office nagged at the back of her mind, and she made note to bring a rag to take care of some of the dust.

A sharp rap on the open door caught Mianna's attention, drawing her gaze to two guards standing there, waiting to be addressed. They were the commanders of the guard force, and both answered to Brunhart. For them to have come directly to her indicated a matter of grave importance, which was further confirmed by their tense stances and somber expressions.

"Commander Bashkir, Commander Kaminski, what have you to report?"

Kalen Bashkir, commander of the cavalry, was first to step forward. He had worked in Mianna's service for the majority of his life, and had gone all gray in the last decade, but for a few reddish patches across the stubble on his chin. He had been a brash young man when Mianna had first taken him into her service, but the years had blunted his harsh voice and withered his frame. He had been openly considering retirement in the recent months.

"Ill tidings, I am sad to say, Your Majesty," Kalen replied, dipping his head in greeting." Three of the guards posted along the roads outside the city were killed in the night. Their replacements discovered them this morning when they arrived for their work."

Disturbed, Mianna set down the papers in her hand. "Three, you say?"

"Yes, Your Majesty."

Mianna frowned deeply. Her guards were well-trained men, and for a death to occur along a guard route was almost unheard of, even with the occasional unruly bandits making their way out of the forests. Three deaths certainly made cause for alarm. "I trust you've left the location as you found it so that a proper inquiry can be made."

Kalen nodded. "Well as we could, Your Majesty. Shall we have Captain Frasch investigate?"

She sighed and shook her head, grabbing a thick fur-lined cloak from where it hung on a rack near the door, wrapping it around her shoulders before stepping out of the office and into the hallway. "He is attending to other matters. I shall ride down to the road to see for myself what transpired."

Dimitri Kaminski, the infantry commander, stepped forward. He was a great deal younger than Kalen, but gray had begun to touch the edges of his dark beard. "I shall question the other guards along the route to determine if they noted anything amiss in the night."

Kalen nodded his agreement. "Aye, and I shall escort you out of the city, Majesty."

"Thank you, Kalen, Dimitri."

Dimitri gave a quick bow before hurrying off to fulfill his task, and Kalen followed alongside Mianna as they briskly made their way down to the stables.

"What is the Captain preoccupied with this day, if I may ask?" Kalen inquired, offering his arm as they passed the gates. Mianna accepted, amused by surfacing memories of times long ago when a young Kalen had attempted rather desperately to win her affections. Though he had long since married a woman from the village and raised a family of his own, fleeting flirtations occasionally persisted.

"He is attending to our guest. Though I believe Albtraum will behave himself once properly influenced, he has left quite the trail of corpses in his wake even in the short four years since his awakening, and the being he houses is frightfully powerful. I would not wish to place any of my men in unnecessary danger, especially not now that we seem to face another threat."

Kalen gave a nod of understanding. "Ah, of course. The Captain is much sturdier than the rest of us. But... if he is truly so dangerous, is it wise for you to take him in?"

Mianna nodded her greetings to the guards who passed them by. "I do not believe he is as he seems to be, outwardly... Take away the daemon commanding him, and you will find not a murderer, but simply a misled and inexperienced young man in need of a place of safety."

The air was crisp and cold on their route to the stables to retrieve horses, and Mianna found that the chill pleasantly did away with the last bits of early morning fatigue that still clung to her. The horses seemed eager to be taken out when they arrived at the stables, taking off at a brisk trot once they had been saddled and mounted.

The townspeople watched attentively as Mianna and Kalen rode past, some stopping to briefly bow. It was a quiet morning, and a sense of peace blanketed the streets of the city. That peace faded into tension as they passed the gates and encountered the full force of the guard scattered along the borders of the city and the road that lead down the mountain. News of the sudden deaths of their comrades had shaken them, no doubt.

When they reached the guard post at the edge of the forest, Mianna noted the large gathering that had formed around the section of road where the incident had occurred, the murdered guards still lying where they'd fallen. A thin dusting of snow had settled over the bodies, but the bright color of the blood across the snow was no less visible.

Kalen was first to dismount his horse and quickly helped Mianna down from her own. She pulled her cloak more tightly around herself as she made her way closer to the center of the gathering, guards parting to allow her to pass with a bow of their heads.

Only one young guard stood fast, blocking her way. "Your Majesty, I would advise you leave this to us, I am afraid the scene is quite ghastly—"

Mianna imperiously motioned the young man aside, and he scurried out of her way. "I am quite certain I can withstand it. Stand aside."

The three men had been killed in quick succession – the first two did not appear to have had the chance to retaliate, as their weapons had not even been drawn. Footprints, covered over with new snow but still visible, led up to the first guard, whose throat had been slit. They did not lead to the second body, but straight past to the last guard.

Mianna looked over the second body, and a guard approached behind her. "Seems to have been a gunshot, Your Majesty."

"That would explain the path of the footprints," Mianna muttered, leaning in to look closer. The dead guard had been shot directly through the eye, leaving a bloody, mangled hole. Long ago, being confronted with something of this nature might have unsettled her, but the years had hardened her to such sights.

The last man had managed to fight back, made evident by the bloodied sword in the snow next to him. His throat had been slit as well, but far less cleanly than the first, a clear sign of resistance. The footprints of the assailant veered off into the forest, along with a heavy trail of blood. Mianna followed it, carefully examining what was left in the snow. The footsteps appeared unsteady, limping... until they suddenly righted themselves, and the blood trail disappeared.

"Has there been any sign of the assailant?" Mianna asked, turning back to face the group of guards gathered around the scene.

One man shook his head. "None, Your Majesty. These men were hours dead by the time we discovered them. None of the guards further along the road reported seeing anyone pass by during the night. We've thought perhaps a group came up through the woods, but there don't seem to be enough footprints..."

Mianna made her way back to the road, stepping carefully around the bodies. "No, I believe the murderer acted alone." She was troubled by what the evidence seemed to suggest – a single assailant, powerful enough to fell three men and escape despite being wounded, leaving a blood trail that faded far too quickly for how grave the bloodstains suggested the wound to be.

She let out a tense breath, looking into the darkness of the thick woods down the mountain, the footprints disappearing into it.

“Have the bodies removed, and see to it the men’s families are notified,” Mianna instructed Kalen as she returned to the path to mount her horse. “Double the guards along the road and at the city gate.”

Kalen looked to her with concern as she stepped up into the saddle of her horse. “Need we prepare for conflict, Your Majesty?”

Mianna shook her head. “No, and it would be best to do away with such thoughts, lest we cause undue alarm. I must see to the arrangements for the families of these men, and tend to important business matters. Please do ensure things run smoothly from here, Kalen, and notify me if anything requiring my attention should arise.”

Kalen bowed his head. “As you will, Your Majesty.”

Mianna set off on the steep climb back up the mountain, her mount ambling along at a labored pace. She was troubled, her brow furrowing as she considered what she’d seen – all the markings of the murders pointed to an immortal assailant, and a message directly targeted at her.

Mianna’s political rivalries were brutal and bloody – the deaths of three men, while they had certainly shaken their comrades, were little more than a formality in the realm of those with the same power she possessed. Given that this had occurred so soon after she had taken in Albtraum suggested that one of her peers disapproved of her actions. The warning, in her mind, was clear as day.

Still, determining where it had come from would prove no easy task. Any one of her peers could have orchestrated such a thing – there were some she suspected more, but with the unity of the Order growing more tenuous by the day, none could be ruled out.

Mianna made her way back into the city, leaving her horse with the guards at the gate of the estate to be led back to the stables. Stepping back into the warmth of the estate walls was a welcome relief, but it could not quell the racing of her thoughts. She had much to consider, but the murders were too fresh in her mind for a clear perspective.

She quickly scaled the steps and made her way back through the halls to her office, finding them empty until she reached the office door. Brunhart stood outside, his stony expression revealing nothing.

"Brunhart," she said in greeting, slowing to a stop before him. "I trust you have been informed of what happened."

He gave a single nod. "I know that Albtraum had no involvement. I guarded the guest hall myself last night."

Mianna sighed. "I did not suspect him. The evidence seems to point elsewhere – but the direction is no less troubling, I am afraid."

Brunhart's tense brow relaxed slightly, if only for a moment. "I suppose it must involve our allies, then."

"Yes, but I have no clear leads as to which. For now, I must assume that none outside of Sylva can be trusted, though my trust was certainly wanting to begin with." Realizing she was speaking her thoughts aloud, Mianna shook her head. "No matter. I shall tend to this in greater depth later. While on the subject of Albtraum, how fares our guest?"

"Well enough," Brunhart answered simply. "He seems to be at least somewhat receptive to working with us." He followed her as she stepped into the office. "He is quite a bit younger than we'd expected."

She considered that for a moment as she sat down at her desk. "Not terribly so."

Brunhart sighed. "His voice still breaks. His practical knowledge of the world seems limited. Take care in your interactions with him, that is all I mean to say."

"Duly noted, Brunhart," Mianna answered with a nod.

"He does seem restless," Brunhart added absentmindedly, sitting down in the chair opposite Mianna.

Mianna gave a soft chuckle. "I can imagine. There is only so long he can be expected to stand being confined to that room, passed between the kitchens and infirmary when he is not. I suppose I can meet with him to discuss more of our plans, since he has behaved himself thus far. He'll need new clothes made if he is to be making any appearances before the people – I will have Joaquin see to the arrangements."

"New clothes will not tame his wildness, nor change what the people think of him," Brunhart pointed out, a slight breath of exasperation surrounding his words.

"Perhaps not," Mianna answered, "But Joaquin will certainly aim to try."

Brunhart stood again from the chair slowly, looking back to the door. "I should address the men about what's happened. Is there any particular message you wish me to deliver?"

Mianna considered what to say. Conflict was imminent, and no matter how much she tried to shield her people from that fact, they would know something was amiss, they would feel the rising tension in the air. Announcing it would cause panic, but she could not simply ignore the possibilities looming over them.

She turned, gazing out the window down at the city. It was beautiful, even from so far away. The streets were clean and orderly, and the buildings were always kept in good repair. The people of the city were proud to call it their home, and Mianna was as well. It stood proud and strong on the face of the mountain, a paragon of all the Order should be.

And yet, it had not always been this way.

She had worked hard to gain their trust. She had taken steps into the mire of humanity, much farther than she thought herself capable, all for the sake of this place and these people. She had become as hard and sharp as a keenly honed blade, and as she had given up pieces of her own humanity in pursuit of her kingdom's greatness, it was as if life had been restored to the city.

Pride and resolve had seen them through much. It would see them through this as well.

"Three men died honorably for their kingdom, and we mourn their loss. However, any enemy who believes that the deaths of three men will in any way intimidate Sylva or its people is sorely mistaken."

As Brunhart exited the office with a nod, Mianna carefully dug through the piles on her desk for a parchment and quill.

The world had begun to move. And she had no choice but to move with it.

Chapter IX

I tire of human trivialities.

Albtraum found himself in agreement with Lucifurius as he was twisted around for what must have been the thousandth time by the tailors Mianna had sent for him. The girls had been hovering around him for the better part of an hour, seeming rather uneasy as they took their measurements, scrawling them on a piece of parchment and speaking in hushed tones to one another. It had been late in the afternoon when they'd first arrived, and they were working solely by lanternlight now.

He watched them with suspicion, which only seemed to heighten their uneasiness as they circled him. Albtraum sat defensively, his knees pressed together, his arms held firmly at his side until he was prodded to stand and pose to be measured. Renegade watched the spectacle curiously, shying away when the tailors tried to approach him.

"How many measurements do you need?" Albtraum finally asked with a sigh, and the girl standing beside him jerked back, startled. It was the first time he'd spoken since they'd arrived; perhaps she thought him a mute.

"I... Master Harlan prefers to be thorough. Clothes should not be ill-fitting for a royal ward... That is what he told us." She moved forward again to measure the breadth of his shoulders, and he straightened his back slightly, trying not to recoil at being touched.

Just as Albtraum was beginning to think this might go on forever, the door burst open and a man laden with armfuls of fabric bustled in, sending the group of tailors scattering.

He was a swirl of vibrant colors, from the many materials he carried to the ornate golden doublet he wore, open nearly halfway down his chest, and a deep red sash looped about his waist. Short waves of auburn hair framed his face, with a striking streak of white that started at his hairline with a single strand of hair and continued all down one side of his face, through his eyebrow, eyelashes, and beard – as though lightning had struck him there. His skin was dark, and his eyes were a bright, piercing blue. He was surveying the tailors as they rolled up their measuring tape and wrote down the last of the measurements they'd taken.

The man laid out the fabrics on the table at the head of the room and took the tools from the girls as they scurried out of the room. He turned on his heel to face Albtraum, pointedly asking, "You are Albtraum, I assume?" His voice carried the slight lilt of a foreign accent, but Albtraum could not place it.

He had an air of disdain about him, giving a tiny sigh of exasperation, when Albtraum only nodded in response. "My name is Joaquin Harlan. You'll see me here quite often, as I assist the queen with most of her day-to-day responsibilities, and also provide her wardrobe. I'll be providing you with a new set of clothes as well." He gently took Albtraum by the arm to turn him around. "Your appearance is, quite frankly, unacceptable, and you're so tall I doubt we'll have anything already made that will fit you."

Albtraum frowned and shifted his weight between his feet, feeling somewhat awkward, unsure of how to respond. Rather than maintaining Joaquin's uncomfortably intense eye contact, he opted to watch the tailors as they filed out of the room, a few casting glances over their shoulders at him as they went.

Joaquin looked up at him, scowling deeply. “What's happened to your face?” He took Albtraum by the chin to examine the gash across his nose better. “This is positively tragic. It may even scar... And you have such nice skin.”

Albtraum sighed slightly, just through his nose, finding that it still stung even after the swelling had gone down and he could breathe normally again, for the most part. “That woman... Ismaire... she smashed my face against a table.”

Joaquin grumbled in disgust, patting his cheek before turning back to the table. “Stay far away from that one. Despite our best efforts she seems intent on remaining *thoroughly* uncivilized.”

He made his way over to the vanity, turning over the mirror so it no longer faced the wall. Albtraum watched him closely as he poured a bit of water into the washbasin from the pitcher the servants had brought in that morning, his curled moustache quirking to the side with his mouth as he tested the water with a touch.

“Well, it’s not terribly warm anymore, but it shall have to do. Come here,” Joaquin ordered, pointing at the stool in front of the vanity.

No sooner had Albtraum cautiously stepped over and sat down than he was suddenly shoved headlong into the washbasin, Joaquin pouring cold water over Albtraum’s head as he furiously scrubbed a bar of soap through the tangled, dirty snarls of his hair.

“How long,” Albtraum heard him hiss, “has it been?”

Albtraum gurgled incoherently, but his voice rose at the end as if in question.

“Since you had a *bath*,” Joaquin clarified.

The soapy water stung as it dripped down from his forehead onto the gash across his face – but that was only the beginning of the torment. *"Stop,"* Albtraum croaked. *"Soap. Soap in my eyes."* His eyes wrenched shut and his jaw clenched.

Joaquin scoffed. "Good. They were likely filthy as well."

The torment continued for some time, Albtraum gripping the edges of the vanity as Joaquin scrubbed away, occasionally letting out a huff of disgust.

The remainder of the frigid water from the pitcher was then dumped over Albtraum's head, rinsing away the last of the suds. When he was finally able to open his eyes, he found himself staring down at a washbasin filled with water that was gray with filth, and so opaque he could not see the bottom of the shallow vessel.

Before Albtraum could grimace at the sight, he was pulled back by the hair, yelping in pain as a comb was dragged through its many mats and tangles. He snarled, gripping the sides of the chair – he had faced pain in many forms throughout his life, often at the end of a blade, and yet this experience was somehow more difficult to bear.

After what seemed an eternity of labored ripping and pulling through the knots, the comb finally passed easily through the strands. Albtraum huffed, glaring back at Joaquin, finding the odd man looking infuriatingly pleased with himself.

"There now, you'll still need a proper bathing, but it's a start." He motioned Albtraum's gaze toward the mirror, and Albtraum blinked owlishly back at the clearest reflection he had ever seen of himself.

He had caught passing glances of himself reflected in standing water and glass windows, but they had been distorted and dim, nothing like the stark reflection of the silvery mirror. His face was thin, set with wide orange eyes that glinted in the dim light, dappled with freckles, and... Entirely softer and gentler than he had expected.

He frowned. Behind his skull mask, he had imagined himself a fearsome creature, but the face looking back at him from the mirror was surprisingly human. Even the shallow gash and dark bruising across his face only served to make him look more pitiful and weak.

“Underneath all that, your hair is a lovely color,” Joaquin commented, smoothing out the last damp, unruly strands with the comb before crossing the room again.

Albtraum sighed, slumping in the chair. His scalp ached from the vigorous brushing, but the feeling of clean, untangled hair was undeniably pleasant.

If they would prefer us to be well groomed when we bring this kingdom crawling to its belly, then so be it. You will be resplendent either way.

“I've brought some different materials for you to choose from,” Joaquin called from where he stood, spreading the fabrics out across the table.

Albtraum curiously made his way over to the dresser, examining the materials suspiciously. There were so many colors... More colors than he had ever seen in one place. The hues were rich and deep, some of the fabrics smooth and solid, others intricately patterned with filigree and floral designs. Gingerly, he ran his fingertips across the surfaces of the materials, finding that each one was softer than anything he'd worn.

Of all the many colors, he found himself repeatedly drawn to a velvety material of a paler blue. He could not place why, but he found the color appealing.

He picked it up and handled it for a moment before handing it to Joaquin, who seemed confused by the action.

"Favor this one, do you?" Joaquin asked, prompting Albtraum to nod again. "You don't speak much," he observed.

"I don't have much to say," Albtraum muttered.

Joaquin picked up the parchment left by his assistants, looking over the measurements that had been made. "The good-looking ones usually don't."

Albtraum eyed Joaquin pointedly, feeling somehow that he was being mocked.

"It'll be at least a day or two before my assistants and I can have anything newly made, so I will have to have something close to these measurements sent along to you." Joaquin gathered the fabrics and stepped over to the door, opening it and motioning in the guard who stood outside. "In the meantime, Dimitri here will see you to the bathhouse, so you can make yourself decent for a proper audience with the Queen. I will have the servants deliver the clothes and linens to you there."

As Albtraum was ushered into the hall and the door shut behind him, he could hear Renegade try to rush after him, the pup's claws skittering across the stone floor as he dashed for the door, whimpering pathetically. Albtraum was reluctant to leave him there, but he did not seem to have a choice in the matter.

Joaquin glanced back at the door before turning to the other guard who stood ready in the hallway. "Glen, watch after the dog, will you?"

Albtraum glanced at the young man. Messy curls of mousy hair flopped over his forehead, and he seemed surprised to have been addressed directly. Albtraum had seen him before in the infirmary.

“Ah, of course!” he replied with a wide smile. “Does he have a name?”

“...Renegade,” Albtraum answered as his escort began to lead him down the hall.

“I could never come up with such an interesting name for anything,” the guard, who had been addressed as Glen, replied with a laugh. “You should hear the names I give my horses.”

Albtraum simply looked uncomfortably back at him as he was briskly led away.

Joaquin disappeared in the other direction, and the stern-faced guard marched behind Albtraum, a strong hand resting on the blade at his waist. His tension was palpable.

Clever man.

Despite Lucifurius’ amusement, Albtraum found himself somewhat offended at this blatant distrust. If he truly was supposed to be a guest, he expected the guards should take at least some care to hide their fear of him.

When they reached the end of the hallway, they stood before a great wooden door. Dimitri pushed it open and stood aside, sending thick billows of steam spilling into the hallway. Inside the large room was a bath, set into the stone floor. The bath itself was massive – it reached almost to the edges of the room.

Albtraum carefully stepped inside and the door was quietly shut behind him, leaving him alone in the eerily silent expanse of the bathhouse. He crossed to the other side of the room and undressed, feeling exposed though there was no one to look upon him. He left his clothes in a heap on the edge of the bath, kneeling and climbing into the hot water.

The sensation burned a bit at first, new and sharp, the water coming to just above his waist. But as he sat on the stone ledge against the edge of the bath, the temperature of the water gradually became pleasant, rather than uncomfortable. It felt especially soothing to his feet, which still ached from the ill-fitting boots he had been wearing for so long.

There were nooks carved into the stone at the edge of the bath, where Albtraum found bars of soap. They smelled faintly sweet, and he took one and began to scrub away at the dried blood from the blisters and the dirt caked on his feet. The bandages around his abdomen soaked quickly from the water, but they were wound tight, and remained in place.

He finished scrubbing away at the rest of himself with the soap bar, rinsing his hair out again for good measure, if even just to warm the dampened strands that had grown cold in the chilled air.

After he'd rinsed off, surrounded by scattered suds floating around him, he sank into the warm water, all the way up to his chin, his eyes sliding shut as he felt relaxed for the first time in weeks – the heat of the water had eased the constant tension in his shoulders and his back, and if not for Lucifurius' occasional hums of displeasure at his complacency, he might have fallen asleep there.

He should have remained more alert, he knew. Death lurked at every corner in this place. But he was so very exhausted, and this respite was too tempting to resist.

"Giselle, come to deliver something, have we? Or were you simply here to admire our guest?"

The sound of a voice ringing out, cutting through the heavy silence of the bathhouse, followed by a high gasp of surprise, sent Albtraum quickly backing against the edge of the bath, cursing his vulnerable state as his eyes darted to the open door of the bathhouse.

A servant girl stood there, arms full of linens and clothes. She was turned facing someone who had entered the bathhouse behind her – Mianna, dressed in silk nightclothes, covered by a deep blue robe.

"Y-your Majesty," the girl stammered, quickly bowing her head. "I was..."

"There now, you can be on your way. Albtraum would like to be left alone, I'm sure. I'll take those." Mianna accepted the stack of neatly folded cloth, and the servant scurried away, partly shutting the door behind her.

Albtraum watched Mianna circle the edge of the bath to set the clothes and linens near him. He sank deeper into the water, as though that might offer him more protection. Lucifurius waited, coiled and ready to strike.

"Please, don't let me stop you," Mianna said. There was a laugh in her tone. "You seem to have become quite the subject of talk among my servants."

Albtraum frowned, turning away from her. "Your servants must not encounter much of interest."

Annoyingly, his lack of manners again failed to offend her. "I simply came to look in on you and see that all your needs are being adequately tended to. I would also like to extend an invitation for an audience. Will you dine with me tomorrow?"

He peered up at her blankly. What did she expect him to do? Come alive with enthusiasm? Decline with a snarl?

He simply muttered, "I suppose so, yes."

She smiled, stepping over to the edge of the bath. “Wonderful. In the meantime, please continue to make yourself at home. I can trust you to move about more freely now, but the guards have been warned to keep a close eye on you, so please do not test my patience.”

She looked down on him in such a way that made him uncomfortable, and he pressed himself into the corner of the bath. “Now that you've had a proper bath and new clothes, you should have no trouble finding company with some of the more... socially inclined servants, if that is what you wish.” She smirked and stepped back around the edge of the bath to the door. “Do not hesitate to ask should you require anything else.” She delicately shut the door behind her as she left.

Mianna was certainly mocking him, of that he was sure.

Your lack of caution is becoming dangerous. How long did that servant stand watching us? You were fortunate this time, but next time a blade may find its way to your heart.

Ashamed at his failing, Albtraum quickly dried himself with the linens and hurriedly dressed in the clothes he’d been given. They were finer than what he’d been given before, but fit too loosely on him. He fidgeted with the edges as they awkwardly wrinkled over his gangly frame.

His body felt heavy as he left the bath house, and as he was led back to his room once again, he found the halls to be cold in comparison to the damp heat he'd sat in for the past few hours.

He entered his room in a rush when he arrived, finding Renegade was sleeping soundly, curled up in the center of the bed. He yawned and stretched as Albtraum settled into the covers. The bed had been made with fresh sheets, and against his now-clean skin, the feeling was nigh on intoxicating.

Overcome by some feeling he found unfamiliar, Albtraum reached out to scoop up Renegade, bringing him up close to nestle into the pillows. Renegade licked the end of his nose and whimpered contentedly before snuggling himself under Albtraum's chin.

Lucifurius scoffed in disgust, but Albtraum had scarcely heard it before he drifted off to sleep.

Chapter X

Mianna had offered Ismaire a proper bedroom years ago, and every so often, the offer would resurface. Ismaire had never once considered accepting. She'd always preferred the loft she'd put together for herself in the rafters, away from the commotion of the estate, away from where most people could find her.

Most people, of course, did not include Mianna herself.

"Ismaire," Her voice rang hard and sharp, echoing through the open loft.

Ismaire sighed. "What do you want, Mia?" She rolled over the edge of her bed, out of the elaborate nest of bedding she had constructed over the years, and dropped to the floor to face Mianna, crouched like a cat.

"I thought I had warned you about your informality," Mianna said, but there was a touch of amusement in her expression. "I have matters to discuss with you. Have a seat."

Ismaire rolled her eyes and sat cross-legged on the floor in front of her bed. Mianna stepped up into the loft and stood in front of her, handing her a small, folded bundle of parchment. "I have here a letter from your family, first of all."

Ismaire accepted the bundle, feeling her chest tighten.

"I am not certain yet, but... We may have reason to travel soon, and I imagine visiting your family may be a possibility."

Ismaire swallowed. "Ah. I see."

Mianna gazed at her intently. Like always, she could see right through her. "Do you not wish to see them?"

Ismaire squeezed her eyes shut and shook her head. "No, I... I want to go home, I do. But... I've disrespected everything they gave me, everything they did for me..."

"And that hurt them, I am sure. But not as much as it would hurt for them to lose you entirely, so I suggest you write back. And..." Mianna leaned forward slightly, her posture relaxing slightly. Ismaire did not often see her in this light, when she was not constantly maintaining a regal air, her spine so straight it could snap though she made it look effortless.

"While we are on the subject of atoning for past wrongs, I would again like to remind you that I expect you to remain civil with Albtraum. He is now my ward as well, and I have well enough to concern myself without you posing a threat as well."

Ismaire inhaled sharply to shoot back with an objection, but as she stared up at Mianna, she realized how futile her words would be. She fidgeted with the thick parchment she held. Even though it had traveled halfway across the world, it still held a few grains of sand from the desert, which fell into her hands. "Alright. I will make an effort."

"Thank you. Now, I will leave you to answer your letters. I am sure your family will be joyed to hear from you."

Ismaire turned the parcel over in her hands as Mianna exited the loft, sighing as she anticipated looking upon its contents. She had not so much as visited her home since she first left five years ago, and she missed it, but for the most part she dreaded returning. The words exchanged with her mother over letters had been only half as harsh as the conversation was to surely be face-to-face.

Even harder to accept than her admonishment, though, was her love. Ismaire had received less than a dozen letters from her mother and father in the time she had spent in Sylva, but each one, no matter how pointed her mother's criticisms and scolding, she had always been sure to remind Ismaire of their love for her.

Even Mianna... She had never known Ismaire before she had fallen in with such poor company, and had every right to judge her solely on the deeds she had witnessed. Mianna could have locked her in a cell forever, or even executed her for what she had done, but instead she had given Ismaire a chance to change.

Ismaire would not allow that chance to be taken away from her... even if it meant disobeying Mianna.

She slumped back against the edge of her bed, releasing a sigh of frustration. When she'd first heard the rumors, she sat hoping Albtraum would find his way to their doorstep – she needed to prove to Mianna that she had atoned for her past mistakes, and prove to herself that she was not beyond all redemption. Killing him provided a perfect way to do so. He was an infamous murderer, after all, his crimes more heinous even than her own.

As the rumors got closer and closer to them and finally he showed himself there, she had been just inches from killing him. She'd never expected that Mianna actually *wanted* him, for whatever reasons she had.

He was her chance for redemption, his death the currency to end her debt to Mianna, and she wanted him *alive.*

She furiously ran a hand through her hair, grumbling. She could only hope that he would falter soon – that the monster in him would come back, that they would see him for what he really was.

When he did, she would be ready.

Albtraum stood in front of the vanity mirror, twisting and turning as he attempted to manage the many layers of clothing he had been given. There had been no instruction delivered with the ornate outfit—a doublet of deep violet, a loose, velvety black robe, and a golden silk sash. Even his black trousers and soft cloth shoes had been detailed with delicate embroidery.

He sighed at his reflection. He scarcely recognized himself - dressed in lavish clothing, neatly groomed... positively *presentable*. The mats and tangles were gone from his scarlet hair, and it shone in the light, thick and silky. The queen and her followers had managed, somehow, to tame the wilds from him. His glinting firelight eyes were the only visible remainder of his monstrosity.

Albtraum thought he might be more disappointed to find himself reduced to this state - but the comfort of his fine clothes and the promise of a rich meal awaiting him had occupied his thoughts for the time being. As if to agree, a growl rumbled deep within his stomach.

You have been made to suffer far too many human meals... they are empty of substance. If this goes on much longer, we will find ourselves inexorably weakened.

Lucifurius spoke with strained patience, his tone goading Albtraum to action.
Albtraum knew well that this ruse could not continue indefinitely. He was a captive here—and easy as that was to forget, it was the truth. Already the feel of a blade in his hand seemed a distant, fading memory, and the call of the battlefield no longer sang through his every move.

Renegade was gnawing at his toes, and the pup's teeth were so sharp they found their way through the cloth shoes to Albtraum's skin. He grunted and glared down, prompting Renegade's ears to pin back, his tail giving a halfhearted wag as if in apology.

It was impossible for Albtraum's anger to rise past annoyance - the dog had an inexplicable charm, and loath as he was to admit it, Albtraum had grown attached to him. Perhaps, he thought, he might make a permanent companion of him once he left this place.
It is imperative that we search for a means of escape with all haste. Every day that passes with you in their clutches you become more toothless... Even now, this vermin has more fangs than you.

Albtraum knew Lucifurius spoke the truth, but he found himself hesitant to concede. Giving in meant scorning the possibilities the world of humans held, and he was not yet ready to turn his back on that.

A sharp rap at the door caught his attention, and he turned as the door opened, Brunhart stepping in.

“Well, Joaquin has managed to make you look like a proper royal guest,” he commented with a slight chuckle. “Come on then, I’m to see you off to dine with the queen.”

Albtraum knelt to scoop up Renegade and followed Brunhart out to the hall, shutting the door behind him as he stepped out of the room. Even though it had been but a few days, he felt an ownership of the space. A small fortress in this den of foes.

The setting sun cast an orange glow into the hallway, but the estate seemed far from settling down, guards and servants bustling noisily through the halls as they finished with the day’s work and moved into their evening leisure time. Some of them passed by Albtraum without noticing him, some fell into a hush and stared as he moved past – still others seemed more concerned with Brunhart, quieting and moving ahead with stiff postures, casting him a glance out of the corner of the eye, until they were well past him. Albtraum watched them all as they passed by, so distracted that he did not notice as Brunhart came to a halt, and he walked straight into his back.

Albtraum quickly reeled back, inhaling sharply, fearful of his own inattention. He could just as easily have walked into the end of a blade.

Brunhart seemed to shrug off the collision with only the faintest amusement. “Here you are. The queen is waiting.”

Albtraum stepped past him, setting Renegade down to trot along at his side as he entered the banquet hall. The smell of the food that had been brought out to the table was intoxicating, filling the room and making his mouth water. The table was long, with seating for many guests, but only two of the seats were occupied at the head of the table, by Mianna and Joaquin.

Mianna gave a good-natured smile as she saw Albtraum enter, and Joaquin looked quite pleased with himself, looking to Mianna with a smirk after he'd looked Albtraum up and down.

"I did tell you I could make him worthy of a court appearance, did I not? Although..." He turned back to Albtraum with a frown, rising from his chair with a huff. "You've tied the sash all wrong, just allow me to..."

He trailed off, fidgeting with the length of silk about Albtraum's waist as Albtraum stood stiffly, his arms held awkwardly in the air. When Joaquin had finished, he had seemingly magically produced a neatly constructed knot of the sash. He pulled out a heavy wooden chair from the table, motioning for Albtraum to sit.

He'd scarcely settled into the seat before a servant set a bowl of broth on the table in front of him, and a plate of meat scraps on the floor for Renegade. The pup gratefully tore into the fatty trimmings, crawling onto the plate as he feasted.

Albtraum stared down at the bowl of broth on the table in front of him then glanced across the table at Mianna and Joaquin.

"I doubt this audience was intended solely for the meal," he muttered coldly, reaching for the spoon at the side of the place setting after he saw Mianna do so.

Mianna sipped broth from the spoon and eyed Albtraum as he stirred his own bowl, her expression betraying nothing. The tension in the air was palpable, and Albtraum felt more trapped than ever.

"It can be considered quite rude to some to cut straight to business matters before engaging in socialization, though I do appreciate your pragmatism." There was a teasing lilt in her voice that set him on edge.

He turned his attention to the food then, bringing a spoonful of broth to his mouth. It was a light broth, nearly transparent, but it had a rich flavor and a velvety texture, and for a moment, Albtraum forgot his tension. He glanced about the room to avoid Mianna and Joaquin's curious gazes, finding that much activity bustled just outside the banquet hall, though the hall itself appeared empty with but three occupants at the table.

"I will dispense with pleasantries, if that is what you wish," Mianna declared, breaking the silence. "If I am to be quite brief, I would wish to extend an offer for you to join our Order."

Albtraum started, blinking at her. "Join you?"

Oh, this is quite the development. What fool thing is she planning? Does she truly expect us to be so stupid?

"Yes, Albtraum. Our organization strives to foster balance in this world and all those connected to it, but the voice of a daemon is something we lack. I mentioned previously that your connection to the dark world makes you a valuable ally to us, and I believe your benefits to us could be best utilized if you were to join our ranks."

Has she forgotten my presence?

Albtraum set aside his spoon, and stared down at the table. The ruse was truly being tested, and Albtraum doubted he could continue with it for very much longer, as much as he wished to learn more of this world. They were changing him... Turning him into one of them. As much as he resisted, Lucifurius was right. There had been an undeniable impact.

It was time to put an end to it.

"You must be a fool," Albtraum muttered, leaning back in his seat, eyes still downcast at his bowl. "A fool to think that I would ever join a cause headed by those who have killed and mutilated my brothers and sisters."

Yes. Good.

"The daemon children were a blessing given to you by my father, and they were cast aside as though they meant nothing!" He stood from the table, his shoulders tightening. "He sought concord with your people and he was scorned at every turn. Do not presume to offer alliance now, as though we have somehow forgotten, as though you offer us a favor." His voice was louder and stronger than he had dared to allow in his time here, leaving a sharp silence in its wake.

We must prepare to flee. Find a weapon if you can.

He stood still, staring across the table. Joaquin stared back in shock at his outburst, but Mianna, irritatingly, was unfazed, her posture relaxed and her expression betraying nothing.

"That is what you believe then, Albtraum?" Mianna asked him, setting aside her spoon and standing from the table. "That daemon children were a gift to humanity, and that your father once sought out peace with us?"

"Yes," Albtraum spat back. "And none of your lies will sway me."

He looked behind her then, finding that a few guards had stepped inside the banquet hall, weapons ready. He gritted his teeth. Escape would certainly prove difficult.

"I cannot fault you for that, of course," Mianna answered calmly, waving off the guards, who slowly stood down. "You have known little of the world outside of your father's vision of it. And so, what other truth can you be expected to accept?"

Albtraum narrowed his eyes at her as she spoke. Her composure was both baffling and frustrating, and Albtraum found as he watched her speak that it eroded his conviction. How was she so sure of herself when confronted with the truth?

"I will not ask that you take me at my word. That would be unfair of me. Instead, I will show you the truth."

Albtraum glanced behind himself, finding himself flanked by two guards. He growled. He had missed his chance...

"It will require that we travel beyond the walls of the city, so we must leave it until tomorrow... In the meantime, I will have the remainder of your meal sent to your room. I imagine you might prefer to spend your evening alone."

Mianna motioned to the guards, and Albtraum was firmly restrained by the arms and escorted away from the hall. Renegade ran after him, the guards paying the pup no mind.

You should have run, Lucifurius sighed. *Ah, well. No matter. I am sure another opportunity for escape will present itself shortly... If not, we shall simply have to find a blade and carve one out.*

Chapter XI

The sun had just broken over the horizon when the guards entered Albtraum's room, but he had not slept.

The stale remnants of the meal he'd been brought sat on the vanity. He had tried to resist eating the food, but it had been too tempting, his hunger too great. Renegade looked over to the door curiously as the guards entered. He had spent the night nestled close to where Albtraum sat on the bed, but Albtraum had been far too fraught with tension to stroke the pup's soft fur.

Mianna entered the room after the guards, and Albtraum felt the back of his neck burn with anger at the sight of her. She was dressed in traveling clothes, practical but ornate. Brunhart stood directly behind her.

"Good morning, Albtraum. I would ask if you rested well, but you do not appear to have." Mianna stood aside as more guards entered and surrounded him. "I apologize for the early hour, but I'm afraid our journey will take a great portion of the day. I will ensure your pet is cared for. Let us be off."

Albtraum said nothing, allowing himself to be led away, almost relieved that the ruse had been dispensed with and he was now being fully treated as the prisoner he truly was.

He stared at the stone floors as they made their way through the castle, ignoring the sounds around him as the servants and guards filled the hallways. He would soon be far from this place. He felt his chest tighten with regret that he was unable to take Renegade along with him, but that was how it must be. He could stay here no longer.

The chill of the early morning was sharp as they made their way outside to an assembly of yet more guards with horses at the ready. The beasts shifted, hooves clicking noisily against the cobbled streets, their breath creating great clouds in the cold air before them. There was a small passenger cart, which the guards led Albtraum to, with one sat on either side of him, and three across.

Brunhart sat directly opposite Albtraum, regarding him sternly, but with an underlying emotion Albtraum found difficult to identify.

“I remind you again, boy, we are not your enemies.”

Albtraum glared coldly back at him, saying nothing in response as he turned his gaze to the road ahead.

Mianna and her guards were no fools. They had left no opening – chances for escape were few, if not nonexistent.

Patience, child. Opportunity will present itself. Be on your guard.

Albtraum watched the forests pass by as the group traveled, Mianna riding at the head of the group and a few guards riding alongside the cart. Everything had frosted over in the night, sparkling in the bright morning sun as the frozen trees slowly thawed. It was beautiful, and Albtraum found his mind wandering, anticipating his return to wandering the forests. Unbound by stone walls. Free.

He shifted, his shoulders uncomfortably pressed up against those of the guards, his knees pressed together and his head turned at an angle to avoid looking in the eyes of any of his captors. The sight of them infuriated him.

The roads were well traveled, as made obvious by how smoothly the cart rolled along and the occasional traveler crossing paths with the group. They would veer to the side of the path and bow their heads until Mianna had passed, and Albtraum found the gesture rather odd.

Humans will express reverence for the strangest of things, Lucifurius mused.

The guards remained tense and silent all the way along the road, as did Albtraum. It must have been well over an hour before the road lead them to a small settlement. There were wooden walls, worn but carefully constructed, and the gentle sounds of human activity emanated from within. The sun had risen higher in the sky by now, and the air was warmer, but a deep chill had settled into Albtraum's bones, and his body ached from the uncomfortable seat of the cart.

They came to a stop, and the guards led Albtraum from the cart. He bristled, waiting for a chance – leaving the cart, perhaps, he could reach for a weapon, break loose. The guards were standing farther apart, now, he could break free and run...

Now, child. We will go together.

He readied himself to wrench free of the grasp of the guards—but Mianna's voice ringing out from the village gate captured his attention.

"Have a look then, Albtraum. The results of your father's gifts to humanity."

Curiosity demanded Albtraum turn his head to look upon what she gestured to. Beyond the village's wooden wall was a standard human settlement – or so it appeared on first glance.

As the moments wore on and Albtraum drank in the sight before him, the despair of the village became apparent. There were great gaping holes in the earth, like wounds, that oozed something thick and black. The grasses and shrubs of the area were withered, long dead even before any winter's chill had reached them. The villagers that milled about appeared in poor health, thin-faced and slow moving.

Mianna turned from observing the village to face him. "This is what the lord of all daemons considers his gift to us. Unbidden he reached his darkness into our world, draining the life from it. Impregnating unwilling women with his children, sickening all he can touch."

Albtraum looked across the landscape—blackened with death, the townspeople moving slowly about their daily tasks, hobbled by the sickness that had seeped its way into the very earth.

This was Lucifurius' conquest. The ruin that remained after he had taken all he could, adding it to his own power.

Somehow, Albtraum felt no pride as he observed the crippled village's inhabitants shamble nigh-lifelessly past him. Unease prickled through his mind, along with pity, and perhaps even shame. His sorrow for his murdered siblings was no less, but given that these were the circumstances of their births, he could hardly imagine how any human might consider them a gift. How great and powerful of a ruler could Lucifurius be if all his strength was stolen?

Child. Do not let this witch poison your thoughts.

Albtraum floundered for an explanation... any way this could be a lie. Perhaps the humans had done this, and simply decided to blame Lucifurius?

This could not be, however. The energy exuded by the area was distressingly familiar, the same as the energy that existed within himself.

"I show you this not to shame you, Albtraum. You do not bear the guilt of your father's sins, you are as much a victim as any. But you must understand. You must know the truth." Mianna motioned forward, and the group continued into the village.

Albtraum said nothing, following in a daze, memories of the many he'd slaughtered burning through his mind. Had they been innocent, as these people were? Had they been as unknowing of the reason for their deaths, sacrifices on an altar of stolen lives and false power?

"Albtraum."

Mianna's voice snapped him out of his dark musing, and he looked over at her. She stared back with concern.

"A father's duty is to protect his children. Not to send them by the thousands to die in the clutches of enemies he has made for himself. Not use them as his weapon... as you have been."

Albtraum felt the entirety of what he knew unraveling before him. Desperate, he reached for Lucifurius.

I am nothing to you.

It was a statement, not a question. A wavering, despairing accusation. Albtraum hoped Lucifurius' denial would be all the stronger for it.

Seconds dragged on, feeling like hours.

Finally, a response.

Laughter.

You have always known this, Lucifurius hissed. *Why now does this trouble you?*

Albtraum drew in a shaky breath. *My whole life has been in your service... For your conquest. If I mean nothing to you... What meaning is there? What am I?*

Despair gave way to rage. Something broke within him.

If I have no meaning, then I have no reason to submit. If even you will not dignify my existence, then I will have to do so myself.

Lucifurius' reaction was swift and overwhelming. His words amplified until they drowned out all senses. Albtraum felt as though he was buried, he could scarcely breathe, nothing reached his ears but painful silence, vision blurred until he was blinded. He felt himself severed from every one of his senses, and the world gave way to silent, endless darkness. Nothing remained but the force of Lucifurius' voice and a searing, white hot agony.

You miserable insect. I have warned you before, but it would seem your foolishness knows no bounds. You believe you can stand on your own?! If you believe you deserve to have any more importance than a means to my ends, then you are a fool and I should never have saved you from your mother's clutches.

I thought you the shining example among my children, but it is clear to me now that you are nothing but filth.

You want to serve them? Go on, then. See if they see any meaning in your miserable existence without the meaning I have given you!

When the supernova of pain that had exploded behind his eyes faded, the world came back into focus. He was looking up at Mianna and Brunhart who were knelt beside him, vaguely aware of the twigs and rocks on the ground poking at him through his clothes.

He had fallen unconscious, and was lying on his back. He blinked as he looked up, finding the guards surrounding him, and even a few of the villagers having come over to investigate.

“Are you alright?” Mianna asked him as Brunhart helped push him up to a sitting position.

“I...I...” Albtraum stammered as he looked up at them. Lucifurius had gone quiet, as if the explosion of power had not happened.

The lingering ache in his head and the uneasiness deep in the pit of his stomach, however, said otherwise.

“Have you need of anything for your companion, Majesty?” A villager asked, bowing his head as he approached them. The man looked as withered as the village, deep shadows under his eyes, his face gaunt and his skin pale.

“No,” Albtraum muttered, trying to stand. “No, I—”

“Thank you for your concern, sir,” Mianna answered graciously as she rose to her feet. “A spell by the hearth might do him some good, I should think.”

Albtraum did not object as Brunhart pulled him to his feet, leading him in the direction the villager pointed them in. There was a profound difference in the way Brunhart gripped his arm, compared to the way that the guards had before – as though he was holding Albtraum up, rather than restraining him.

The group made their way to a building at the center of the village. Albtraum realized on entering that it was a tavern, evident by the small gathering of villagers and the rows of tables along the walls. Despite the conditions of the village and the surrounding land, the inside of the tavern was warm and pleasant, a strong fire burning in the center of the room and the smell of rich food wafting through the air.

Albtraum all but collapsed into a chair near the fireplace, his body heavy and weak from Lucifurius' attack on his essence. Only Brunhart and Mianna had followed him in, and Mianna took a seat across from him, observing him carefully.

"Something seems to have come over you. Are you quite alright?" Mianna asked, settling into the wooden chair.

Albtraum let out a breath, looking into the fire. He folded his arms against himself. "I did not know."

From the corner of his eye, he could see Mianna's expression soften, if only slightly. "Of course you did not. You could not have. I assume Lucifurius was the cause of your collapse."

Albtraum nodded. His head swam, still thrumming with ache.

Mianna looked around the tavern, seemingly unfazed by the sidelong glances directed her way and the whispering of the patrons. "This village was first stricken fifteen years ago. Young women suddenly bearing horned children, the earth decaying and infertile, sickness overtaking all who resided here... We offered them a place within Sylva's walls to escape the conditions here, and many accepted, but still more stayed. They are proud of this place... They have made it their home and their grave."

Albtraum listened to her and fidgeted uncomfortably, the world around him feeling suddenly nebulous and surreal. He could hardly imagine being so bound to one place, having spent his life roaming, always moving, always alone but for...

He drew in a breath, stopping himself. He did not want to think about Lucifurius. He did not want to think about life without Lucifurius.

“This is not the only city your father has drained the life from, or impregnated with his children. There are many across the world... More evidence every day of his rotting soul. He is no noble ruler seeking to reclaim something stolen from him. He is a withering god desperately clinging to something he should have let go of long ago.”

Her words had to be falsehood, and yet Lucifurius had not denied them. Faced with a challenge, Lucifurius had only confirmed Albtraum’s burgeoning doubts. Aching emptiness filled him.

Albtraum could never imagine a life beyond what he shared with Lucifurius. It seemed nothing could go on.

And yet, it had.

The world persisted. The gentle sounds and smells of the tavern enveloped his senses.

Another existence remained with these people. Lucifurius had called it a lie, but how was the life he provided founded in any truth when it was so easily dismantled?

Emptiness gave way to exhaustion. But this was the exhaustion of a battle ended... not of a defeat.

“I will return to your city with you,” Albtraum said quietly, standing from the chair. “I will offer what you require of me.”

This, it seemed, was the first thing he had said that truly surprised Mianna. Her bewildered expression gave way to a warm smile, and she stood as well, extending a hand. "I am so glad of this partnership, Albtraum. I hope that you will find it mutually beneficial... You are a great boon to us, but we also aim to offer you a chance at the life you deserve, guided by your own will."

Though he understood her words, he had little concept of what a life guided by his own will might look like. But something about the idea was enticing all the same. Awkwardly, he accepted Mianna's outstretched hand, gripping it timidly in agreement.

They left the tavern, and the guards awaiting them eagerly, seeming to sense Mianna's triumph as they made their way back to the wagon. Brunhart remained close at Albtraum's side, but it did not seem to be for the purposes of restraint. The guards gave Albtraum a wide berth, but it did not seem to be out of fear.

The road here had been strained and silent, but the road back saw the group conversing comfortably, never addressing Albtraum directly but seeming to accept his presence.

As they reached Sylva's walls once again, they felt far less a prison, and far more the beginning of something new.

CHAPTER XII

Albtraum was left largely to his own devices in the days that followed, and he was glad of the fact. Having disposed of the lie that he would cooperate with Mianna's wishes and having truly agreed to follow her, he was not sure what to do, how to act. He stayed in his room most hours of the day, a guard or servant occasionally leading him through the gardens to walk Renegade. His meals were delivered to him three times daily, and he was regularly informed by all who interacted with him that if he should require anything he need but ask.

He had no earthly idea what someone in his position *should* require, and he spent most of his time in anxious anticipation, waiting for a sign of the way forward. He had never before realized how truly dependent he was upon Lucifurius' guidance until now, that he was devoid of it.

Lucifurius had been silent since the trek to the corrupted village. At times it almost seemed he was gone... but his presence was undeniable, looming at the back of Albtraum's consciousness, watching everything he did. The silence was almost more powerful than his voice had been.

Albtraum laid quietly in his bed, awake but unable to raise himself just yet. He was sunken comfortably into the downy mattress, Renegade curled up beside his head on the pillow. A knock at the door awakened the pup, and he sprang up, running to the end of the bed and yipping, full of fervor but not very threatening.

Albtraum got up, opening the heavy wooden door to find Joaquin standing there, an armful of leather-bound books almost obscuring his face from view. Without asking to be let in he pushed past Albtraum, setting the stack of books on the dresser.

“Good morning,” he chirped, too energetic. He was dressed just as lavishly as he had been each time before, this time in a deep red tunic with shiny golden trim. “The servants have informed me you have been spending all your time in this stuffy old room. Can you read?”

Albtraum was somewhat taken aback by the sudden nature of the question, and took a moment to respond. “Yes,” he mumbled, rubbing his eyes. “I suppose I can.” It was a skill that had been implanted in him by Lucifurius; he could not remember a time when he had not had it.

Joaquin smiled. “Wonderful. We have a rather extensive library; I’ve selected some books you might take interest in. I thought you might enjoy having something to do while we make preparations, rather than just twiddle your thumbs for the next few months.”

Albtraum examined the tall pile of books and picked up the book on top, a small volume simply etched with the title *The Prince.*

“Oh,” Joaquin interjected, stepping closer. “I must have taken that by accident – it's Machiavelli, he's dreadfully tedious.”

Albtraum shrugged. “I can read it and see for myself.” He set it back down on the dresser.

Joaquin sighed. “Alright, but *please* don't let it turn you away from the other books if you dislike it.” He turned, motioning for some servants outside to come into the room. They were carrying neatly folded stacks of clothing, which they carefully laid out on Albtraum’s bed.

“I’ve started working on a wardrobe for you, as a ward of the queen you will need to be decent even while traveling and going about your daily business." Joaquin gestured to the clothes as the servants left from the room. Renegade sniffed at the freshly tailored fabrics, and Joaquin tried unsuccessfully to shoo him away.

Albtraum picked Renegade up from the bed to set him down on the floor as he looked over the clothes laid out on the bed – the coat, made from the velvety blue material he had chosen, was the first thing to catch his eye. Beside it was a vest, a dark umber color, and an ivory-colored cloak. There was a pair of canvas trousers and two pieces of leather leg armor, attached to a finely pressed belt. A riding outfit, if what he'd seen so far of human attire was anything to go by.

There were a few other sets of clothes with simpler designs but intricate embroidery – Albtraum had to wonder how they'd had time to do all this in the space of a few days. A few more pairs of canvas trousers and a black tunic paired with a dull red velvet shirt to be worn underneath. Two other loose tunics, one blue and one gray, that would have been plain if not for the embroidery that had been threaded through them as well.

"This, of course, is only what I have made for the moment, I have every confidence I can produce a full wardrobe for you before we set off on our travels," Joaquin mused.

"I am... certain you can," Albtraum replied, somewhat bewildered.

He looked over to find that Renegade had trotted over to the door, yipping at a guard who stood there.

"Hello there, Renegade," the guard said as he knelt down, extending his hand to be sniffed before scratching Renegade between the ears. Albtraum had seen him before, guarding the infirmary, and he had looked after Renegade once before. He looked up when Albtraum stepped out into the hall, pushing messy curls of mousy hair out of his eyes as he stood. He was tall, but still a touch shorter than Albtraum.

"Ah, hello! Aleksandra sent me up, she wanted to look you over again and make sure everything is healing properly. You're Albtraum?" He extended a hand. "I'm Glen Harlowe. Normally I guard the stables, but..." He trailed off as Albtraum did not take his hand, simply staring at him.

Joaquin stepped out into the hall after Albtraum, chuckling. "He's still adjusting to civilized life, so be patient with him. Albtraum, why don't you spend some time out and about today? I'm sure it might do you some good."

Glen nodded. "I can escort him around for the day! Well, let's go and have you looked over, shall we?" He started off down the hall to the stairway and Albtraum followed after him, picking up Renegade as he went.

Glen did not say anything else on their way down to the infirmary, but he kept looking back at Albtraum as if he were about to. When they reached the infirmary it was empty, and the doctor seemed to be waiting for them. She sat Albtraum down on one of the benches as he entered without so much as a greeting, cutting off the bandages around his abdomen. It stung when the air hit it, but Albtraum tried not to wince.

"Better," Aleksandra said after looking over the wound, "but you should still try not to overexert yourself." She re-bandaged it and poked and prodded at his face for a moment. "This will be less likely to scar if you don't pick at it, so don't touch it."

Albtraum stood again as the doctor went back to her work and turned back to Glen, who was on his knees, playing with Renegade.

“I need something to eat,” Albtraum informed him quietly, adjusting the hem of his shirt, which had caught on the bandages.

Glen stood suddenly. “Oh, of course! It's still breakfast at the mess hall, so there'll be quite a crowd, but... We could go into the city, if you'd like.”

Albtraum found the permissiveness with which he was allowed to roam around quite overwhelming, hence why he had kept to his room. But the prospect of venturing somewhere outside the castle walls intriguing, and having a guide made it far less intimidating.

“We can go to the city,” Albtraum repeated in agreement.

“Follow me, then.” Glen started in the direction of the front gate, Albtraum trailing behind him, Renegade scampering around his feet.

The chill in the air was milder than it had been in days previous when they stepped out into the courtyard, and the sun was shining. Albtraum found it hard to believe he'd only been closed off in the estate for a few days – it felt like a small eternity since he'd seen the outside. They walked down the hill into the lower section of the city, the street merchants and townspeople watching them as they passed.

Glen stopped at one of the buildings on a street corner, pushing the door open and waiting for Albtraum to walk in ahead of him. It was dark inside and the air was thick and smoky, and the sounds of chatter spilled out into the street as the door opened. The smells wafting from inside made his mouth water.

Albtraum stood inside the crowded building, picking Renegade up to keep him from being trampled underfoot.

“Ah, Noman!” Albtraum turned around as Glen made his way to a large table at the center of the floor, where a lone guard sat drinking from a tankard. Albtraum had seen him before too – he'd escorted him to the symposium hall the previous night. "Your day off, is it?"

"Yes," the older man said gruffly, setting down his drink. His long black hair was tied back, and he was dressed similarly to the other people in the building, in plain work clothes. "You're still working, though."

"Well, I'm just escorting him around for the day." Glen nodded to Albtraum. "We came down to get some pie."

Noman nodded. "Just finished mine."

Glen motioned for Albtraum to sit, and he did, holding Renegade in his lap.

"They have the best meat pies here," he said excitedly, sitting down next to Albtraum as a man approached the table with two tankards, setting them down at the table.

"Brought a friend with you, Glen?"

"Guest of the queen's," He answered, but the man already seemed to know. "Have Annette make us a pie each, would you, Maks?"

"Of course." The man turned back and disappeared into another room.

Noman nudged Albtraum's arm with an elbow. "Drink up, boy."

Somewhat annoyed at the command, Albtraum picked up the tankard and drank from it. He recoiled, spluttering. He had nearly choked himself on a large gulp of the bitter drink, and half of it ended up spat back into the glass.

Noman was chuckling. "You'll get used to the taste."

In smaller sips, it was tolerable. It warmed up his chest as he drank, and the feeling was not entirely unpleasant. Thought Albtraum did wonder if he was being poisoned.

“So, Al – Can I call you Al?” Glen asked, taking a drink from his own tankard. Albtraum shrugged. “What do they have you here for? You don't... You don't need to talk about it if you don't want to, of course, I only thought I'd...”

“I'm not entirely sure of that myself,” Albtraum muttered in response.

“They've said we may be traveling soon, which is exciting, it's been so long since I've even been down the mountain.” Glen reached over to pet Renegade, who was pacing across Albtraum's lap, trying to climb over his arms.

Albtraum sat up quite quickly when someone set a steaming pie in front of him with a spoon, and he quickly dug into it.

There were potatoes in the pie, but Albtraum avoided them easily – the rest of the pie was delicious. After every few bites, he'd stop eating to feed a morsel of meat to Renegade. Glen ate at his own, watching them with a grin.

“Good, isn't it?” His smile widened when Albtraum nodded. “Most people love Annette's pies.”

Noman stood from the table and patted Glen's shoulder. “I'd best get on with my day, I'll see you boys tomorrow.” Glen waved as he stepped out.

“Don't like the potatoes?” Glen asked when he turned back to the table, pointing at Albtraum’s mostly-empty bowl with his fork. Albtraum shook his head. “I'll eat them, then.”

"Do you know all the people in the city so well?" Albtraum asked curiously as he watched Glen finish off the potatoes in the bowl. The concept of having so many connections and relationships was staggering, but all the many people in this place seemed to be quite closely acquainted.

Glen's eyes widened a fraction. "Oh, well, not *all* of them. Annette and her son Maks looked after me when I was young, so I know most of the people who visit here. And the guards I work with, of course."

"Glen," came an old woman's voice behind them. "You've got two dishes in front of you and your skinny friend here's got none – I know you love to eat, but I never raised you to be a thief."

"I didn't want to waste the potatoes, Annette," Glen laughed. "He doesn't like them."

"That so? I'll give you a chicken pie next time then, dear, it hasn't got any potatoes. I reckon I've got some scraps for the pup, too." She stepped away from the table.

"We can come back tomorrow to get another pie if you like," Glen said to Albtraum as he watched to woman walk away.

"Alright," Albtraum replied. The woman had returned with parchment-wrapped package, and Renegade sniffed excitedly at it as she placed it in Albtraum's hands.

"Don't be a stranger, either of you. Glen, you never told me your friend's name?"

"Oh, this is Albtraum. Al? Al." He grinned. "We'll be back tomorrow, Annette."

“You're going to get fat if you keep eating my pies every day, Glen, and then you won't be able to find a girl to marry you. Look what's happened to Noman,” Annette said with a huff as they stood to leave.

“In Noman's defense, I don't think finding a wife has *ever* been a concern of his,” Glen chuckled. Again, he opened the door and waited for Albtraum to step out ahead of him.

It had grown even warmer in the time they’d spent inside, the sun shining warmly upon the cobbled streets, melting the lingering ice that had built up there. Renegade eagerly tried to reach the package of scraps in Albtraum’s hand as they walked, though Albtraum held him tucked in the opposite arm.

“We don’t *have* to come back tomorrow, of course. I just thought you might like more time out of your room, and maybe you can try a chicken pie!”

Albtraum wondered how he was expected to respond – and so he did all he could think to, briefly nodding.

You will never be one of them. You are so pathetic you cannot even become a human.

Albtraum slowed to a stop at hearing Lucifurius speak. He had not believed he was gone, or that he would remain silent, but...

“Al? You alright?”

Albtraum looked over to Glen. “I... I need to go back to my room,” he muttered quickly.

Glen’s brow furrowed. “Are you sure? Do you need to see Aleksandra again?”

"No, I..." Albtraum let out a breath. "I just need to lie down."

"Alright. It was good to meet you, Al. I'll come by to guard the door later if you need anything else."

Albtraum stared back at him, then hesitantly nodded once more before scooping up Renegade. "Good to... meet you as well."

He rushed back up to the castle and through the hallways to his bedroom, seemingly unnoticed by the people he passed. The castle walls seemed safer somehow, but he knew there was no safety from Lucifurius. He was everywhere, entwined with Albtraum's very soul. They were never apart... There were no lengths he could go to that would offer escape.

Lucifurius was laughing. *You exchange pleasantries and wear their garb and eat their fare as though you can be one of them. But you can never be.*

As he drew a shaky breath and took a step to ascend the stairs to his bedroom, he was startled to find himself face to face with Mianna. She seemed nearly as shocked as he was to have run into him, but regained her composure in an instant.

"Ah, Albtraum, good to see you," she greeted.

"Ah, hello..." he was not sure how to address her, so he settled for how he had heard everyone else do so. "Your Majesty."

She smiled and waved him off. "'Mianna' is just fine. After all, I'll be more a mentor than a ruler to you, anyhow. Which is precisely what I wished to discuss with you. Perhaps you and your dog would like to join me?" She held out her hand for Renegade to sniff, and he wagged his tail and nuzzled into it.

He looked past her up the stairs. Solitude had sounded inviting, but...

"Yes, that would be fine," he muttered in reply.

"Wonderful! I was on my way to the aviary." She motioned for him to follow her, and they climbed the staircase.

"I'm afraid I am not familiar with what an aviary is," he said after a few moments of silence passed between them.

"Think of it as a very large bird cage," she explained. He expected she might have expressed some exasperation with him for not understanding, but her tone was light and friendly. "I keep several falcons much the same as you keep your dog."

Albtraum had never conceived birds might be kept as pets, but then, he supposed there were likely a great many things he still had to learn about the human world.

She led him down the hallway to a room that was, just as she had described it, rather like a large birdcage. Huge, towering windows looked out over the expanse of the mountains before them, and above him windows looked up to the sky.

There were a few nests on large poles around the room, and from them he could hear the chittering of the birds. Mianna pulled on a thick glove from a table sitting next to the door, then gave a sharp whistle and extended her arm.

A hawk swooped down from one of the nests and gracefully landed on her outstretched hand, prompting Renegade to yip in alarm. The hawk seemed mostly unfazed, but regarded the dog carefully.

"This is Aidan, the most well trained of my birds," she explained. "He often delivers messages for me, albeit over short distances."

Albtraum managed to calm Renegade and regarded the bird curiously. He had only ever seen falcons at a great distance, and was intrigued at how comfortable this one seemed in Mianna's presence. She softly stroked its head before thrusting her arm up to send it flying back to the nest.

"I had thought pigeons or ravens were more commonly used to deliver messages," Albtraum commented as Mianna removed the glove and took a seat in an armchair near one of the windows.

"I prefer my messages to be clutched in larger claws," she replied with a slight smirk.

He watched her, somewhat uncomfortable. She acted human, sounded human... but everything in him knew she was not. Even now, as he tried to ignore it, he could sense the power she held, though he no longer had the slightest desire to claim it. If Lucifurius did, he did not express as much.

Even as an ally, something about her set him on edge.

"Ah, but I should inform you of what is to come. You have been patient, of course, and there is much you have overcome in the past days."

He waited for her to continue.

"You are a curiosity, to me, Albtraum," she muttered, deviating from the previous subject. "You speak so little, yet I know there is more you can say."

"Perhaps I've just grown accustomed to silence," he offered half-heartedly, stroking Renegade's head.

“Perhaps. But I am afraid what I have to propose demands you find your voice.” She motioned for him to sit, and he did.

There was comfort in taking orders. As much as Lucifurius’ control had become stifling, without it, he felt lost.

“I see no need to mask the truth. If I am to trust that you will be honest with me, I must offer you the same. The Order to which I belong, to which my kingdom belongs... it is crumbling. You saw the corruption of the village we visited—Sylva hangs by a tenuous thread, and I fear it may follow suit. Those I once called allies, I cannot trust. As it stands, Albtraum... you are my most valuable asset.”

He hummed out a contemplative sound. “If you think I can provide you with insight as to Lucifurius’ every thought, I—“

Mianna held up a hand to stop him. “I know you cannot.” Her voice was hardly above a whisper. “But you can do something more.”

“...Which is?”

“You can take his place.”

Albtraum sat unmoving. His eyes scanned the room, as if searching for an answer. He waited for a retaliation from Lucifurius, but none came. “I cannot,” he answered. “I...”

Mianna stood. “It is your decision. I will not stop you if you refuse. But I implore you, Albtraum, we need your help.”

He shook his head. “I know I promised I would help you, and I intend to, but... I am not what he is.”

“You are not, no. And that is precisely why you are ideal to do this.”

Albtraum let out a trembling breath. “How am I to... how? He is as a god, an army unto himself, and I ...”

“You have defied him.”

Albtraum let out a breath in a rush. “Only because he has, for some reason, *allowed* it...”

He could hardly conceive of such a thing. The mere fact that he had refused to follow Lucifurius and somehow still continued existing had been difficult enough to come to terms with, but this...

“I will not ask that you make a decision now, but I would ask for the moment that you at least join us on our travels to the other kingdoms. I have informed them of our impending visit in the coming months, and seeing the state of the Order as it is now may yet convince you.”

“I...” He lowered his shoulders as he realized how tense they had become. “I can do that much, at least.”

“Good. I believe on our travels, you should have ample time to learn. And I sense something in you, Albtraum... I believe you will lead well. I suppose I must convince you of that just as I must convince my peers.” She laughed softly. “Now, I'm sure you'd like to get back to exploring Sylva yourself, and I encourage you to continue making yourself at home.”

He nodded. Renegade had settled into his lap, drifting off to sleep. Mianna left him there with a nod in parting.

Home. Before, he'd never thought such a thing possible, but now, it was all he could bring himself to want.

Chapter XIII

Mianna expected, as always, to find her office a flurry of dust and chaos when she entered it, but was rather surprised to find it tidy and organized, and Joaquin sitting at her desk, looking over letters and documents. He was dressed crisply and formally, as he always was, and Mianna found herself wondering whether she had ever seen him looking anything but perfectly kempt in the many years they had worked together.

"Good morning, Mianna. We've heard back from the other kingdoms," he informed her, holding out a few of the parchments to her. The seals were broken. "They have all expressed eagerness to meet with our new charge, everyone seems quite intrigued by him. Though Camlion seems a bit more eager to meet with *you.*"

Mianna glanced over the letters, raising an eyebrow. "He always does, doesn't he?"

Joaquin chuckled. "I wonder how many more times you'll have to let him down gently before he takes the hint?"

"He may never learn, unfortunately." She circled the desk to sit down as Joaquin stood up from her chair.

Weeks ago, after Albtraum had agreed to join her, free of any ruse, she had decided to organize a tour to the other Order kingdoms. Tensions were high, and she needed as many on her side as she could gather—as well as more information about who sought to rise against her.

Returning to the thought of the attack, she looked back over to Joaquin. "Have you had any further insights as to who killed our guards?"

"I am afraid not... Every one of them is equally suspect in my mind. None of them have ever had an abundance of respect for your rule." Joaquin smirked. "And I daresay your audacious lack of offense at that disrespect has done little to improve your relations with your colleagues."

Mianna smiled in return and set the letters down among the pile of documents on the desk. "That said, I am glad that Albtraum has made himself fully willing to follow our directives. With possible enemies on all sides, we need as little resistance as possible from within. The servants inform me he has been quite take with the books you brought for him, he was reading Machiavelli this morning."

"He was?" Joaquin gasped, almost horrified. "I added it to the pile accidentally... I never thought he would enjoy such tedium. I never finished *The Prince,* myself. I do hope he has moved on to the others by now. Chaucer, Virgil, Boccaccio, Ovid... That should keep him occupied for quite a while, I imagine, until we leave. A proper noble should be well-read."

"A sentiment I fear Ismaire still does not share."

Joaquin heaved a great sigh. "I have long since given up on that girl. In any case, I have the tailors working on my designs, Albtraum will need more clothes. We cannot make a good impression if we parade him around looking like a commoner."

Mianna smirked. "'Commoner' seems to be quite a broad term to you, Joaquin. You thought the pope dressed like a commoner, when we met in Rome."

“The fault is all his. So many changes have been made to the church practices through the years, and I haven’t the slightest idea why ridding the traditional garments of that *ridiculous* hat was not among them.” Joaquin crossed the room to open the curtains, and the light filtering in was still dimmed by the overcast sky.

Specks of dust that Joaquin had brushed away from the desk glinted in the dim rays, and Mianna absently thought that the office was due for a dusting. “Well, it truly doesn’t matter at this point what impression he does or does not make. The tour is a formality, a goodwill gesture. I have the final say of who we put in power, and that will be so regardless of whether they are convinced or not.”

“And will it be him?” Joaquin inquired, glancing at her from where he stood.

Mianna made a sweeping gesture. “Clearly, we have an abundance of alternate options.”

Joaquin smirked at her sarcasm, quirking his moustache to the side. “Surely there can be none better, not after the *vision* you had.”

“It wasn’t a vision, Chronus *came here* and spoke to me. If that doesn’t speak to the dire nature of the situation, I don’t know what will.” Annoyance edged into her voice, though not for Joaquin.

He sighed. “You need not convince me. I only wonder if the others believe you as well.”

“They have a right to be skeptical, of course. Chronus rarely appears before members of the Order, and only in the most dire of circumstances.”

“All the more reason we must make a good impression.”

Mianna was about to respond when she saw one of her guards passing by outside the door. “Glen,” she called, and he turned around, stepping into the office.

“Yes, Your Majesty?” He unconsciously straightened his coat as he stepped up before her.

“I hear you’ve been spending some time with our guest?” she asked him.

“Oh, yes,” Glen answered, relaxing slightly. “He doesn’t talk too much, but he still seems to be willing to cooperate and I haven’t had any troubles with him.”

She smiled. “That is good to hear. I thought I might ask you to take some time to ensure that he has some knowledge of horsemanship. I imagine he may need to ride at some point soon.”

Glen grinned. “Of course! The weather’s been warmer lately, and it’ll give the horses more chance to stretch their legs.”

“Wonderful. You are dismissed, Glen.”

He turned and left the office with a nod, and Joaquin took a seat on the other side of the desk. “Well, I’d best get this place in order, and then I ought to make you a new set of outfits for the journey, since they’ve already seen the travelling clothes you have.”

“I am sure I have something I haven’t already been seen in,” she assured him as she stood. “But if you insist, I will not refuse new clothes. Just take care not to overwork yourself.”

“My dear, you cannot know me as well as you claim to if you think I can be overworked.”

With a laugh, she left him in the office, and left to the throne room, where she had meetings to conduct with her citizens. She had always held them herself, rather than having delegates speak for her. Some in her employ considered it undignified, but Mianna found over the long years of her rule that the more she showed herself before her subjects, the more they had come to respect her.

It was bright in the throne room, the back wall being almost entirely comprised of intricate iron-framed windows. There was a decent gathering of people, and the chatter ringing through the high ceilings fell to a scattered hush as she entered. The gathered townspeople began forming lines to speak to her as she climbed the steps at the head of the room and took her seat on the throne.

She nodded to the first man in the row, a farmer she recognized was from the outskirts of the town. His clothes were not as fine as some of the inhabitants of the inner city, but it was clear he had made an effort to look his best.

"Your Majesty," he said in greeting, bowing his head. "We anticipate a rainy summer, which could mean a surplus of some of our crops. We might bring in more revenue by accepting an advance on our anticipated harvest from towns that import our goods."

Mianna considered what he proposed for a moment before adding, "However, if your prediction proves false, you may not have enough crop for yourself after promising an amount to your importers."

"That is the risk, Your Majesty."

"I leave the decision to you," Mianna said. "If you offer your crop at a profit and end up without enough for yourselves, you will not have the assistance of the royal treasury. However, you should no doubt be able to provide for yourselves well enough through the winter with the extra money you'll have made, should it come to it."

The man nodded again. "Of course, Your Majesty. We appreciate your leniency."

He stepped out of the way and allowed the next in line to step forward. This time a whole group stepped forward. There were four of them, all boys, a bit dirty and rough around the edges, and Mianna noticed the guards on either side of her move their hands to their swords. She smirked at their cautiousness, thinking it unlikely these boys were capable of causing any real trouble.

"What can I do for you?" she asked as the boys seemed to consider who should speak first.

They looked back and forth at each other for a moment before the shortest, a somewhat dumpy young man with dark hair, stepped forward.

"We'd like to join the royal guard," he said, clearly trying to sound confident, though his voice rose at the end as if in question, rather than a demand.

She raised an eyebrow, leaning back in the throne slightly as she looked over them. "How old are you, good sir?"

He seemed slightly embarrassed, looking at his shoes before answering, "Fourteen."

She nodded. "And your friends?"

He seemed to hesitate. "Thirteen."

She sighed. “I take it none of you have families who’ve tried to talk some sense into you.”

“We’re orphaned, ma’am,” one of the others said. His voice was high and unsteady. “We found our way here from the villages down the mountain.”

The first boy spoke up again. “We’ve been getting by on odd jobs around the city, but we’d all like to do something more.”

“I see.” Mianna shifted slightly. “And I suppose you are aware that I do not hire men who’ve not yet seen twenty winters into my guard.”

“We’re all good with swords, ma’am,” he pleaded, looking defeated.

“Better young men than yourselves who claimed to be good with swords have come to me to join the guard, and I have turned them down also. If you’ve need of better work you can work in the estate kitchens, assist the blacksmiths, or help the guards in the barracks. In seven years’ time, if you’d still like to join the guard, you may meet with me again.”

Mianna waved them off in dismissal, but they stepped forward. “Other kingdoms let men as young as we are fight for them!”

The guard to Mianna’s left did draw his sword, then, and stepped forward. “Watch your tone, boy! You speak to the Queen!”

Mianna stood, waving the guard off. “If I took offense to every citizen that ever spoke to me out of turn, I would never have time to get anything done. Please.” She turned back to the boys, and her tone hardened. “Other kingdoms are desperate for fighting men and care nothing for their citizens. I prefer not to hire boys into my ranks, as I would rather have a strong royal guard force than a large one.”

The boys backed down slightly, looking sheepish.

"Now, you can speak to the estate servants if you wish to work among them, or, if you would like to push this matter further, I will be sure you can find no work in the city either. You are dismissed."

The boys shuffled off, and Mianna sat back in her throne.

"Forgive my outburst, Your Majesty," the guard muttered.

"Quite alright. Do be sure you defend Sylva's people with the same zeal in my absence." Mianna watched as her servants spoke with the townspeople who had been waiting; often their concerns did not need to be addressed by Mianna directly, and having the servants to sort them out helped expedite her audiences.

"Absence, Your Majesty?"

"Yes, we will be visiting the other kingdoms to gather support for our cause. And given all that has happened of late, I fear we may face more attacks in an attempt to dampen my resolve. I will need every man in my employ to defend the kingdom to the utmost of their abilities."

"Of course," the guard answered. "We will not allow ourselves to be intimidated by those who wish to do us harm."

Mianna nodded in agreement. "And ensure that anyone who tries does sorely regret it."

It was early morning, still dark enough that the chess board in Joaquin's room was illuminated almost entirely by candlelight, but the faint glow of the sun had begun to creep its way into the windows.

"Checkmate," Brunhart informed Joaquin brusquely as he placed a bishop before Joaquin's king.

The pieces were almost comical, viewed side by side on the board together. Brunhart's were well-crafted, but worn and rugged, carved of dark wood. He'd made them so long ago, he could scarcely remember what they'd looked like when freshly carved. Joaquin's were marble, patterned with gold designs that still managed to exude opulence even as time and use had begun to wear them away.

Joaquin sighed deeply, knocking over his own king with a careless flick of his finger. "I truly thought I had you, that time. Ah, well." He gathered his pieces and placed them back in their box – also carved marble, so heavy Brunhart wondered how he carried it anywhere – and stood from the table. "I have much to do, as much as I'd like another game, I fear we would be here all day." He brushed a white-streaked strand of hair from his face.

"True enough."

"You're planning to look after Albtraum today, are you?"

Brunhart nodded, gathering his own pieces into a threadbare cloth sack. "After I've organized the men this morning, yes. I doubt he needs the supervision, but he's seemed..."

"A bit overwhelmed," Joaquin finished for him with a light chuckle. "I suppose I've not helped with that much, but I believe I am coaxing him out of that nigh-impenetrable shell of his. Slow though it maybe."

"Perhaps you are."

Brunhart left Joaquin to his work, and set off to his own. He made himself busy in the guard barracks, assigning duties to the guards who were to remain in Sylva during the queen's excursion, when he was approached by the cavalry captain, Kalen Bashkir. The infantry lieutenant, Noman Grouser, was readying for his daily duties, checking over his weapons and strapping on his pauldrons.

"Captain Frasch," Kalen greeted calmly as he approached. At least in appearance, he was older than Brunhart himself, with ashy blonde hair that was almost all gray now - but Brunhart remembered when he had been a young recruit. He wore the gray coat of the guard uniform, but not the deep green cloak over it. He had likely not gone out on his first watch yet. "I was wondering if I might have a word with you."

"Of course," Brunhart replied, and the young guards he had been speaking to stepped away as the older captain stepped up to the table.

"I've mentioned to you that I've been considering retirement," he reminded Brunhart, taking a seat at the table.

"I hope you're not planning on informing me of its start, not right before the queen sets out on an extended absence," Brunhart asked, wondering where this was headed.

"No, no," he assured Brunhart, waving him off. "Rather that I would like to recommend someone for my replacement."

"Who might that be?"

"Glen Harlowe," Kalen answered, nodding to where he stood over at the door to the barracks. He seemed distracted, talking with some of the other guards and glancing out of the doorway down the hallway ever so often.

Brunhart could not hide his surprise. “Him?”

Kalen chuckled. “He’s a bit flighty and softhearted, but he’s good with horses and lances alike, and a hard worker. I can tell you’re not convinced, but just bring him along with you on your journey, give him a chance to prove himself.”

Brunhart sighed, retrieving his sword from the weapon rack as Kalen looked over the guard assignments laid out on the table. “Alright. If I find he’s not up to the task I will choose my own replacement, so you know.”

“As I expected.” Kalen heavily placed his hand on the table and stood. “Do let me know if there is anything else I can do for you before you set off.”

“Are you not accompanying us?” Brunhart asked.

“We should keep both captains here in the city, and Grouser said he wanted to go with you. Says it’s been a while since he’s been out of the city. I, on the other hand, am content to remain here.”

“Not only that,” Noman added from where he was lacing his boots on a bench nearby, “The men said they could use a break from my griping.”

Brunhart sighed. “So you’ll come with us – and gripe on the road.”

He grinned. “Of course.” He stepped over and patted Brunhart’s arm, then walked out to the hallways to begin his day’s work.

Brunhart turned his attention once again to Glen, who was dressed in his stable clothes, and not his uniform. He was already supposed to have started his watch, and he was not even scarcely ready. Brunhart grumbled to himself and walked over to confront him.

"Glen," he started sharply, and the young guard turned around to face him, startled. He had been conversing with someone standing outside the door. "I suppose you won't mind explaining to me why you are not prepared for your duties this morning, especially not after I've just come from hearing Captain Bashkir sing your praises."

"Oh, I'm sorry, Captain," Glen stammered. "I forgot to inform you – I'm going to the fields today, the queen requested I teach Al how to ride before we set off." He motioned behind him.

Brunhart suddenly noticed that Albtraum was standing just outside the door, dressed in travelling clothes that looked to have been made by Joaquin, for the delicate golden embroidery of the trim and the rich quality of the fabrics. His hair had been tied back. He looked uncomfortable. He looked from Glen to Brunhart, seeming unsure of what to do.

Glen was looking up at Brunhart. "Sorry – you said Captain Bashkir mentioned me?"

"Never you mind," Brunhart said with a sigh. "I suppose the queen's orders do take precedence over your regular duties, but you must inform me from now on."

"Of course, Captain, and I'm sorry for any inconvenience I might have caused you."

"I'll come with you, if you'll have me," Brunhart said with a nod.

"That's fine by me," Glen agreed, and stepped out the door. "Well, we'd best get going before we lose too much daylight."

They made their way from the barracks to the halls of the estate to go outside, crossing the path of guards and servants as they always did.

Brunhart noted that most no longer seemed to gaze at Albtraum with suspicion, rather nodding in greeting as he passed by.

Albtraum followed behind Glen and Brunhart walked at his side, noting that the pup he'd given him was trotting closely behind them, tail wagging and pink tongue floppily out of a happily smiling mouth. Brunhart could not help but chuckle at the sight. He had grown in the past weeks, his paws too big for his body and all of his movements clumsy as he tried to navigate his increasing size.

They left the estate and walked down to the small field just outside the estate courtyard, where the stables were. The sun was shining brightly, and Brunhart could hear the horses shifting and neighing as they approached. Glen led Albtraum into the rows of stalls, and Albtraum looked warily at the horses.

"This gelding here is Grey. He's my horse." Glen stopped at the stall, and Brunhart watched as Albtraum stopped beside him.

Grey was, as his name suggested, a speckled grey horse, a sturdy beast, if perhaps a bit too well-fed. Brunhart knew Glen to dote on all the horses, but Grey belonged to him, and Glen almost always came down to the stables with pockets filled with treats for the horse.

"Grey will help teach you how to ride, he's very gentle." Glen hopped over the stall wall and began working to saddle the gelding, stroking his mane every so often as he did.

Albtraum shifted from foot to foot, looking skeptical. "I'm not sure I trust these things."

"Ah, don't worry," Glen assured him. "They're just like dogs, only a bit bigger!"

Albtraum glanced back at his dog, who was sat on the floor, curiously watching the horses. "I… I don't think they're like dogs at all."

Glen opened the stall gate, and the horse carefully stepped out. Taking the reins, Glen led the horse outside, onto the field, and Albtraum followed him out, the pup still trailing him.

Brunhart stood on the outskirt of the field, watching them. Albtraum seemed nervous as Glen locked his hands together to boost him up onto the horse's back, and he took a long time to steady himself once he was sat in the saddle. The pup was dashing around the horse, nipping at its heels, but the larger beast seemed entirely unfazed.

They were far enough away that Brunhart could not hear them speaking, but he watched as Glen placed the reins in Albtraum's hands and held a firm hand on his arm to keep him steady as the horse started forward slowly.

Brunhart thought back to how distrusting he had been when Albtraum first arrived, that he had viewed him as a threat and wanted nothing more than an opportunity to remove him from their company. As he'd been around him more, though, it had become far more obvious that the boy was just that – a boy – and ever since their visit to the corrupted village, he had been much more receptive, if quieter and more nervous.

Albtraum weaved in the saddle a few times as they rode around the open field, but Glen helped to steady him again. They rode back and forth, in circles, Albtraum mounted and dismounted a few times, to get a feel for it. He seemed somewhat more comfortable as the time passed.

After a while, Glen and Albtraum both walked back over to where Brunhart waited, sitting on a bench against the stable wall. Glen led the horse behind him.

“Time for a break, I think,” he said as he led the horse back into the stable stall and took off the saddle.

Albtraum stopped next to Brunhart, kicking at the dirt. His stance hinted at discomfort.

“I’m hungry,” he informed Brunhart.

Brunhart could not help but smile. “I am not surprised. What would you like to eat?”

Albtraum looked down the road towards the city. “A pie,” he said after a brief pause. Then, after another thought, “Two pies.”

Brunhart chuckled. “That hungry, are you? I take it you’re referring to Annette’s pies, then, I’m sure Glen has introduced you to them.”

He nodded as Glen stepped outside to join them. “Are we going to get pies from Annette?”

“It would seem you’ve given Albtraum a taste for them,” Brunhart answered with a nod as they started down the hill. Albtraum held Renegade as they walked, stroking the pup’s fur.

“I’ve meant to thank you,” Albtraum said suddenly to Brunhart as they walked. “For... Giving me a chance to resist him, and stand on my own.”

Brunhart was taken aback by the sudden nature of his statement, but responded with a slight smile. “You are welcome. I hope that you will take this chance to do better.”

Albtraum nodded back at him. Though Brunhart was not completely sure, he thought this might have been the first time he’d seen the boy smile.

Chapter XIV

As the strands of days slowly turned to weeks and then to months, Albtraum became gradually more comfortable with his surroundings. At times Lucifurius seemed distant enough that Albtraum lent almost no thought to his presence.

Still, nervousness gnawed at the back of his mind. Lucifurius grew restless at times, and as he did, Albtraum was never far behind in his own restlessness. Their stances had forever morphed in his mind. Instead of standing side by side, they faced one another. Opposition.

The pains Lucifurius caused him were a constant reminder of this. Nothing was ever to be the same between them, moving forward.

And Albtraum was not certain if that excited or terrified him.

He was thumbing through the pages of a book one afternoon, having returned from having a meal in the town with Glen, when he heard a sharp rap at the door. He'd scarcely taken a breath to answer before Joaquin barged his way in. Albtraum had come to learn that the man seemed to enter most rooms this way, and nothing he barged in on seemed to have disturbed him enough to break the habit.

He carried armfuls of clothing. He had done so often over the last few weeks – and Albtraum had more clothes now than he was quite sure what to do with. He set down his book and curiously stepped over to examine them, nearly tripping over Renegade as he did.

“I believe you should have a complete functional wardrobe now,” Joaquin said excitedly, showing off the pieces he carried by laying them flat over Albtraum’s bed.

“Did I not have a functional wardrobe before this?” Albtraum’s eyes widened. “These are certainly... elaborate.”

Joaquin seemed mildly offended at his tone. “Of *course* they are. You can’t attend talks or social events dressed in your everyday attire.”

Albtraum didn’t know what talks or social events entailed, but if there was a code of dress he figured it must involve a fair degree of tedium. “Well then... thank you.” He’d heard humans expressing gratitude and had begun trying it out himself. Lucifurius, as with most human behaviors, found it grating and pathetic. Albtraum had grown fond of the way it seemed to make people light up when he said it.

“Of course, my dear.” Joaquin began folding the clothes again. “I’d recommend you start packing, since we will be setting out tomorrow.”

“Tomorrow?” Albtraum asked, somewhat jarred by the realization. His brow furrowed. As much as he wanted to see what else existed in the world of humans, he had grown somewhat comfortable with his routine in Sylva. He wandered into town with Glen from time to time, explored the estate with Renegade, spent the hours reading and whiling away the hours with the books Joaquin had given him. Most people gave him a wide berth, but others were friendly. He had enjoyed his time here... sometimes he almost forgot about Lucifurius.

“Yes, all of our arrangements have been taken care of and it would not do to delay any further.” Joaquin patted Albtraum’s arm, seeming to sense his concern. “You’ll be travelling as a royal ward, so you can look forward to similar accommodations to what we've provided you here. Some of the inns along the way have—"

"And when the business is concluded?" Albtraum asked him, interrupting. "What then?"

Joaquin seemed a bit taken aback. "Well- I suppose you'll go on staying here, or wherever else you might like to go. Is something the matter?"

Albtraum swallowed hard. The future was a nebulous, dark mass – he could not see past it, he could not see through it. The uncertainty terrified him, as though if he moved from his place he might plummet into a pit of nothingness.

"No, nothing. Just... Mianna has not given me much direction."

"You'll have to forgive her for that. She's torn in many different directions at the moment. Though, the fact she's left you to your own devices means she trusts you, so I'd imagine you do not have much to concern yourself with." Joaquin stepped aside to allow Albtraum to fold the remainder of the clothes as a servant stepped in to clean the room. Albtraum had deduced from a few scant interactions with her that her name was Giselle -she was always tending to the guest rooms, but Albtraum imagined this was mostly a formality to keep him from feeling awkward about her presence.

She nodded in greeting and smiled slightly in Albtraum's direction as she entered the room. This was an improvement from their previous interactions – at the very least, she no longer seemed afraid of him.

"Mianna trusts me with a great many things, it would seem," Albtraum sighed, returning his attention to Joaquin. "More than I trust myself, perhaps."

"Well, perhaps you might try trusting her judgement, then. Haven't grown bored of Machiavelli yet, have you?" Joaquin asked him with a slight smirk as he saw that *The Prince* lay open on Albtraum's dresser.

"No," Albtraum replied quietly. "I find his writing quite interesting."

Joaquin grimaced. "To each his own, I suppose. I've always preferred poetry to dull technical prose."

He noted that Joaquin had stopped talking after a short while, and stood curiously watching him carefully fold and stack the clothes that had been brought in.

"What?" Albtraum asked, somewhat defensive.

Joaquin seemed started slightly, as if Albtraum had pulled him from deep thought. "Oh, it's nothing. I only thought... Ah, it's nothing of importance. Do you have any business to finish here in the city before we set off?"

Albtraum shook his head, stroking Renegade's head as he paced over to beg for attention. He was scarcely a puppy anymore, his head reached Albtraum's knee.

"Wonderful, then, you can take the rest of your time here to relax before we leave. Your injuries haven't bothered you at all?"

Albtraum considered the question, unconsciously moving a hand to the location of the wound in his gut. It twinged from time to time as he moved about, but no longer required a bandage. The scrapes and bruises he'd picked up before arriving here were gone entirely, and the once-nasty gash across his face had faded to a barely visible nick on his nose. Yet, he had thought for a time that he might never be rid of these injuries.

Was this how slow the wounds of humans healed? Albtraum did not know, since Lucifurius had always healed any wounds shortly after he'd acquired them. Though this pace of healing seemed agonizing, it was at least preferable to being at the mercy of Lucifurius' whims.

"No, they do not."

"I'll leave you to it, then," Joaquin said, bringing Albtraum out of his own thoughts. He started to walk towards the door.

"Wait," Albtraum blurted, and Joaquin stopped, looking confused. "You don't have to. I..." He was unsure of what to say.

"Why don't you come with me," Joaquin suggested, looking the slightest bit... smug? Albtraum wasn't sure.

Albtraum stood, and Renegade jumped at his legs. He followed Joaquin out of the room into the hallway. It was still early in the day – light from the windows flooded the spacious hall.

"You seem to be opening up the more time you spend here," Joaquin observed as they walked.

"Opening up?" Albtraum questioned with a raised eyebrow, unsure of what he meant.

"There's more and more to you each time we speak," Joaquin clarified, gesturing vaguely at him.

"There's no more to me than there's ever been," Albtraum muttered.

Joaquin looked at him, smiling a bit distantly. "Ah, you'll understand what I mean someday." The expression slowly morphed into a concerned frown. "How much of your mind... do you share with him, really?"

“Lucifurius?” Albtraum asked, and Joaquin nodded.

You don’t truly know, do you? And that... That terrifies you more than anything.

Albtraum sighed and tried to ignore him. “None of it. He can see my thoughts, and he can speak into my thoughts, and he can hurt me, but we are... separate beings. He can’t control me.”

Oh, the stories you tell yourself... They would be amusing if they were not so pathetic.

“Hurt you?” Joaquin’s concern seemed to grow.

“Yes, when I do something that displeases him, he can make me feel pain... Worsen pains that already exist, or make new ones. Mostly splitting headaches... as if hearing him ramble all hours of the day was not headache enough.”

My, what a wit you have! Lucifurius snarled in the back of his mind, sardonic and venomous.

Joaquin did not seem amused. “Inform us of these pains from now on, if you would... We may be able to help ease them.”

Albtraum was not sure they would be able to, but he nodded in response all the same. He watched Renegade trot beside them as they headed down the stairs.

Joaquin stopped a few times as they wandered the estate to issue instructions to the servants they encountered. Albtraum noted that they were near to the guard barracks, and wandered over to see what was happening there as Joaquin lectured a particularly empty-headed looking servant about cleaning up the dust in the guest halls.

There were shouts and laughter from inside as the men were watching each other take part in sparring matches. Some men leaned on the fencing of the sparring deck – a raised wooden platform contained by short railings - some stood back, half-watching, conversing among themselves. Albtraum noted Noman in the ring, and he seemed to be giving a difficult time to the young guard who stood against him.

A few of the men looked over as Albtraum stepped into the barracks. He noted that the tension that seemed to build around his presence in the weeks before had lessened, and perhaps had even gone entirely. For the most part, the guards no longer seemed to consider him a threat.

Brunhart and Glen were among those watching the sparring, and Brunhart approached as he noticed Albtraum enter the room.

"Finished your preparations for the journey, pup?" he asked, turning to stand beside Albtraum and continue to watch the spar. Brunhart patted Albtraum's shoulder, something he'd been doing often whenever they were together. Albtraum was not sure of the purpose of the gesture, nor the nickname, but he didn't dislike it.

"Not just yet," Albtraum answered. "But there's not much left to do."

He hadn't noticed Joaquin entering the room behind him, and started when he spoke. "We are getting his belongings packed, you should ensure your men do the same soon. Mianna wants to be sure we start on our journey early so as not to be on the road long after dark," he said to Brunhart.

Albtraum watched the sparring carefully. Noman was a skilled combatant – he was older, slower, and heavier than his opponent, yet he still managed to outmaneuver the younger man, easily pinning him against the edge of the ring to deliver a "killing" blow with the wooden weapon he used.

Noman stepped down from the deck after the young man as he exited the ring, grumbling, rubbing his new bruises. Noman huffed and scanned the room, settling on Albtraum.

"Al, why don't you get in there and fight a few rounds!" He exclaimed, grinning. "I'm getting tired of winning."

Albtraum looked to Brunhart for permission, and found him frowning.

But Joaquin answered before he could. "He's only just recovered from the injuries he had, and you'll ruin the clothes I've made!"

Noman rolled his eyes, but Brunhart spoke up. "No, he should stay in practice for combat. It wouldn't do for him to be unable to defend himself."

"I'm capable of fighting," Albtraum answered.

"Let's see, then."

Brunhart stepped up into the sparring ring despite Joaquin's huffing and muttering of disapproval and Albtraum hesitantly followed, instructing Renegade to stay. Brunhart motioned for Albtraum to take a weapon from the racks that lined the back edge of the ring, and Albtraum picked up one of the wooden swords that hung there.

"No," Brunhart said, shaking his head. "Get a real sword."

Albtraum frowned and went to pick up one of the swords from the real weapon rack. He lifted it and nearly dropped it, the tip sinking into the wood of the deck.

Startled, he tried again to lift the weapon. It was heavy – much, much heavier than he ever remembered any sword being. He could hardly lift it and keep it steady, much less wield it as he had before.

Was it simply that he hadn't handled a weapon in so long? He'd spent years fighting, it seemed drastic for him to have lost so much progress so quickly. This had once been as easy as breathing, why now was it so difficult...?

Lucifurius answered his wandering thoughts with a low, mocking laugh. *You think the strength with which you cut down our foes was your own? You think you can do anything on your own, without me? You are nothing without me. You'd be dead in a ditch with no one to remember your name long ago without me to guide you.*

Albtraum tried to hold the sword steady. Brunhart stepped over and took his hands, showing him how to grip.

"And stand a bit lower," he offered, demonstrating the stance. Albtraum tried to imitate him, but between his growing distress and Lucifurius' constant taunts, he found it difficult to even focus on what Brunhart was saying to him.

As much as he'd tried to resist the things Lucifurius said to him, he was no longer able to deny that the words carried some truth. He was weaker since they'd begun to separate. His body had been irreparably damaged. And even these people he was growing to trust... Even they had wanted Albtraum only because of his connection to Lucifurius, even if they were in opposition to him.

Brunhart stepped in front of him. "Albtraum?"

Albtraum looked forward to meet his gaze, feeling disoriented. "Yes?"

Kill him, Lucifurius growled. *Let me guide you again. Kill him. Kill him. KILL HIM.*

Albtraum let out a tense huff of frustration and shoved the sword in his hand back onto the weapon rack, scratching anxiously at his arms with his now-free hand.

"I..." He started to explain himself to Brunhart, who looked back at him curiously, but all the words that came to him evaporated into a sigh. He picked up the sword again, but Brunhart shook his head and took it from him.

"We don't have to do this right now," he said gently. "Something's clearly got you in a state. You'll not learn anything if your head's not clear." He patted Albtraum's shoulder again. "Care to get something to eat?"

Albtraum nodded, and Brunhart guided him back towards the door with a hand on his shoulder. Glen had moved to standing nearer to Joaquin, and held a squirming Renegade in his arms. He handed the pup back to Albtraum.

"Perhaps you just need something lighter than a sword," Glen suggested in greeting.

"Perhaps," Albtraum agreed, feeling miserable. A dull headache burned behind his eyes.

Joaquin put his hand on Albtraum's unoccupied shoulder. "Or perhaps it's best to not worry about these things for now. There's plenty of time to learn everything, but I daresay your etiquette needs some work before we visit other royalty."

The way they behaved around him felt odd. Some small part of him still felt that he was wrong to disobey Lucifurius, but... they treated him with such care and concern, where all Lucifurius ever seemed to do of late was cause him pain and harm him.

Worry not, child.

They will realize, soon, how pathetic you are. They will abandon you, like all things will. All things save for me.

Chapter XV

The sun had barely risen by the time Albtraum was abruptly awakened, shaken by the shoulder somewhat un-gently by Joaquin. It was still dark in the room.

"Good morning," Joaquin greeted somewhat breathlessly, setting the candle in his hand on the nightstand. "We've got to get ourselves on the road quite soon."

Albtraum mumbled incoherently as Joaquin tugged him out of bed by the arm and helped him out of his bedclothes, which he held awkwardly in his hands as Joaquin rifled through his wardrobe attempting to decide what he should wear. The clothes still held the warmth of the bed, and Albtraum found himself wanting to crawl back in and sleep longer.

The chill of the room and the uneasiness of standing there in his smallclothes did nothing to help this fact, and he sleepily rubbed his eyes as Joaquin tossed things at him – trousers, a tunic, boots, an overcoat – He fumbled to put them on and then stood still as Joaquin fussed over the wrinkles and circled him to tie back his hair.

"There now – check over the room and be sure you haven't forgotten anything," Joaquin instructed him. "We will not return for quite some time."

He did so, finding nothing but Renegade still curled up on the bed. Albtraum called to him, patting his knee, and Renegade hopped down from the bed and followed along as they left the room and headed outside.

He had become very obedient in the months Albtraum had spent with him, training him to follow simple commands. Rarely did he stray from Albtraum's path in recent days.

The guards had begun gathering in the courtyard, packing their belongings into their saddle bags, helping the servants load the rest of the cargo into the carriages. There was a damp chill in the air, and breath from the men and horses alike still clouded in the air. Joaquin handed off Albtraum's belongings to him and scampered off to direct the servants as they worked.

Albtraum found the horse that had been assigned to him, an easygoing chestnut mare named Clover. Glen had picked her out himself, and Albtraum had practiced riding her enough to be comfortable on a longer excursion. He began packing his saddle bags with books and an extra cloak Joaquin had made him for colder weather.

Renegade waited behind him, and Albtraum scooped him up to set him in the space in the saddle behind where he would sit. The pup squirmed but settled in after a moment, and Albtraum scratched at his ears before climbing into the saddle himself.

He noted Mianna at the head of the group, already settled in the saddle of her own horse, watching the servants load the carriages, occasionally speaking to one of the guards.

They were men Albtraum had seen often as he went about his relatively routine existence within Sylva's walls, but he knew only some of their names, and hadn't taken the time to speak to any of them. Mianna looked quite regal among the rest of the people in the courtyard, none of the exhaustion of the early morning showing on her carefully composed expression.

On one of the wagons was a huge cage, and Albtraum very briefly wondered what it could be for until he heard the cry of a hawk above them, and looked up to find it circling the group. It must have been Aidan, Mianna's prized bird.

Ismaire came out of the estate before long, looking sour and annoyed as she packed her own saddle bags and mounted her horse, specifically avoiding looking in Albtraum's direction. Her clothes were plain and practical, almost as though she thought herself a soldier, and Albtraum was certain her satchels and pouches contained all manner of small weaponry.

Mianna led her horse around to face Ismaire.

"Remember what we discussed," Albtraum heard her mutter to the young woman. "You've written to your family, I assume?"

"Yes," Ismaire huffed in response.

"Good. They'll have plenty of time to prepare for our visit, as they will be one of our last stops on the journey."

Albtraum watched curiously as Ismaire finished her own preparations and mounted her horse – she rode astride it in the saddle, and not side-saddle as the other women did.

Brunhart had joined the group by the time Albtraum had gotten mounted and settled, calling roll from a parchment in his hand as everyone mounted and readied to leave.

"...Mellimend, Yorke, Branco, Grouser, Harlowe..." He sighed in frustration as he looked over the list of guards accompanying them, then around the courtyard. "Where is Glen?"

“Haven’t seen him,” Noman grunted in response.

Mianna shrugged as Brunhart looked to her.

“Well, we can’t afford to delay. He can catch up.” Brunhart mounted his own steed, a massive, broad-chested black warhorse.

Albtraum frowned at that, looking around for him. “But...” He’d been looking forward to Glen being one the journey with them – the more familiarity, the better, in his eyes.

“He’ll catch up,” Brunhart assured him, starting his horse off down the road. Albtraum kept checking over his shoulder for Glen – after a while he glumly accepted that he might not rejoin the group.

Mianna had waited to ride alongside Albtraum as he hung towards the back of the group. She started her horse forward as he approached, offering a smile in greeting which he returned with a curt nod. He had begun to understand human social niceties – performing them, of course, still felt awkward and unnatural.

“You seem to have grown rather fond of this place and its people,” Mianna pointed out.

“I have,” he answered, seeing no reason to lie. Though he still felt out of place among the people of the city, and fondness was not a concept he was well versed in, it felt right to describe his moderate comfort here. Just a few short months ago, he might never have imagined that he would feel so attached to stone walls and human companions.

He hadn’t spoken with Mianna in weeks – when she had proposed that he take the place of Lucifurius. The conversation seemed a distant memory now, but he had not forgotten it, and he was certain she had not either.

“Good,” she answered warmly. “I must say, I am rather impressed with how you’ve gotten on. The other rulers will quite like you, I think.”

“Joaquin says I’ve got etiquette to learn before I meet them,” Albtraum said, fidgeting with the sleeves of his coat.

Mianna nodded. “He is right. Thankfully, you’ve plenty of time to learn on the road. I have things to teach you as well. And our first host is probably the most forgiving of the lot.”

“Forgiving enough to host someone like me?”

She smirked. “There’s quite an air of mystery about you, Albtraum. Nobility find that intriguing. Intriguing enough to perhaps look past the more... colorful parts of your history.” She motioned to him. “Besides, your time in Sylva has made you almost an entirely new man. Without your ghastly mask and coat of grime, no one will ever recognize you.”

“Perhaps not. I mean, I... I should hope not.”

Mianna chuckled. “We shall speak more later, Albtraum.”

She left him then, as he was contemplating her words, and rode ahead into the group, conversing casually with the guards and her servants.

They had nearly arrived at the city gates when a rider on a horse came galloping up to the group. Albtraum recognized the horse as Grey – and the rider as Glen. He had a large satchel over his shoulder.

“Sorry I’m late, Captain!” he called to Brunhart at the head of the group. “Annette made pies for everyone for the road – here’s yours!”

Brunhart looked to be ready to lecture Glen, but just sighed and mumbled his thanks. Glen weaved his way through the rest of the group to hand out the pies. Albtraum felt the corner of his mouth quirk up in a half-smile as Glen made his way over with a pie in hand. It was wrapped in parchment paper and pleasantly warm in his chilled hands as he accepted it.

"And here's one with no potatoes for you!" Glen said to him.

"Thank you," Albtraum said around a bite of the pie. He struggled for something else to say. "I was worried you weren't going to come," he decided on, feeling a bit silly.

"I wouldn't miss this," Glen laughed. "I've never been on an excursion this long, I've been looking forward to it ever since it was announced." He ate his own pie, and Albtraum settled into silence as he listened to Glen talk aimlessly about the horses and the road ahead.

After a while had passed and Glen had fallen mostly silent, Albtraum reached into his saddle bag to withdraw the book he was currently reading – Chaucer's *Canterbury Tales* – and he continued to read through it, occasionally looking up and around the group, quietly observing the behavior around him. There was an air of excitement about the guards and the few servants that had joined them, but Albtraum wasn't sure if he quite felt the same. Renegade squirmed and shifted, and Albtraum reached behind to scratch his ears and feed him the last few bites of pie he had.

He distantly noted that he recognized the road they were on, the same one he'd taken to enter Sylva with Lucifurius' guidance. It seemed hardly the same now... winter had warmed into spring, the trees dancing with shining green leaves, the ground sprouting with grass and flowers. It seemed peaceful, a kind of peace he had never stopped to consider before in his life, when every step he took was towards another kill.

The road wound down the mountains and into the forests, the air's damp chill becoming sharper as the group ventured beyond where the sun's warm rays could penetrate. Albtraum knew the path – and he recognized the structure they passed along the road. The temple.

The aura it exuded was just as familiar – but no longer did it feel welcoming. It was malevolent and unsettling, and Albtraum felt the back of his neck prickle with icy dread.

"Did you know of this place? This was one of the first rifts that appeared in our world," he heard Mianna say from where she'd ridden up behind him. "The temple was built to contain it... To observe it. It's been abandoned for years, and we of the Order are forbidden from entering."

Albtraum wondered who there was to forbid Mianna from doing anything. She seemed to be a high authority.

Nothing but delusions of grandeur. She is but an insect compared to the power I wield, Lucifurius commented.

Albtraum gritted his teeth. Lucifurius did not often speak of late... and when he did, there was nothing left of the comforting familiarity it once made him feel.

I suppose that's why she commands a whole kingdom and you command one boy, he shot back.

Everything went white for an instant.

Your boldness is not amusing, child. Either you will learn your place, or you will die with the rest of them.

Albtraum blinked through the dizzying pain, finding himself disoriented and confused as he looked around the forest floor.

He'd fallen from the horse. Renegade stood beside him, licking his face as he sat up.

"Are you alright?" Mianna asked him as she dismounted from her own horse, an emotion in her voice that he couldn't read. One of the guards who'd been following on foot offered him a hand up, which he accepted as Brunhart rode up behind his horse to investigate.

"I..." He stood, leaning on the guard's arm for support. He looked up, seeing that the group had stopped, everyone glancing curiously at him. Joaquin had appeared to dust him off and straighten out his clothes. "It's fine. I upset Lucifurius." He reached for him in his mind, trying to gauge his mood – but Lucifurius had withdrawn, silent.

That wracked Albtraum's nerves far more than Lucifurius' ire.

Mianna's brow furrowed at him, waiting for further explanation, but he simply waved her off and walked back to mount his horse. He glanced around awkwardly at the many concerned eyes on him, dipping his head as he lifted Renegade back into the saddle before mounting himself.

"You alright?" he heard a voice inquire. Glen.

He nodded, feeling embarrassed, glad when the group's collective eyes looked away from him. He noticed Ismaire watching from a distance, disdain pouring from her very presence. That, compared with everyone else, almost felt like a relief.

Lucifurius had reduced him to little more than a frail child in their eyes. He despised being viewed this way, being vulnerable.

Brunhart rode closer Mianna and Glen mounted their own horses. "You can ride in the carriages if you need to," Brunhart said to Albtraum, reaching over to pat his shoulder.

“One of the servants can trade places with you,” Joaquin added from where he stood near one of the carriages. “You only need ask.”

“I’m fine,” Albtraum assured them again, and they seemed to relent.

Lucifurius was silent all the rest of their time on the road that day.

Once again, it did not feel like a relief.

The chill in the air had turned bitter by the time they reached the inn, and Brunhart was glad to be inside again. The inn had been largely empty before the group arrived, but now bustled with activity, the guards eating and drinking in the inn’s dining hall, tired from the long day on the road.

The innkeeper was discussing something with Mianna, and Joaquin was looking about the place with mild disdain. It was comfortable and well-kept, if a bit small, but obviously not up to Joaquin’s somewhat outlandish standards. Brunhart spotted Albtraum among the guards in the dining hall.

“Always a pleasure to have you, your Majesty,” the innkeeper said in closing to Mianna. Brunhart recognized him, but he had been the son of the innkeeper the last time they’d passed through here. He nodded in greeting to Brunhart and stepped away to let them converse.

“We’re keeping a good pace,” Mianna said casually. “It should only be a few weeks before we reach Terce.”

Brunhart nodded and started to shed some of the layers of his uniform, folding them over his arm. He looked back over his shoulder at Albtraum, watching him eat with the servants and guards.

"You seem quite taken with him," Mianna commented, looking in the same direction Brunhart was.

"Well, he does need supervision and guidance," Brunhart answered simply.

"Speaking of which," Joaquin interjected, "we should be sure to educate him further before we reach Terce."

"About the Order?" Mianna asked with a frown. "I'm not sure divulging information about our organization's plans to him while he still houses Lucifurius is a wise idea."

Brunhart felt something bristle in him, finding something about Mianna's tone distasteful. "We can't expect him to trust and follow us if we aren't willing to give some amount of trust in return."

"There is, however, also the fact that Lucifurius seems to be taking out his displeasure at being trapped by us on him," Joaquin sighed.

Brunhart looked back over to Albtraum again. Though he had recovered quickly from the day's earlier incident, he still seemed shaken and nervous, even now.

"There is that," Mianna answered, more quietly.

"It can wait for the night," Brunhart said decidedly. "It's been a long day on the road."

He left Mianna and Joaquin to discuss arrangements with the servants and stepped into the dining hall, sitting down across from Albtraum. He looked up upon noticing Brunhart, but seemed distracted, swept into the chatter of the guards around him. The hall was noisy, fifteen men making almost as much noise as one might expect from a hundred.

"If you're a daemon, then, what can you do?"

"And where are your horns?"

"And what is he, then, what can he do?"

There had been a swirling of questioning and confusion for months, ever since Albtraum's arrival in Sylva. In close quarters with him, the men were even more curious, naturally – and bombarding Albtraum with questions. Still, he seemed more comfortable than he had at any point in the day thus far.

"I don't have any interesting answers, I'm afraid," he muttered. "Lucifurius is my father... but, lacking a body of his own, he forces me to share mine. I can never remember having had horns, but there are remnants of them..."

A few of the men clambered to feel Albtraum's head, and he allowed it – even seeming somewhat amused as a few withdrew with nervous chuckles or mumbles of astonishment.

His amusement faded as he continued speaking. "As for what Lucifurius can do, through me..." he shut his eyes and shook his head. "He is dangerous. I fear what he may cause me to do..."

"I would like to see him try," one of the men snorted, taking a swig of his ale. "Daemon or no, how much can he do, really, without a body?"

Albtraum seemed to be considering an answer when Brunhart cleared his throat to announce himself, and the men slowly returned to conversing among themselves as he took a seat across from Albtraum.

The men had stew and bread set out in front of them, and most seemed to be close to finishing their food by now, but Albtraum had hardly touched his.

Brunhart leaned over the table. “Are you feeling alright?”

Albtraum frowned, but nodded. He tore off a piece of bread and reached under the table, Brunhart assumed to feed Renegade.

He sat back again. “Your episode earlier startled us, that’s all.” He still felt concern lingering in the back of his mind, but tried to put it aside.

“I argued with Lucifurius when I shouldn’t have. He’s done that for as long as I can remember, when he’s displeased enough.”

Brunhart sighed, accepting a tankard and bowl from one of the servants. “Well, take care not to go out of your way to displease him, then.”

Albtraum watched him eat silently for a few minutes, picking at his own bowl. “I need to learn how to fight again,” he said abruptly.

Brunhart looked up from his bowl. “You shouldn’t be worrying about that now, there are many things that require your attention and there are plenty of guards to protect you.”

“I don’t want to have to rely on others to protect me,” Albtraum said, somewhat more forcefully.

Brunhart thought about the months he’d observed Albtraum up to now, how already he was a far cry from the feral, unwashed vagabond who’d turned up on their doorstep. For him to learn to fight again would of course be useful, but Brunhart felt wary of taking him back to the place he'd been before, even in such a small way.

Still, Albtraum did have a point. They could not eliminate the possibility of situations in which he would be without protection.

"If we have the time, we will," Brunhart relented.

Albtraum looked content with that answer, and continued to slowly eat from his bowl.

Glen came up to the table with his own bowl as they ate, nodding to Brunhart in greeting as he sat beside Albtraum at the table. "I've gotten the horses all settled for the night," he reported, slightly out of breath – the stables were down the hill a ways from the inn itself. He looked to Albtraum as he dug into his food. "You want to bunk with me for the night? You can tell me all about that book you're reading."

"You could read it yourself," Albtraum suggested.

Glen shook his head. "Never learned. Not really necessary for working in the stables, you know? Maybe you could teach me."

"I am not sure if I know well enough myself, I... didn't really learn." Albtraum seemed uneasy.

"You'd make a fine teacher, I'm sure," Brunhart assured him. Albtraum shrugged in response.

Glen dragged Albtraum off upstairs as soon as they'd both finished eating, leaving Brunhart at the table with the few guards that remained, talking and drinking.

Brunhart noticed Noman move down from his seat at the head of the table to sit across from him. He had already stripped down to his underclothes and taken off his boots.

"Feeling at home, are you?" Brunhart commented with a raised eyebrow.

Noman gave a low chuckle. "We won't always have inns on the road, so I'm just enjoying the indoors while I can." He nodded in the direction Albtraum and Glen had gone. "He's certainly seeming different, eh? Hard to believe there's a daemon in him now."

"Not just in him, he's one of them too," Brunhart muttered. "Though that hardly seems to matter."

"You certain of that, Captain?" Noman seemed surprised.

"Does he seem like a threat to you?"

Noman sighed. "That could be exactly what he wants you to believe."

Brunhart shook his head. "He's only a boy. And we need to treat him as such if he's to come through this successfully."

"So long as he keeps acting like one, there shouldn't be a problem," Noman said with a shrug. When Brunhart looked sharply at him, he laughed. "I'm not going to *do* anything, Captain... A bit touchy on this one, are you? You are right, though, I don't think we've got anything to worry about from him."

"Lucifurius, of course, is another matter." Brunhart stood. "I should make sure tomorrow's arrangements are prepared."

"I need a few more drinks in me before bed," Noman said, waving him off.

Brunhart climbed the stairs to the bedrooms upstairs, speaking with the soldiers to be sure they knew their duties for the next day – navigation, managing the caravans, guarding the wards.

It was warm in the inn, with all the fireplaces roaring, and by the time Brunhart made it to the room he was staying in with the other guards, he was glad the day was over.

He was just climbing into his bed when he looked up and noticed Albtraum and Glen sitting on one of the beds against the wall, leaned against each other, fast asleep. The book Albtraum was reading was open on his lap.

Brunhart was about to reach out to wake him, but he seemed to be comfortable where he was, and instead Brunhart pulled off his boots, set the book on the night stand, and tossed a quilt over them both. Albtraum stirred slightly, but settled back against Glen's shoulder.

Something in him railed against this journey, against taking Albtraum across the world to be touted to nobles and royalty before being sent to rule over a world he'd never even seen. He deserved a proper boyhood, more than being used as a political prop.

But he was, of course, the only option they had at present.

Brunhart crossed the room back to his own bed and settled in to sleep as the rest of the guards did around him. As he looked up at the log ceiling in the dark, he could only hope he'd be able to provide Albtraum with what he needed in the time they had.

Chapter XVI

After another few days of travel, the weather turned.

It was ironic, Ismaire thought, that they be caught in the rain on a night they had to make camp, when all the nights they'd spent in inns the weather was still fair. The tents were holding against the downpour so far, but the chill of the damp air was hard to banish. She had spent the vast majority of her life surrounded by nothing but desert sand, and even with so many years spent in Sylva, she could never get used to the cold and the rain.

She looked around the tent-covered area they'd set up, frowning at the pitiful little fire that crackled in the center. Her gaze travelled to one of the other tents. where Albtraum was sitting on a cot across from Joaquin, wrapped in a cloak, listening intently as Joaquin spoke animatedly about something. She scoffed. He'd gotten *quite* good at pretending, but the ruse had never fooled her.

She wrapped her arms around herself and shivered, feeling miserable. Sleep was not likely with the way the rain was keeping up, so she resigned herself to keeping watch with the other guards who were patrolling the camp.

"What do you think you're doing?" Brunhart asked her gruffly as she stepped up beside him, pulling up her hood to shield her from the rain.

"Keeping watch with the rest of you," She answered, her tone matching his.

“The last I remember, you are a royal ward and not among the employ of the guard force.”

“I’m not going to mill about *reading* like Bonehead’s been doing,” she said, looking up at Brunhart.

“Back in the tent,” he grumbled at her.

She huffed, and stepped back under the shelter of the tents, but this time she stepped over to the side Albtraum was sitting on. She’d keep watch in her own way if Brunhart wouldn’t allow her to do it with the rest of the guards.

Albtraum looked up when he saw her approach, but otherwise didn’t acknowledge her. His dog was curled up under the cot, sleeping soundly, perhaps the only creature who could sleep soundly during such a storm. Glen was a few tents away, trying to calm the restless horses.

“You’ll enjoy Terce, I think. The king can be exhausting, but the city is so interesting, since...” Joaquin trailed off. “Ah, well, I’ll let you see for yourself. It’s quite the sight to behold.”

Albtraum nodded in response as Joaquin glanced over to Ismaire.

“Ah, Ismaire, we were just speaking about Terce. Perhaps there is some information we should go over with you as well.”

“Mianna’s explained everything I need to know already,” she retorted.

“I meant the nuances of etiquette,” Joaquin snorted. “Something I have seen absolutely no evidence you understand in the slightest.”

“I address them by Your-Royal-Greatness and try not to spit on the floors. It’s really not that difficult.”

“If only it were that simple,” Albtraum muttered.

Ismaire watched him suspiciously, wary of his attempt to relate to her.

Albtraum yawned and rubbed his eyes, shutting the book in his lap and setting it aside in the pack at the head of his cot. He blinked at Ismaire a few times, aware of her staring.

“You should sleep,” Joaquin said decidedly to Albtraum.

Albtraum nodded as Joaquin handed him a blanket for the cot, and he settled in to sleep. Joaquin watched him with a slight smile, and not the slightest hint of leeriness or suspicion.

What was it about Albtraum, she wondered, that had them all so smitten? Why was she the only one who could see him for what he was?

She settled into her own cot as Mianna finally joined them in the tent.

“This rain is dreadful,” Joaquin commented to her.

“Believe it or not, I have slept in worse,” Mianna said to him with a sigh, having a seat on one of the cots. “Comfortable enough, Albtraum? Ismaire?”

Albtraum mumbled something back sleepily. Ismaire grunted.

Mianna turned to face her, speaking in a low voice. “It’s important that you remember your eventual station as we move forward. Making a good impression on the other kingdoms will make all of our future dealings in this matter much simpler.”

“I know,” Ismaire muttered. She pushed herself up on her elbows and looked over at Mianna, lowering her voice even further.

"But there are more important things to worry about than etiquette. And one of them was invited along on this expedition."

Mianna frowned in response, looking over to Albtraum as Joaquin settled in to sleep himself. "Your concerns are misdirected, Ismaire."

"I don't believe they are. You're too soft."

Mianna let out a laugh, stifling herself when she realized it had come out louder than she had intended. "I've been accused of being many things, by many people, but I don't believe 'too soft' has ever been one of them."

Ismaire had expected to be executed the snowy spring day Mianna had captured her, many years ago. She had sat in a cell for days, whiling away her time with thoughts of escape. When Mianna had finally come for her... it was not to escort her to the executioner, but rather to inform her that she had been designated to head a revolt, and offer her the chance to atone for her wrongdoings. This had ostensibly been the case for Albtraum as well, but how could a *daemon* possibly conceive of betterment, of atoning for what he'd done? His deeds ran through his very blood.

Ismaire felt her frustration welling up in her chest, and ran a hand through her hair. *Can't you see I'm only trying to protect you?* But the words died before she could say them.

Mianna seemed to read her thoughts anyhow. Her tone was softer as she spoke. "You seem to forget who the ward is in this arrangement, Ismaire. The time of my life for others to concern themselves with watching out for me is long past."

Ismaire squirmed and shifted, uncomfortable. She hated being talked down to this way, and by Mianna, of all people. For all the command she exuded, Ismaire could not help but feel protective of her. Especially after all she'd done, and the second chance she'd provided, away from the mistakes Ismaire had made...

Mianna was one of the last few people who saw any good in her. And Ismaire was not going to let that be taken from her by this monster Mianna had insisted on taking under her wing, no matter how human he increasingly acted.

Ismaire settled back into her cot and watched the guards mill around the camp site as she tried to quiet her thoughts, listening to the rain fall on the tent covers as she drifted off to sleep.

The rain had stopped by the morning, but a chill still hung in the air, and the ground was soft and damp. The guards and servants were shaking out belongings that had gotten wet in the rain.

Ismaire was one of the last to get out of her cot, pulling on her boots and trying to rub the sleep out of her eyes.

Albtraum was standing off at the edge of the camp with the guard he'd seemed to have made friends with, Glen. They were tossing a fallen branch into the bushes, and Ismaire wondered what the purpose was until she noted that his dog was chasing the branch, returning with it to be thrown again.

It seemed to be such a useless creature, but Albtraum was obviously no fool. His mutual affection with it had earned him favor with anyone who witnessed it, and Ismaire found herself astounded at how gullible they all were.

She scowled as she packed her belongings and readied her horse for the journey. Their charted course would put them in an inn tonight, and Ismaire was glad for it – though she'd grown up in tents and spent most of her childhood wandering with her family, it had been in a much warmer and drier place than here.

As they set off, Ismaire rode into the middle of the group, looking around at the guards as they rode forward. So far it was quiet today, as the storm had kept anyone from getting much sleep and they were not in the mood for lively conversation.

Ismaire sighed. If she was going to prove herself, she would need support.

She rode up in between two guards who were talking, with whom she had sometimes sparred, figuring they would be a good place to start. Their exchange ended abruptly as she placed herself between them, and she nodded in greeting.

"Piotr, Edmund."

"What is it, Ismaire?" Piotr asked with a sigh. He was not much older than her, but already looked far too perpetually tired for his age. The dark hair that fell across his face and cast his eyes in a dark shadow did nothing to help that fact.

"What do you think of the ward?" She asked, trying to seem casual, looking around to see if he was within earshot, relaxing when she did not see him.

"She's a bit of an annoyance, and needs to stop butting into others' conversations," Edmund grumbled with a slight sneer, amused at his own jest. He, unlike Piotr, was the very picture of a noble knight – but his teasing and boyish grin belied an immature nature.

Ismaire narrowed her eyes at him. "Hilarious. I mean the daemon."

Piotr shrugged. "He minds his business, and he's caused no trouble with us. I've only heard of daemons, never met one before, so I suppose I do find him to be of some interest. Probably more so if he'd actually had horns."

Ismaire huffed and shifted in her saddle to get more comfortable. "Really? That's all? The fact that he's a murderer hasn't bothered you at all?"

Edmund turned to her, his amusement fading. "If it's that much of a bother to you, I should remind you that many of the men in our ranks come from less than saintly backgrounds. And didn't you move slaves, if I'm recalling correctly?"

She frowned deeply, frustrated at her continuous failure to find any common ground, and huffed. "Yes, everyone is aware of that."

They rode on in relative silence a while longer – Ismaire deciding to spend more time observing the guards to see who may be more likely to sway to her side – before Glen came riding up, straight to the head of the party, where he steered his horse in front of Brunhart and Mianna, bringing the group to a slow and awkward stop.

He was too far away for Ismaire to hear what he was saying, but she picked up a tone of alarm. Brunhart turned his horse back and set off in the opposite direction at a trot, ordering a few of the men to follow him. They split off from the road into the woods in different directions.

Ismaire rode her horse up next to Mianna's, glancing over at her friend with the raise of an eyebrow. "What's going on?"

"Albtraum's gone missing," Mianna said with a mildly affected sigh. "He's probably just wandered off the path a bit too far, but he could put himself in danger if he gets too far away."

Ismaire scoffed quietly to herself. Put *himself* in danger – as if some poor travelers were not in more danger from the daemon on the loose.

"I'm going to help them look," she said abruptly, spurring her horse to a gallop before Mianna was able to say anything to stop her. She veered the horse off into the trees and rode until the forest became dense and thick enough that she had to dismount.

She started forward into the trees on foot, but hesitated, turning back to her saddle bag for her dagger. Mianna had advised her against bringing any weapons, saying they were more likely to cause trouble than protect from it, but Ismaire had of course snuck one into her belongings anyway.

She stopped periodically, listening for any unusual sounds. She could hear running water close by, and the guards calling for Albtraum a short distance away.

She moved in the direction she heard the water from, finding the trees thinning and opening up to a wide, fast-moving river.

Ismaire walked along the bank, still looking and listening, her dagger clutched loosely at her side. Perhaps she'd be so lucky that Albtraum had gotten himself so lost he would never be found, or better yet, that he'd fallen into the river and drowned...

But her hopes were dashed when she saw the bright scarlet flash of Albtraum's hair through the trees up ahead, at the crest of the river's falls.

She could see as she approached him that he was somewhat disheveled, carrying the dog under one arm, breathing heavily as he climbed up the hill from the river bank.

He seemed startled when he came to face Ismaire. "I... Renegade ran off," he said simply, staring back awkwardly at her.

They stood there in uncomfortable silence for a prolonged moment, and Ismaire realized as she heard the guards calling for Albtraum, nearly too far away to be heard over the roar of the river, that she'd stumbled upon the perfect opportunity. He was alone. Unarmed. Everything about his current state was unprepared for an attack. All she'd need to do was lash out with the knife, and keep pushing until she'd shoved him over the edge of the falls... It was doubtful they'd ever find him.

She gripped the knife tighter.

And stood fast. As if paralyzed, she simply stood, staring him down. She could not move. All she could see was the messy strands of his scarlet hair and the mud on his dark coat. The dog dangling awkwardly in his looped arm, its paws dirty, a panting grin as though it were immensely proud of itself.

He stood there – tall, narrow, perhaps even a bit delicate – looking nothing like an ancient monstrosity that had snuffed out the lives of thousands, but rather an ordinary, even somewhat charming young man.

It seemed like an eternity before he cleared his throat and said, "We should go and rejoin the others," before continuing to scale the hill.

She turned to watch him go, dumbfounded at herself, how she'd simply stood frozen, unable to attack him even though she'd had the perfect opportunity. Was it possible that whatever spell he'd put Mianna and the whole of Sylva under had begun to take hold of her as well?

Ismaire found herself unable to answer that for herself and swore to herself as she tucked the dagger into the pack on her belt, following after Albtraum to reunite with the traveling party.

Chapter XVII

The group's travels continued uneventfully over the next few days, taking them along picturesque and peaceful mountain roads well-travelled by merchants and couriers. Albtraum had scarcely walked the roads before, when he travelled alone with Lucifurius, as they had valued a certain degree of stealth.

There was still something that felt unnatural about walking alongside humans. They spoke with him, tended his needs, asked of him his thoughts and opinions. At times, he was almost overwhelmed by it.

He had become especially fond of Joaquin and Brunhart, often drawn to spend time with them. They were all too eager to teach him more of the world he had entered, and Albtraum might have found himself quite lost without the instruction. He had thought, for a time, that Lucifurius' knowledge was infinite, that he had learned all he needed to of the world and its people. But there were intricacies in everything, most of which he had been thus far blind to.

The air had begun to warm in the midday sun, thick with the smell of damp foliage as they entered a village to rest the horses before continuing the next stretch of their travels. Albtraum could see smoke billowing over the stone walls, and people moving about in the spring sun beyond the gate.

"Well, can't speak for you lads, but I could certainly use a drink before we continue on," he could hear Noman saying from where he rode at the head of the group. "Anyone care to join me?"

"Yes, think I will," Piotr, another of the guards answered. Albtraum had noticed that he often seemed rather sedate – in the few times he had spent with Piotr and his closest friend, Edmund, Piotr had done little of the talking.

"Suit yourselves," Brunhart replied flatly. "But I trust you'll not indulge enough to compromise your duties."

"But that's only when it becomes enjoyable, Captain!" Edmund joked as he handed off the reins of his horse to Glen, who was gathering the mounts of the group to lead them to the horse troughs against the walls of the village. Renegade gave the horses a wide berth but trotted around them as if trying to herd them closer.

He saw Ismaire walking together with them. She avoided crossing paths with him so much that at times he almost forgot she was there at all... Which was far preferable to her constant attacks.

Albtraum dismounted his own horse, following after Glen. "Will you join them?

"Me? Ah, no, don't think so," Glen chuckled. "There'll be time for ale tonight, and the horses need my attention. You?"

Albtraum shook his head. "No, I..."

It dawned on him, as he gazed at the gates they passed through, watching the guards jovially walk through to the tavern, that he had an unsettling memory of seeing them before.

We know this place. You remember that hunt... do you not?

Albtraum started at Lucifurius' observation. The village was indeed familiar – he recognized it as the first place Lucifurius had led him to kill, years ago. The cobbled streets bustled with activity, more than he'd seen when he'd last passed through. On the outskirts of the town, the smithy stood – it had been long since abandoned, grass and weeds growing around its perimeter.

Something felt knotted and tense in Albtraum's gut as he remembered the first kill he'd made there – but the memory was hazy, flat – as though it had been a thing he'd witnessed, and not a thing he'd done.

It seemed that had been an eternity ago, but Albtraum still felt the discomfort of the recollections creeping up the back of his neck.

He realized Glen was staring, slight concern wrinkling his brow, as he waited for Albtraum to continue.

"I'm a bit tired," Albtraum answered, trying to offer a reassuring smile but feeling it form into more of a grimace. "I'll wait here."

He turned, then, without offering further explanation, and returned to the group of carriages and wagons waiting at the gate. Brunhart was speaking with another guard as he tended a damaged carriage wheel – Lev, Albtraum thought he had heard him called. So many names he'd learned, just in the space of a few weeks.

Mianna stood behind one of the carriages, likely to avoid drawing unnecessary attention, conversing with one of her servants. Albtraum approached them cautiously, not wishing to interrupt, but Mianna quickly took notice of him.

"I had thought you would join the others in the village," she pointed out. She was watching the skies, as did the servant girl perched on the carriage behind her.

Albtraum simply shook his head. “I have passed through this place before.”

Mianna seemed confused by his statement for a moment before realization crossed her features. “Well, if you’re concerned about being recognized, I don’t suppose you should be.”

Albtraum stood stiffly, watching Renegade follow the horses. “It’s not that. It’s...” He frowned, the sentence dying off before he was quite sure what he wanted to say.

Mianna looked at him curiously, then glanced away, brushing a few stray chestnut curls from her face. “I understand it must be difficult to revisit an era of your life you have left behind, and would rather leave where it lies. But you are on a new path now... at least, I hope you consider yourself to be?”

“I am,” he confirmed, tugging at his gloves. He turned his gaze upward, finding Aidan circling high above the group.

The sight of him called to memory the last time they had spoken in earnest, in the aviary. He had still been avoiding Mianna, lest the topic should come up again, but... Sooner or later, he was going to have to address it.

Albtraum cleared his throat. “I would like to know more about your intentions for me, and more details as to what exactly your Order is.” He stood straighter and turned to face her, somewhat uncomfortable with his own assertiveness as he continued to speak.

Mianna nodded. “Ah, yes. I did wonder how long you’d be content to sit with the information I’ve already given you. I am encouraged that you seek to gather more information before making a decision – all the more reason I feel you will make a good ruler.” She motioned for him to follow her as she walked back to where the horses waited. "There is much to talk about – and some things even I am not fully knowledgeable about – so I suppose I've simply not been sure where to start. There are centuries of history to cover..."

"The fundamentals would be a good place to start, I'd wager," Albtraum replied simply as he mounted his horse, and Mianna mounted hers.

She laughed. "You really are all pragmatism, aren't you? That will serve you well in political endeavors."

The men had started to return from the tavern, and everyone prepared to leave again. He watched as the servant whistled, and Aidan swooped back down to the cage. Renegade had hopped up to sleep on one of the wagons. Albtraum was all too glad to leave the familiar village behind.

"There are a precious few people in the world who have been granted immortality. We estimate there are less than a score of us across this world. Some of us are more powerful than others – and the most powerful among our number are members of the Order of Azoth."

"And I suspect you are among the most powerful of this Order?" Albtraum asked casually, feeling a numbing pain prickling at the back of his neck as Lucifurius seethed.

"Only in this world," Mianna replied simply. "That is where the matters of the Order become somewhat more complicated – There lies another world beyond the Rift."

Albtraum thought back to what she'd told him before. "Where I came from?"

"Yes, though from what you have told us, you have no memory of that place, correct?"

He shook his head. “Nothing before Lucifurius guided me.”

Mianna looked out ahead to the road, taking the reins to guide her horse closer to Albtraum’s. “It is possible he has suppressed your memories. In any case, that is of little concern to us, as all that matters now is the path we take from here.” She turned back to him. “I get too far ahead of myself, though.”

As Albtraum listened, he found himself in admiration of how authoritatively she spoke. He had once thought Lucifurius a formidable master, but his erratic temperament and lack of composure was a far cry from Mianna’s coolly unwavering command.

Careful now.

Albtraum ignored the ringing in his ears. “Explain immortality to me.”

“Simply put, we are immune to the effects of time, and death in most of its forms. How exactly an immortal can be killed depends upon their position in the hierarchy of the Order.”

“The very lowest members of the Order are called Wanderers, although not all of them are without connections. We are not entirely certain of how most of them are immortalized, but unlike most others, they return from the dead to live again.”

“Return from the dead?” Albtraum asked with the raise of an eyebrow.

“These are exceedingly rare occurrences, but they happen seemingly at random. In many cases, they come under the employ of the Order. Brunhart and Joaquin are two such cases, both older than even myself.”

He glanced back at the two of them, Joaquin speaking animatedly to Brunhart as he watched carefully over the group. He gave Albtraum a nod in greeting when their eyes met, which Albtraum was quick to return.

"Just how old are you, exactly?" he asked Mianna as he turned around again.

"You'll not want to form a habit of asking a lady her age, but this year marks one hundred thirty-six for me."

Albtraum stared in surprised, blinking curiously at her. "That's..." He shook his head, looking forward again. "Quite a number of years."

She chuckled. "Brunhart nears two hundred, and Joaquin refuses to indulge me with specifics, but I've managed to deduce he is well into his sixth century."

The idea of such a lengthy existence was staggering to Albtraum. He could scarcely wrap his mind around it. It occurred to him that he was not even entirely certain of how old he himself was – he had a vague idea what the length of a year felt like, but trying to multiply it over in his mind so many times...

He was glad for the distraction from that particularly complex train of thought as Mianna continued speaking.

"Before I tell you more of the Order, though, there is more I must tell you about yourself."

Albtraum could not keep himself from smirking at that. "I suspect I must be the only person alive who must be told his own story by someone else."

Mianna returned his amusement, but it was strained – masked by something else. “You might find yourself surprised, Albtraum. I do not wish to overwhelm you, but... as you have no doubt realized, there is much that Lucifurius has kept from you... His true name, for a start.”

Albtraum frowned. One of only two names, including his own, that he had known for years... and that, too, was false.

As though you were ever worthy of knowing it.

“Z’xolkuloth is the ruler of the dark world, and the progenitor of all daemons. Lucifurius, or so he calls himself, is only a projection of Z’xolkuloth...Or rather, Lucifurius is a part of him. He has divided his own essence and used it to possess other bodies, but he does have a body of his own. As I understand it, he seeks to create a body for each part of his essence, to render himself invulnerable.”

“*Each* part?” Albtraum questioned with the raise of an eyebrow. “There are others?”

“One other that we are aware of, as well as Z’xolkuloth himself, residing in the dark world.” Mianna delivered the information with a sort of careful gentleness, as though she knew he might find it burdensome.

Familiar hurt bubbled up in Albtraum’s chest – he had always thought, and Lucifurius has always spoken as though there were only ever he and Albtraum. They were alone against the world. Albtraum had been the chosen favorite, the only vessel worthy of Lucifurius.

More lies were stripped away every day.

“Z’xolkuloth,” Albtraum repeated. “So, that is his true name, then, and he is using another being as a puppet as we speak, just as he uses me.” He tried to ignore the growing ache that burned through him as Lucifurius stewed in his anger.

Mianna shook her head. “You are no puppet, Albtraum. I am sorry if I’ve soured your mood... Perhaps we can lighten it. There are many more complex matters to discuss and I have much to teach you, but since we will be working together, we should also get to know one another.”

Albtraum wrinkled his nose and scowled, looking forward over the head of his horse. “I’m not much for socializing.”

“Well, that will come to you with practice. You might start by telling me more about yourself?” She looked at him expectantly, and he felt as though he’d suddenly forgotten every word he knew.

He stammered a few times before managing to mumble, “Haven’t we just established that you know more of who I am than I do myself?”

“There is more to you than your practical capabilities and where you came from, which is all I am currently aware of. For example, your interests, your talents, your relationships with others.”

Albtraum’s mind was distressingly blank. He looked around at the landscape as if hoping it would give him an idea of what to say. His gaze settled on Joaquin, who had ridden ahead of them, casually conversing with one of the guards. Brunhart rode silently still a ways behind them.

“I... suppose I have gotten on well with some of your citizens.”

Mia smirked, following his line of sight. “I should say so. Joaquin positively adores you, these days you’re all he seems to talk about. And I’ve never seen Brunhart go so soft for anything. And you seem to be making friends among my guard... I must say, I had my doubts about you, when we first took you in. But you’ve exceeded my every expectation.”

Though her comments about him had made him uncomfortable before, he found himself pleased with the praise and the confirmation that his fondness for his companions was well and truly reciprocated. “Is that so?” he replied, trying to seem unfazed but finding it hard not to beam.

“We did very well in choosing you for this position, and I believe you will grow into it even more the more you learn.”

He looked ahead thoughtfully, focused on nothing in particular. “Reading,” he said abruptly, and Mianna looked back to him. “To answer your question. I do enjoy reading. Lucifurius taught me many things, but he has also kept me from many things... Reading allows me to think with another mind, I suppose.”

“What an interesting way to put it,” she said with amusement. “You seem to have gotten quite good at commanding your dog, as well.”

Albtraum nodded. “I find it good to have him around. He makes for good company.” He sighed. “There is not much else, though. I’m afraid my experiences have been limited only to endless killing under Lucifurius, and the last few weeks I’ve spent in your kingdom.”

“Then you should be looking forward to having more experiences. You have the whole world before you, and practically endless time to take it all in.”

Albtraum nodded absently, still considering her words. Feeling uncomfortable as the moment of silence between them grew, he cleared his throat. “And what of you? Whatever little you know of me, I know nothing about you.”

“Mine is a rather more long and complicated history,” she replied, straightening out her dress as she shifted and settled into her saddle. “The brief version is that I was once a bastard peasant girl – I was raised by the village healer, my family all died when I was very young. It was just my luck, however, to be the bastard of a king, and when his reign ended, the Order tracked me down and placed me in his throne. Since then, I have ruled Sylva, a job I quite enjoy."

"Your kingdom does seem prosperous," Albtraum commented, attempting to imitate her earlier complimentary exchange. He squinted at her statement. "Bastard...?" He'd only ever heard the word hurled as an insult.

"My parents were unwed," she explained. "Many societies have a stigma attached to this status."

"Interesting." Albtraum looked down. "I... apologize that you lost your family."

"It no longer troubles me. I have had a great many years to make my peace with their loss."

Albtraum thought about family, and parents, and his thoughts wandered back to Lucifurius as he stirred at the back of his mind. "Lucifurius... or, I suppose Z'xolkuloth is my father, so I am afraid the notion of family is rather foreign to me."

"By blood," Mianna confirmed with a nod. "But I assume you do not consider him as such."

Albtraum had only a vague idea of what the usual relationship between parents and children was like, based on his observations of Sylva's citizens over the last few weeks and the passages he'd read in books.

But he knew it was nothing like what he had with Lucifurius.

"I do not," Albtraum said firmly, looking up again.

Because you are so much more than my child. Our souls are bound together, we are one and the same, we are as if extensions of each other...

Albtraum found himself repulsed by the thought, and tried to focus on something else to quiet Lucifurius. He looked over at Mianna, and found himself at a loss as she stared back waiting for him to speak, fern-colored eyes glimmering in the sunlight.

He turned slightly in his saddle to face her, waiting for the drone of Lucifurius' voice to fade out. "Tell me more about yourself."

Chapter XVIII

"My brother and I were both children of the King of Sylva who ruled before me, and one of his courtesans. My brother was eight years my senior, and my mother died before I can remember. My brother raised me with help from the village healer... When he came of age, he was conscripted to fight for the Sylvan army. He planned to confront our father about our existence, but he was killed in a battle before having the chance to speak to him." Mianna felt the ghost of an ache at the recollection, but the memory was so distant now it lacked any of the sharpness it had once had.

She watched Albtraum as he listened to her, his eyes glinting reflectively in the rapidly dimming light like those of a nocturnal creature. It struck her for a moment how normal he looked, despite everything – riding in his tailored travelling clothes, with his hair braided back, loose strands dancing in the breeze almost playfully. He was almost passable for an ordinary young man, but still there was an unfamiliarity to him, an almost alien sort of beauty in his features.

But for all that, it was his naiveté that Mianna found most endearing, and he seemed genuinely interested as she spoke.

"After my brother's death, I was adopted into the family of the village healer, whose daughter my brother had been engaged to be wed to. Years later, the King of Sylva died, and I was found by the Order and groomed to act as his replacement. The man who taught me was Arion Raekyn. He held the throne of Terce, which Camlion Roane now possesses." She nodded to Albtraum. "He was one of the greatest champions for your alliance with us... In fact, his opinion swayed me to your side."

Albtraum looked quite perplexed by this. "He did not even know who I was, nor I him."

Mianna shrugged, breathing out a slight laugh. "That was Arion. He had such faith in you and the potential for your rule."

"It would seem I have lofty expectations to uphold," Albtraum sighed, shoulders slumping slightly. "If he no longer rules Terce, what became of him?"

Mianna looked ahead again, noting that they neared the next village, where they'd be stopping for the night at the inn. "He was a Shadran. They are a race from the dark world which you hail from. He abdicated his throne four years ago and left to the dark world to fight for your cause. I have not received word from him since... I have no choice but to assume he is dead."

Albtraum looked uncomfortable. "All this death. Does it not bother you?"

Mianna considered his question. Arion's loss still hurt – four years was not long in relation to the life she'd lived, and there had been no confirmation, only a slow, dawning realization that Arion would likely not be returning.

"It does. But Arion knew what he was doing. He was aware that death likely awaited him there." She let out a breath, and it made a faint cloud in the chill of the evening air. "And when you have lived as long as we have, you learn not to define things by their endings."

Albtraum frowned deeply, and she found his expression hard to read. "I had no idea," he muttered faintly. "A man was there fighting and dying for me, and I had no idea. I was not even aware there was a cause to fight for."

Mianna tried to sound reassuring. "You cannot be blamed. Lucifurius kept you locked within his own mind... You were unaware of a great many things, among which was your own existence for a time."

Albtraum did not seem entirely convinced, and fell quietly pensive as they continued along the road to the inn. "Lucifurius told me he created other beings to reside in the dark world. I assume he referred to these... Shadrans?"

"Ah, yes. You may have a chance to meet a few of them in Terce. Some of Arion's Shadran vanguard still serve Camlion."

Mianna looked forward again and noted Brunhart riding against the path, turning his horse to ride next to Albtraum's. He handed him a leather sheath. "I came across this in the market where we stopped for supplies," he explained to Albtraum.

Mianna had never seen Brunhart so engaged, so... happy. He'd been a stoic man – and a rather cheerless one, she suspected – all the many years she'd known him. Albtraum had brought out an entirely new side to him.

Albtraum removed the sheath, revealing a slim dagger. He looked back to Brunhart for explanation, holding the weapon as though it might bite him.

"It's lighter than a sword, and you've got a long enough reach to use it effectively. I'll teach you how to use it well once we reach Terce."

Albtraum sheathed the blade again, tucking it into one of his saddlebags. "Thank you, Brunhart."

Brunhart reached over and patted his shoulder. "Of course, pup." Mianna had heard Brunhart affectionately address Albtraum this way in the last few days, and Albtraum seemed to enjoy being called by it.

It was quite cold when they reached the inn, and Albtraum was quick to go inside, having forgotten to wear his cloak. Mianna followed after him, meeting Joaquin at the door.

"You're not wearing your cloak!" he exclaimed, sweeping an arm around Albtraum and rushing him through the inn to the fireplace. "You're going to catch cold..."

Albtraum looked annoyed, but he could not keep laughter from his voice. "Truly, Joaquin, you'd be shocked to hear the things I wore and the cold I stayed out in before..."

"I would be!" Joaquin interjected. "Just thinking of it makes me shudder." He sat Albtraum down at the fire, motioning Mianna over to sit with them. "I assume the two of you still have things to discuss."

Mianna sat, unwrapping the shawl from around her shoulders as she did. "Yes, now that we've spent some time socializing I should get back to teaching you the things you need to know about the Order."

"Perhaps the origins of the organization," Albtraum sighed as he watched the guards file into the inn, discussing amongst themselves their sleeping arrangement for the night.

Mianna smiled. Albtraum's interest was encouraging, and she settled into her seat more comfortably as she readied to tell him more. "Well, that is something I can speak on."

"The story of Septimus and Ishtar," Joaquin sighed. "Mianna, I do so love this section of our history, please allow me to tell the tale?"

Mianna shot a wry look his direction, well versed in his passion for dramatics and stories. "I'll remind you, Joaquin, that not only does this history belong to our Order, but my own family..."

"But you tell stories as if delivering a lesson in arithmetic," Joaquin groaned. "Do your family's memory this one service, and let me tell the story to our dear boy here."

Mianna huffed, but couldn't keep the amusement from her face. "Alright, then, go on ahead. Do be sure to mind the facts as well as your theatrics."

Joaquin glared at her before turning slightly so that his body faced Albtraum. "Septimus and Ishtar were the founders of our Order as it is today. Ishtar was Mianna's grandmother..."

Mianna noted something change in Albtraum's expression. It was clear he tried to keep it from showing, but he blanched slightly, and seemed to be almost too focused on Joaquin, staring intently at him. Joaquin was, of course, too wrapped up in storytelling to notice.

Joaquin told the story, his voice thick with melancholy. "Many hundreds of years ago, the Order did exist, though its goal was then to make contact with the other world. They erected a temple around the first rift, the only known connection to it. Septimus and Ishtar were lovers... She walked the path of light, those who sought to learn all they could about the other world without ever entering it, keeping their distance, relying on conjecture. Septimus walked in the dark. A scholar. He wanted to immerse himself in the dark world to learn what he could of it--"

"And Lucifurius took control of his mind," Albtraum interjected.

"Yes," Joaquin answered with a frown. "Don't tell me you've heard this story before?"

"No, I..." Albtraum shook his head. "Go on."

"Septimus resisted Lucifurius as long as he could, but eventually the strain became too much. He began slaughtering innocents under the daemon's control. Ishtar despaired to find a way to separate them, and there was none apart from the death of Septimus. Still, she tried. She spent her every moment trying to find a way. Septimus had himself chained beneath the temple where she and her colleagues stayed... But the newly formed Order learned of this, and they ordered her to kill him."

"And so, Ishtar drove her own blade through his heart, Septimus offering himself as a sacrifice to hinder Lucifurius if even the smallest amount... After this, Ishtar made a pact with a being of the other world, and crafted the Order as it is today. She sought to keep a balance in the world, waiting for the one who would replace Z'xolkuloth's place on the dark world's throne, ending his corruption... And it was you, Albtraum. We've all waited all this time for you."

Mianna listened as Joaquin finished telling the tale, and Albtraum's expression had turned worried. Silence hung between them for a long time, the only sound being the crackling of the fire.

"There's not a way to separate us?" Albtraum said quietly after a long time.

Joaquin frowned and started to speak, but Mianna beat him to it, finding herself reaching over to place a hand on Albtraum's arm. "You have the potential to become his equal, Albtraum. A human cannot separate themselves from Lucifurius' control, no... but you can. That is why you are the one we chose."

The tension in his shoulders appeared to ease, but the frown in his expression remained. "I am not his equal. I will never..."

"No," Joaquin interrupted. "Nothing about you is equal to him. You are more than he is, or ever will be."

His words seemed to connect with Albtraum, and his nervousness seemed to melt away – Mianna watched them curiously, in awe of the close bond they already seemed to share.

It seemed Albtraum was building himself a family, one by one.

Albtraum had grown weary of the road by the time he was informed they would be arriving soon in Terce. He wondered how he had spent his life up until now constantly moving – for years, he had never spent more than a day in the same place, and now travel was somewhat exhausting, if highly interesting.

They paused at the crest of a hill to ensure the whole party was still together, and Albtraum rode his horse over to the edge of the path to look down on the city, amazed at its size. He could hardly see its end on the horizon. Until now, Sylva had been the largest civilization he'd visited – but this place was easily five times its size. The air was much warmer here than it had been in the mountains, and the landscape was lush with vegetation. Even from this distance, Albtraum could hear the activity bustling in the expanse of the city below.

"That's where we're going?" He asked over his shoulder to Joaquin.

Joaquin chuckled. "Oh no, my boy, not to that city. We're going underneath it."

"Underneath?"

"Terce is underground," He heard Ismaire snap from a short distance away. Her short tufts of hair ruffled in the slight breeze. "An Order city would never be so conspicuous."

Albtraum bristled at her sharp tone, but kept quiet. He would gain nothing from confronting her. He looked down and watched Renegade scratch at his ear, trotting circles around the horses' legs.

Mianna rode to the front of the group. "I've sent word ahead, so we should go down to the gates. Camlion will be waiting for us, no doubt."

They moved away from the sprawling city, circling around its border. Albtraum felt nervousness tighten his chest as they rode on, wondering how he might be received by the people here. Joaquin had taught him how to speak nobly, how to avoid causing offense... and yet he worried still that he might forget or overlook something.

They continued away from the city for a long while, until the walls were a distant sight and the roads were mostly clear of travelers. The road soon disappeared entirely, but a faint path grown over with grass and flowers led them into a ravine, at the end of which stood a large gate.

The gate was open, soldiers clad in bronze and leather stepping out to assist the party in entering the doorway. The inside of the entranceway was dark, but Albtraum's eyes adjusted quickly to the dimmer light.

"Welcome back to Terce, Your Majesty," a guard who appeared to be of high rank greeted, helping Mianna down from her horse. He was stocky and heavily armored, with dark hair. "How was your journey?"

"Pleasant and uneventful, thank you, Guilliaume," Mianna answered cheerily. "Camlion waits for us in the courtyard, I assume?"

"Yes, he has been quite looking forward to your visit. We will take care of your horses and equipment, you and your company can head that way where the King awaits you."

The pathway was long and slanted, opening up into a larger room below. The rest of the group dismounted and walked into the open area, the Tercian guards tending the horses and carriages. Renegade walked behind Albtraum, wagging his tail and sniffing the air. The footsteps of the group echoed loudly off the cold stone walls, and Albtraum found the amplified sound grating.

We could make these halls echo with different sorts of sounds... The music of death and despair.

But not so grating as he found Lucifurius' interjections.

There were a multitude of guards in the wide, open hallway. Albtraum had thought the underground might be quite dark and cramped, but the hall opened to high ceilings with many hanging chandeliers, bathing the room in a soft, warm light.

Standing in the center of all the guards was a young man, and Albtraum assumed from his lavish attire that he was their king. Despite this, he appeared barely older than Albtraum himself, only the whisper of boyish stubble growing unchecked on his chin. His ashy blonde hair stuck out every which way in wild curls, longer pieces falling over his golden eyes.

A wide, childish grin split his face when he saw Mianna, and he stepped forward with his arms outstretched, sweeping her into a rather undignified embrace. "Mia! It's been ages! I'm so glad you made the journey." He was barely taller than Mianna, but still lifted her slightly off the ground. She looked exasperated, awkwardly patting his shoulders as he set her down.

"Good to see you as well, Camlion. May I introduce Ismaire Uemytlach and Albtraum, our wards."

Albtraum nodded in greeting, and Ismaire grunted out a sound that might have been "hello".

As they were led away from the courtyard and into the section of the underground city that housed off the royal estate, Camlion took Mianna by the arm, a gesture she accepted stiffly. "How were the roads, then? Anything interesting? Or... anything amiss?"

Mianna eyed him carefully. "Amiss? Why, should there have been?"

"Ah, well..." Camlion slowed to a stop, awkwardly glancing back over his shoulder. Albtraum unconsciously raised an eyebrow as their eyes met.

"Mia, surely we can discuss this once you've all had time to settle in?" Camlion questioned with a chuckle.

"We can discuss it now, Camlion, since you were so keen to bring it up," Mianna replied sweetly, but Albtraum could sense the edge of her words.

"Yes, er... Well, this is a bit awkward, but... it seems you were right about the corruption spreading from the dark world. As it happens, a rift has opened up in one of the outer sections of the city, and sickened some of the townsfolk. We've cleared the people out, of course, but—"

A rift. Another place Lucifurius had poisoned. Albtraum felt his chest tighten at the thought.

"There is a rift in Terce, and you did not think it prudent to contact me immediately?" Mianna pulled away from Camlion's grasp and stared him down in admonishment.

"I did not wish you to worry! Besides, I have the situation under control."

Mianna let out a huff. This was perhaps the closest Albtraum had seen to her losing composure, but in an instant, her frustration melted, and she offered a curt nod. "Perhaps you are right, Camlion, perhaps it might be better to discuss this after we have settled ourselves."

As the group was dispersed, the Sylvan servants were quick to usher Albtraum through the halls, navigating them easily. They must have been quite familiar with Terce's layout, Albtraum realized. The overall atmosphere of the place felt quite similar to Sylva, lacking only its tall windows and sweeping, spectacular views, but there was something cozy and comfortable about the firelight and enclosed spaces.

We are creatures of the dark, of course. It is only natural you should feel more comfortable here. You will be more powerful, as well, especially now that I have begun to claim this place as my own... The perfect time to kill again and rebuild our bond.

Albtraum drew a shaky breath and tried to ignore Lucifurius entirely, a feat that was impossible, but the effort seemed to quiet him all the same. Albtraum was led down a hallway to a small but well-decorated room by the servant girl assigned to him, and he patted his leg to call Renegade to him, removing his cloak and messily folding it over his arm before setting it on the dresser. More servants entered the room carrying his belongings.

"Can I fetch anything for you, my lord?" the servant girl asked, and Albtraum looked over awkwardly, unsettled by her formality.

"I have all I need here," he said quietly, relieved when she gave a brief curtsy and left the room with the rest of the staff attending his things.

The bedroom was small, but comfortable. Candlelight kept the windowless space softly lit, glinting off the stone walls and floors. This place almost made Albtraum feel like an animal in a den, huddled down under the earth. Renegade sniffed curiously at the bedding, continually interested in his ever-changing surroundings.

Albtraum felt restless in the room, comfortable though it was. He opened the door, calling Renegade to his side, and made his way back to the main hall.

He had known that Lucifurius had immense power… he had once taken comfort in the thought, been in reverence of it. But the knowledge of the rift made him fearful, knowing that this world he had come to consider his own was under threat.

As the moments wore on, Albtraum found himself restless from travel, and there was little of interest to him in the small bedroom. Calling Renegade to his side, he quietly exited the room, following the hallway back out the way he'd come to the courtyard.

He was relieved to find Mianna conversing with Joaquin, Brunhart standing nearby and listening in. They looked up as Albtraum approached, Mianna offering a gracious smile in greeting.

"Ah, Albtraum. Are you finding your accommodations acceptable?" she asked him, her tone light but somewhat breathless, masking underlying emotion.

"Yes, of course. But on another matter… did I hear correctly earlier, that there is a rift here in Terce?" He asked the question carefully, feeling as though perhaps he should not be asking.

Mianna merely sighed and nodded in response. "Yes… I haven't the slightest idea why Camlion did not see fit to inform me before we arrived.

Are you feeling any ill effects? I recall you collapsed when we drew near the rift outside of Sylva... And in the afflicted village we visited."

Albtraum grimaced slightly at the memory. "Ah, that... I provoked a reaction from Lucifurius on both occasions, I don't believe it was to do with our proximity to the rifts..."

But of course. You know the force of my power even without such augmentation.

"Still," Joaquin spoke up, clearing his throat, "You should exercise caution. Perhaps it would be best if you stayed behind when we investigate tomorrow..."

"No," Albtraum said quickly, stopping him. "No, I... I should be there."

"He is right, Joaquin. Perhaps it is only Camlion... But Albtraum must appear capable if we are to convince everyone of his capacity to assume the throne of the dark world," Mianna agreed.

Their discussion was interrupted when a few Tercian guards approached, bowing quickly to Mianna. Now that Albtraum got a better look at them, he could see that their uniforms were quite similar to those of the Sylvan guards, with only small differences.

"Your Majesty, the King would like a brief audience with you, in private," one informed Mianna.

"Ah, I expected he would. Will I see you in the dining hall this evening, Albtraum?" Mianna asked.

Albtraum nodded. "Yes."

Looking pleased, Mianna followed the guards away as Joaquin went back to directing the servants. The Sylvan guards overseeing the work of the servants transporting the group's belongings seemed tense and on edge. It was the kind of demeanor Albtraum saw often in men at war... Poised to attack, looking for threats around every corner, the tightly wound knots of their shoulders easing only in the presence of those of their own kingdom.

It was not the behavior Albtraum would expect of people among friends, on a simple diplomatic mission.

Brunhart himself did not seem to share the concerns of his men, whatever they might be, at least outwardly. But Albtraum noted the way he casually swept his eyes about the room every so often... How, even after shedding his cloak and riding gear, a sword remained fastened to his belt.

Albtraum considered asking what had them all so alert, but knew he was unlikely to receive a proper answer. He was only barely their ally himself. He fidgeted with his sleeves.

"Brunhart, do you think we might practice with the dagger you got for me?" he asked after a brief silence.

Brunhart smiled slightly, an expression that always looked lopsided because of the scar running from the corner of his mouth. "That is a good idea. I'm feeling restless from our time on the road myself, and some sparring will surely help us rest easier tonight."

Albtraum hurried back to his room to fetch the dagger before returning to follow Brunhart through the royal wing to the guard barracks. Brunhart informed one of the men they'd be sparring, and the man motioned them into the sparring ring with the raise of an eyebrow. Renegade flopped down against the edge, panting. His tail thumped noisily on the hollow wood of the deck as he wagged it.

Albtraum unsheathed the weapon and examined it. “Are you sure I shouldn’t be learning how to use a sword?”

“Daggers conceal easier, it wouldn’t do for you to be seen walking around with a sword on your belt in the position you’re in.” Brunhart stepped over and took Albtraum’s hand, showing him how to grip the dagger’s hilt. “It’s easier to wield, too.”

He stood back. “You’ll not want to hold it too high, your arm will tire quickly. Too low, and you won’t be able to parry your opponent’s attacks.” He took a wooden practice sword from the rack. “Let’s try.”

Albtraum felt a familiar and yet somehow entirely alien feeling as he fell into the stance of battle once again after neglecting it for so long. Brunhart lunged forward and took a swing, and Albtraum moved to block it, catching the wooden blade to his arm. He winced, and Brunhart chuckled.

“This is why we’re practicing now… Try to angle your dagger more with your opponent’s blade, you’ll avoid ruining your own edge, and more importantly you can catch them with your guard.

They practiced the parry a few more times until Albtraum was able to execute it with a moderate rate of success. He found it hard to believe he’d once done these things with such ease.

But then, he supposed, it hadn’t really been him then.

Do not be so sure.

Brunhart moved to demonstrating how to attack with the weapon, and Albtraum found he moved much more nimbly than he had with a sword, even when under Lucifurius' control.

"You'll have an advantage over those with larger weapons," Brunhart explained. "You can swing shorter, while they leave themselves open." He held the practice sword up again. "Go ahead."

Albtraum lunged forward as he'd practiced, easily evading the wooden blade and lashing out with the dagger, startling himself as he caught Brunhart in the arm.

He stepped back, letting his weapon clatter to the floor, watching the bloodstain spread across Brunhart's sleeve.

"I... I'm sorry, I..."

Almost. Almost. Almost. Pick up the knife. Attack him again. Do not stop until we are one again.

Brunhart waved him off. "It's nothing. Truly." Albtraum watched in awe as the wound rapidly closed, leaving only a faint bloodstain on Brunhart's sleeve.

"We can keep going," Brunhart encouraged, retrieving the knife and holding it out to Albtraum.

Albtraum shook his head. "I don't..."

He invites it! And you throw away this perfect chance as though it were nothing! Have you any idea the power he could bring to us?! He is an army unto himself! Kill him, you fool!

Trembling, he turned away from Brunhart. "I can't... Not now. I..."

Brunhart placed a hand on his shoulder. "If you truly wish to learn, you will need to fight past your hesitations. You could not harm me even if you wanted to, so you should practice as though I were an enemy."

Lucifurius laughed, a more acrid and searing laugh than Albtraum had ever heard before. *He believes it, he truly believes he is safe from us.*

Albtraum pushed Brunhart's hand away, more forcefully than he wanted to. "You don't understand," he muttered. "You don't know what he can do... He's..."

Brunhart stepped closer to him, speaking with careful patience. "Albtraum, you must not let Lucifurius intimidate you, and you must not listen to what he says."

"Do you not think I am *trying?!"* Albtraum exclaimed suddenly, stepping away. "Do you not think I would prefer not to listen to his endless talk, keeping me awake through the nights, speaking over my own thoughts? You have no idea the lengths to which I have gone to defy him, and to serve the purposes of your Order, or the lengths I will have to go to still!"

Brunhart seemed largely unfazed by Albtraum's sudden shouting, but his expression had fallen slightly. He sighed and seemed to be preparing to answer, but was interrupted by the timid voice of a servant standing in the doorway. Albtraum had been so swept up in his distress that he had not even noticed her enter.

"Sirs, her Majesty the Queen requests your presence in the banquet hall," the girl said, giving a quick bow. "Discussions with the King are to be held, and a feast will be served."

"We will be there shortly," Brunhart said, dismissing her.

Albtraum opened his mouth to say something, to apologize for shouting, or further explain his reasoning. But the words never came, and the slight confusion and disappointment Brunhart regarded him with killed any further chance of finding them. Renegade watched curiously, no doubt startled by the suddenness of the outburst.

You have reminded him of what he has always known... You are a beast, a monster, and no matter what they do, they cannot tame it out of you.

"We should go to the banquet. I am sure you are quite hungry, we were on the road most of the day," Brunhart suggested gently.

Miserable and ashamed, Albtraum followed him out of the room.

CHAPTER XIX

Mianna followed Camlion into his office, having a seat in one of the armchairs across from his desk. The royal quarters had been rebuilt in recent years, and the floors were no longer dusty and barren, nor were the tapestries and décor threadbare and dirty. Arion had always found himself too occupied to tend to his own spaces, and so Mianna and Joaquin had arranged to have them finished in a way befitting royalty.

Arion had kept the space immaculate after that, something the Tercian servants continued on doing to this day. Mianna almost expected to find him sitting at the desk in the royal office.

But of course, when they entered, it was empty.

Camlion dismissed his servants and sat himself down in the armchair next to Mianna, turning toward her and getting comfortable. "You're looking quite well. I've been looking forward to your visit ever since you informed me you'd be coming."

Mianna nodded. "Thank you, Camlion. Unfortunately, I have come for more than a mere social call, and we have important matters to discuss."

Camlion smirked at her. "Surely there can be socializing once our business is concluded, Mia."

Mianna regarded him coolly. Camlion had been chasing after her ever since he'd first met her, when he was a young boy under Arion's mentorship. Though she'd refused him repeatedly, his confidence that he somehow had a chance to woo her never waned.

"Camlion, I'm afraid the matter is rather serious. Especially since a rift has now appeared in Terce."

"I do understand your alarm, truly. But it seems to be small, and we have already moved the people away! We could contain it, like the one outside of Sylva..."

"And more will only keep appearing. As they did in Sylva. The more corrupt he becomes, the more rifts will appear, the more people Z'xolkuloth will sicken and impregnate."

Camlion frowned and slowly tapped at the arms of the chair, pondering. "Is it truly as bad as all that? I thought those were just stories people told to explain outbreaks of disease and ill-begotten children."

"It seems especially naïve of you to deny the influence of the dark world when you have it in your own court," Mianna rebutted calmly. Arion had mentored Camlion for years, offering him the throne when he had left to head the resistance in the dark world. Some of his fellow Shadrans, members of his vanguard, had stayed behind, and remained in Camlion's service.

"Castus and Nestor consider themselves subjects of Terce now! But... I suppose you are right, it's just so ghastly, I shudder to think it might be true..."

Mianna sighed. "Well, now you can see that it is. Our Order was founded to manage the corruption Z'xolkuloth spilled into our world, but I believe now the matter has become grave enough that we must instead turn our efforts to stopping that corruption at the source. Z'xolkuloth, and even Azoth... They must be replaced."

Camlion's eyes were wide. She almost pitied him – the young man had come from humble beginnings, and managing a kingdom alone was proving to be a difficult undertaking for him – much less becoming involved in matters of such a massive scale.

But she herself had not been so terribly different, and they had been mentored by the same man. Camlion was going to have to grow up some time or another.

"There is someone in the Order who knows what I am planning to do, who opposes me."

Camlion sat forward, his eyebrows raising in surprise. "You don't think that I might betray you, Mia?"

Mianna regarded him carefully. She had intended to question him about his potential involvement in the murder of her soldiers, but she hadn't truly suspected him... His haste to assert his innocence, however, before she even had the chance to explain what had happened...

"Certainly not. Should I, Camlion?"

"No, of course not. The decisions you have made for this Order have always been sound ones, and I would never think to challenge you. Though this does complicate matters, does it not? If we cannot even trust our own, how can we possibly hope to effect change within the Higher Order?"

"Somehow, we must. Z'xolkuloth has been left in his position far too long. As the pieces of his soul gather power, his corruption spreads to others. It will not be long before we are affected ourselves."

"Well, you have made progress in hindering him, have you not? What was his name... does he not house Lucifurius? All you have to do is keep him alive and the piece of Z'xolkuloth's soul within him will lose its power and remain trapped there," Camlion replied, seeming to think himself quite clever. He spoke to her with a reassuring, if mildly arrogant tone, as though she had come to him for advice.

Mianna let out her annoyance in a short breath. "Surely the fact that I've brought him here should be your indication that I do not plan to—" She looked down as he leaned forward to pat her arm, cutting her off.

"Really, Mia, I wondered why you've been parading the poor man around as a ward. I'm sure he's a fine man in an unfortunate position, and with your soft and kind nature you would not want to deny him his freedom... But surely one man's fate in relation to that of all of the world's is a small price to pay?"

Mianna frowned, making a note to herself to appoint less sycophantic advisors to attend him. Clearly, he was not being challenged by anyone nearly as much as his brash young ego required to remain under control. "Hindering the fragments of Z'xolkuloth's soul does not halt the spread of corruption, it only slows it. Keep in mind that you have held your office for four years, Camlion, and I have held mine more than a century. I am your friend, but I am also your superior, and I do not much care for how cavalier you are when we meet."

Camlion moved back quickly, his confidence melting under the slight heat of her words. "O-of course, Mia. Forgive my rudeness."

She resisted the smirk that threatened to creep into her expression. "Albtraum is far more than just the newest vessel of Lucifurius. He is a daemon."

"Truly?" Camlion looked unsettled.

"He is our first hope for placing control of the dark world in better hands. And I doubt we will have such a perfect chance again. Chronus herself foretold to me that he would come."

"I... see." Camlion sighed and leaned back.

Mianna stood, circling around the room. "I believe that Azoth himself has also been compromised. He has withdrawn more and more from the Order, and seems concerned only with his own gains. He has not participated in our governance since long before you took your throne." She looked over the desk, noting that it seemed much neater than her own back in Sylva. "This rot will only continue to spread the longer we allow it to continue. We must stop it at the source, and that begins with Azoth and Z'xolkuloth."

"So then, your other ward..."

"Chronus informed me of her as well. She has potential to assume the role of Azoth. The both of them will require a rather involved mentorship before they can assume these positions, however. I will require the full support of the Order of this world."

Camlion looked thoughtfully at the floor for a moment before standing. "Whatever you should require from me, Mia, you have it." He stepped over and took her hand. "You know I would wage an endless war for you, I would go to the ends of the earth."

She leaned away slightly, carefully pulling her hand from his grasp. "That won't be necessary, Camlion," she said, now unable to conceal her amusement as she chuckled lightly. "But I would like you to make them both feel welcomed here. We've only discussed the Order's future briefly with Albtraum and Ismaire."

"Of course, it would not do to set them on edge before they fully understand the duties before them. I was educated for many years about my position," Camlion commented.

"And I fear we may not have the luxury of such time."

"Let us get on with it, then." Camlion guided Mianna out of the office with a hand on her shoulder. "I've prepared quite a large feast for your arrival. I hope your party brought their appetites."

"I am quite sure they have."

Albtraum was almost glad for the sudden commotion of the dining hall as he entered. He'd had a few moments to change his clothes and leave Renegade in his quarters, and he and Brunhart had parted ways without much conversation after, the awkwardness in the wake of Albtraum's outburst persisting.

Inside the dining hall was a flood of people, the fine silks and rich colors giving them away as nobility. He gazed out over the crowd, finding that a great many of them had gathered near the head of the great wooden table, where Mianna stood surrounded, people clamoring to speak with her. She smiled, her gracious air never falling even as Albtraum estimated the socialization had to be becoming tedious.

He'd lost count of the number of cups of wine he'd had, seeing as every time he finished what he had a servant appeared from thin air to refill his cup, but it was enough to make his head feel foggy. Much to his relief, no one had approached to speak with him, but he was drawing many curious stares from the Tercian guards and townspeople, making him uneasy. One group in particular, comprised of several young girls, was almost certainly following him as he moved about.

Albtraum was finally able to stop the servants from refilling his wine, handing off his cup to one of the serving girls, who wordlessly accepted it with an amused smirk. Albtraum remained where he stood, listening to the musicians play over the roaring chatter of the crowd.

Music was perhaps one of the strangest things he'd encountered in the world. It served no purpose, yet he found it enjoyable, the melody taking his mind away from the discomfort of being surrounded by so many people.

Brunhart emerged from the crowd, looking somewhat tired himself. He wasn't in his guard uniform, which was unusual, but Albtraum supposed even he had to stop working at some point.

"Well, this is extravagant enough to please even Joaquin, I'm sure," Brunhart muttered as he stopped to stand beside Albtraum. "Mianna did mention there would be a welcoming party, but I must admit, I was not expecting so many people to be here when we arrived..."

Albtraum wondered if perhaps it would be better not to respond – but Brunhart was not Lucifurius. They did not communicate with seething silence. "I am sorry I shouted," he muttered abruptly.

Brunhart seemed perplexed for a moment before chuckling. Relief flooded Albtraum, he instantly felt the tension in his shoulders ease. Brunhart was not angry.

“Men have done far worse than shout at me with no apology. I only ask that you remember we wish to help you… Not control you as Lucifurius has done.”

Albtraum nodded, feeling a lump form in his throat. Perhaps an effect of the wine. “Mianna has been teaching me of the history of the Order. I’ve had a lot to mull over.”

“Undoubtedly. It’s quite a lot to take in.”

“And she said before that you are almost two hundred years old?”

He nodded. “Yes, that I am. Though to be honest with you, most of those two hundred years have been something of a blur for me.”

“How did you come to be involved with the Order?” Albtraum asked curiously, realizing the topic hadn’t ever come up in their conversations.

Brunhart looked forward at the swarm of nobles before them. “I was a sword for hire and had proved myself to be difficult to kill, so I was sent after Joaquin by someone who wanted him dead. I would later learn that he was immortal himself… As well as in Mianna’s service, and under her protection. She is a more powerful immortal than I am. She gave me two choices: serve the Order, or face death once again, with no chance to return this time.” He looked back to Albtraum with a faint smile. “And naturally, it’s not difficult to scale the ranks when you outlive everyone you work alongside.”

“I see,” Albtraum replied. “And your work is important to you?”

“I wouldn’t say it’s anything I’d have chosen for myself. But I’ve grown into it, and it does give me a sense of purpose.”

Albtraum considered that. “I hope I can find that with the Order as well.”

Brunhart looked back at Albtraum with an expression he found difficult to read, as if he was unsure of what to say.

Deciding to break the silence before it stretched on any longer, Albtraum spoke up again. “You’re a Wanderer… Does that mean you died?”

Brunhart’s brow furrowed. “Yes.”

Albtraum felt he was perhaps prying too deeply, but curiosity overwhelmed his instinct to leave the discussion where it was. “How did it happen?”

“A mercenary company was passing through my village and asked me to join up with them. I was tending my family’s farm with my wife at the time, and she was with child. Naturally, I turned them down, thinking nothing of it. But a few days after that, they came to my home, dragged my wife and I from our bed, and slashed her throat in front of me, I suppose thinking it would rid me of my attachment to the life I had.”

His voice seemed just slightly strained, but he otherwise delivered the information with careful neutrality, much as Mianna had when relating her own personal history.

Just as Albtraum was beginning to wonder if he would continue or not, he gave a humorless scoff. “I stood no chance when I fought back, which of course I knew. There were six of them against only myself. But at that point, I had nothing to fear. Everything I had was taken from me, and if I was to die, I would be all the better for it.”

A voice from years ago rattled through Albtraum's mind. *Fear, why is there anything to fear now? My sons are dead, you've taken everything from me!*

Lucifurius seemed to remember as well. Or perhaps he had been the one to bring the memory back to the forefront of Albtraum's mind.

You see... You are the same breed of walking filth to him as the men who destroyed his life. And you had the utter gall *to think he could possibly care for you.*

Albtraum had been trying to ignore Lucifurius, but he found himself shooting back a response before he could stop himself. *No. I did not choose to kill anyone. I was merely your weapon, but I'm not any longer, and I never will be again.*

He braced himself for pain, but Lucifurius stayed unnervingly docile. *We shall see about that.*

Brunhart was looking at the ground, not having noticed Albtraum's distress. "They killed me too. After that, I... vaguely remember meeting with Death himself, that he encountered me and decided he did not want me among his collected souls that day. When I awoke, my wounds had healed, the men were gone, but I had come back alone. My wife and our unborn child were still dead."

"Ironically enough, after that, I did take up work as a mercenary. Though it took me a great many years, I hunted down the men from that day. They were all retired by then, thinking they'd die fat and happy in their beds rather than on the end of a blade... I've taken comfort in knowing how terrifying it had to be to see my apparent specter come back to kill them."

Brunhart turned back to face Albtraum and started slightly. “Oh, pup, I… I am sorry. I don’t mean to bring up such a grim subject at a celebration meant for you.”

Albtraum noted that his expression must have betrayed his feelings of uneasiness, and tried to unfurrow his brow. “It’s alright, I did press you.”

Brunhart patted his shoulder. “I don’t wish to trouble you.”

Albtraum nodded, feeling the grogginess the wine had brought about in him again. Before he could consider it, he heard himself blurt out, “Am I the same as them, then? The ones who killed your family?”

Brunhart’s eyebrows raised in confusion, and he seemed to struggle for an answer. “Well, no, why would—“

“Albtraum!” a voice cut through the chatter, interrupting them. Mianna emerged from the crowd. She had changed since their earlier meeting, now dressed in a velvet gown the same color as the wine that was being served, patterned with an intricate gold filigree with a delicate silk sash tied around her waist.

Her mouth quirked to the side in a smirk as she looked over Albtraum and noticed the gaggle of young women watching him from a short distance away. “I see you’ve attracted quite a following.”

“I hadn’t noticed,” Albtraum lied, too quickly. Mianna’s wry smile only widened.

“Let’s hope that charisma follows you to your office,” she quipped. “I wondered if you might like to have a dance with me.”

“Dance?” Albtraum had only a vague idea what she meant by that, and shifted uncomfortably.

"I'll need to teach you, of course." She linked her arm through his. "I'm going to steal him away for now, Brunhart."

Brunhart did not seem to return her amusement, and simply nodded in acknowledgement.

Albtraum was pulled along by Mianna closer to where the musicians were performing and she stopped, turning to face him. She took hold of his hands and pulled him into position.

"Here you are, like this," she instructed, showing him how to move in time with the music. He found no difficulty in following the rhythm, but found the movements awkward as she guided him.

"So intense!" Mianna exclaimed playfully, motioning to his scrunched forehead. "Your movements are so stiff. Try to relax yourself."

He tried to do as she suggested, loosening the tension in his shoulders and letting his arms lower slightly. He found it easier the longer they practiced, allowing Mianna to direct his movement until he felt he was able to keep the pace himself.

You once let me guide you this way. We danced a different dance. And we can do it again.

Albtraum focused on Mianna to quiet Lucifurius. She appeared aloof, as though the dance was effortless for her – in truth, it probably was. A century was a long enough time to perfect any kind of craft or skill imaginable.

Through the mild haze of his thoughts, he distantly thought that he enjoyed the closeness and contact. Mianna was one of the few people he'd gotten close to who hadn't often touched him in some way – Brunhart's pats on the back or shoulder, Glen's excessively tight hugs, Joaquin's fussing over his hair and clothes.

She was quite different from the others, though. Something about her seemed much more strange and otherworldly. Though she was outwardly charming and friendly, there was a distant coldness in the way she interacted with others – as though she were keeping everyone at arms' length, no matter how close she got to them.

Lost in his own mind, he stumbled slightly, nearly tripping over himself before Mianna caught him around the waist.

"Careful there," she laughed. "Had a bit too much wine, have you?"

"...Yes," he admitted, steadying himself. He quickly started to pull back, but Mianna's grip remained where it was.

"I dare say you have quite the knack for this," she praised. "You should—"

She was cut off when Camlion approached them. His casual grin wavered as he took in the sight of them, but he remained pleasant as he spoke. "I hope the festivities are to your liking, Albtraum. I apologize if I seemed to ignore you before. I've simply never met someone like you, and there has been much going on..."

Albtraum blinked at him. "It's... alright. And yes, the celebration has been enjoyable. The wine never stops flowing, it seems."

Camlion laughed, though Albtraum didn't think he'd said anything particularly amusing. "I am glad for that. I look forward to a prosperous reign from you, Albtraum. And if anyone can teach you how to be a successful politician, it's this one," he motioned to Mianna with a wink. "You're in the best of hands."

"I thank you for that glowing endorsement," Mianna chuckled.

"On that note, it would seem it is time for us to eat," Camlion chirped. "And I would like to introduce you to Castus and Nestor, Albtraum – if I am not mistaken, they will be the first beings from your world you have met?"

"They are Shadrans?" Albtraum asked. "Yes... Lucifurius is the only other being I have—"

Camlion's expression fell, as though he'd seen something ghastly, and he was quick to interrupt. "They will be wanting to meet you as well, I am sure! I will go and fetch them, they can join us at the table." Without another word, he hurried off.

Mianna hadn't moved from where she stood with her arms wrapped around Albtraum's waist the entire time they'd been conversing with Camlion, but she pulled back once he'd left. "Well, it seems we should find our places at the table," she said cheerily as she walked away. "Perhaps you can try out your new dancing skills on one of your devotees over there after the meal?"

Albtraum let out a strained laugh that was more of a cough than anything. "I wouldn't want to subject anyone else to my footwork at this stage..."

He moved to his place at the table, following Mianna – it was strange, eating among royalty, seated alongside them, servants curtsying as he passed. He'd been treated well in Sylva, but it had been somehow more practical... with less decorum. He found himself missing that familiarity.

Ismaire was seated a few spaces down from him. He looked away to avoid meeting her eyes. She was dressed in a simple jacket and trousers, but the jacket was embellished with a lace sash and jeweled adornments in a clear attempt to make her seem more refined than she did usually. It was only mildly successful, dampened by her constant scowling and careless posture.

Brunhart sat just next to her, Joaquin at his other side. They smiled in greeting as Albtraum sat, Joaquin seeming utterly in his element as he accepted a glass of wine from a servant.

"Hope you brought your appetite, dear," he chuckled. "If there is one thing I do enjoy in Terce, it is the food."

Albtraum sat up straighter as a small bowl of soup was carefully placed in front of him, and he was drawn in by the rich aroma, carefully sipping from a spoon as Joaquin had taught him to do.

Ismaire immediately began eating, taking nearly-overflowing spoonfuls, but Albtraum eyed the soup suspiciously.

"What is this?"

Camlion was about to answer as he joined them at the table, but Joaquin did first. "*Vichyssoise*, my boy."

"Soup made with *pomme de terre*," Camlion added.

As Albtraum's confusion grew, Joaquin explained. "Apples of the earth."

"Do apples not grow on trees?" Albtraum questioned.

"It's a rather unnecessarily complicated manner of calling a potato," Brunhart sighed.

Albtraum's nose wrinkled. "But *why?* A potato is nothing like an apple. Apples are sweet, potatoes taste of soil and despair."

Mianna laughed, perhaps even a bit ignobly, but Camlion appeared offended. "Perhaps to your unrefined tastes, but *pomme de terre* is the backbone of most every dish we prepare here."

Albtraum attempted to conceal his disgust. Joaquin had ingrained it into him – it was rude to refuse food. "I see." He continued to sip down the soup, hoping for the next course of the meal to be more satisfying.

"As riveting as I am finding this lively debate about vegetables, it would seem Castus and Nestor are here to meet Albtraum." Mianna gestured to two figures who approached the table, and Albtraum looked up at them – and found himself somewhat stunned at what he saw.

The two men were tall, although shorter than Albtraum himself. They dressed in the same uniform as the Tercian guards, but they were obviously not human in the least.

They had night-black skin and silvery-white hair that was braided and tied back elaborately, revealing long, pointed ears that pricked and swiveled like those of animals. Their eyes were reflective, like Albtraum's – but lacked an iris or pupil, making them appear unnaturally large above smooth faces that lacked a nose or mouth. The taller of the two had golden eyes, the other a deep violet.

Albtraum knew he was gaping, but he could not stop himself as he took in the sight of them. He felt some deep familiarity... and yet, at the same time, they were unnerving, like nothing he had ever seen before.

Lucifurius hissed, long and slow. *Traitors. I gifted them their wretched existence... and they offer themselves to my enemies. Just as you have.*

The violet-eyed Shadran gazed back with the same intensity, then gave a curt nod. “Good to see you again, Your Majesty,” he said to Mianna. It sounded as though he spoke just as a human would – and yet, Albtraum knew he could not have, not lacking a mouth as he did.

Mianna nodded in return. “Nestor. I trust you are well?”

“Yes, quite so.” Nestor turned his eyes to Albtraum once more. “This is him? The daemon Chronus has chosen for the Order?”

“Yes, though interestingly enough he has never met one of his own kind, nor any of yours,” Mianna explained.

“I pray you’ll be worth Arion’s sacrifice,” the other Shadran – who Albtraum assumed was Castus – spoke up. His golden eyes were narrowed, and his tone was ever so slightly acidic.

“Come now, Castus, I am certain he will be. Especially with Mianna’s expert guiding hand,” Camlion interjected.

“Certainly, Your Majesty.” Nestor gave a brief bow. “We shall leave you to your meal.”

Albtraum felt a small surge of panic as they turned to leave – he had been so dumbfounded by their alien appearance he had not said a word, but he was eager to learn more of the place he’d come from and its people. “Will you not join us?” he blurted abruptly, suddenly aware of his own volume as a few people glanced his way.

Castus turned and glanced back at him. “Time spent in the dark is all we require for sustenance.”

Albtraum struggled to think of any other reason to ask them to stay as they again turned to leave, and Mianna offered him an encouraging smile.

“I am sure you must have a great many questions... But we shall have more time to speak with them later.”

Albtraum leaned back in his seat, realizing how in his surprise he had leaned forward suddenly.

He watched them weave through the crowds, no one paying them any mind. He wondered how that could be, when they had such an unsettlingly inhuman appearance – but he remembered, as Mianna had explained it, that one of them had been their king not so very long ago.

He felt uneasy at the thought of inching closer to the dark world, to anything Lucifurius had created, and yet... in the same moment, he found himself overtaken by curiosity, falling into silent contemplation as everyone at the table bustled around him.

CHAPTER XX

It was still relatively early in the evening when the feast drew to a close - it was difficult to tell for certain, with no windows to the outside, but it had been midway into the afternoon when they'd started. Mianna had chatted with some of the nobility who passed by her seat to greet her, but the meal had overall been uneventful.

She glanced beside her to where Albtraum and Ismaire sat. "Albtraum, I thought perhaps you and Ismaire might join me after the feast, I believe there are some things we should discuss before our travels take us further."

Mianna watched as Albtraum glanced in her direction in response to the question, pulled from his reverie as he was watching the feastgoers around them. Brunhart had returned to issuing orders to their guards, and Joaquin was speaking with one of Camlion's treasurers. Ismaire, still picking at the last scraps of lamb roast on her plate, scoffed quietly.

"I have an office here – Arion provided it to me so I would have a place to work when I visited. If you're quite finished dining, we can talk Order history over some wine."

Albtraum seemed to perk up at that. "Oh, yes. I would be quite interested to hear more."

"Well, follow me, then. Ismaire?"

Ismaire set aside her silverware. "Hmm, fine. Suppose I don't have much socializing planned for the evening. Let me change out of this damn jacket, though... I'll meet you there."

Ismaire rushed off to her room, and Mianna stood from the table to lead Albtraum to her office, feeling a pleasant comfort in the warmth of the hall and the gentle chatter around her as the feast slowly dispersed and the guests returned to their homes. Albtraum seemed to be growing gradually more comfortable, perhaps from the encouragement he'd received from Joaquin and Camlion, perhaps from the wine; she could not definitively say.

Still, an uneasiness picked at her. As much as she wished this to be a pleasant visit, the alarming knowledge of the rift so close by, and Camlion's nervous behavior set her on edge. She had known that conflict was fast approaching, but this felt... unpredictable, unfamiliar, and she felt herself unprepared. More than ever, she had to make reliable allies... and for the moment, Albtraum and Ismaire – teachable, young, receptive – were the best chance she had.

The old wooden door to the office was heavy, but she opened it delicately, leaving it cracked just slightly so that Ismaire could make her way inside more easily when she returned. There were a set of great velvet-upholstered armchairs arranged in a circle and she stepped over to one, sitting down and sinking into the deep cushions.

Albtraum sat across from her somewhat awkwardly, still somewhat clumsy in his slightly drunken state. "Ismaire, ah... seems not to make use of the etiquette Joaquin has taught us."

Mianna raised her eyebrows. "Well, it's little surprise you noticed that. I certainly hope she does not plan to continue such boorish behavior when she assumes a position of power."

Albtraum shrugged, offering a faint, lopsided smirk. “I don’t suppose anyone would be able to stop her, though.”

“As if anyone could stop her *now.*” Mianna chuckled in response, glad that Albtraum’s mood seemed to have brightened. He was often quiet, pensive… but there was a wit about him, and he did seem capable of good humor on occasion. “We can get started ourselves while we wait. Ismaire already knows most of the basics. I’ve told you much about the Order, but there is doubtless little you truly understand, based on what I’ve told you.”

Albtraum breathed a single laugh. “Well, I… Yes. I’m relieved it wasn’t just my own incompetence.”

Mianna shook her head. “They are complex matters…I will explain in full detail.” She settled back into the chair. “I told you already of the Wanderers, but there are a great many more layers to the Order. Above the Wanderers are the immortals of my own rank, the Earth Immortals. We are entrusted to overseeing the operations of the Order in this world – Camlion and the other rulers we are visiting are my peers. Of the four of us, one is given moderate authority over the others, a position which currently belongs to me. We possess the ability to kill immortals below us, and each other… But only if Azoth himself, our leader, should sanction it.”

“Bringing me to the next rank, the Higher Immortals. At present, there are three: Z’xolkuloth, Azoth, and Theoria. Above them are the True Immortals… beings who cannot be killed or destroyed, no matter the method. They are Chronus and Necros.”

“At the inception of the universe, we believe there were initially only five beings. The first was Chronus, and she watches over and directs the flow of time. Second was Z’xolkuloth, and he created the matter of the universe. After him came Theoria, the keeper of all memory. The final of the four beings was Necros, the embodiment of death. Azoth, the last, was intended as a mediator, to keep balance."

"Z'xolkuloth created Luxiscura, the other world I have informed you of. Half is shrouded in darkness – a realm they call Hatheg Kla, the world of your birth - the other in light – called Oraspectus. And between them exists a middle realm."

Albtraum watched as she spoke, occasionally breaking eye contact, but seeming attentive. He fiddled with the hems of his sleeves.

She sighed. "Z'xolkuloth was not always corrupt, you see. He filled Luxiscura with a great many creatures, among them the Shadrans who serve him. There were also the Middle People, among whom is Azoth himself. Z'xolkuloth called himself Khthon, and was the god-king of Hatheg Kla. Azoth was appointed to rule the Oraspectus from the middle realm where he resided. Together with Chronus, Necros, and Theoria, they formed the Order, and tasked themselves with ensuring balance in the universe."

"After a great many millennia, the Order learned that the equilibrium of our world was in jeopardy... Knowing he could not hold the balance himself, Azoth chose a human member of the Order to rule over Oraspectus... My grandmother, Ishtar. He himself would govern only the middle realm. Chronus gifted four members of the Earth Order with immortality, and they held the balance of this world. Of the four, one was always slated to be an Oracle, the only people who can communicate with Chronus – we do not know why, but only a small number of people are able to understand her or see her. I am one... Arion was as well."

"Meanwhile, Azoth struggled to control Oraspectus and the middle realm both. His power and influence waned, and with the balance disrupted, Z'xolkuloth slowly became corrupt. He separated his soul from himself in an attempt to cleanse it, but the corruption ran deep, and the soul fragments gained their own sentience, calling themselves Skulthur... and Lucifurius. They attached themselves to hosts and scoured any place they could find for life forces to drain in order to gain the power to create bodies for themselves. Z'xolkuloth himself became inert, and the corruption seemed to halt for a time."

"But corruption continued to slowly spread to all members of the Order. Azoth has sought a successor to Z'xolkuloth for centuries, but a daemon must hold Hatheg Kla, and all of Z'xolkuloth's children were either dead by his hand, nowhere to be found, or would have been worse rulers than their father."

"Corruption overcomes all of us at one point or another. It overcame Ishtar, and the Earth Order... Our lives grow shorter each cycle. I am the third of my position, as are most of my colleagues respective to their own positions. Camlion is the fourth of his line. When we become too corrupt to rule, we must submit to death, and a replacement is chosen for us."

Albtraum looked somewhat alarmed. She understood this, having felt it herself as a young girl, when Arion taught her of the Order... immortality was not so magnificent as it seemed at first glance. "So then... You..."

Mianna gave a slight smile of reassurance. "Fear not, Albtraum. By my estimation, in our current state, I have several years before my own corruption overcomes me. But once you succeed, our time will be greatly lengthened, perhaps indefinitely. Unfortunately, Azoth is beyond such salvation, as is Z'xolkuloth, and the light world has gone ungoverned for over a century."

Albtraum frowned. "I've only just begun to understand the size and scope of *this* world, Mianna. Lucifurius often talked to me of the dark world, but this is..." He shook his head. "I'm not sure I can get my mind around all this."

"You will be able to make more sense of it, in time. You will be going to the other world yourself, once you are ready."

"Will we, now?" Ismaire's voice sounded from the doorway.

Mianna turned to face her. She'd changed back into more comfortable clothes – loose fitting trousers and a shawl draped over her shirt and bodice. They were some of the few clothes she'd accepted from Joaquin, and odd amalgamation of courtly attire with desert garb, but Joaquin, of course, made the styles bend to his will as he always did.

"Ismaire, so nice of you to join us. We've just gotten to the section of the discussion which contains information you haven't already heard."

Ismaire snorted. "Thank all the gods for that." She plopped down in the armchair next to Mianna.

"Now, Albtraum, the first thing we must do is fully separate you from Lucifurius. Once he has a body of his own, he can be destroyed, and his soul fragment will return to its original body," Mianna continued.

"Z'xolkuloth," Albtraum said with a nod. "I assume the same process will need to be repeated with the other fragment?"

"Indeed. But he seems to have avoided our world for a great deal of time, and likely prowls the dark world. In fact, he may already have his own body."

"Wonderful," Ismaire commented. "So we're going to have to track the bastard down?"

"I suspect that once Lucifurius is destroyed, the other fragment will reveal himself to deal with the threat Albtraum poses. By that time, Albtraum should have connected with the rebel army that waits for him in Khanda Ura, capitol of Hatheg Kla," Mianna explained.

"If an army waits for me," Albtraum murmured, "should I not go to them now?"

"They have waited centuries for you, Albtraum, I am sure a few more months will not be a concern. It would not do to rush things, as we could potentially undo years upon years of work."

Albtraum slumped in his chair, surely overwhelmed by all Mianna told him. The limitations that had been imposed on him until recent months had made his world miniscule, microscopic – and taking in so much more must have been a great deal to bear.

Still... he was going to have to learn, and if he was to be a successful ruler, there was far more ahead to endure. She had to prepare him for that.

"Once you have succeeded in overthrowing Z'xolkuloth, you will need to appoint Ismaire in Azoth's position. Ismaire, in the meantime, you will remain with the Earth Order as an ambassador. There is likely to be a great struggle as we go about this, and we shall need all the support we can get."

She scowled. "An ambassador. Bonehead gets to dive right into the glory, and I have to wait around as a useless figurehead?"

"*Albtraum* must ensure that the greater threat has been dealt with before you can assume your duties in full, yes," Mianna said pointedly.

Ismaire seemed to be contemplating a comeback, but simply grumbled unintelligibly and crossed her arms.

Mianna's brow furrowed with concern. "And if glory is what you draw from the tasks that lie ahead, perhaps you are not the correct choice for this position."

"No, I..." Ismaire huffed. "I'm just talking. I don't like sitting and *waiting*."

"There will be work to be done here in this world, Ismaire, I assure you," Mianna said to her. "Now, there is one other matter we must discuss, the three of us. The two of you are allies, and it is high time you started acting like it. Ismaire, I understand Albtraum's past is of concern to you, but your behavior since his arrival is not acceptable."

Ismaire looked affronted. "What would you have me do, Mianna? Link arms and sing ballads of undying friendship with him?"

"As if I'd wish to," Albtraum grumbled in response.

"Albtraum," Mianna said in warning. He shrank back slightly at her tone. "What concerns you so, Ismaire? Perhaps it might be best for Albtraum himself to address your worries."

Ismaire shifted, turning slightly more towards Albtraum, keeping her arms firmly crossed over her chest. "He's murdered innocents, and shows no remorse for what he's done. He came into my home unannounced, and I was expected to treat him as a guest of honor."

"*My* home," Mianna corrected tersely. "Which, I will remind you, you found because you were sent there to gather *slaves*."

Ismaire's mouth snapped shut. She was ashamed of that, deeply, and Mianna knew it – some part of her disliked using it to rein Ismaire in, but when she became dogmatic enough, there was little else that she responded to.

Albtraum spoke up then, audible only because the room had fallen into dead silence. “I did not… choose to do what I did. But at that time, I… There was no alternative. Killing was the only thing I knew of the world. The prospect of it – now, I despise it. It terrifies me.”

Ismaire eyed him suspiciously. “That’s certainly convenient,” she muttered.

“It’s the truth,” Albtraum shot back, more forcefully. “I… care for the people I have met here, and my only want now is to assist this Order they belong to. If – if Chronus chose me for this, then this must be my purpose.” He stared down intensely at the floor beneath his feet. “Perhaps it is the way I must make my amends for my past actions.”

Ismaire opened her mouth to say something, but closed it after a moment, her words seeming to escape her. Mianna waited patiently as they both sat in reserved silence.

Ismaire stood and turned towards the door. “I will be civil with you going forward,” she said carefully. “We will work together as associates, but we will never be more than that, do you understand me? I will never call you my friend.”

She walked out, shutting the door behind her.

Mianna sighed deeply as Ismaire left, rubbing her temples. “Well,” she said with feigned cheeriness, “at least we seem to have made a spot of progress.”

Albtraum made no attempt to hide his exasperation. “At least there is that.”

Albtraum was aware of the early hour only by the sound of the servants rustling about outside his bedroom door. He had not slept, his mind roiling with the deluge of information Mianna had imparted to him.

He felt restless, and rose from the bed, having already dressed hours ago. Renegade stretched as he woke and lazily dropped down from the bed to trot after Albtraum as he made his way to the door.

As he pushed the door open, he startled a servant girl who was passing by. "Oh! *Pardonne-moi, mon seigneur*... I hope we did not wake you..."

"No," he replied somewhat flatly. "I was awake." He'd understood most human languages before through Lucifurius, but some of the words he heard spoken here were unfamiliar, meanings inferred only through context.

"Shall I fetch someone to..." She paused, looking him up and down. "You've dressed already..."

"Yes," he answered, unsure what she expected of him.

"You still do not think yourself a noble, clearly," a voice sounded behind them in the hall. "Odd for a daemon."

Albtraum glanced over his shoulder – behind him stood the golden-eyed Shadran he'd met the day before – Castus. Renegade wagged his tail, seeming unbothered by his appearance, though something about it still unsettled Albtraum deeply.

"I seem misaligned with many expectations," he said quietly, turning to face Castus as the servant girl scurried away.

Nestor approached behind Castus, dressed in a plain riding outfit and carrying a sword. He gave a brief bow as he stood before Albtraum. "We will be going to investigate the rift on the outskirts of the city today, Most High. Will you be joining us?"

Albtraum nodded, somewhat taken aback by the formality he'd been addressed with. "Yes, I plan to."

Shadow-dust and moonlight... and treachery.

Albtraum inhaled deeply, trying to calm the racing of his pulse as Lucifurius spoke.

Castus still regarded him coldly, his ears pinned back. "Yes, I suppose you should know more of the place of your birth, even in such an indirect way."

"Castus," Nestor interrupted. "Mind your tone, you speak to the Khthon."

Castus somehow conjured a scoff. "He is not Khthon yet."

"You are right," Albtraum answered, clearing his throat. "I... do not mind if you wish to call me by my name, as I haven't yet assumed any titles."

"You really are a strange daemon. You are supposed to demand I call you Khthon, not concede that it's not yet your title." Castus' largely featureless face somehow bore an expression of annoyance.

“Be that as it may, my dissimilarity from the rest of my kind seems to be the reason I was chosen for this position.”

Castus’ ears pricked up. He made a soft chuckle. “Well, you’ve your wits about you, at the least.”

“Good morning, Albtraum,” another voice rang through the hall. Mianna. She was dressed in travelling clothes, though they were lighter than what she’d worn in the days before. Castus and Nestor both stepped aside with a nod as she approached. “I see you are already making friends with your subjects.”

“Well... They aren’t yet my subjects, and Castus at least doesn’t seem to consider me a friend.”

Nestor snickered at that, his smooth face wrinkling slightly as a human’s might in the midst of a laugh. His ears lowered after a moment. “It’s a shame. Arion would have liked him.”

Mianna smiled sadly. “He would have. Ah, well... I came to inform you we were preparing to leave for the city outskirts, but it seems you’re already quite prepared. Let’s be off then, shall we?”

He followed her back to the courtyard, glad to see that most of the Sylvan guard was joining them that day. The men stood close together, conversing with one another, mostly keeping to themselves as the Tercians worked around them. Ismaire, in particular, was watching them warily. Their horses had been saddled and waited to be mounted, Glen carefully stepping around them, patting their necks to calm their agitation at the echoing sounds around them. Noman and a few of the men waved as they approached.

Albtraum felt a sense of comfort at the gesture, and returned it. He made his way over to his horse, Clover, allowing Mianna to step over to talk with Ismaire before they departed.

"Morning, Al!" Glen called, walking over. "I'm still trying to work through *Canterbury Tales* –" He withdrew the volume from his satchel, thumbing through it for a moment before holding it up, pointing at the print on the page. "What's this word?"

Albtraum looked where he pointed. "Ah...*surgery.*"

Glen chuckled. "I'd suppose Aleksandra would box my ears if she knew I'd gotten that one wrong."

"We might practice with an easier book, you know..."

"Oh, but I like this one so far! Besides, you're a great instructor, so it hardly feels difficult." Glen hopped onto Grey's back.

"Well, I'm glad for that." Albtraum looked down at Renegade where he stood between the horses, peering up at them. He waited attentively as the rest of the group mounted their horses.

The sound of a rider approaching on his other side alerted him, and he turned to face the newcomer, finding himself faced with Nestor. "Shall I ride with you, Most High?"

"'Albtraum' is fine," he muttered in response. "And yes, if you would like."

"All due respect, but you should begin growing accustomed to your titles. You will wear them better then when you truly do carry them. But if you wish, I will call you Albtraum for now."

Glen had ridden ahead with Brunhart and Noman, leaving Albtraum to converse with Nestor. As comforting as he found the presence of his friends – were they his countrymen, now? – he was excited for the chance to ask Nestor about the dark world.

"I have not even met one of my own brothers or sisters..." he said as they started forward. "Much less one of your number."

"So you are curious, is that what you are saying?" Nestor asked, one ear cocked towards Albtraum as his gaze remained locked forward on the road.

"I was that obvious about it, was I?" Albtraum laughed.

"Hm, only a little. What would you like to know?"

Albtraum considered that. "Well... first of all, I suppose... how do you speak?"

Nestor glanced at him. "Not as humans or daemons do, clearly, as we lack the means to physically produce sounds... We can speak directly into the minds of others, much like your father does... The difference is we cannot do so covertly, nor across long distances. Effectively... it is the same as having an ordinary voice."

"I see." Albtraum was fascinated, enough that he felt only a slight pang of unease at Nestor referring to Lucifurius as his father. "And daemons... you live alongside them?"

"In the dark world, Shadrans are forbidden from holding any position of power above a daemon... we were created to be their servants. Daemons are immortals of a sort... they do not age past adulthood, but they are not impervious to death. We are just the same, and so we make ideal servants to them... and, as it so happens, to the immortal leaders of the Order."

"And that is why you now reside in Terce?"

"I was a rebel warrior in the dark world alongside Castus and Arion... we came here to seek the assistance of the Earth Order, and they gave Arion the kingdom of Terce to govern while we searched for a daemon to follow. Many daemons seek the throne... and so they gather armies behind them, fighting and killing one another... and we follow the victor. There are still loyalists to Z'xolkuloth, of course... but the dark world is desperate for change. You are our most promising hope."

"Ah, well that is..." Albtraum looked down at his hands on the reins. "...certainly a great expectation to live up to."

"I believe it is warranted. And you can only hone your effectiveness from here."

"Very well said, my friend," Joaquin's voice sounded behind Albtraum as he and Mianna rode up alongside him. "If you'd be so kind, might we steal him away for the moment?"

"Of course." Nestor nodded to Albtraum. "It was good to speak to you, Albtraum." He rode ahead on the path, leaving Albtraum in Mianna and Joaquin's familiar presence.

"Joaquin wished to make sure you were alright," Mianna informed him. "Since we are journeying to the rift today."

"Yes, I haven't felt unwell at all." He did feel a tightening in his chest as his thoughts wandered to Lucifurius, but he shoved down his worry. "We were just speaking more of the dark world... And of Arion."

"Yes, Castus, Nestor and Arion were childhood friends, and fought together much of their lives," Mianna confirmed. "So when he says Arion would like you, that is certainly high praise."

"Well, it's true, isn't it?" Joaquin agreed.

"We can't ever know, I suppose..." Albtraum muttered.

"No, it's true," Mianna said resolutely. "You even remind me of him in many ways. Arion was sometimes too soft-spoken for his own good, but... When he needed to be heard, he made himself be."

"If only he'd imparted a *modicum* of that quality onto his successor," Joaquin groaned under his breath, and Mianna snickered. Albtraum glanced ahead on the path where Camlion was conversing animatedly with Brunhart, though at this distance it was difficult to tell if any real conversation was indeed occurring.

Albtraum found himself looking at the sights as they passed – the great cavern continued, and it was filled with markets, houses, people bustling about on cobbled paths that lead even deeper into the earth, lit by torches and lanterns. The ceiling of the cavern was so high that Albtraum at times almost forgot they were not beneath open sky.

Some of the people bowed and waved as their king passed, and Camlion seemed to delight in the attention.

"Do the people of your kingdoms know much of the Order's affairs, or the other world?" Albtraum asked Mianna.

"They are aware of it, and of our immortality. We allow mortals to reside in our kingdoms in exchange for a certain amount of discretion, of course." Mianna waved as some of the people they passed recognized her and pointed. "The world is not accepting to all people... and some of them tend to take refuge in our kingdoms when they stumble upon them."

"Like I did," Albtraum mused.

"Quite so," Mianna agreed with a smile. "Ah, now if you'll excuse me, I should speak with Camlion before we arrive..."

Albtraum nodded as she went, and rode on in silence, observing his surroundings as they descended the curving path leading deeper still into the caverns.

Chapter XXI

"Mianna, I have told you several times now, the situation is under control. So why is that beautiful brow of yours still furrowed so?"

Mianna stared ahead, irritation keeping her from meeting Camlion's gaze as they conversed. She had been pressing him further about the rift, and he had been evasive – like a child hiding a broken heirloom. "It sounds to have spread rapidly, and that is alarming."

"We moved people away, only a few were sickened, but they've recovered… and I don't believe anyone has fallen pregnant."

"Camlion," she sighed, bringing a hand to her forehead. "There are forces at work here you do not understand, which you seem to have gravely underestimated. You should have informed me immediately."

"Well, I can't very well go running to you every time a problem arises," Camlion pouted.

Mianna let out a sustained breath. He was right, of course, but that was given that he was capable of handling problems on his own, in a manner that did not result in disaster.

"Well, I suppose we shall just have to go there and investigate to truly see just how bad it is."

The falling look of concern across Camlion's face did not fill her with confidence.

It took them not quite an hour to reach the part of the city touched by the rift – Mianna could tell immediately, as the lanterns in the area had been extinguished, and the path faded into total darkness. It was an eerie sight... Not many things made her feel deep unease at this stage of her life, but this made her feel like a frightened child facing the unknown of the night.

The voices of the party fell to a hush as they slowed near the empty buildings. The horses shuffled to a stop, whinnying nervously at the palpable tension in the air. A few Tercian guards approached the darkness with torches, the flickering light of the flame slowly illuminating the sight of the rift before them.

Mianna could not stop a slight gasp from escaping her lips as she looked upon it.

A huge crack like a great, gaping maw had opened in the face of the rock, glittering masses that looked like gemstones speckled across the inside. It must have been twenty feet across. A thick, syrupy substance like clotting blood oozed from it like a great infected wound, pooling at the base of the wall in a great dark puddle. Inside the chasm, the torchlight revealed only black, endless darkness. She heard a chorus of gasps and murmurs behind her as the Tercians and Sylvans alike as they examined the sight before them.

"Camlion," she finally stammered out as she dismounted her horse and took a few steps forward. "This rift is *massive—*"

"Yes, but it hasn't spread any further in some time," Camlion answered, his voice low. "And we've forbidden anyone from entering this part of the city.

Mianna pressed her lips together. "Well, you did that right, at the least." The mere feeling of the air in this place was enough to send shivers down her spine, though the air was somewhat warm.

The group chattered in awe as they all moved closer to the rift on foot. Albtraum looked dumbstruck, Joaquin following him closely as he cautiously approached.

"Albtraum?" she asked after him. "Are you alright?"

He glanced back over his shoulder at her, pushing his hair away from his face and nodding. "Yes... it's merely alarming."

Her gaze turned back to the rift. "That it most certainly is," she muttered.

Castus stood the closest to it, closer than even the torchbearers dared approach. His feet were just inches from the pool of dark liquid on the cave floor. "It first appeared some months ago," he called back to Mianna. "Around the middle of the winter."

"Not many people lived in this part of the city anyhow," Camlion said quickly. "It was relatively easy to find lodging for them elsewhere."

"You'll get my praise for tending quickly to your people, but not for your mishandling of this in every other manner," Mianna said coolly, staring up at it.

Camlion sighed. "I... should have contacted you sooner about it, I apologize—"

Camlion was cut off by a shout from ahead as a few of the Tercian guards suddenly bolted away from the rift, and Mianna saw Albtraum struggling with Castus before it.

She took a step forward, about to call out, but her voice died out in her throat as she watched. Albtraum wielded a dagger, lashing out at Castus, who dodged his attempted strikes with some difficulty, attempting to wrest the weapon from his grasp.

Internally, she chided herself. How stupid could she have been, not to consider this as a possibility? Castus seemed to understand his need to hold back, however, and did not seem intent on harming Albtraum as they scuffled.

Albtraum swiped forward, again missing Castus narrowly. His eyes were wild and unfocused, an animal malevolence in them that she did not recognize. He snarled as Castus evaded him.

"Lucifurius," she whispered, half to herself and half to Camlion who had grabbed her arm in his panic. "He's taken hold of him again—"

The Tercians and Sylvans alike seemed dumbstruck, unsure of how to respond. Mianna considered intervening herself when suddenly Castus darted back, and she watched as Albtraum collapsed on his back.

She was relieved, but only for a moment.

Mianna had thought that Albtraum might have lost consciousness, as he had before in the presence of rifts – but she saw that he now held the dagger to his own throat.

Castus stood back, watching with the rest of the Tercians. No one dared breathe.

The guards then shouted in alarm as the great crack in the earth split wider, and a low, droning roar sounded from the depths of the rift. The flames of the torches flickered so low they offered almost no light at all.

Albtraum remained where he was, straining to keep the dagger where it was as the very earth seemed to shudder with the activity of the rift.

Mianna felt herself take another step forward, but Joaquin was faster.

Child. Let go.

Albtraum strained, holding the sharp edge of the blade to his throat. Every fiber and sinew in him was screaming, drawn to its limit against Lucifurius. He could hear the roar of the rift above him, drowning the shouts of the guards in a sea of deep, relentless sound.

You will end us both. Stop this foolishness at once.

Albtraum shut his eyes, feeling the blade break his skin, hot blood spilling over. *I will—*

"Albtraum!"

He felt his arm wrenched away from his throat, and in the split second he lost focus, Lucifurius took control again. He felt himself shove someone to the ground, his arm slamming the dagger down with a crunch as it scraped against bone—

As the howling of the rift faded to silence, Albtraum stared down in horror at the dagger embedded in Joaquin's shoulder.

He breathed heavily. His fist was clenched so tightly his fingers had gone numb. He felt tears prick the corner of his eyes.

"No… I…"

He remained frozen in place, feeling himself trembling.

"Joaquin…"

Joaquin drew deep, shaking breaths himself, his eyes wide with panic. Albtraum had shoved him to the ground, stabbing the knife into his shoulder, knees pressed into his elbows, crouched above him. Blood pooled beneath them, and Joaquin's eyes spilled over with tears.

"It's alright, my boy," he gasped, his voice trembling. "You're alright."

Albtraum's attention was suddenly drawn behind him as he heard the familiar clang of blade against blade – Brunhart stood with his sword drawn, crossed with the blade of an axe wielded by Castus.

His hand released the handle of the dagger, and he scrambled away from Joaquin, stumbling and falling on his knees. Someone roughly hauled him up by the arms, and chaos ensued around him.

The hands that gripped him were those of Tercian guards, but they were soon rushed by the Sylvans. Curses were shouted, blows exchanged.

We are close… so close…

"That is *enough!*"

Silence fell, so sudden it had a weight. Albtraum turned his gaze to the source of the cry, and saw Camlion standing beside Mianna, eyes narrowed.

"Castus," he continued. "You are under arrest for attacking a royal guest."

Castus stood fast as the Tercian guards suddenly accepted the order and seized him, his ears low. "As you wish, Your Majesty."

Albtraum whimpered, feeling his legs weaken under him. Someone kept him from falling to the ground.

Castus glared at him as he was hauled away. "You are nothing but a pathetic child on the leash of your father," he snarled. "And you will never be fit to be Khthon."

Albtraum was rushed back to the royal estate, quickly pushed into a carriage and led away from the site of the rift. He was in a daze, without sense of time nor place until he found himself in his quarters, lying curled on his side on his bed. He was distantly aware of Renegade's presence as he panted at the end of the bed.

The room felt as though it were spinning.

Surely now you realize the futility in this, Lucifurius hissed. *The only power you hold over me is to end your own miserable life.*

Albtraum curled further in on himself. *Perhaps that is the only power I have, but it is power all the same.*

He was startled by a knock at the door, and suddenly sat bolt upright, standing from the bed.

The handle of the door turned and opened, and he felt himself weaken again – with relief this time, rather than panic – as Joaquin stepped into the room.

Joaquin greeted him with a concerned smile and quickly made his way over to him – Albtraum struggled for words, but they all died on his tongue, and all the strength melted from his body until all he had the power to do was bury his face in his hands and sob.

Humiliated, he turned away, horrified to find that he could not stop himself from crying. He curled in on himself.

Oh, for that moment all he wanted was to melt into the ground.

"Albtraum," he heard Joaquin say, his voice high with concern. He felt his hand on his back, and flinched from his touch. "What is the matter?"

Albtraum turned around, attempting to scrub the tears away from his face. His eyes hurt, his cheeks were burning, and he could hardly see through the newly forming tears in his eyes. "F-forgive me, I didn't mean—
"

Joaquin cut Albtraum off when he pulled him into himself, hard. Albtraum started to pull back, but found himself desperate for the comfort, and felt his body all but go slack in Joaquin's arms as the last of his sniffles died down.

"Joaquin," he choked out, finally. "I... I am sorry, I am so..."

"*Shh,* boy, it's alright." Joaquin stroked his hair as Albtraum leaned into him. "Nothing more than a ruined doublet, I assure you." He drew back, motioning to the hole where the dagger had been – without a trace of a wound beneath it.

"Good," Albtraum groaned breathlessly. "Good." He took deep breaths to steady himself, slumping back down on the bed.

"Whatever is the matter, my dear?" Joaquin asked him gently. "Everything is alright. No one was harmed."

Albtraum shook his head. "I lost... control of him. I could not stop him... And now..." he squeezed his eyes shut. "You are afraid of me."

Joaquin's eyebrows raised. "Of you? Oh, my boy, no... I feared only that I'd not be able to stop you harming yourself." His hold on Albtraum tightened. "Many years ago... before I was immortal... My brother chose to die rather than fall into the hands of an enemy, and I was unable to stop him. I feared I'd lose you the same way..."

Albtraum leaned in as Joaquin embraced him once again. He felt he should push away, he was dangerous, after all...

Instead, he sat on the edge of his bed, miserable and ashamed as Joaquin comforted him.

He looked over to the door, finding it still open, Mianna watching them with concern.

"Mianna," he said hurriedly, standing and pulling away from Joaquin. "I... I cannot apologize enough for what..."

Mianna held up a hand. "There's no need," she said gently. "I only came to make sure you are alright. Brunhart wanted to look in on you as well, but he did not wish to overwhelm you."

"I am fine," Albtraum said, his voice cracking on the last word. He grimaced. "Fine. I fear I have made things much worse for everyone..."

Mianna sighed. "Well, not necessarily. And while I certainly do not wish to make light of your distress... I believe it may have been what Camlion needed to see, to finally begin taking all this seriously."

Joaquin chuckled. "He was refreshingly speechless all the way back here."

Mianna nodded, a small smile breaking the tension on her face. "Yes... and our men were quite impressed with your bravery. To be so ready to endanger one's own life to protect others is a noble quality for a leader, to be sure."

Albtraum turned away from her, sullen. "I do not deserve such praise. I should have been able to force him back."

He felt Joaquin's hand on his shoulder. "You are far too hard on yourself, my dear. You have nothing to prove to us, we only wish to help you—"

"I am terrified of him," Albtraum blurted before Joaquin was finished speaking. "I fear that I may be too weak to control him. That he might overthrow me in my own mind and..."

You stupid, useless dreg. This is the path you have chosen for yourself. You alone made the decision to turn against me. Do not presume to whinge your fears to our enemies now as though you have any right.

Pain like boiling acid rose up behind his eyes, and he let out a breath as nausea overtook him. He sat back down on the bed.

"You should be more concerned about the harm he's doing to you," Joaquin muttered.

“I will assist you in destroying him,” Albtraum said to Mianna. He shook his head, scarlet strands falling over his shoulders and partially obscuring his face. “But you should find someone else to head this revolution of yours. I am clearly not strong enough.”

She was silent for some time. “Albtraum, you were sent to us by Chronus herself. She saw something in you and knew you would be the one to lead the dark world away from this path of rot and corruption.”

“You keep telling me of all these people who have believed me to be an answer to this, but how can they?” He scoffed bitterly, shoulders tense. He could feel tears forming in his eyes again. “None of them knew me. None of them saw who I was, or... How weak I am. How am I to trust their judgement of me?”

“You are not,” Joaquin said abruptly, and Mianna and Albtraum both peered curiously at him.

“Joaquin...” Mianna murmured, but he seemed to be paying no mind to her.

Joaquin sat, stroking Albtraum’s hair again. Albtraum tensed slightly at the contact before lowering his shoulders, exhausted.

“Trust in our judgement of you. We can see you would succeed, Albtraum.” Joaquin wrapped his arm about Albtraum’s shoulders. “It may seem insignificant to you, but how you’ve resisted Lucifurius... No one he had hold over before you could have hoped to accomplish what you have.” He chuckled. “And they had a mind to themselves *before* he took possession of them.”

Mianna interrupted them then. “Lucifurius is not a complete entity on his own. He has only half of a mind, half of a soul, and no body to house it.

But you are a complete being, and your potential far exceeds what he could ever dream of attaining."

Albtraum looked from Joaquin to Mianna, sighing. "Truly?"

Mianna smiled, nodding solemnly. "Truly."

None of them said anything else, and after a while Mianna stepped away, leaving them there. Joaquin stayed at Albtraum's side until he was finally too worn down to stay awake any longer, and sank into deep, dreamless sleep.

Chapter XXII

Brunhart doubted, as he looked around the guest barracks, that any of his men had slept. He certainly hadn't.

They had all seen rifts before – the one near Sylva, at the least – but this had likely been the most harrowing they had come across, and the incident with Albtraum certainly hadn't helped matters. At the start of the journey the mood among the guards had been cheery, but this had sobered them considerably. Brunhart drank down a swig of ale with his breakfast, listening to the chatter around him.

"Must be hard carrying around that thing," he heard Edmund muttering.

"The nerve of that Shadran, too, going after a royal ward with an axe... What was he thinking?" Piotr agreed quietly.

This was the only place the men had been able to speak freely since their arrival. Mianna had been quite adamant that her men have their privacy – and so the Tercians gave the guest barracks a wide berth. Still, they spoke in hushed voices, and the air around them felt tense, an edge of uneasiness laying heavy on them.

Edmund turned his attention to Brunhart. "Captain, do you suppose Terce may have had something to do with the murders? It was an immortal assailant who killed our men, after all... And given some of what has happened..."

Brunhart cleared his throat. He'd anticipated such questions from his men – the murders had shaken them all, and the incident at the rift had certainly stirred up those feelings once again.

"I don't believe any possibility can be ruled out at the moment."

As the men considered his answer, a voice near the door drew Brunhart's attention. Albtraum stood in the doorway, speaking to Glen. He looked drawn and tired, but he was dressed for the day, his hair loosely braided back as Joaquin had taught him to do, and Renegade stood at his side.

"I just wanted to make sure everyone was alright," he could hear Albtraum saying to Glen. "I know some of you got caught up with the Tercians..."

"Yes, of course, we're all fine! What about you, though? Your neck! You really almost did cut your throat!"

Albtraum's hand unconsciously moved to the shallow slash across his throat. It was faint, barely visible, but an unsettling remnant of the previous day's events. "It's nothing, truly..."

"Glad you're alright, Al," Edmund called out to him from where he sat at the table. The other guards murmured their agreement, and Albtraum looked somewhat surprised, but nodded in response to them.

"Good morning, Brunhart," he muttered as he stepped over.

"Good morning, pup. I did look in on you yesterday, but you were asleep."

"Yes, I was exhausted... I apologize."

Brunhart sighed softly. “No need for that. Are you feeling alright?”

Albtraum looked miserable as he accepted a tankard of ale handed to him by Noman. “Yes, though I was called to an audience with Mianna and Camlion, and I am feeling rather uneasy about it.”

“Her Majesty will stand behind you, you can rest assured of that,” Piotr told him. The men had gathered around the table to join in the conversation, and Albtraum seemed to balk slightly at all the eyes on him.

“I appreciate your willingness to defend me, but I...” Albtraum trailed off, and the others interjected.

“Think nothing of it,” Edmund said quickly. “You’re a man of Sylva now, same as us, and we stand with our own.”

“Aye, that we do,” Noman agreed. “Sylva has long been a place for those who, for whatever reason... didn’t fit, elsewhere. Camlion, and those two Shadrans, for that matter... they can’t understand, not really.”

“And it’s a shame, because Arion did,” Piotr commented with a sigh. “He was the one who helped make Sylva what it was. Even the Queen was once an outcast with nowhere to go... just like the rest of us. Arion was the one who took her in and taught her.”

“Well, Camlion is not Arion,” Edmund muttered. “And his people can see that every day.”

Albtraum listened to them speak attentively, keeping quiet and looking to be deep in thought. Glen patted his shoulder.

“Sylva is your home too. We’ll look out for you same as we would for any of us.”

Brunhart finally cleared his throat to speak up. “They are right. You need not worry.”

Albtraum nodded slowly in response, taking a drink of ale. “I suppose it is just... frightening. Not even being in control of my own mind or body.”

“You took it back, though, yeah?” Edmund pointed out. “Lord of all Daemons and he only had you for a minute. He’s no match.”

Albtraum clearly couldn’t keep himself from chuckling lightly. “It is rather more complex than all that, but... I feel I should live up to your confidence in me.”

“There, that’s the spirit,” Noman said.

The topic of conversation shifted to travel preparations then, and Albtraum listened to the men chatter for a while as he finished his ale.

Brunhart leaned in slightly to speak to him. “You are alright, though?”

He nodded again. “Yes. Mostly, I was terrified I had hurt Joaquin...”

“He was half to hysterics after they dragged you off. If Camlion hadn’t arrested Castus, Joaquin might have just taken matters into his own hands.” Brunhart smirked. “Really, though... he was worried.”

Albtraum’s brow furrowed in mild confusion, but he seemed to accept it. He drank down the last of his ale before standing from the table, leaving Renegade curled up at Brunhart’s feet. “Well, I should not keep Mianna waiting... Thank you all for reassuring me.”

The men bid him farewell, and Brunhart watched as he walked off, his posture exuding more confidence than it had when he walked in, if only the barest amount.

Albtraum gritted his teeth as he entered Camlion's office led by a guard, who kept him at arm's length as he opened the door and ushered him inside where Mianna sat conversing with Camlion across his desk, a slight frown wrinkling her brow.

Albtraum nodded in greeting to her, feeling slightly nauseated and unable to look at Camlion for fear of what he might glean from his expression. This entire excursion had been meant to make a good impression on the other kingdoms, to show them Mianna had made the right choice...

He questioned how he might convince anyone of that when he scarcely believed it himself.

Mianna's expression brightened as Albtraum stepped in, and she motioned for him to sit. He did so, shakily exhaling as he finally looked across the desk at Camlion. Anxiety quickened his pulse further as he saw that Castus sat at the back of the room behind him, his long ears angled low.

"Good morning, Albtraum," Mianna greeted. "I was just speaking with Camlion about yesterday's events—"

"Yes," Camlion interrupted quickly. "Allow me to first ask – are you unharmed?"

"I... Yes," Albtraum answered, mildly stunned at the question. He had expected Camlion might level an admonishment at him. "Yes, I am fine. And you, Castus? I did not injure you as we fought?"

Castus seemed equally surprised to have been addressed, and his ears pricked forward slightly. "No, Most High. You did not."

Castus was notably chastened from the way he'd acted the day prior, but Albtraum knew enough to know it was ingenuine. After the scathing remarks he had made... his heart could not be so quick to change.

"You need not put on airs with me, Castus," he said, his voice quieter than he wanted, but firm. "I know how you feel about me. You've been quite clear."

Camlion fell silent and glanced back at Castus as Albtraum spoke to him. Castus sat straighter, and spoke up, his eyes narrowing, his smooth face strangely expressive. "Well, if we are to be honest—"

"I believe we should be, don't you?" Albtraum asked him. It was bolder than he had dared to speak before, but Mianna watched him carefully, as if intrigued by what else he would say.

"Quite. My feelings have not changed; I believe you are unfit to lead the dark world. You are a child, with no knowledge of your own homeland. You are to govern our world, and yet Nestor and I are the only native beings of that world you have ever had any sort of contact with. And what happened at the Rift..."

He should not be surprised. He knows what I am capable of.

"How can you be expected to lead when you carry your own opposition? When he is interwoven into your very being, how can you be certain the decisions you make are your own, and not merely thoughts he has given you under the guise they are your own?"

Albtraum pondered his words. It was a weighty consideration... But he felt strangely confident, in a way he seldom had before, that it was not the truth.

The irony was not lost on him that as he considered this, a sharp pain lanced behind his eyes. In punishing him for asserting himself, Lucifurius only deepened his surety.

"It would be a waste of my breath and all of our time for me to try to convince you of my ability, Castus. Perhaps I am not the most fit for this position, but I am the one who is here. I will head this cause, with the help of the Order and my mentors. Whatever I need to know that I do not, I will learn. I do not need your approval, or your respect to do so. You can join me... or you can stand aside."

Castus stared back, his golden eyes betraying nothing. It was uncomfortably silent for a long while before Castus stood, turning to Camlion.

"Am I dismissed?"

Camlion frowned back at him before giving a long sigh and waving him away. "Go."

Castus gave a curt bow and swiftly exited the office. Camlion huffed.

"I apologize for his rudeness, Albtraum. He will be removed from his position at once—"

Albtraum shook his head. "I have no need to see him punished."

Mianna finally cleared her throat to speak up, raising an eyebrow. "But we will keep in mind who denied us support."

"And I will never be among that number, truly," Camlion said quickly, pressing a hand to his chest. "Whatever needs you have of me, consider them had."

"Thank you, Camlion." Mianna stood. "We really should be preparing to leave for Nerea, now, I believe."

"Ah, of course. Well, I'm sure you'll have no objections from Malklith. Albtraum seems every bit as capable as any of us, and with you to guide him I am sure he will accomplish great things."

Albtraum nodded, feeling somewhat unsure of himself yet again, as Mianna exited the room and motioned for him to follow.

When they were out of earshot from the office, she grinned, clasping her hands together. "*That* was positively marvelous, Albtraum!"

He grimaced, sheepish. "Was it? I failed to sway Castus to my side. And Camlion's praise felt oddly... hollow."

Mianna's grin turned to a smirk, and she nodded. "Good you noticed that. Camlion is... embarrassed at what he's allowed to happen here, with the rift, and I believe he hopes that placating us with sincere-sounding support will lead us to be more forgetful about the whole thing."

"Well, you hardly strike me as the forgetful type."

"You observe correctly yet again. Ah, but... even if Castus remains unconvinced, you have realized something vitally important to ruling successfully, and that is... not everyone will follow so easily, and you cannot waste time convincing all of them. Sometimes you simply must move on. You could rule as a tyrant, you could force them into submission, but you only breed resentment with such action."

Albtraum was particularly struck by her words as he found his thoughts wandering to Lucifurius. He had done just that... and lost Albtraum's loyalty utterly as a result.

You will soon see I have no need of diplomacy.

He gazed off down the hall as they walked back to the guest quarters, sighing. "Even so... Given what happened, I've surely only given Ismaire more reasons to despise me as well."

"Perhaps not. She had oddly little to say when we made our trek back yesterday. I'm not sure she expected you would go to such lengths to resist – I'm not sure any of us expected that, really." Mianna fell silent for a moment before continuing. "Although, I hope in the future you will perhaps not rush so quickly to suicide. You are very valuable to us and our cause."

Albtraum grimaced, watching at the guards and servants milling in the halls as they passed. "At the time, it seemed my best option. Lucifurius has much to lose if I die, it seems."

The utter gall *of you. There have been other hosts before, and if you die, there will be more after. You truly think yourself so necessary?*

Albtraum clenched his jaw. *Why did you stop me, then?*

A long while passed. Silence.

Mianna glanced at him as they walked. "And past that... You have people who care for you, now, and they would most certainly be pained to lose you. Even I have come to consider you something of a friend… And that does not happen often."

Albtraum found himself surprised by that. "Well… It will be good to be among friends as we continue forward, then."

"On that note…" Mianna slowed to a stop, and turned to face Albtraum as he matched her pace. "You have had much to endure as of late, and Joaquin has been pestering me about it, so… I thought tomorrow when we leave for our next destination, we might first spend some time in Paris."

Albtraum raised an eyebrow. "Paris?"

"The city above Terce. There is much to see there – theaters, shops, the architecture… It's truly like nothing else. And there will be no duties to attend to, so we can enjoy ourselves. Would you like to go?"

Albtraum scarcely had to consider it, and found himself quickly nodding at the chance for a diversion. "Yes, I would."

"Wonderful. I shall see you tomorrow then, when we leave for Nerea."

They parted ways then, Mianna returning to her quarters and Albtraum wandering back to the guard barracks where the Sylvans surely still waited.

He let out a breath and tried to ease the tension in his shoulders, but found it difficult. It had been heartening to hear that so many people truly did care for him, beyond his practical use to their cause… but there was more than ever before that Lucifurius now posed a threat to.

The home he had found – not just in Sylva itself, but with its people – he could hardly fathom there had been a time when he had another purpose in life.

He was disrupted from his musing when he crossed paths with Nestor, who looked startled to see him, and gave a quick bow. “Most High. I am glad to see you are well.”

He nodded. “Thank you, Nestor. As I finished telling Castus moments ago, however... There is no need to feign formality.”

Nestor’s ears drooped. “Please, do not doubt my sincerity. Castus and I may be close, but there are many things that... over the years, we have disagreed on. This is yet another. He believes that you cannot control Z’xolkuloth, but...”

He looked down. “Castus has not seen what becomes of most in the throes of Z’xolkuloth’s control. I have. And I have not seen any resist with the fervor you have – nor with as much success.”

Albtraum shifted, unsure how to respond. “At times I feel it is all I can do just to... keep my own thoughts separate from his.”

“Yours is a... unique and fascinating scenario. You never knew anything before his control, and now you defy it. Others... well, perhaps their lack of familiarity with him was their undoing.”

“Perhaps.” Albtraum sighed. “Regardless of that, I have no other choice but resistance.”

“Then it seems you have no choice but to succeed.”

“How do you suppose I will? I would be the first, would I not?”

Nestor’s ears twitched up slightly. “Most of your brethren are entirely unlike you. Fighting for power, for their own glory, some not even knowing why they fight. Certainly, some have had good intentions... but Shadrans do not rally behind good intentions. They rally behind power, and a real possibility of success. And with the backing of the Order... you have that."

Nestor stepped past him before he had the chance to respond. "Good day, Most High, and I pray many victories come to you.

Chapter XXIII

Ragged breaths clouded in the air before him as Septimus fell to his knees into the frozen dirt. He looked at his fingers splayed in the earth before him – covered in blood, blood up to his elbows, and he did not know whose it was.

You have gotten careless.

"You are the one controlling this damned body!" he screamed back, his voice a harsh rasp, cutting through the silence of the cold air.

You are still resisting.

"You promised this wouldn't... You promised, no innocents –"

You still believe you have any right to make demands of me?

Septimus trembled as he sat back on his knees. Much of the blood, he could now tell, was coming from shallow wounds across his arms. He must have tangled with someone – but his memory was hazy, and nothing tangible remained. Had he killed the person who'd done this?

As he struggled back to his feet, he heard a shout echo across the trees – he knew the moment the sound reached his ears whose voice it was, and turned.

"Septimus!"

Ishtar stood in the snow, her breath clouding before her, two temple soldiers standing several paces behind her. Septimus recognized the soldiers – supporters of hers, men who were sure to never speak of this meeting.

He hated them for it – he hated her for it – though, did he? She was hiding him from the Order, because they would kill him if they knew. And he dearly wished they would.

"Ishtar," he answered, his voice cracked and raw. "Please, do not..."

"You're injured," she informed him forcefully, stepping forward as he stepped away.

Memory clawed its way back to him. "I should be dead – I should be – Why did you stop that man?!" His voice sounded alien to his own ears. His words laced with Lucifurius' venom.

But the venom drained away as he collapsed again. He'd taken a knife to the gut as well – he could feel it now. His eyes traced the path of the blood running from the blade in Ishtar's hand.

If only she'd been the one to seek me out, *Lucifurius sneered.* At least this one has mettle.

"He was going to kill you – and if we do not see to your wounds, you will die still –"

"As it should be," he groaned. His vision blurred, he could feel his heart sputter in his chest, and relief flooded him... but it dissipated as his eyes righted themselves, the beat of his heat corrected itself... and surely, if he examined his wounds, he would find they were beginning to heal.

Do not venture to believe you can escape me.

"Septimus," Ishtar pleaded. "We can overcome him still – and I cannot lose you, especially not now that I..."

She trailed off, and a painful silence hung between them, but he knew. As greatly as he wished not to, he could no longer deny the growing of her belly, the increased protectiveness of her guards.

"No..." He raised his eyes to hers. "It would be best, love."

The soldiers had moved forward. He could hear shouts in the distance, and saw the glow of more torches. One of the men gripped her arm.

"My lady, the Order's forces have arrived. We must flee, or—"

Septimus had not even the breath to cry out in protest before he had snapped to his feet, once again Lucifurius' marionette. He rushed Ishtar, wrenched the short sword from her hand, and thrust it into the gut of the soldier beside her. He could make out bewilderment in the man's emerald eyes before he collapsed to the ground.

"Fauto!" Ishtar cried out, trying to push Septimus aside.

He gripped her shoulder and shoved her to the ground beside the collapsed soldier. As the second man who had stood behind her drew his sword, and hesitated... Septimus closed the gap with inhuman speed, drawing the blade of the sword across his throat.

He gasped, gargled, and fell forward, clinging to Septimus' tattered clothes as he slid to the ground.

Septimus felt his head turn to the approaching army, as Lucifurius made use of his eyes to observe them – and then he turned, and ran, Ishtar's broken sobs the last sound he heard before his mind went to darkness once again.

Mianna had been in a bad temper since they had journeyed to the rift. Camlion's incompetence had proved not just irritating, but dangerous, now – even Albtraum's skillful first dealings in the political world were not enough to assuage her concerns.

"A braid today, my lady?" one of Mianna's servants asked as she finished with the ties on her dress.

"Yes, thank you, Adyta. I should think that would be best for a day in the city." Mianna had never been a vain woman, but she could not help but frown as she examined her reflection in the mirror. Travel and the stresses of her dealings with Camlion had taken their toll on her complexion, and her exhaustion wore plain on her features in the form of tired eyes and pale cheeks. A few days' rest would cure her, but still, she was annoyed to not look her best.

She sat still as the servant braided her hair and watched as they finished packing her belongings. After they had finished, she followed them to the courtyard, glad to at last be leaving the dismal halls of Terce. She had once found this place to be comforting, cozy – but without Arion here, it felt like little more than a network of dark caves.

As the guards prepared for their return to the road, Mianna observed them. For the most part, they were milling about anxiously – but they stood attentively, bowing their heads as they saw Mianna had joined them. Joaquin was already seated in a carriage, working away at something with a needle that looked to be a guard's jacket.

“Ah, Mianna, there you are,” he chirped. He finished his stitch, breaking the thread with his teeth before placing the needle back in his supply box. “Piotr, I’ve finished,” he called, and the guard strode over to retrieve the coat.

“Thank you, Master Harlan,” he said with a slight smile as he pulled the coat back around his shoulders. “Must have torn it on the road,” he said in explanation to Mianna before bowing slightly and returning to his horse.

“So, where shall we go today, then? The Louvre?” Mianna asked with a smirk as she stood beside the carriage.

Joaquin snorted. “Please, my dear, you know I cannot enjoy the ostentatiousness of Parisian nobility. The theater, perhaps – I sent two of our servants out yesterday to gather some information as to what is happening in the city. *Andria* is on at the theater... I thought Albtraum might enjoy it.”

“Ah, that’s Machiavelli, is it? I am certain he will.”

As they spoke, Mianna saw Albtraum and Brunhart approaching from the hall, trailed by Renegade and a few guards who carried Albtraum’s belongings.

“I apologize for the delay,” Albtraum yawned as he approached them. He looked exhausted, dark circles ringing his eyes and his posture somewhat slouched.

“Oh, not to worry. We are still preparing to leave,” Mianna answered. “You look as if you haven’t slept at all.”

“I slept... a small amount, perhaps. I am not sure. I was rather restless.”

Joaquin opened the carriage door. "Well, ride with us, then. You should have enough time for a rest before we reach Paris."

Brunhart set to gathering the party to leave, as Albtraum settled in to the carriage, Renegade curled up at his feet.

Mianna heard a voice calling out to her from the royal halls - and had to keep herself from grimacing as she saw that Camlion strode toward her.

"Ah, Mianna, I am glad I caught you before you set off! Do enjoy Paris for me, won't you?" Something about the way he spoke urged an invitation to accompany them, but Mianna merely smiled coolly in response.

"Thank you, Camlion. I am looking forward to showing Albtraum around the city – he has never been to one quite so large."

"Ah, well, should be exciting!" Camlion was visibly disappointed Mianna had not responded to the wordless plea of his tone. "Well, as for your travels - I've hired the finest vessel and crew to see you all to Nerea, and I've already made arrangements with a stable I own on the port to tend your horses and caravan."

"Thank you, Camlion," Mianna said quickly. "Now, we really should be going—" She was cut off when Camlion took her hand and pressed something into it, her brow furrowing in confusion.

"I had this made for you," he told her with deep solemnity.

Mianna opened her hand and examined the thing he'd given her – a huge gold ring set with a dark emerald.

"Oh... Thank you, Camlion." She smiled tensely, putting the ring on her index finger. "I will wear it well."

"As you do all things," he muttered, taking her hand and bringing it to his lips, holding the position uncomfortably longer than necessary.

Albtraum let out a faint sigh of what Mianna could only assume was irritation, and it was as if he'd stolen the sound from her own lips.

She cleared her throat. "Well, I will inform you of any updates in our planning. As we've discussed, please do not make any changes to your usual operations. No new allies, trade deals, nothing of the sort." She tempered her tone was as if she was speaking to an overzealous child.

"Of... course," Camlion replied, seeming embarrassed. He looked over to Albtraum. "It has been a pleasure meeting you," and then to Ismaire, where she sat mounted on a horse among the guards, "And you as well, Ismaire! You two will work wonders for our Order, I'm sure of it."

Mianna opened the carriage door to get inside. "Well, we must be going. Farewell, Camlion."

He caught her arm and kissed her on the cheek. "Be sure to write to me as soon as you've reached Nerea safely."

Mianna merely brought her hand to her cheek as if to wipe the kiss away. "I will," she answered with a businesslike tone. She dropped somewhat ungracefully into the carriage beside Joaquin, gathering her skirts behind her.

They sat in silence until they passed the gate, Mianna pulling Camlion's ring from her finger and holding it out in her palm. "It's positively *garish,* isn't it?" she laughed, "It's so large, it would overpower *anything* else I wore."

"Mianna, how cruel!" Joaquin gasped, but he was snickering as well.

"Feel how heavy it is!" She exclaimed to Albtraum, who held out his hand to accept it. His eyebrows raised in surprise.

"I don't suppose this might be the vessel he told you he'd arranged," he quipped with a smirk. Mianna and Joaquin erupted into giggles.

"Oh, Albtraum, the wit on you," Mianna said, glad that there was some humor beneath his layers of quiet seriousness.

"It truly is hideous," Joaquin sighed. "It looks like something *he'd* wear. What was he expecting, that you'd throw yourself into his arms and beg him to ravish you?"

"I believe he hoped for exactly that," Mianna said with a nod. She took the ring back from Albtraum. "Ah, well. It may make an interesting conversation piece on my desk at home. I daresay the fashionable people of Paris might frown upon this, so I shall leave it behind."

Joaquin reached over to pat Albtraum's knee as he seemed to notice that he was nodding off. "Get some rest, my dear. You'll need your energy for Paris."

Albtraum nodded his agreement, and rested his head on the wall of the carriage to sleep.

Albtraum felt he had scarcely closed his eyes before he felt the carriage stopping again, and he started awake, rubbing his eyes as he looked out the window.

They had stopped at a pub just inside the city gates, which bustled with activity despite the early hour. Slowly, he stepped out of the carriage as the group discussed what to do – some of the guards wanted to stay at the pub for the day, and Ismaire with them, but others wished to venture into the city.

Albtraum simply stood, still half-awake, blinking as the group bustled around him, discussing when the group would reconvene. The servants chattered excitedly about their day in the city, but Albtraum still felt too bewildered by the mild chaos around him to share in their emotion.

"Shall I take the dog?" Piotr asked, kneeling to scratch Renegade's ears. As the only animal companion amongst the group other than the horses and Mianna's hawk, he'd gotten quite popular, and his tongue lolled from his grinning maw as he relished in the attention, gazing up at Albtraum as he did.

Albtraum nodded. "Of course. That would probably be better than taking him through the city, I wouldn't want to lose track of him."

He caught Ismaire's eye as she walked to the door of the pub. Rather than glare at him as she had before, she frowned, and quickly looked away – her expression denoting more nervousness and apprehension than the hatred and rage he was used to seeing from her. She hurried into the pub, the door almost closing in the face of the soldier behind her.

Albtraum sighed, hoping that Ismaire's feelings toward him were not shared but better hidden among the rest of his company. He had been moved by their vocal support, and somehow... he knew it was genuine.

But he also knew how terrifying it had been to be back in Lucifurius' clutches once more, as well as how unsettling it must have been to witness. They would have been right to fear him. Perhaps they did.

Nonetheless, he took a breath to steady himself, and joined the group gathering beside the pub. Joaquin was speaking about the theater, Brunhart listening with only barely feigned interest as Mianna brushed a few loose strands of hair from her face. Her clothing was practical and perhaps a bit understated, but still held a regal air, her dress made of a deep blue velveteen hemmed with slivery patterns.

Joaquin, on the other hand, seemed to have dressed with the intention of drawing as many stares as possible, in a deep wine red cloak stitched with delicate gold embroidery, fastened with a delicate gold chain, worn over his gold satin doublet. Somehow, he still managed to wear the outfit without it looking garish.

"Well then, shall we be off?" Joaquin said to the group. He looked to be barely containing his excitement at venturing into the city, gazing out across the river and the winding streets before them.

Albtraum saw that Glen and Noman had joined them as well. "This is the first I've been to France!" Glen exclaimed as he looked out at the city.

"You'll soon see you haven't missed much," Noman muttered in response.

"Ah, that's right – you're from Paris, aren't you, Noman? Have you missed it?" Glen questioned.

"Missed? I was born here, lived here a while. Wouldn't consider it anything like a home. I'd just rather be out in the open air than a stuffy pub," he answered gruffly.

They started down the road into the city, and Albtraum was surprised at the size of it. Until now, Sylva had been the largest city he'd seen... but it could be walked across in the space of less than an hour, and Paris extended as far as his eyes could make out into the distance.

“What shall we do first?” Joaquin asked as he turned around to face the group, deftly walking backwards, his cloak whirling around him dramatically with golden threads shining in the sunlight.

“Perhaps something to eat,” Brunhart suggested. “We left Terce in such a hurry we did not have the chance for breakfast.”

“Crepes!” Joaquin declared, turning around again, leading them onward. *“En avant!”*

Albtraum was amused at his excitement, and followed along as they walked together. The people they passed in the street stared... and as they did, Albtraum noticed they seemed much more ragged than the inhabitants of Sylva, even at the furthest edges of the city.

They continued on down the street for a while before coming to the corner, where a small building stood, warmth spilling out the open door into the cool spring air. With it came the scent of food from within, and Albtraum found his stomach growling at the savory aroma.

Joaquin bounded inside, returning later holding an armful what appeared to be some sort of rolled-up pastries.

“This is quite the same principle as the meat pies you enjoy back home,” Joaquin informed Albtraum, handing him one of the warm rolls before distributing them among the group. Albtraum examined it curiously, finding it to be filled with cheese and spices, and what appeared to be lamb. He bit into it.

“Better than potato soup?” Joaquin asked him with a smirk.

Albtraum nodded, mumbling through the bite in his mouth, “Much better than those boiled stones someone had the audacity to call food.”

"Oh, come on now, I love potatoes," Glen chuckled. "But I may have to ask Annette if she could make something like this when we return home..."

Though the crowds of people had first made Albtraum uneasy, he soon found a sort of relaxed peace at the sound of many voices overlapping as they continued through the city. Joaquin had to stop to look at every street merchant and vendor, some of the servants looking with him. The guards seemed perplexed by this, and merely stood watch.

Joaquin gasped, scrambling over to a vendor who was selling different types of cloths and fabrics. Albtraum watched him pick up rolls of fabric and dash back over, wrapping them around Albtraum before running back.

"Are you going to make *more* clothes?" Albtraum called after him as he ran back.

"Of course! We have many more occasions to attend and you've already been seen in those."

As Joaquin and the servants browsed through the wares of the street shops, Albtraum walked down to the nearby river, trailed by Noman and Glen. Brunhart was discussing something with the other few guards who had followed along while Mianna chatted with her servants.

"Perhaps we should find some books while we're in the city?" Glen suggested. "We'll have plenty of time aboard the ship to read, so..."

"Ah, yes," Albtraum agreed as he sat down by the water, listening to it rush over the rocks. "A ship... that will be interesting. I've never been on one."

Glen nodded. "I haven't been on one since I came from Nerea years ago, and I don't remember much of it."

Albtraum looked over to him, mildly surprised. “You’ve been to Nerea?”

Glen nodded, his amber curls bouncing in the slight breeze. “That’s where I was born, as a matter of fact! Lived in an orphanage there until I ran into the path of the royal Sylvan escort, walked right up to Captain Frasch, and told him I wanted to be a soldier.”

Noman chuckled. “I remember that. I was barely a new recruit at the time. You hardly came past Brunhart’s knee.”

“’Course, Her Majesty told me I was too young, but she offered me a job helping the stable hands since I seemed so eager to go with them. Annette and her son Maks took me in, and I’ve lived in Sylva ever since. Sometimes I forget I haven’t lived there all my life!” Glen smiled out at the horizon. “It’s become my home, though. There’s no place on earth I love more!”

“The infirmary, specifically,” Noman sighed.

Glen looked embarrassed, and Albtraum raised an eyebrow. “The infirmary? Why there?”

“Because Aleksandra’s usually there,” Noman teased. “Sometimes we thought Glen here might’ve had a weak constitution for all the times he went to the infirmary ‘injured’… turns out he just wanted an excuse to see the doctor.”

Albtraum was able to vaguely piece together what Noman meant as Glen scowled, his face flushing. “You have feelings for Aleksandra?” he carefully asked.

Noman snorted. “Of course he does. Anyone with eyes can see that. Are you ever going to marry her, Glen, or just endlessly pine over her?”

"I will as soon as I've secured a higher position! I want to be a worthy partner to her..." Glen shook his head. "She's accomplished so much as Sylva's doctor, and I'm just a guard."

"Well..." Albtraum hesitated, feeling perhaps it wasn't his place to speak on the matter, but something in him urged him on. "If you're as good a partner as you are a friend, I am certain you'd be more than worthy enough to her."

Glen looked taken aback, but he smiled. "...Thanks, Al. I'm glad you think so."

Noman gave a hearty laugh. "Well Glen, the boy's a sap, but you'd do well to listen to him. Ask for her hand before you're both gray."

Albtraum turned to Noman as Glen wrangled with his embarrassment. "What of you, Noman? What story does your life tell?"

"Good *God,* man, you really have been spending too much time with that flowery-headed seneschal. Just hear what he's done to your *language."* Noman chuckled. "In truth, I've got nothing as tragic or exciting as most of the people you've met here. My family is still alive, although we haven't spoken in some years. I'm the heir to a rather large estate, though when the time comes I'll probably just pass it off to the closest nephew I've got."

"A noble?" Albtraum questioned, genuinely surprised. "I'd never have pegged you for it."

"Good! Then I'm doing something right, I suppose."

Albtraum watched as Glen kicked at the river stones. "What brought you to Sylva, then?"

"I ran away from home when I was a boy. I'd already been betrothed largely against my will to some other noble girl who was doubtless as unhappy with the whole thing as I was. My parents offered to find another noble daughter to marry me off to, one I'd prefer more, but..." He sighed, his voice lowering. "That was a hopeless venture, since it's men I would have preferred. I told my family as much, and they promised they'd 'keep my secret', so as not to bring any scandal to me or the family..." He scoffed. "I didn't want secrets. So I left."

Albtraum listened to his story with a furrowed brow. Though he had grown accustomed to living with humans, he realized he still knew precious little about their world, much less that of humans who came from outside Sylva. "Why would your preference have brought scandal to your family?"

Noman gazed intently at him before his eyes widened slightly as he realized Albtraum's question was in earnest. "Ah, well... I don't think you know how encouraging it is you had to ask that."

Glen chuckled. "It's alright, I didn't understand it either. But... in many places outside the Order, marriage... and love for that matter, is very strictly controlled."

"But that's when I stumbled on the city accidentally, and I suppose I just never left," Noman continued. "There are others like me in Sylva... Joaquin, for one. I don't have to keep secrets."

Albtraum listened to him talk, noticing that Joaquin had returned suddenly, motioning Albtraum over. His arms were burdened with heavy fabrics, soft and intricate patterns that glistened in the sun. The guards struggled behind him with heavy trunks filled with his other purchases.

He was showing a deep green material to Mianna when Albtraum stepped over. "What do you think, Mia? A dress from this material?"

She smiled lightly and ran her hands over the emerald-colored velvet. "Such a lovely color," she mused. "Perhaps for autumn, once we are back home?"

"Wonderful idea, my dear," Joaquin agreed with a grin. "Now... shall we head to the theater? I believe they'll be showing the play soon..."

"Ah, yes! I believe you'll enjoy this one, Albtraum." She rushed over and took him by the arm, startling him slightly, but he walked along with her. "You're already quite well acquainted with the playwright, I believe."

Albtraum could think of only one author of whom he had read all the works he could get his hands on. "...Machiavelli?"

"Yes! It is an adaptation of another work... But it's certain to have his flair."

"We'll be seeing Joaquin's purchases to the caravan, I suppose," Brunhart called.

Joaquin whirled around to face him. His cape made him look like a flag in the wind. "Brunhart! Do come to the theater with us. You could do with some culture. And surely there are enough hands to handle six measly trunks without your supervision."

"Measly...?" Glen muttered as he lifted one, particularly burdened by its weight.

"A whole cadre of guards and servants is not well suited to a theater, beside the fact that I find plays tedious and overblown." Brunhart chuckled. "You enjoy yourselves, though. We will meet you at the city gates later."

"For shame, Brunhart! Alas, you will remain an uncultured lout to the end of your days." Joaquin's brow was furrowed in mock disgust, but his amusement was clear, the ends of his moustache quivering with suppressed laughter.

Brunhart simply rolled his eyes as he turned away.

Mianna hurried along, tugging Albtraum with her, and he could not help but be swept into her excitement. They made their way through the streets, many people casting prolonged looks their way. They were out of place here... not enough that the slight stares gave way to gawking, but enough that Albtraum could sense it.

"I am interested to see what you make of the play," Mianna said as they turned a corner to walk down another stone-cobbled street. "You are a newcomer to the consumption of theater, but... as you seem to be of a philosophical mind, I believe you will have much to say on it."

"You think me philosophical?" he asked her with a raised eyebrow, following along with Mianna's arm through his as Joaquin rushed ahead.

"You are quite thoughtful and intelligent, and all the reading you've done has only sharpened your wit," Joaquin interjected.

They think your intelligence your own. How amusing.

Albtraum started at Lucifurius' voice, fighting to keep his expression and posture carefully neutral. He had been enjoying himself, and for a moment he'd almost forgotten about Lucifurius. Almost.

"Where is the theater?" he asked Joaquin, eager for more distraction.

"Right this way," Joaquin replied, waving Albtraum along into the large building before them.

Mianna finally released his arm, and they moved into the theater, an usher stepping up to guide them, somewhat surprised at their appearance as Joaquin said something to him in French. The elderly man led them to a box at the back of the dark theater, where the three of them sat together and waited for the start of the performance. The hum of low chatter surrounded them.

As the actors took the stage, Albtraum observed them carefully. Their tones, movements and dress were exaggerated, clear and ingenuine replications of human behavior. Albtraum wondered if he appeared this way to those around him – an obvious imitation.

The play was a story about marriage, a concept Albtraum was aware of, but still did not quite understand. From the tale that played out before him, it seemed needlessly complicated, and though it was meant to be rooted in love, it appeared to be more of a business transaction, the interactions more riddles than relationships.

"I much prefer the city theaters to the dull performances at the palace," Joaquin whispered to Mianna, and she nodded.

"Why is that?" Albtraum asked, keeping his voice low and his eyes turned to the stage.

"The palace performances are better to look at, certainly, but they lack in honesty. Well, all theater does, of course, but—" He pondered a moment. "Sometimes, an abundance of polish and perfection becomes a bore."

Albtraum found himself growing restless as time wore on, but the play did hold most of his attention. It continued its meandering tale of tested loyalty, kept secrets, and politics – finally culminating in two weddings, a happy end for all.

The sun had begun to set by the time the play had concluded, and they shuffled out of the theater carefully, out onto the streets again. Crowds still gathered along the edge of the streets despite the time.

Joaquin still had spring in his step as they made their way back to the main road, though Albtraum felt somewhat exhausted. "I thoroughly enjoyed the performance! Machiavelli's writing is often so dull, it's wonderful to see the man was capable of creativity as well."

"It was certainly... complex," Albtraum replied, still unsure how he felt about the whole ordeal. "It seemed to me the story could have been rather a bit shorter if they'd all merely been honest with one another..."

"There is no theater in *that,* my dear," Joaquin chuckled. "Try to abandon some of your boundless practicality the next time we see a play."

"It was interesting, though." Albtraum looked out across the wide river into the distance as they walked, where he could see a massive palace dimly lit by the setting sun. It was unlike anything he'd laid eyes on before.

"What is that?" he asked, slowing to a stop.

Mianna stepped over to stand beside him as Joaquin attempted to hail a carriage to see them back to the inn at the city gates. Her jade eyes reflected the distant lights of the palace as she gazed out at it.

"That is the Louvre. It is the palace where the nobility live, much like the estate in Sylva," She answered simply.

"It is... nothing like the estate in Sylva," Albtraum muttered as he stared at it. Heavily guarded, separated from the rest of the city, looming over it.

In Sylva, there was no such separation. Townsfolk, farmers and merchants freely entered the estate to discuss business with the tradesmen and scholars there, guards standing as guides and protectors rather than a wall of separation.

"No, you are right." Mianna turned and faced out at the streets, leaning against the railing of the bridge. "I did not wish for Sylva to become like most kingdoms."

Suddenly, the sights he'd seen before – the ragged townsfolk, the worn down buildings – were thrown into a sharp relief, in stark contrast to what lay before him.

"The ruler of this city cares nothing for the people outside the palace."

You see now... Humans are not so perfect as you think them to be.

Mianna seemed somewhat surprised at Albtraum's sudden declaration, looking over at him, but she sighed, her expression falling back into stark neutrality.

"Yes... this is the way most cities operate. Kings allowing their greed to drain the people they rule over in the name of power they can laud over other kings who do just the same." Albtraum watched her as she turned her eyes back to the people on the street. "I was not born into the nobility. I consider myself the same as any person who lives within Sylva's walls. I am a shepherd... not a subjugator."

Albtraum's brow furrowed, and he shot back a sharp response to Lucifurius' taunting.

As if humans are all the same... As if I have not found goodness and love among them. Those I have found are nothing like these corrupt and greedy kings. Just as I am nothing like you.

Acidic pain bloomed through his skull. *We shall see.*

Mianna gently took Albtraum's arm. "Come, it seems Joaquin has found a carriage."

He followed after her into the darkness of the street, the chill of the air suddenly feeling sharper around him.

Chapter XXIV

It was a few days later when they reached the port, and Brunhart had found himself caught in a storm of chaos as they struggled to board the horses at the stable and gather the group and their possessions to board the ship.

He turned back from issuing orders to his men to face Albtraum where he stood on the edge of the path looking out over the sea.

"It's so vast!" he exclaimed, his voice muffled as the sea breeze snatched at his words. Renegade stood beside him, sniffling the air.

Brunhart watched him as he gazed out at the waves, forgetting about the rest of the group for the moment. He found himself longing for simplicity, wishing he could have come to the port with Albtraum merely to gaze out onto the water and breathe in the soft, salty air as they listened to the lively chatter of the crews that paced the docks.

But of course, they were still on business.

Albtraum turned around to face him. "Can I go down to the shore?" he asked, his eyes so bright they looked to be lit up with fire.

Brunhart felt something in him soften at Albtraum's innocent tone. "Alright. Try not to be long, we do need to be boarding soon."

Albtraum nodded his thanks and scampered down to the shore, Renegade running to keep up.

“I must say, it’s been surprisingly enjoyable, helping guide him through becoming human,” Brunhart heard Joaquin chuckle as he approached from behind. “I hope we will have some more time to show him more of the joys of the world before he is entrenched too deeply in Order politics.”

Brunhart frowned. “It does seem unfair that this is the only way he’s allowed to experience these things.”

Joaquin watched Albtraum walk along the shore, up to the ramp of the ship where he conversed with Edmund and Glen as they waited for the ship to be ready for departure, standing just where the waves could not touch their boots. “I’ve never really considered the prospect of having children in my life... but I somehow feel as if all my many years have led up to this chance to look after him.”

Brunhart was mulling over Joaquin’s words when their conversation was interrupted by the captain of the ship they were to board. He was a stout man, and his clothing was threadbare, but he’d clearly made good effort to make himself presentable. “Are you Sir Frasch?” he asked Brunhart.

“I am,” Brunhart replied.

“We’re ready for the lot of you to board,” the man said with a nod.

Brunhart looked back at the guards gathered behind him, who nodded their acknowledgement and moved to gather the group and the last of their possessions.

As he walked to the port to board he saw Albtraum had wandered further down the shore and was now crouched on a rock that rose from the water, holding Renegade in place. Brunhart's pace slowed as he realized Albtraum was speaking to someone, a rough-looking man in dark clothing.

Brunhart froze, his gut twisting. Somehow he was struck with the sudden feeling that he knew exactly what the man was doing – because he'd done it before himself in his days as a sellsword.

Albtraum was in a precarious position. The overhang was far from the path, far from where anyone was paying attention. It would be a simple thing for him to slip and fall into the waves...

As Brunhart lurched forward to run toward him, he saw Glen and Edmund quickly approaching the man, Edmund's hand on the hilt of his sword. Even from this distance, Brunhart could see tension wind into the man's shoulders – and he ran off, disappearing around a corner. Glen and Edmund quickly flanked Albtraum, their stances defensive – and Brunhart felt a sense of relief at the sight.

Their interactions had been casual on the journey thus far, and often to a degree that Brunhart might have called unprofessional – but they were still guards, after all, and Albtraum was still a ward of Sylva. They had not let friendship cloud their sense of duty... or perhaps it had even strengthened it.

Albtraum looked surprised at their sudden shift in behavior, frowning in the direction the man had run off in. Glen and Edmund stood down, but only slightly, as Brunhart approached them.

"What was that?" Albtraum asked, bewildered.

"Particularly bold pickpocket, perhaps?" Edmund suggested. "In any case, Albtraum, do try to keep your wits about you... Given all that's happened, it seems the world is not particularly safe for any of us at the moment."

Brunhart cleared his throat. “Yes, Edmund is right. You must be careful.”

Albtraum was noticeably troubled as he led Renegade back toward the ship. Glen followed close behind him as they boarded, and Brunhart cast one final look in the direction the man had disappeared, an unsettled feeling winding itself into the back of his mind.

Albtraum hurried up the ramp to the ship, carrying Renegade in his arms as he had refused to set foot on the ramp. Edmund and Glen appeared easygoing once again, leading him to wonder if their sudden shift in attitude had happened at all.

In truth, Albtraum hadn’t thought much of his encounter with the strange man on the shore until he’d seen the way he’d run as soon as Edmund and Glen approached. He’d thought it odd, perhaps, that the man approached merely to ask where he was going from the port... but he had not considered the possibility of a threat. How could he, when he felt he was a threat himself?

I truly miss those days. I feel like a fool, having to constantly worry when some human weakling might strike us down and condemn me to wandering once again.

Albtraum tried to push the thought from his mind, leaning against the ship’s railing, finally setting Renegade on his feet. He was mesmerized by the movement of the water on the horizon, having never seen so much of it in his life. It seemed to stretch on into eternity.

He watched as the servants and guards carried the group's supplies down below deck. They had been moving around so much, and Albtraum was somewhat weary of it by this point, but he found the new sights and experiences to be worth the tiring nature of the travel.

"You alright there, Albtraum?" he heard Edmund ask him.

Albtraum blinked at him before realizing he must have still seemed shaken by the incident on the shore. "Yes, of course," he answered. "I suppose I was just... caught off guard."

Glen joined them then, his expression darkened. "Well, after what happened in Sylva before our journey... I believe we should be careful."

"What happened?" Albtraum asked him.

"Three guards were murdered. No one is certain, but... We think the murderer may be immortal... someone who works for one of the Order kingdoms."

Albtraum vaguely recalled hearing about the incident in passing very early on in his stay in Sylva. At the time, the significance had not registered to him, but now that he knew Sylva's people – knew that the guards were close, that they considered one another to be a family – he felt somewhat ashamed the the gravity of those occurrences had not struck him sooner.

"Y-yes, that's right... I am sorry. That must have been difficult."

Glen looked more somber than Albtraum had ever seen him, and Edmund nodded. "They were good men. Didn't deserve what happened to them. Even more reason why *you* should be careful, we don't want to lose any more of our countrymen."

When the ramp was raised and the ship set off, Albtraum found his footing lurching beneath him, and would have fallen on his face if not for someone catching him by a handful of his tunic.

"Careful there," he heard Noman's voice warn as he helped Albtraum right himself. "If you do that near the railing you could go overboard."

"I'm fine," Albtraum assured him, shifting in place to counteract the rocking of the ship. "This is strange," he muttered. "I've never stood on anything so unstable..."

"I think it's sort of fun!" Glen exclaimed, seeming to have returned to his ordinarily cheerful demeanor. "If you close your eyes, it sort of feels like you're flying!"

"Another good way to end up over the railing," Noman huffed.

Brunhart returned then, running a hand through his hair, his shoulders slightly raised with tension. "Most of the arrangements should be taken care of. The journey will take us about a week, so we should settle in and get as much rest as we can now."

"We got anywhere to spar?" Noman asked him. "All this travel's got me restless."

"Ask the crew. Perhaps they have some room in the cargo hold."

Noman headed off to do so, and Albtraum looked back and forth from Glen to Brunhart. Glen seemed to recall something. "Oh, Al, I found a book at the market in Paris when you went to the theater. I think it was... *The Divine Comedy?*"

Albtraum nodded. "Yes, I believe that was among the books Joaquin gave me... but I left it back in Sylva. Still, perhaps we should work through

Canterbury Tales first..." He turned back to Brunhart. "Seems Glen and I will be reading for now."

Brunhart finally seemed to have relaxed. "Alright. Be careful near the railings. I believe I could use some sleep, but don't hesitate to come find me should you need anything."

Albtraum and Glen weaved their way through the bustling crew and servants to one of the higher decks, where they sat against the mast and Albtraum continued guiding Glen through the book, Renegade curled against Albtraum's leg. Albtraum himself had already read through the book three times in the time it had taken Glen to get through half of it, but it was alright by him, as he quite enjoyed the story and seemed to pick up on new details each time he read through it.

Glen had memorized his letters, and was slowly working through piecing words together. Most common words he was already doing quite well with, but some of the more sophisticated words were still giving him trouble.

The sun beating down went from pleasantly warm to hot after a while, so hot Albtraum found himself removing his coat. A vague malaise twisted in his gut, and he squirmed uncomfortably in place as Glen recited the words on the page. Renegade paced around him anxiously, panting in the heat.

Eventually, Albtraum's distress distracted Glen from his reading. "Are you alright, Al?" he questioned, setting the book down. "You don't look too good."

Albtraum brushed sweaty strands of hair away from where they'd stuck to his forehead. "I'm not sure... Suddenly I feel ill."

Albtraum felt bile rise in his throat suddenly, and he made a clumsy dash for the railing, barely managing to get there before his stomach abruptly emptied its contents.

Glen followed after him, patting his back sympathetically. "You must be seasick..."

"Seasick?" Albtraum managed to choke out as he spat repeatedly, trying to get the foul taste out of his mouth. "Is the sea air poison? I did not feel ill at all the entire time we spent at the port."

Glen shook his head. "No, no, it's the rocking of the ship upsetting your stomach."

Albtraum wiped his mouth on his sleeve, feeling much more uncomfortable in the heat of the sun. Without thinking, he scrambled to pull his tunic off, finding little relief once the air hit his skin.

He sighed, stumbling back over to the mast and all but collapsing against it again. "Let's continue... it might take my mind off it."

Glen looked concerned, but sat down beside him and continued to recite from the book.

Albtraum's nausea only increased as time went on, such that he couldn't stop himself from letting out an audible groan from time to time. Renegade stood in front of him, peering curiously at him.

Albtraum heard footsteps scaling the deck, and looked over to see Ismaire approaching him. She looked at him awkwardly, as if she'd stumbled on a wild animal she hadn't been expecting.

She appeared to be debating whether or not to address him before frowning and saying, "Can't handle the sea, can you?"

Albtraum grumbled at her. “And you can, I suppose?”

“Actually, yes,” she replied, almost preening. “Spent quite a lot of time on boats, I’ve had my sea legs under me for ages.”

“Well, all due congratulations to you,” he muttered sardonically, feeling ill enough he could not spare any energy towards being pleasant. The heat of the sun was greatly uncomfortable and he felt as if someone had liquefied his insides.

She scowled. “Just look at the horizon,” she mumbled before continuing up to the front of the ship.

Despite his bitterness towards her, Albtraum tried to do as she suggested, to no avail. Glen tried to pat his back comfortingly, and though Albtraum appreciated the gesture, the contact only served to heighten his discomfort, the touch lancing through him like a shock.

Albtraum heard another set of footsteps come up behind him and glanced up to find Joaquin looking down on him with concern.

“He’s feeling seasick,” Glen explained before Albtraum could.

“I can see that,” Joaquin sighed, kneeling down. “My boy, what have you done with your clothes? You’re going to burn to a crisp in the sun, pale as you are. You should lie down until you’ve gotten used to the feel of the ship.”

Albtraum did not argue as Joaquin led him below deck, Glen calling after him, “I’ll keep practicing!”

It was much cooler below the deck, thankfully, and Albtraum found his discomfort just slightly relieved as they headed into one of the rooms and he unceremoniously flopped onto the bed. He regretted his carelessness, however, as the sudden movement shook up his stomach again.

Joaquin sat on the bed beside Albtraum, moving his head to his lap, smoothing back his hair. "It will pass soon enough, my dear.

Albtraum hadn't noticed Renegade follow them in, but the pup's head suddenly appeared over the edge of the bed, and he crawled over the edge to lay next to him.

"No one else seems to be having as much trouble," Albtraum groaned, embarrassed, throwing an arm over his eyes.

"Because we've all been on ships before, Albtraum. You can't expect to be perfectly well-suited and ready for every single thing you encounter."

Albtraum was about to answer when Joaquin's eyes lit up and he suddenly appeared excited as a servant entered the room to drop off Albtraum's belongings. Albtraum noticed a new case atop the pile, which Joaquin motioned to be handed over to him.

"Speaking of which...I saw this at one of the merchants in Paris, and I simply had to get it for you." Albtraum sat up carefully as Joaquin opened the case, revealing a stringed instrument. It had been decorated with a gold foil pattern and polished to a glossy shine, emphasizing the rich shade of the wood. "It's a violin. I thought you might like to learn how to play."

Albtraum gingerly lifted the instrument from the case, admiring it. "I suppose I will need something to do on the journey."

One of the servant girls handed Joaquin a similar case, from which he pulled another violin. It was well cared for, but still showed signs of wear. "I thought against bringing this along, but I am glad I decided to ignore my better judgement! I will teach you. You're well on your way to becoming a properly cultured leader."

Joaquin took the bow of his own instrument and showed Albtraum how to hold it, then drew the bow across the strings, producing a smooth, sweet note.

Albtraum tried to imitate his motion. What followed was one of the most horrifying screeches he'd ever heard. Renegade leapt up, his ears twitching before firmly pinning back. Albtraum winced.

Joaquin shot him an encouraging smile. "As I said... You cannot expect to begin anything with proficiency. Not to worry, my dear. Your playing will be, at the very least, tolerable by the time the sun sets tonight!"

The rest of the ship's passengers would have begged to differ.

Brunhart lay back in his bed, trying to listen to the sound of the waves outside the window of his room, but finding the gentle hiss of the water drowned out by the repetitive notes floating from the open door across from his own.

These had been largely the only sounds he had heard for the past two days. Joaquin, for whatever reason, had decided that Albtraum might like to learn how to play the violin – and unfortunately for everyone aboard the ship, Albtraum had indeed become rapidly, deeply fascinated with mastering the instrument.

And little else had held his attention since.

It had been a relief, at first, when he'd learned to play smoothly – but now, the deftly played notes were almost as grating as the beginning screeches had been.

Finally, Brunhart stood, crossing the hall to Albtraum's room. Albtraum's back was to the doorway and he sat on his bed, hunched over the violin, playing a quick scale, his shoulders tense with concentration.

As he paused to take a breath between scales, Brunhart carefully took the bow from his hand. Albtraum whirled to face him.

"Brunhart, I was practicing," he protested with a frown.

"You've played the same thing perfectly at least a hundred times," Brunhart informed him gently, but with slight exasperation. "Trust me, I have been counting. Your last mistake was nearly an hour ago. Surely you've earned a break."

"Only this scale," Albtraum answered. "I haven't even begun to put the notes together yet." He made a grab for the bow, but Brunhart held it out of his reach.

"How about," he started, setting the bow on the nightstand, "we practice more with your dagger?"

Brunhart almost immediately regretted the suggestion when Albtraum shrank back as if he'd been threatened. "I... I don't think that I should."

"And why is that?" Brunhart asked, sitting beside him as he hastily put away the violin in its case.

Albtraum shook his head. "You don't understand. When I have a weapon in my hands again, he... Lucifurius..." Albtraum looked up, scratching at his arms. "If I were to hurt anyone—"

Brunhart frowned, patting his knee. "I understand your fear, but there's no need for it. Lucifurius' threats are empty. You are far stronger than he is."

"And I think you have far too much faith in me," Albtraum muttered.

Brunhart stood up, looking down at him. "Well, if I were to trust you as little as you trust yourself, I still know you cannot best me." He left out, of course, that this was a fact he hoped to change. "If you truly can't have any faith in yourself, then at least have faith in me."

Albtraum blinked up at him as if realizing something, and some of his fear seemed to lift. "...Alright." He stood and started out the door, but Brunhart caught him by the arm.

"You're not to let any worry for me stop you from learning properly, you understand?" he said firmly. Then, gentler, "But if he hurts *you*, we're going to stop."

Albtraum nodded hesitantly before they headed down a level to the cargo hold to spar.

Albtraum had learned how to hold the dagger correctly, and his movements were naturally nimble and fluid. His height and thin frame, however, made him somewhat gangly, and his attacks were often imprecise as he seemed to not fully comprehend where all of his limbs were as he fought.

Brunhart found himself more concerned as time passed that perhaps *he* was the one holding back too much – a drawback he knew he could not remedy, as he could not imagine hurting Albtraum in any way, even if the purpose was to educate.

Albtraum finally landed a blow on Brunhart's side, between his ribs, sinking the knife in to its handle. He froze with a sharp inhale, anxiously looking Brunhart in the eye.

Albtraum was not the first to use Brunhart as a living practice dummy. He'd long been giving his men the advantage of practicing with real weapons, free of any fear that they could cause him any lasting harm. And it had helped him, as well. Though immortality allowed him to heal his wounds rapidly, they still caused him pain in the time they existed. After taking so many, however, the pain was quite easy to push through.

Brunhart gave a slightly breathless chuckle, wincing as he pulled the knife out carefully. He breathed in and out a few more times, foamy, pinkish blood bubbling at the corners of the wound before it sealed off, feeling like nothing more than the chill of an unexpected touch.

He patted his side and returned the knife. "Well done, Albtraum. Anyone else would have been regretting challenging you about now."

Albtraum's uneasiness melted away slightly, and he looked pleased with the praise. He fought more enthusiastically after that, but Brunhart could see clear as day that he tensed and hesitated just before striking. He only hoped this would change in a real battle.

"Albtraum!" a voice sounded from the top of the stairs, but it did not break his focus as he lashed out at Brunhart again. Looking over Albtraum, Brunhart saw Joaquin storming down the steps to the cargo hold, his eyes narrowing at the scene before him, Mianna following close behind. He looked quite a bit more disheveled than Brunhart was used to seeing him, his hair tousled and ruffled up by the sea breeze and his outfit missing a layer or two after the midday heat. Mianna was in much the same state, her hair tied up in a loose updo, slightly frizzy curls escaping and framing her face.

"What happened to practicing your music?!" Joaquin exclaimed, and Albtraum did stop and turn to face them then, panting with exertion. He straightened and tried to hide his exhaustion upon seeing Mianna.

"Leave him be, Joaquin," Brunhart grunted. "I had to tear him away from the damn thing – this idea was mine and mine alone."

Albtraum looked back sheepishly to Brunhart. "If it's all the same to you, I would like to stop."

Brunhart shrugged, nodding his head. "Alright then."

"If you're torn between music and combat, might I suggest a compromise?" Mianna chimed in. Albtraum's full attention turned to her. "The sun is setting and the air's grown cooler, it's the perfect time to have a dance up on the deck."

Brunhart sighed. "I would not call that a compromise."

"Why not?" Joaquin demanded. "It's a well-known fact that every artful combatant must have the skill to dance with grace as well!"

"Combat need not be artful," Brunhart said flatly, resisting the urge to roll his eyes. "Unless you'd like your opponent to run you through while you're busy executing an elaborate flourish."

"A dance does sound nice," Albtraum blurted, interrupting them, his tone sharp with nervousness.

Joaquin took him by the arm, leading him up the steps. "Then dance we shall!"

Much of the traveling party was on the deck when they arrived there, enjoying the cooler evening air. Glen had been looking after Renegade, who looked thrilled to see Albtraum, dashing over so quickly he nearly crashed into him.

Joaquin reappeared with his violin, settling himself up against the mast as he started to play, softly at first as if the music were a suggestion.

Brunhart sat down beside him as his playing increased in volume and Mianna took Albtraum by the arm to lead him. Albtraum looked quite happy as Mianna conversed with him, and Brunhart could not help but feel the same, watching him enjoy himself.

"You're quite the natural at this, I must say," Mianna praised as Albtraum followed her footwork to the cadence of Joaquin's playing.

He looked down in concentration, her praises only serving to make him more nervous. "No, no. I am rather amateurish compared to all of you..."

"Albtraum." She cut him off, and he looked her in the eye. He was still looking down – she was a good deal shorter than he was. "We are centuries old. You've had a lifetime of experiences to make up for in just the short time you've been with us, so by that measure-" she raised his arm with her own and twirled underneath him "-you've done marvelously. I cannot wait to show you off in Nerea."

Albtraum fell silent for a while, enjoying the sound of Joaquin's masterful playing and his closeness with Mianna.

"We should take tomorrow to rest. We've been pushing through so quickly, we've barely had a moment to breathe. What say you and I look through the books you've got and find something to read together? We'll have some wine and lounge the day away."

Albtraum felt something well up within him, something that felt like panic without the prickling of dread. Happiness? Excitement? He blinked hard, trying to clear the fuzziness in his head – it felt like one of the balls of thread Joaquin used was looping around his brain.

"Yes," he answered, embarrassingly aware that some time had passed since her question, and she was looking at him expectantly. "That sounds... wonderful. Truth be told, that is my ideal course of action for any given day."

She gave a hearty laugh. He loved the sound, the way it floated over the music, brazen and unfettered. "Oh, you're a boy after my own heart, Albtraum."

She started to pull back as Joaquin's playing changed tempo. "I'm sure you'd like to have a break," she said with a gentle smile.

He gripped her hands in hers tighter. "No," he said quickly, his voice cracking as he did. Mortified, he cleared his throat. "What I mean to say is... I was quite enjoying dancing. We can keep going."

She looked pleasantly surprised, and stepped closer to him again. "Well, alright then. Whatever you'd like."

What had driven him to her of late, he wondered? He found himself somewhat desperate for her attention and approval. Of course, he felt that with Joaquin and Brunhart, and even Glen and the other guards, to an extent – but it was different than how he felt towards them. He found himself somewhat hurt and perhaps a touch jealous when she lavished affections on anyone else – he had been glad to see her turn down Camlion's constant flirting.

His friends – no, *family* – were important to him – so deeply important that he could scarcely consider living without them. But Mianna had been the first to show him any kindness. The first to treat him as an equal. If not for her, he'd never have found any of the things that mattered to him at all.

He realized, as he considered the situation, that he had agreed to Mianna's plans in part because he wanted to please her. He had no desire for power – though he did dearly wish to protect his new world from the festering corruption that threatened it... Mianna most of all.

Why had she become the center of all he is actions? Why did he feel he would go to any measure just to make a moment in her presence last a while longer?

Lucifurius hissed an answer. *Because you have completely lost all touch with what you were meant to be. This rift can never be mended. This indisposition is a sickness unto death.*

Albtraum felt Lucifurius' words weigh down the airy happiness that bubbled up from within him, nearly crushing it out entirely. Of course, he could never truly have what he wanted. He'd never have a moment alone with *himself,* much less Mianna or anyone else.

"You seem to be quite deep in thought," Mianna commented, breaking him away from his own musings. "What perplexes you so?" she asked, playfully reaching up to tap his furrowed brow.

“I...” He considered explaining, but found himself stiffening and pulling away instead. “Perhaps you were right. Perhaps I do need a break.”

Her happiness dropped into concern. “Are you quite alright?”

He started to move in the direction of the stairs. “Yes, it’s nothing. I’m still just feeling a bit seasick.”

Mianna frowned in disappointment. “Well, alright. Have one of the servants bring you some tea, it will help soothe you.”

He nodded quickly, wanting to be anywhere but the deck at the moment. He started down the stairs, feeling his body tremble so much from anxiety that his teeth chattered.

“Albtraum,” Mianna called after him.

He looked up. “Yes?”

“We’re still going to have wine and read tomorrow, yes?””

Albtraum blinked at her, then nodded. “O-of course. Yes.”

She smiled again. “Good! Then I will see you tomorrow.”

Albtraum was glad to have ended their interaction on a slightly more pleasant note, feeling relieved as he descended into the cool darkness of the middle quarters. He stumbled his way into his room, slumping down into a heap on his bed.

A moment later, Brunhart knocked at his half-open door. “Albtraum? Are you alright?”

“I’m fine,” he shot back, his words snapping with tension. He let out a breath and repeated, gentler, “I’m fine.”

Brunhart pushed his way into the room slowly, frowning with concern. Close behind him followed Joaquin, shoving his way into the room much more forcefully.

"What's the matter?" he asked in near-panic.

Brunhart remained much calmer. "Was it Lucifurius again?"

Albtraum shook his head. "No... well, yes, but... not why I left, I mean..." He let out a sigh, irritated at himself for being unable to even string together a proper sentence.

The worry in Joaquin's expression relaxed into something else, and the ghost of a smile quirked his moustache up slightly. "Oh, I believe I know exactly what's going on here, Brunhart."

"And what might that be?" Brunhart looked at him with ready exasperation, though he hadn't explained himself yet. Albtraum sat with his shoulders hunched, looking at the both of them, wanting to curl into his bed and disappear.

Joaquin's expression split into a grin. "I believe our dear boy has just had his first foray into falling in love."

Chapter XXV

Ismaire huffed as she sat on a wooden crate, watching as Piotr took her place to spar opposite Noman.

She was glad to be stationary, at least relatively so, for a time – and even more glad she did not have to behave herself before royalty. She had missed sparring with the men, drinking ale and speaking however she pleased. Though it had been rather warm for most of their voyage, a heavy rainstorm had brewed overnight, and a damp chill hung in the air below deck, and the men had chosen to warm the blood in their limbs with mock-combat.

"We're visiting your home after Nerea, aren't we?" Edmund asked her somewhat breathlessly as he sat down beside her. Piotr had bested him earlier, and he had seemed uninterested in taking up a false weapon to continue after that.

She frowned. "I wish you'd stop reminding me of that. Gods, Mother will kill me." She groaned, rubbing her forehead. "Her last letter wasn't as angry as some of them have been, but she hasn't had a chance to express her disappointment to my face just yet."

"She's still your mother," Edmund said with a shrug. "Besides, you've made a better woman of yourself now, wouldn't you say?"

Ismaire frowned. "I hope so." *Still haven't managed to convince the lot of you that you've taken in a wild beast, though.*

Ismaire turned around when Edmund stood suddenly, bowing his head. "Your Majesty," he said in greeting, and Ismaire found herself facing Mianna. She was still dressed mostly in sleeping clothes, though she'd thrown a robe around herself to ward off the chill of the air.

"Good morning, Edmund. Ismaire." Mianna smiled, and Ismaire turned her attention to her own feet. She'd been having particular difficulty being in Mianna's presence of late, in large part due to her frustration and Mianna's continued insistence on accepting Albtraum into Sylva's fold. Especially after the incident in Terce... how could she not see how dangerous he was? How was she this *blind?*

"Good morning, Mia," Ismaire muttered.

"I wished to look in on you, as we haven't spoken much in a while. Also, I am not sure if the guards informed you, but..." She trailed off. "At the port, before we left, there was a suspicious man who approached Albtraum. Given that we still are unsure who murdered our guards in Sylva, you should be cautious as we travel. There is still someone who means us harm."

"You don't have to tell me to be careful, Mia."

Mianna sighed. "Just because you are immortal does not mean you cannot be captured or have some other misfortune befall you. I have some business to attend to, so I will speak with you again later."

Ismaire fell silent as Mianna walked away again. Edmund sat staring ahead for a long moment before sighing and turning his gaze back to Ismaire. "You don't have to do this, you know."

Ismaire looked pointedly at him. "Do *what?*"

"Punish her for disagreeing with you."

Ismaire felt her face flush with frustration. “I am not punishing her.”

“Then why is it that the more time she spends with Albtraum, the more you avoid her? You could have gone into the city with them back in Paris. Instead you sat in the pub and moped. So you don’t like Albtraum, what of it?”

“It’s more than just not *liking* him, Edmund! He is dangerous, I know the lot of you have forgotten that because he acts innocent. But I thought what happened in Terce may have woken you all up to that fact.”

Edmund opened his mouth to answer, but the words left him, and all he could do was let out a sustained breath. “Ismaire… have you considered that your feelings on this matter might be clouded?”

“No, I have not. Because they are not.”

She expected him to continue arguing, but he laughed at her. “You really are a child, aren’t you?”

“Call me a child all you like, Edmund, I won’t be the one waking up with a knife in my back.” She crossed her arms, scowling mightily, and watched as Piotr and Noman finished their spar and stepped away from the makeshift ring the men had set up.

“Perhaps not,” Edmund answered. His mouth remained in a hard line, but there was still a laugh in his voice. “But I won’t be the one with such a stick up my arse.”

She grumbled. “Joke about this all you like, but I will never trust him. And you’d do well to do the same.”

“Mmhmm.” Edmund sighed once more, and stood again. “I am going to get a drink. I believe you could use one.”

Though Ismaire wanted to continue arguing, she knew it was a fool's errand. "Fine." She stood as well, following Edmund to the meal hall of the ship.

She would merely have to wait until Albtraum lost his grip on his façade once again.

Albtraum had considered jumping overboard to disappear into the sea so many times that at this point, he was starting to actually think it might be a viable alternative to what was ahead of him.

Joaquin had offered to rearrange his room so that it appeared "as welcoming as possible", as he put it. He had promised it wouldn't take more than a few moments, but they were approaching an hour. Renegade anxiously paced around, distrustful of the movement of so many large objects.

"It's not any more welcoming than any other room on the damn ship, Joaquin," Brunhart sighed from where he stood in the doorway.

"There is an art to furniture arrangement, you know! I know *you* haven't moved a thing in your room back in Sylva after *fifty years,* but some of us actually want to be comfortable."

"It's perfectly comfortable," Brunhart grumbled, almost too quietly to hear.

Albtraum sighed heavily, crossing his arms close to himself to warm his hands. The air had grown cold quickly, an almost alarming change from the hot sun that had warmed the ship before.

"I think you've done enough, Joaquin," he said, standing from his bed to shoo Joaquin out of the room. "Besides, she will be here soon and I don't need an audience."

Joaquin chuckled. "Yes, of course, we'll leave you alone. I have a gift for you first, though." He scampered across the hall to his own room, returning after a moment with a robe, which he handed to Albtraum.

It was clearly not new, Albtraum could tell as much by how worn it was, but it was still soft and velvety, and the rich dark red and gold pattern was still visible on the fabric. Albtraum pulled it on around himself, finding it quite comfortable, if a bit too short on him.

Joaquin answered his questions before he had the chance to ask. "I made that robe for someone long ago, but he didn't properly appreciate it, so I stole it back for myself. It's always brought me luck and I hope it will do the same for you now. And—" he produced a crystalline bottle from behind his back, filled with dark wine "—this. *Vin Bordeaux*. You had better enjoy that, now, it's been aging nearly twenty years. That wine is as old as you are."

Albtraum accepted it with a hint of exasperation, but was for the most part grateful. "Thank you, Joaquin. Now—"

"Yes, yes, we're going." He pushed Brunhart out of the room, shutting the door behind them.

Albtraum sat on his bed waiting anxiously for some time. He felt tension wind into his gut and his shoulders, and he fidgeted with the duvet.

He considered picking up a book to pass the time while he waited, but none looked appealing through the haze of his anxiety.

Renegade climbed up onto the bed with him, nudging Albtraum's hand until he scratched between his ears.

After a while he thought that perhaps Mianna might have forgotten the plans they had made. Or perhaps she had never intended to come at all. She was a queen, after all, she had endless matters to attend to and an endless array of people vying for her attention.

A knock at the door came, snapping him out of his preemptive disappointment. "Come in," he called, trying to relax back against the pillows so as not to appear as tense as he actually felt. Renegade trotted over to the door, tail wagging.

Mianna stepped into his room. She had not changed out of her sleeping clothes – she had only wrapped a large velvet shawl around herself. She still looked more dignified than most people did in full finery, Albtraum thought.

"Albtraum, I do apologize," she said as she rushed in and shut the door. "I slept quite a bit longer than I intended, and I had to speak with Ismaire." She greeted Renegade by stroking his head and he leaned against her, panting happily.

"..It's alright," Albtraum replied, mostly relieved that she had come at all. "You likely needed the rest."

Mianna stepped into the room, approaching the bed where he sat. "Ah, I suppose you are right. We have been forging ahead quite quickly, and I have not been sleeping well. There is much on my mind... How I will navigate the future, with war a looming inevitability, and no certain hope of any support from my Order peers."

She sat beside him, leaning back into the mound of pillows Joaquin had set up on the bed. "But enough about business matters. That is all we've discussed, it seems like. That and the grotesqueness of the Louvre." She smirked.

Albtraum suddenly forgot all conversation topics he'd considered beforehand. He watched Renegade settle into the bed between them. "Well, I... er..."

She smirked at him. "Poor thing, I've kept you so focused on business it's all you remember how to talk about." She motioned over at the violin sitting on top of Albtraum's belongings. "You've taken up playing the violin, haven't you?"

Albtraum blinked at the violin, feeling foolish. "I can only play scales thus far."

"That's quite impressive for only a few days of practice." She leaned over to pick up a book from the pile at the end of his bed. "What of your reading? Surely you've got something there to talk about."

"I quite enjoy Chaucer. And Machiavelli, of course. I've been working through the *Divine Comedy* with Glen, but Dante is rather a bit too dramatic for my tastes." He thought, staring at the stack of books and trying to remember what he'd enjoyed. "Some books about the stars, and medicine... Though all that's rather over my head."

Mianna rifled through the stack until she found the book on medical treatments. She opened it and thumbed through, scanning the pages. "I was raised by healers. They taught me quite a bit of medicine."

"Did you know many societies labelled healers as witches and tried to banish or kill them? Seems a very odd way to react to them saving more lives." Albtraum caught himself and grimaced, remembering that Mianna was over a century old and likely knew any of the facts he found interesting. “Ah... of course you knew that. I’m sorry.”

“Do go on,” Mianna urged. “I’m sure there’s got to be *something* you know that I don’t.”

Albtraum’s eyebrows raised and he reached for the wine bottle, pouring it into the glasses Joaquin had left for him. “I think that’s going to take some time.”

Mianna accepted her glass as he handed it to her. “Generous servings. I can see Joaquin taught you to pour. I’m sure you can tell me something I didn’t already know before I’ve finished my wine.”

“Well, alright.” Albtraum settled comfortably into the pillows opposite where Mianna sat, and took a drink from his own glass. The wine was rich and sweet. “Let’s see... There are some astronomers who suggest that the heavens are part of an ever-changing system, and that the other bodies of the universe perhaps do not orbit our world.”

Mianna nodded. “Yes, and to go a step further, we of the Order are actually certain they do not. Free of the fetters of religious doctrine, the Order has been able to uncover much more about the way the world works than any other society.”

“Why do the churches put such effort into suppressing the spread of knowledge and understanding?” Albtraum pondered. “From what I understand of their God, he does not seem the type to wish his people to limit themselves.”

Mianna shrugged. “I’ve watched the churches for many years... It all comes down to the human need for control and power. It’s always seemed to be more about that than the message of the religion.”

Albtraum's mind flickered back to Lucifurius, suddenly concerned by how quiet he'd been. The same concept applied... Lucifurius had been trying to suppress his knowledge from the start.

"I've hoped that Sylva could become a place unburdened by the limitations the churches place on everything," Mianna continued. "What one is allowed to study, or believe, or who to love."

Albtraum nodded. "Noman mentioned something of the sort."

Mianna smiled sadly. "Yes, although it saddens me that people like Noman and Joaquin were forced to deny pieces of themselves... I am happy to provide some kind of haven for them within the walls of my kingdom. As well as to encourage the scholarly pursuits... especially of medicine. What Aleksandra and the healers who work with her have been able to accomplish as Sylva's doctors is beyond compare... and all because she's been allowed to study corpses, which is forbidden in most other places."

Albtraum considered that. "Even death cannot stop the church's control, then."

"Another reason we immortals must keep ourselves hidden from the world... Most societies might consider us abominations, and the attacks might never end."

Albtraum shifted, looking at her as his brow furrowed. "Does it not grow wearisome? Working to protect a world that you can never reveal yourself to?"

Mianna simply shrugged. "I have grown used to it. The relationships I have with my people are all I need. The rest of the world will never know just what I do to serve them, but that is the burden we bear as the Order."

A brief silence hung between them as Albtraum moved to change the subject. "On to Machiavelli, I suppose... did you know he was close with Cesare Borgia, and much of the writing of *The Prince* is based upon his time spent in politics?"

Mianna smiled sheepishly at him. "I've actually met with Machiavelli on several occasions, and Cesare Borgia and I... courted, for a time."

Albtraum tried to push down his displeasure at the idea of Mianna courting anyone, burying it with his interest in Machiavelli. "You knew Machiavelli? What was he like?"

"Quite mysterious," Mianna answered, swirling her wine before taking a deep drink. "And perceptive. There were times I worried that perhaps he'd caught on that I was not entirely what I seemed."

"I wish I could have met him," Albtraum sighed, leaning his arm on his leg and propping his chin up on his palm. "Most people think *The Prince* is something of a set of instructions for a tyrannical rulers, but I think it's more of a warning to those under them."

"You see, there's something I didn't know about," Mianna said with a bright smile. "Quite clever of him if it's true, isn't it? I'd wager most corrupt nobility already know about the tactics he describes, but commoners might be unaware."

"It's certainly given me some things to consider avoiding in my own future rule," Albtraum said thoughtfully.

Mianna sighed. "I know I did promise no talk of business, but..."

Albtraum reached over with the bottle to top off her half-empty wine glass. "Your work with the Order is your greatest joy in life, I can see that much. It would be cruel of me to expect you not to talk of it." He did enjoy watching her talk about it, he thought. Something about her passion and enjoyment made some feeling of similar happiness rise up in him.

She raised her eyebrows and sat back with her wine. “Well... If you insist. I was going to inform you a bit about Nerea before we reach it. Unfortunately, it is more like Paris than Sylva... Nerea is the main hub of the Order’s monetary resources, and Malklith Bishop, the king, taxes his citizens heavily and cares little for them. At times he borders on tyranny. Our relationship as peers has never been close – he holds no respect for me or my position. He thinks me as wild and uncontrolled as my father, which...” She sighed as she trailed off.

“My father... not many know this, but he, too, was a host of Lucifurius. Though I never met my father personally, he – and his ill deeds under the control of Lucifurius – they hang over my head to this day.” Her voice was softer, oddly less confident. “He became more and more violent and destructive until Arion, the person closest to him in the world... was forced to end his life.”

You have heard this story before.

Do you expect it will ever end any differently?

Albtraum blinked at her, shocked. He’d known there were others – of course he had. He had always been the “favorite”, of course, but Lucifurius had spoken often in passing of his other hosts.

Faced with the knowledge of *who* one of the hosts had been, however...

“He was a good man at heart, or so Arion told me... but even at his best, he had a hideous temper, and he was said to have been prematurely affected by immortal corruption even before Lucifurius had taken hold of him. To the rest of the Order, surely... it had seemed he simply lost control over time, becoming more and more violent."

Albtraum sat silently for a long time, staring at his hands as he bit his lip. Another who had experienced the same torture of Lucifurius' relentless voice – and had succumbed. So far, none had successfully shaken his control, and that terrified him.

As the silence began to stretch long enough that Albtraum feared Mianna might think he was no longer listening, he spoke up. "I am... I am sorry, Mianna."

She looked at him with confusion. "You've done nothing warranting an apology."

"I know, but only – I only wish your lineage was not interlaced with so much pain." The last words were silent, addressed to Lucifurius. *That* you *caused.*

"All of us have had pain in our pasts. Mine, all things considered, is mild compared to Arion's dealings with my father. He loved him, dearly, and watched him transform into a monster. I merely bear the mark of his corruption for all eternity. At least in Malklith's eyes." She chuckled, and Albtraum felt his dampened spirits lighten slightly at the sound. "I should be the one apologizing... Thanks to me, you'll not have an easy time convincing Malklith you are worthy of a position with the Order."

"Well, it will only be more of a challenge for me to meet, then," Albtraum answered, mustering all the confidence he could into his voice.

"And meet it I am certain you will. You are becoming a model future ruler."

"I should think I have you to thank for that," he mumbled into his wine glass as he took another drink.

Mianna reached out to stroke Renegade's fur. "Well, you've been an excellent pupil."

Renegade stretched and rolled over, his tail flopping against the bed. "He quite likes you," Albtraum observed.

Mianna looked lost in thought. "Brunhart mentioned he was quite... *unkind* before you took him on. Seems you two have brought out the best in each other."

Albtraum considered an answer, but Mianna interrupted his thought. "Oh! Your braid has come loose," she pointed out. "Come here, I'll fix it for you."

He silently followed her suggestion, patting Renegade so he'd move out of the way. He sat himself down with his back to Mianna and she set her wine glass on the night stand, carefully undoing the escaping braid and running her fingers through his hair to comb it out.

It was soothing when Joaquin fixed his hair, but something about the way Mianna's fingers felt was different – intoxicating, almost. He closed his eyes, feeling his shoulders relax as she delicately picked through the tangles in his hair.

"Ah, your horns," Mianna muttered, almost too quiet to hear, as her fingers brushed the side of his head, just above his ear. "I'd forgotten – daemons have horns. That must have been where yours were... They were broken off?" She gently ran her fingers up toward the top of his head, where more horns had presumably once been.

His hand unconsciously moved to the places she touched, and he felt the area of his scalp she's brushed against. There were hard, raised round parts of his skull – three on each side – that he had never paid much mind to, and he felt the slight protrusions absentmindedly for a moment.

He finally shrugged, shaking his head. "I've never had horns in the time I can remember."

Mianna turned him back around, deftly braiding his hair. Tighter than Joaquin braided it. "How far back do you remember?"

Albtraum sighed. He had spent a lot of time trying to extend that window of time, but try as he might, anything that happened before Lucifurius had taken hold of him was an ocean of black.

"Not far, I'm afraid. My memory begins when Lucifurius first guided me."

Mianna tied the ribbon around the end of the braid. "You were thirteen, I estimate. Based upon the information Chronus imparted to me. She said you were born late in the winter. I still wonder how she found you... How she knew you would be the right one."

Albtraum had been wondering the same himself.

"I have... memories that are not my own," He blurted after another brief period of silence. Mianna said nothing, but he could almost feel the questioning in her gaze. "I thought them dreams at first, but they are... the memories of Septimus and Ishtar."

He finally turned back around, and Mianna sat stunned and wide-eyed.

"I... also have had dreams of them," she said slowly, "that felt more like observations of another's memory. I suspect some aspect of my immortality causes this – some part of the connection I bear to them as my grandparents."

Albtraum was surprised by this, but a wave of relief also overtook him – he was immensely glad for the commonality. "Perhaps some residue of

Septimus' memory persists in Lucifurius. Perhaps I see it because our minds are so closely entwined."

"Perhaps." Mianna let out a long breath. "As much as I've told you of the Order, there is... still a great deal I cannot explain, knowledge that I do not have access to. In fact, sometimes I... I wonder if this is the right path at all, when I face so much opposition... I wonder if I am leading us all to ruination."

Albtraum sat forward. "You are fighting against corruption, and doing the best you can to protect your people... I fail to see how this could ever lead to ruin."

She smiled softly. "You are right. I am letting my mind wander directions I should not. Ah, but here I am, talking Order business again." Mianna picked up her wine again. "Well, you've unveiled my greatest passion in life, so it's only fair you tell me your own."

"Mine?"

What was it that truly gave his life meaning? Long ago, it had been killing for Lucifurius... But that wasn't anything he'd chosen, and he certainly did not derive any joy from it. The very thought of it made him feel cold and sick and anxious.

"...Everyone I've met since you took me in," he answered with finality. "Everyone who's... been kind to me. You all could have turned me away, or killed me, but you... You gave me a chance to find out who I was. And I owe it to Sylva – to all of you – to protect that. I was nothing before I met all of you."

And you are nothing still.

Mianna beamed at him. “I am glad to hear it. You have a good heart, Albtraum – and it will make you a good leader.”

Albtraum looked down. “I sincerely hope it will.”

“And I will be glad to call you an ally when you are.” Mianna wrapped a throw around her shoulders and curled up in the pillows. “Now, I’m sure you might like to hear more about Machiavelli…”

Chapter XXVI

Though Ismaire was more accustomed to travelling on a ship than many of her companions, she was still glad when they finally reached Nerea's docks. The warm sun of late summer did not reach here, at least not this day, as a persistent, drizzling rain fell over the small island that the kingdom of Nerea stood proudly upon.

Ismaire pulled her cloak around herself as they docked, trying to ward off the damp chill of the rain. There was a fish market flanking the docks, though it did not seem particularly busy, any potential customers perhaps driven away by the cold.

The Sylvans were gathering off the docks, huddled beneath the small overhang of a fish stand. Out of the corner of her eye, she could see Albtraum walking over to join them. Glen waved him over as he saw him.

Ismaire sighed to herself as she descended the ramp. Everyone was insistent upon accepting him – she was far past the point of being able to convince them otherwise. Perhaps it would be better if she did as well... outwardly, at least.

Since convincing them normally clearly was not an option, Ismaire had resolved to be civil with Albtraum while she waited for him to show his true face once again. She'd be ready this time – not dumbfounded into inaction as she had been at the rift in Terce. Perhaps he would see through her, but... Mianna, at least, might be more receptive to the truth if Ismaire had appeared to at least try to accept him.

I wanted to believe him, Mia, I did. But it seems he was never to be trusted from the start.

"...It's damn cold," she muttered as she joined the group, waiting for the royal escort to fetch them.

"It's going to be well into winter when we get back home," Piotr pointed out. "Perhaps you should brace yourself."

Albtraum had fallen silent as she had walked up, and she was annoyed – it was almost as though he *knew* what she was planning, and would not give her a chance to practice civility.

"What about you, Bonehead? Prefer colder or warmer weather?" Gods, the lengths she was stooping to.

He looked somewhat shocked to have been addressed by her, and blinked a few times before he answered. "...The cold. You can always put on another coat, or warm yourself by a fire. But the heat can be inescapable."

She snorted. "Right."

"And I haven't worn that skull mask in *months...*"

Ismaire was interrupted from responding then when Mianna joined them. "The escort's arrived," she announced. She wore a hood, but her hair was damp, her curls tighter. She looked much more rested than she had all the time they spent in Terce, and Ismaire was glad for it. Perhaps now she might look at things with a clearer mind.

"Ismaire, Albtraum, as we've discussed, please do keep your behavior as proper as possible while we are here. Nerea's nobility is much more strictly adherent to tradition than that of Terce."

"Of course. I know now that the best course of action, when in doubt, is simply to feign a smile and nod agreeably," Albtraum joked with a half-smirk.

Mianna giggled, even though what he'd said wasn't particularly amusing. She was too kind for her own good. "Well, Joaquin will be glad to see you've remembered the most important rule of etiquette."

Ismaire could hear a chorus of chatter from up ahead on the road, and she saw a procession of carriages leading down to the docks. The man who stepped out to greet them, she could only assume had to be Malklith.

He was dressed in all manner of expensive-looking clothing – she'd venture to say *gaudily,* she hadn't much listened to Joaquin speaking of fashion, but she could tell that much. He had light hair, blue eyes, a neatly trimmed beard – like one of those men the stories called handsome, but Ismaire had never been capable of judging such things for herself.

"Ah, Mianna, dreadfully sorry to have left you out in this rain. I am glad you made it in before the seas grew too rough."

The way he spoke was far different than Mianna, or even Camlion, for that matter, but Ismaire could not define how, exactly. Mianna's smile, of course, betrayed nothing, and even Albtraum seemed not to react much to him, perhaps more focused on his own behavior than on reading the man before him. It was no wonder – maintaining the air of humanity above his monstrous core was a monumental task.

"Malklith," Mianna said, and her voice was all honey and flowers, "there certainly isn't room for my whole escort in these carriages."

Malklith seemed taken aback, his blue eyes darting to where the guards stood. "Well, it would be a waste of such comforts on people such as them, wouldn't you agree—"

Something changed then in Mianna's expression. It was slight, almost imperceptible... But plain as day as Ismaire looked at her. Anger. Rage, even. She inhaled slightly, cut off as Joaquin laid a hand on her shoulder.

"—And besides, their accommodations are a good deal closer than the palace. A small bit of rain certainly never harmed anyone," Malklith finished.

"Accommodations? My escort will not be permitted within the palace, then?"

Malklith seemed surprised. "Why, heavens, no... only nobility stays within the palace, of course. We have our own guards, you'll be perfectly safe, of course. Your wards can stay in the palace, and the rest of your company will stay in the accommodations we've arranged."

Mianna drew herself up coldly. She was capable of looking quite terrifying when she wished to, in spite of her ordinarily mild demeanor. But Joaquin, again, stopped her.

"It will be quite alright, my dear. Malklith is right, the palace is no place for non-nobles." The plea in his voice was obvious.

Malklith chuckled. "You'd do well to listen to your right hand, Mianna. Seems Arion never did manage to tame the wilds out of you fully."

Mianna's ire seemed to evaporate, but annoyance lingered as she climbed into the carriage with Malklith, Ismaire and Albtraum, leaving the rest of the group to make the trek in the rain.

"You might even find yourself begging to snap up our servants when you've had some time with them. I've even had my tailors make up some clothing for all of you, to get you out of that Sylva drab," Malklith chattered on.

Ismaire frowned. Drab? The clothes Joaquin and his tailors designed were comfortable and practical, and that was more than enough for her. She even considered the things Mianna and Joaquin himself wore to be lavish... Nothing like the laughably overwrought visual assault that Malklith wore. Indeed, he seemed to not even be able to sit comfortably in what he wore.

"That was kind of you, Malklith," Mianna said sweetly.

No one in Sylva had ever taken issue with the way Ismaire dressed – and Joaquin, though they often hadn't agreed about fashion, had been very accommodating in the outfits he designed for her, managing to keep his beautiful shapes and embellishments while leaving the fit loose enough to be comfortable for a desert dweller such as herself.

Here, she could practically feel Malklith's eyes dipping over her disapprovingly.

"You are Ismaire, yes? I can certainly tell you are from a desert nation."

"That's rather the idea," she muttered.

"Well, you will not have to wear your old clothes here. Sylva is quite renowned here in Nerea for its... *frugality*. An admirable trait, but as they say... When in Rome..."

Albtraum gazed at Malklith through narrowed eyes, his scarlet brows creased in irritation. "This is not Rome."

"Goodness, you're certainly the serious one, aren't you? It is an expression, to say that, ah... When you are a visitor, you should match your behavior to that of your host."

The rest of the carriage ride was oddly silent, but Malklith grew more animated as they drew closer to their destination, pointing out new construction that had taken place recently – new embellishments to the walls, to the cobbled streets, to the gardens. Ismaire would not have been surprised if the stones beneath the carriage were eventually paved in gold as they neared the massive palace.

His voice was thick with self-congratulation as he spoke, and it was as if he found himself quite charitable as he showed them the intricate grounds surrounding his home. As though they, poor plebians that he saw them as, were being graced with such wondrous sights as they had never had the chance to see.

Ismaire was speechless – and perhaps she appeared to be in awe, but she was in fact baffled. Sylva was not a poor kingdom – far from it. The estate had nothing like the splendor of Nerea's palace, but it had a dignified beauty all its own, and those who worked there took excellent care of it. Like any kingdom, some citizens were more wealthy than others, to be sure – but even those who worked the fields and farms, who would have been considered peasants elsewhere, generally wanted for very little.

And yet, Malklith treated them as if they had clawed their way here from absolute destitution.

They had reached the palace – finally – and Ismaire steeled herself for what was to come. As Albtraum gazed up at the sight before him, a single sound escaped him, almost too quiet to be heard.

"Ugh."

Well, Bonehead, genuine or not, seems that's one thing we can agree on.

It was evening when Mianna found herself standing before the door of Malklith's office - she'd shoved her way inside once and shouted at him, decades ago, but now she merely brought her hand to the finely-polished wood to knock.

"Come in," he answered cheerily, and she stepped inside. "Oh, Mianna! You've finished with the tailors, then – did the dresses need many alterations?"

"Not many, and they may have one ready for this evening's meal." She suppressed revulsion at the thought – the bright blue dress, covered in gold chains and jewels, had been horribly uncomfortable. "I trust you've been well."

"Yes, wondrous news since I last wrote you – Elemnestra is with child."

Elemnestra – Malklith's stern-faced, statuesque wife. Mianna had long suspected that she controlled far more of Nerea's political dealings than Malklith cared to admit – or perhaps even realized. She smiled slightly. "Congratulations to you. When will your child be born?"

"Ah, in the winter, most likely."

"On another topic... I wanted to discuss a matter with you privately – I don't wish to alarm your dinner guests or your wife."

"Certainly, what is the matter?" He set aside the papers he had been thumbing through.

"A rift has appeared in Terce."

Malklith's eyes widened, and a silence fell over them for an uncomfortably long moment before he sighed. "Mianna... You must cease this nonsense about the corruption of the dark world. Such hysteria is ill-befitting a monarch."

"Write to Camlion, then, if you do not believe me."

Malklith's voice softened. "I have no doubt there is indeed a rift in Terce. What I do believe is that your fears are baseless. Rifts have often appeared in many places, and the problem is easily solved by simply moving away from the area it has corrupted. We are to carry out the will of the Order, not question it."

"And what of the people who cannot uproot their lives, Malklith? What of them?"

His mouth drew into a frown. "Your concern for the lesser stock of this world is becoming more irritating than it is charitable, Mianna."

Mianna's breath hitched in her throat.

She wanted nothing more than to take him by the collar of his ridiculous coat, and put his ridiculous head through the *ridiculous* stained glass that looked out over the city, dyed too deeply to actually make out any detail in the distance.

But she could not. Malklith's monetary resources were sorely needed, and she could not afford to let personal feelings prevent her from securing support for what lay ahead.

Still, some part of what she was feeling must have shown on her face. Malklith stood, sighing once again. “That is an ugly expression for a woman, Mianna.”

Mianna had to stop herself from gaping at him. “Chronus herself has recommended this, Malklith. This was not some decision I pulled from the air.”

“And? Chronus has long been suspected of attempting to force a schism in the Order for her own gain. Do not tell me you intend to follow in her footsteps.”

“I am simply... concerned, and if you had seen what I had, then surely you would be as well.”

“I understand your fears, Mianna, truly I do. If I had a father who had succumbed to corruption so swiftly as yours, I would fear for myself. Perhaps... something in you feels you are destined for the same path as him. But only the most weak-willed immortals are bound for corruption.”

Mianna wanted to tell him in no uncertain terms that if that were the case, perhaps it was he who should be the most afraid. Instead, she simply waited for him to go on.

“I would be happy to lend Sylva the monetary resources it needs to flourish, but only if you put this ridiculous plan for war out of your mind. Camlion warned me you would be going on about this, but I had no notion of the extent.”

She had expected as much – she had *known* Camlion’s honeyed, saccharine support could not be genuine, but it stoked the coals of her anger all the same.

"I am not opposed to the daemon working alongside us – an ambassador to the dark world would be useful, certainly. And the matter of Lucifurius... I will concede he is a threat that must be dealt with. But I doubt it will come to war." Malklith sat back down at his desk.

She huffed – she could not appear to be giving in so easily. "Perhaps you are right. But there is still one other matter – an assassin who murdered three of my guards in Sylva, and who my men suspect may have stalked us to the port. A suspicious man approached Albtraum."

"An assassin? Well, that is a matter of some alarm."

"Yes. And more alarming still... Evidence suggests the assassin was immortal."

Malklith blinked at her. "Immortal? Are you certain?"

"Fairly so."

He let out a breath. "Goodness." His reaction seemed genuine, but Mianna was a skilled enough liar herself to know this meant nothing.

"I am certainly not accusing you of anything, but still..." She cast her gaze at the floor, then back to Malklith.

"Well, should we be in the midst of a schism, I will always stand for the Order's best interests. You can rest assured that I am someone you may rely on."

"I appreciate that, but my greatest concern for the moment is my servants. I am worried the assassin may strike once more, and without the benefit of your guards force's protection, I fear they are vulnerable..."

"Understandable, but we have stationed guards at the guest estate. They will be well looked after, I can assure you."

"No intended disrespect, Malklith, but..." she crossed her arms. "I saw the guards that were stationed there – it was hardly an adequate force, especially for a group of people who may be targeted by an assassin—"

Malklith stood once more. "Mianna, you simply *must* cease panicking over every little thing. Beside the point, is your guard captain not immortal as well? And the seneschal? Surely, they are not in such great danger that I must send in the entirety of my royal guard."

Mianna pressed her lips into a hard line. His disrespect for her had not changed. Even as she had grown older, even as she had become every bit the refined royalty she should have been.

Perhaps the fact that she had been an unruly young woman when they'd first met had nothing to do with it. Perhaps he never would have respected her at all.

"Run along now, would you? I shall see you for dinner."

Mianna held her tongue once again, nodded, and turned to leave.

Albtraum darted away from the door as he heard indication that the conversation was ending, making sure to stay on the rich plush carpets that lined the stone floors to dampen the sound of his footsteps as he rounded the corner away from the door. He was glad, for the moment, that the guards had taken Renegade with them – he may have made all manner of barks and whines and potentially given him away.

The halls were blindingly white, made of polished marble. The light from the gilded lanterns reflecting from their shining surfaces almost hurt to look at.

He heard the door open – and he was safely out of sight. He sighed.

Some part of him felt guilty – he was spying on Mianna, after all, even if his intention was purely curiosity about her dealings as a ruler.

That, and he did not trust Malklith... and his intuition, it seemed, was correct.

You see... She went to this man to beg for his money like a dog for scraps. She is the same as them – she is the same as all these lofty humans you have decided to morally object to.

Albtraum shut his eyes tightly, and drew in a long breath.

"Ah, Albtraum!" Mianna's voice startled him, and he whirled to face her. "I apologize, I meant to find you and Ismaire both – but I had to discuss something with Malklith first."

Albtraum inhaled to reply, weighing what to say next. Honesty, ultimately, won out. "...Ah, yes, I... was listening at the door."

She smirked at him. "Well, well. Eavesdropping? I daresay you're quite ready for court politics. And did you hear anything that interested you?"

"N-not particularly, although, Malklith..." he grimaced.

"You need not say more." She chuckled. "I am certain we are in agreement." She was smiling, and seemed at ease – and Albtraum found himself even more irritated that Malklith had deigned to say anything about her could be considered "ugly", no matter what her expression had been.

Mark my words, child, I will end this witch's miserable existence and free you from her wretched grasp.

"Forgive me if I am being dense, Mianna, but… What need would you have of monetary assistance from Malklith? Sylva did not seem to be in need of resources when we left…"

Mianna walked with him back to the guest quarters. "You are correct, Sylva is not particularly wanting for any monetary aid at the moment – at least when it comes to our economy." She lowered her voice. "War, on the other hand… is another matter entirely, and I am afraid we lack sufficient resources for me to lead my people to battle with full confidence."

Albtraum let out a shaky breath. "So, it will come to war, you believe?"

Do you fear what I will do to that miserable hovel you call a home?

She nodded solemnly. "Yes. We of the Order had been prepared for such a possibility since Ishtar held the throne – although Sylva's coffers were all but stripped bare under my father's rule. A proper fund for war can take many decades to accrue even once a kingdom is economically stable, and unfortunately, it seems I am out of time. Not to mention the prospect of war seems to be no longer supported by my peers of the Order."

They, at least, know well enough to tuck tail and hide.

Albtraum crossed his arms to hide the shaking of his hands, and tried to keep his expression neutral. Very rarely did Lucifurius speak anymore unaccompanied by searing pain. "So then it would be best to convince Malklith that Sylva is indeed a poor kingdom."

"Precisely what I wished to discuss with you and Ismaire. Though, I do not imagine it will be difficult – he seems to think Sylva quite a poor kingdom no matter what we do or how we present ourselves."

Albtraum looked around more closely at the hall they stood in. It truly was like nothing he had ever seen... a positively obscene display of wealth that was nigh-nauseating to look at. It would not be difficult to act awestruck – in some ways, he truly was.

His attention was turned suddenly to the door to Ismaire's room, and he could not keep his eyes from widening as she staggered into the hallway.

The tailors had finished with the alterations to Ismaire's dress – and mercilessly laced her into it. The dress was a deep violet color, with so many frills it was difficult to make out any detail of the shape of it, and many hanging strands of pearls. Ismaire seemed to have trouble walking, hobbling out to where Albtraum and Mianna stood with a huff.

"Oh, my." Mianna grimaced. "I suppose this is what we have to look forward to this evening."

Ismaire glared at the floor. "I certainly hope you get what you came here for. I can barely get a damn breath in."

Albtraum sighed. "I don't suppose what they have prepared for me will be much better."

“You’ll get trousers, at the least. Lucky bastard,” Ismaire snapped, but her tone was oddly less pointed than it normally was. Perhaps he was beginning to make progress in becoming her friend.

“Well... As Malklith said, I suppose... When in Rome.” Defeated, he began to walk back to his room.

He could hear the laugh in Mianna’s voice as she called after him. “Try not to move too much once they’ve gotten you into your clothes. We will see you for dinner.”

Chapter XXVII

The dining hall was quite crowded when Mianna, Ismaire, and Albtraum arrived together, an unusual sight to Ismaire, as Nerea's palace had before seemed quite desolate for how reclusive all the resident nobles were. A slight hush fell over the hall when they entered, many staring and murmuring as they attempted to size up the newcomers.

"Certainly hope I'm not going to have to make conversation tonight," Ismaire muttered to Mianna as they stepped past the door and into the chattering sea of aristocracy.

"But of course not," Mianna chirped, smiling amicably at the people who stared in her direction. "You are a woman. Your function is merely to follow the conversations led by the men."

Ismaire had to hold back a laugh. "Oh, good. Bonehead's in charge of that, then."

"Doubt I'll have much more to say than you would," he responded, almost under his breath.

Ismaire found almost all the nobles there to be dressed just as ridiculously as she was, though she somehow still felt out of place. Her spirits were somewhat lifted by the fact that Albtraum's outfit was almost more laughable than her own – a powdery yellow satin overcoat with almost as many frills as her dress. Mianna, of course, managed to wear her own finery as well as she could, her hair styled elegantly with a gold pin.

Ismaire picked out Malklith's seat at the head of the table and plopped down three seats away from him, leaving room for Albtraum and Mianna. To her annoyance, Albtraum sat next to her.

The servants circled the table serving a clear broth to start the meal. Ismaire detested the way nobility ate their meals – everything divided into courses, too much food at the end of it. By the time she would be finished with the broths and breads, she would have no room in her belly for anything else. Not that she had room for much of anything at all with how tightly cinched the dress was.

"Can I ask something of you, Ismaire?"

Ismaire's eyes darted over to where Albtraum sat beside her. This was perhaps the first time he had ever spoken to her directly. As he politely sipped his soup, he gazed out at the people seated around the table, and Ismaire could see that some of the women sitting opposite them were chattering in hushed tones to each other, casting thinly-veiled gazes at Albtraum.

Resisting the urge to roll her eyes, she answered his question. "What is it?"

"You are immortal. I... I remember that much, from before, when we fought."

Damn. It seemed an eternity ago, and she had almost forgotten how badly he had managed to injure her in their first encounter. Not that any injuries she sustained had mattered in years.

"...Yeah. What of it?"

"Did you die?"

She looked at him again, then, and found herself looking into his eyes – she did not look away, though she wanted to. They were the color of flames, and seemed almost to glow in the light of the chandelier above them.

"What?"

"Like the others. They died before becoming immortal. Did you?"

She looked away from him again. "...No. I didn't." Another thing she felt some manner of guilt over – she hadn't really earned the right, had she?

"How, then?"

"There's this... ability immortals of Mia's rank have. I think she calls it Imbibing. She took my hand in hers, cut our palms, our blood mixed, and... That was that. The wound closed up, and every one I've gotten has ever since. Think they can only do that once... She said something about Chronus asking that she do it, to protect me."

"I see." He nodded. "Well, I am glad you did not have to experience death, then."

He was trying to make conversation, and at first she felt irritated by it... but she remembered that she'd tried to do the same when they had first arrived. It was certainly a topic of much more depth than the weather, as she had brought up... But he was trying all the same.

She had begun to wonder – begrudgingly – if perhaps she *was* wrong about him. He'd had plenty of chances to do all manner of violent and unseemly things – and yet he hadn't. He had been avoiding her, not trying to make trouble – and at the slightest inclination that she was extending an olive branch, he seemed to gladly accept it. His potential motives were becoming more difficult to parse, leaving fewer and fewer possibilities – most of them leaving him, in fact, not a monster at all.

She fell silent as the servants delivered the next course of the meal and Mianna took her seat on the other side of Albtraum, nearest to Malklith.

The low chatter at the table continued on, droning, for some time as the third and fourth courses of the meal were laid out. Ismaire had lost her appetite at the second, but continued to take bites as she could stand it – Mianna, after all, had told her she had to mind her manners.

"So then, Albtraum, Ismaire... how are you liking Nerea?"

"Oh, it's wonderful," Ismaire said with as much feigned enthusiasm as she could muster.

Albtraum nodded. "Yes, certainly like nothing I've seen before. Sylva simply does not compare."

Malklith sipped at his wine, humming his agreement. "It is a shame, because Sylva could be as great as Nerea – it is a *larger* kingdom, in fact, so there is no reason the estate should not be as splendorous – perhaps even more, if Mianna can conduct herself in the right way." He smirked in Mianna's direction, and Ismaire felt a strong desire to shove his face into his food.

Mianna gave an affected sigh. Were she not a queen, she may have acted on the stage, Ismaire thought. "You are right, of course. In fact..." She sighed, and Ismaire's eyes widened as she saw that Mianna's glistened in the candlelight. *Tears?*

"When Ismaire first came to us in Sylva, we could not even feed her the proper meals a royal ward should expect. Yes, she ate nothing but pierogis for weeks." Her voice quivered.

Ismaire could have snorted at that – she'd eaten pierogis for weeks entirely by choice, because they reminded her of the goat cheese and flat breads she'd eaten as a child. But then, she supposed the best lies were half-truths.

"Yes, and it was the same when I first came to Sylva as well," Albtraum murmured. *You too, Bonehead?*

"Well, Mianna did the best she could, certainly," Malklith said, his tone agreeable but dripping with scathing judgement.

The table went back to idle chatter, and the meal continued. Ismaire was glad when they finally came to the lamb roast, which she'd saved the barest amount of room for, but by the time they got to the tarts for dessert, she was too full to eat.

Albtraum had left scraps on his plate for most of the courses, but he'd inhaled the tarts, and sat looking longingly at the ones left untouched on Ismaire's plate.

Raising an eyebrow, she pushed the delicate saucer toward at him. "Go ahead," she grumbled.

He seemed genuinely surprised. "Oh. Thank you."

She scowled to herself – she could scarcely see him as the monster any longer as he happily devoured fruit tarts and left the corners of his mouth stained with berries.

She agreed with herself that, for the moment... perhaps she no longer had the need to watch him so closely. Perhaps she could give him a chance... as Mianna had, once, for Ismaire herself.

When the meal had finished and Albtraum was feeling more unnecessarily stuffed than he ever had in his life, Malklith and his wife, along with a small group of nobles, led them to a spacious sitting room where the servants continued to serve wine.

They talked at length about all manner of things that seemed entirely inconsequential, and Albtraum found himself quite lost in the conversation, constantly looking over to Mianna for guidance – but finding her equally glassy-eyed and disinterested.

"We may make a trip to Sylva in the springtime to see what you can do with Nerea's assistance," Malklith said to Mianna, gesturing to her and almost pouring his wine onto the fur carpets beneath them.

Mianna gave a tight smile. "But of course. The spring air would be good for Elemnestra and the baby too, I am certain."

Ismaire silently drank her wine, peering out over the edge of the glass with perpetually narrowed eyes. She was not concealing her displeasure well… but luckily, no one seemed to have taken notice, the nobles laughing loudly at some joke Malklith had made.

Elemnestra caught Mianna's attention, prompting her to step off to the side where they could converse more easily – and leaving Albtraum fully alone. Feeling somewhat helpless, he looked back and forth from Mianna to Malklith – and ultimately settled on Malklith. He could not rely on Mianna forever… He had to demonstrate some degree of self-sufficiency.

"Ah, Albtraum, you've not had proper conversation with men of your station before," Malklith barked, his words slurring together ever so slightly. "Come, join us."

Albtraum nodded and sat opposite him and two other noble men who seemed to be equally intoxicated.

"You seem to be the only one here with any sense. Tell me, you don't support Mianna's ridiculous bids for war, do you?"

Albtraum found himself bristling with irritation – but he did not want to jeopardize the support they stood to gain.

"To be truthful, I cannot say. I do not know enough about it. My battle has been internal."

"Ah, right, right. You're the host of Lucifurius, are you? Tell me, how *does* it feel to be host to the Lord of all Daemons?" Malklith leaned in closer, and Albtraum could smell the wine on his breath.

"I... I am not sure I would know how to explain it... this has been my reality as long as I have memory."

And you are a fool to so fervently seek the unknown of a life beyond me.

"*Bah,* you're no fun." Malklith waved him off.

Albtraum feared that perhaps he was losing Malklith's attention – and support, by extension – so he cleared his throat to speak up again.

"So, ah... Admittedly, Sylva has been my first experience dealing with the inner workings of a kingdom... Nerea is obviously quite different. Perhaps you could explain why?"

That certainly seemed to pique his interest, and he leaned back over. "Well, in truth – Ceallach here, my treasurer, is better equipped to answer that." He gestured to the man sitting beside him – he was reedy and dark-haired, wine glass gripped precariously between bony fingers.

The man cleared his throat. "In short, proper taxation of a kingdom's citizens. It is well known among the Order that Mianna has never kept a proper head about her shoulders – seeing things always from the perspective of the peasant—"

"Because she is one. Let us not mince words." Malklith scoffed, casting a scathing look in Mianna's direction. Albtraum took a breath to steady himself.

"Regardless," Ceallach continued, "she has given far too much power to those beneath her. She believes she may foster loyalty by allowing her subjects to keep much of what is owed to her station."

"And that is why," Malklith interjected, "Sylva's estate looks the way it does. Poor boy, you've never had the proper treatment your class demands."

"Mmh." Albtraum's gaze wandered over to Mianna, who met his eyes with a knowing frown and slight raise of an eyebrow as Elemnestra continued to chatter on. "So then – proper taxation is the way you've funded all this? Are you not concerned your subjects may find this unfair?"

Malklith scoffed. "Of course not. Good God, we should discuss extending your stay here in Nerea – if only to clear out the utter *nonsense* Mianna has been filling your head with. No, of course they do not consider it *unfair*. Sylva's countrymen may, because for nigh on a century they have been allowed to have that which they have no right to. It is the duty of those of a lower station to serve their betters – and the people of Sylva have long since forgotten that. And look where it has left that wretched kingdom." Malklith was no longer speaking in hushed tones, his voice was certainly loud enough for Mianna to hear.

When Albtraum glanced back at her – partly to subtly signal to Malklith that perhaps he should keep his voice down if he planned to speak with such open offensiveness about Mianna's kingdom, and partly to gage her reaction – he was surprised to see her watching Malklith with mild amusement, swirling the wine in her hand.

She had no reason to be offended, of course. Malklith's words were utterly empty, flatly untrue. And yet Albtraum himself could not keep an acute defensiveness from rising in his chest, threatening to burst out into some of the more colorful insults he'd picked up from Joaquin. The man was everything Machiavelli had described in *The Prince* – selfish, cruel, and dominating.

"Well," Albtraum finally replied, trying to keep the strain in his voice from sounding too obvious, "Perhaps your monetary assistance will show Mianna what she has been missing, and motivate her to pursue the correct path."

"We can only hope," Malklith said finally, sounding exhausted.

The conversation had begun to die down – and the sun had long since set. Albtraum hoped they would perhaps be retiring for the evening soon – he wanted nothing more than to strip the uncomfortable coat from his body, with its irritating seams and too-short sleeves.

He saw a servant approach him – a young man, perhaps younger than himself – and he bowed his head before gesturing to Albtraum's empty glass. "More wine, my lord?"

He weighed the consideration, furrowing his brow. "Yes, thank you." He held out his glass to be filled, frowning as he noticed the boy's hands shaking. The flow of the wine slipped over the edge of the glass ever so slightly – a minor error resulting in only a drop of wine falling to the pad of Albtraum's thumb – but he'd scarcely felt the warmth of the liquid on his skin before the boy seemingly panicked, dropping the entire pitcher into Albtraum's lap.

The wine splashed everywhere – nearly soaking him entirely. It was warm – a warmth that was nauseatingly familiar.

Ah...

Albtraum sat frozen, his breath hitching in his throat as once-distant recollections surfaced close enough he felt drowned by them. Blood. Death. The endless presence of Lucifurius, everywhere he turned. There was a look of horror on the face of the servant – did he know, somehow? Could he sense this?

There is a knife on the table behind you, you saw it when you stepped inside. But you've no need of a weapon... Join with me again... and we can kill every one of them with our bare hands.

Albtraum merely sat motionless, his eyes wide and unfocused, his limbs devoid of feeling. The servant stammered something – an apology? He could not tell—

Something shattered the haze that had enveloped him – the voice of the treasurer, Ceallach.

"You useless goddamn lout!" he roared, and there was the heavy sound of a blow against flesh, a yelp – and the servant felt to the floor. Ceallach had taken the pitcher from Albtraum's lap and beaten the servant over the head with it.

Control snapped back to Albtraum's body, and he swiftly stood, watching as Ceallach readied to strike the servant again. Malklith watched with complete detachment, and Albtraum could already hear the sound of Mianna and Ismaire's footsteps as they scrambled over.

The man's earlier aloof demeanor had morphed into an ugly snarl, and Albtraum scarcely had time to consider what he was doing before he caught Ceallach's arm, twisting it to the side and shoving him against the wall. The pitcher clattered to the floor with a clang. Ceallach screamed.

This one. He is cruel even to other humans, yes? A pitiful waste. Surely his death would be a boon to your miserable human world. All you must do is break his worthless neck.

Albtraum gripped Ceallach's arm tight in his fist, hard enough to bruise. The man's expression had again morphed – this time to fear. Albtraum stood face to face with him – not even daring to breathe – for a long moment before roughly pushing away from him, sending him tumbling to the ground as Albtraum took several steps back.

He breathed again – too fast. Panicked. The servant still cowered on the floor, peering out from behind his own defensively raised arms.

Albtraum felt his own heavy breaths nearly forming into sobs, tears prickling at the corners of his eyes. A hand brushed his arm, and his gaze snapped that direction – Mianna.

"It's alright, Albtraum." Her voice was quiet, soothing.

Malklith was laughing – the sound was sharp and infuriating. "You've still got much to learn, clearly – concerning yourself with the plight of a damn servant. Mianna really has turned everything in your head to mush, hasn't she?"

Albtraum swallowed hard. His throat had never felt so dry. “Mianna, I am sorry, I must take my leave for the night.”

She patted his arm reassuringly. “Of course. Send a servant to find me if you should need anything.”

He nodded once, and rushed out of the room. The wine soaking his clothes had grown cold in the night air. He wandered half-aware for some time, making several wrong turns, before he once again stood before the door of the room he’d been given to stay in. The gilded door loomed over him in hideous mockery as he rushed inside it, slamming it behind him and collapsing to his knees on the floor, finally letting out the strangled sobs he’d been holding in.

You cannot keep this up forever, child.

It must have been mid-morning when Albtraum finally awoke, signaled by the rays of sun that had crept across the floor to settle on his face.

He sat up, rubbing the sleep from his eyes and the ache from his neck. He’d not even made it to his bed – and he was still in his clothes from the night before. The wine had dried stiff, staining the yellow satin of the overcoat.

He clumsily undid the fastenings of the coat, pulling it off with a huff before stepping back over to where the trunk of his belongings had been left, his own clothes neatly folded on top of it. He was glad that the wine had not ruined his own clothes, but even if it had, it was no reason for Ceallach to attack the boy as he had.

Albtraum changed back into his clothes, leaving the others in a crumpled heap on the floor, much how he'd slept the previous night. His head felt full of thick fog.

He grimaced at himself in the mirror – his hair was unruly, his eyes ringed with dark circles. He did his best to comb out the tangles and splashed some water on his face from the basin in hopes of banishing his apparent exhaustion.

Cautiously, he opened his door – No one stood directly outside his door, though there was a servant at the head of the hallway – an older woman with streaks of gray in her hair.

He approached her carefully, trying to make his footfalls heavy enough that the sound of his footsteps would be obvious. The last thing he needed was anyone else to be afraid of him. He cleared his throat quietly, and she turned around.

"Excuse me," he murmured. "Where might Mianna have gone?"

The woman did not seem afraid of him. Perhaps no one had warned her about him. "The Queen? I believe she went to the tearoom. It is down the hall that way." She pointed him in the correct direction.

Albtraum nodded. "Thank you."

He walked with purpose, passing a few people along the way who gave him curious looks. He did his best not to meet their eyes. Eventually, he came to what he assumed was the tearoom, as Mianna sat inside, thumbing through a book.

"Mianna," he said in greeting, stepping inside.

She looked up, seeming somewhat startled. "Oh, Albtraum! Are you alright?"

He nodded, stepping over to where she sat. "I... I believe so. Please... forgive me, this is the second time in a row I have embarrassed you..."

Mianna was quick to cut him off. "Please do not apologize."

"I felt I must. I do not even have Lucifurius to blame for my outburst this time..."

Her brow furrowed. Her expression was impossible to read. "I... No, I did not think that he was. And still, you have no need to apologize." Something in her tone sounded... relieved.

"I will apologize to Malklith eventually, I swear it," he said solemnly. "But now, I... need some time away from this place, to clear my thoughts. I am afraid I would come across quite uncharitable now if I tried to speak to Malklith."

Mianna sighed, a slight smile quirking up her lips. "I can hardly fault you for that."

"So then, by your leave, I would like to spend a today in the guest estate."

"You'll hear no objections from me. Ismaire also wished to spend her day in the market, so I'll have sufficient reasoning to complain to Malklith that he's made the two of you feel quite unwelcome." She set aside the book in her hands, and he glimpsed he cover – *Discourses on Livy*. He smirked slightly. "That man – Ceallach – his behavior was reprehensible, even Malklith must see that."

Albtraum's voice fell to a murmur. "Yes... I was quite shocked."

"Well, do tell the others I said hello, and please thank them on my behalf for so admirably putting up with Malklith's nonsense. I shall see you tomorrow, then."

"Yes. Thank you, Mianna."

Albtraum left the tearoom to retrieve his trunk from the bedroom – it was heavy, but not unmanageable. The rest of his belongings were with the servants, he supposed.

As he neared the main door, he ran across Ismaire. Her eyes widened as she saw him.

"Oh. You leaving too, Bonehead?" It irked him that she still insisted on such a juvenile nickname, but he put aside his irritation.

"Yes, I fear I will jeopardize our goals even further if I have to face Malklith again at the moment."

Her eyebrows raised once in agreement. "Yeah, I'm feeling much the same. It... It was good... what you did back there, I mean. Starting to maybe change my mind about you."

He tried not to grin too widely at that, but was unable to keep at least a slight smile from his face. "I do understand why you haven't trusted me, but... Truly, I do not mean you or Sylva any harm. I consider it my home and my people."

She huffed. "Yeah... Don't push it. See you." With that, she brushed past him, disappearing around a corner.

It seemed progress had at last been made.

At that, he continued his trek to the exit, a man he assumed was a soldier stopping him as he reached the massive gate. His clothes were particularly flashy for a guard, and did not seem to offer much protection – or maneuverability.

"My Lord," the man said quickly. "You are not due to leave this place for some time yet, I thought."

"I am simply going to spend some time at the guest estate," Albtraum answered.

The guard seemed quite confused. "Ah, well... Allow me to escort you, then."

Albtraum thanked him, and followed after the man as they walked down the cobbled path that led to the estate. He had not offered to help with the trunk – but Albtraum was mostly unbothered by this. If the man were to assume Albtraum was the same as any of the other nobles here... he could not blame him for not wanting to put in more effort to help than strictly necessary.

The man left Albtraum at the door to the guest estate. It was much more modest than the palace – but still far more elaborately decorated than it needed to be.

He stepped inside – the windows in the hall were open, and a cool breeze was blowing in.

"Hello," he called, setting his trunk on the floor and shutting the door behind him. He could hear the skittering of claws on the stone floor – and Renegade burst out from an open doorway to run toward him.

Albtraum laughed, crouching to greet the dog, rubbing between his ears as he whined happily in greeting. He looked up, finding Joaquin had stepped out as well.

"Albtraum! I was not expecting to see you today."

"I hope I am not intruding." He stood once again as Joaquin embraced him in greeting.

"Not at all, dear boy. Is everything alright, though? You look positively terrible." He patted Albtraum's cheek.

Albtraum gave a deep sigh. "Truthfully... No, I am afraid." He shook his head. "There was an... incident, last night, I lost my temper with Malklith's treasurer after he assaulted a servant for accidentally spilling the wine. I tried to hold myself back, but.... The lot of them are truly insufferable, Malklith most of all. I threw the treasurer to the ground."

Joaquin's white-streaked eyebrows raised. "Even *I* would not consider physical violence over wine. Perhaps you could have restrained yourself more, but... It sounds as though the man got what he deserved. Surely even Malklith can understand that."

"I hope he will. But I cannot face him just yet. I cannot stand being in that place, and... hearing the awful things he keeps saying about Sylva, and Mianna."

"I've been fortunate enough that I've never properly conversed with the man, though from all I've heard, I imagine a bed of thistle might make for better company."

"Truly." Albtraum huffed. He finally followed Joaquin into the guest quarters – and they were much more pleasant than the palace had been, with doors leading out to a balcony that overlooked the cliffs that dropped off to the sea below. Doors to the bedrooms were open, revealing them to be empty. “Where has everyone gone?”

“Brunhart took some of the guards to the market – I suppose Noman got the idea in his head to cook something for us tonight.” Joaquin chuckled.

“That sounds wonderful. For now, however, I should like nothing more than a long nap with a window open, so I can sleep to the sound of the ocean.”

“That, we can certainly give you. Come along.”

Joaquin led Albtraum to an unused room, and he promptly flopped into the bed. The linens smelled slightly stale, it had clearly been some time since they’d been used. But it was far better than a gilded marble floor, and he soon found himself drifting off to sleep.

Chapter XXVIII

Brunhart was sitting against the wall with a block of cedar in his hands, whittling away at it absentmindedly. It had been a while since he'd done any wood carving, and he was glad to have the time to indulge in an old hobby and listen to the sound of the waves crashing against the rocks below.

Albtraum was standing at the balcony, looking out over the sea. He had been quiet for a while now – Brunhart had questioned him about what had gone on with Malklith, why he was here – but he'd been hesitant to speak on it.

Up on the top floor of the estate, they were mostly isolated from the low chatter of the men downstairs as they assisted Noman with the stew he had taken it upon himself to make – although the occasional burst of laughter or shouted word rose up to them from time to time. Joaquin had himself gone to the nearby market to look for more materials, promising he would return in time for dinner.

Brunhart was always happy for Albtraum to have more time spent away from business – he wanted him to have as much time as possible to spend behaving as an ordinary young man, and not endlessly worrying over the fate of the world, politics, and diplomacy.

"Enjoying yourself there, pup?" Brunhart asked over his shoulder. Albtraum was just out of his view from where he sat.

"It's much better to look at when you're not being rocked about," he answered quietly, his voice slightly muffled by the wind.

Brunhart chuckled. "Never much cared for ships or ocean travel myself."

He continued to work on the wood block, unsure of what, exactly, he was carving. Sometimes he had to find it along the way. "I know Joaquin has likely been pestering you about it, but I haven't had the chance to speak with you about things are progressing with Mianna."

Albtraum sighed. "Truthfully, I am not sure. This may be a fool's errand... But I believe we've become good friends, at the least."

Brunhart raised an eyebrow. "Well, she'd be a fool not to have you. If she can't see that, she doesn't deserve to have you."

A few more moments of silence stretched on before Albtraum spoke up again. "You spoke of your wife before. What was she like? How did you meet?"

Brunhart stopped carving for a moment as he considered Albtraum's question. The memories of his life before immortality were old and dull, but they did still ache to recall. Still, he could not deny Albtraum's curiosity.

"I was working my family's farm, and she'd always come by to buy the milk I got from my cows," he answered. "I was unfriendly to her, as I was to everyone, but she persisted trying to converse with me every time she paid me a visit. Eventually, I realized I wanted her there with me always. We married not long after that."

Brunhart felt a smile form as he went back to carving. "Her name was Anya. She was the only reason I ever spoke to anyone in that village, though I'd lived there my whole life... Dragged me out and forced me to socialize. She was a kind soul. Always looking out for everyone else. She'd have liked you, I think."

"Really?" Albtraum asked, sounding genuinely surprised.

"Of course," Brunhart replied gently. His hands slowed in their work as thoughts that had been lingering in the depths of his subconscious for quite some time rose to the forefront of his mind.

He considered how to word his feelings before going on. "You know, Albtraum... I find myself often thinking that had our child been born, it... Might have been someone quite like you."

Albtraum's voice was barely audible. "You think that? Truly?"

Brunhart found himself nodding, though Albtraum could not see him from where he stood. "Truly. After all this, you know... I've come to think of you as my own son."

Brunhart set aside the block and listened over his shoulder, eager for Albtraum's response.

Some foolish part of him hoped that perhaps Albtraum might change his mind about Mianna's cause so that he could properly raise him, keeping him away from the burdens of otherworldly politics. He wanted life to be simple again, to be quiet and carefree, and Albtraum deserved that above all else.

But he knew that this cause was important... and it had given Albtraum a sense of purpose.

But as he waited, all he was met with was a thud and a startled yelp from Albtraum.

Brunhart's blood froze in his veins.

The wood block in his hand clattered to the floor as he leapt to his feet, rushing around the wall to the balcony –

Albtraum was no longer standing there – and in his place, a dark-skinned man dressed in dark, ragged clothes.

Brunhart recognized him as the man they had encountered in the port town – the world seemed to go out of focus around him as he pieced together what had undoubtedly just happened. In a reflex of pure instinct, he hurled the carving knife in his hand at the man. It hit him squarely in the eye, and he staggered back, but did not fall.

Brunhart swore as the man pulled the blade from his eye and the wound healed instantly – he was immortal, no doubt. The two of them stood frozen, each waiting for the other to move. The man bolted.

Brunhart considered, for a fraction of a second, whether to go after him before deciding that Albtraum was infinitely more important. He lurched over to the edge of the balcony, looking down – his heart sank. He could not make out any sign of Albtraum through the foaming waves crashing against the rocks below.

His heart pounding with fear, Brunhart turned on his heel and ran as quickly as he could down the stairs and out the main door, ignoring the startled and inquisitive looks of the Sylvans he passed by.

Once he'd made it outside, he dashed around the building, stumbling down to the crags that sloped to the sea. It was steep – and a long, *long* way down.

There was no time for caution – so rather than carefully climb down, he jumped.

He let out only the barest grunt as he landed and felt a bone – or perhaps two – snap in his leg. He had to wait only the briefest moment for the broken bones to right themselves before he sprinted straight to the choppy waters crashing on the rocky shore.

He looked up, panting hard – he was directly under the balcony Albtraum had been thrown from. Desperate, panicking, he whirled around in place, searching for any sign of him, reaching down and feeling through the water.

His head snapped up as a flash of red caught his eye – Albtraum, caught in a wave, hanging just under the water's surface.

In water too deep to move quickly, Brunhart stumbled over to him, hauling him up out of the water. He was unconscious. A deep gash in his forehead oozed blood, quickened by the seawater dripping off of him.

Fast as he could, Brunhart made for the shore, holding tightly to Albtraum's inert form. He tripped, nearly falling, as he reached the shore, bogged down by his soaking wet clothes and Albtraum's weight in his arms.

He fumbled as he dropped Albtraum onto the rocks of the shore out of the water's reach, looking him over.

His chest seized with terror – Albtraum did not seem to be breathing.

Instinct took over and Brunhart rolled him over, facedown, thumping his back with the heel of his hand – hard enough to hurt, but he had to make him breathe.

Time was agonizing. The thought finally reached him – he hadn't been fast enough, the fall was too great...

But then Albtraum coughed and spluttered, gasping as seawater and blood poured from his mouth onto the rocks. He tried to push himself up, but weakly grunted, crumpling back in on himself.

"What happened...?"

"It's alright," Brunhart answered hoarsely, helping pull him to his feet. Relief flooded him, weakening his knees – the last thing he needed right now. "Never you mind. It's alright, I've got you." Albtraum struggled to stand, so Brunhart easily hefted him onto his back.

He carefully climbed the steep hill to the path, rushing straight to the palace. No one in the guest house could provide Albtraum with the medical attention he needed.

"Captain?" he heard someone shout ahead of him, alarmed. Edmund. "Captain, what's – is he alright?"

"Where is the assassin?" Brunhart demanded without answering, carefully shifting Albtraum on his back to better hold him.

"We only got a glimpse of him, he rushed out so fast, and then you—"

"Do not stand there, *go after him!*" Brunhart shouted, and Edmund did not wait to be told anything else.

When he finally reached the gate, the guards stepped in front of him. "Good sir, you are not permitted within the estate walls, as I'm sure you've been informed," one of the armor-clad men said, holding up a hand to stop him. "State your business."

"State my business?!" he snapped back. He was dripping with seawater, his mouth in a snarl, he must have looked half mad. "My boy's been injured, are you blind?!"

"You aren't permitted to enter the estate," the other repeated more firmly.

Brunhart shoved past the men, who seemed at a loss for what to do, into the foyer. "Get me someone to see to him. *Now!*"

The guards nervously scampered off, and Brunhart stood, huffing in frustration, though his anger melted into worry as the atmosphere fell silent, and there were no sounds left to drown out Albtraum's pained moaning. They were both soaked to the bone, and the air in the room was cold. Albtraum shivered.

"We'll get you taken care of, don't you worry," Brunhart murmured, tone softening again.

After what seemed a veritable eternity, Malklith entered the foyer, Mianna following close behind. Her eyes widened as she took in the sight before her. "What's happened?!" She rushed forward to meet them.

"Someone pushed him over the balcony," Brunhart explained. "Immortal. Someone who knows us. He escaped." He shook his head. "I am unsure how badly hurt he is, but it is not good."

Malklith stared at them – with hardly the concern or interest Brunhart might have thought appropriate for the sight of his noble guest having narrowly escaped death. "I shall send a doctor to the guest house. You take him and head on back there—"

"So your guards can allow in another fucking *assassin?!"* Mianna spat at him.

Malklith regarded her with his eyes narrowed, incensed – as though he'd witnessed outrageous behavior from an unruly child.

"None of your doctors will see him. I have knowledge of healing – I'll tend him myself."

Brunhart bristled at that – he questioned if Mianna's medical knowledge was sufficient, but... His disdain and distrust for Malklith meant that his doctors, whoever they may be, hardly seemed a better option.

Mianna huffed, her voice strained as she spoke to Brunhart. "Come, let us get him to my quarters."

Malklith scoffed at her. "Do as you wish. But you intend to share your bed with him? That is *hardly* proper."

Mianna turned back sharply on her heel to face him once more – her gaze was fire and poison.

"*Fuck* your propriety."

As they made their way to Mianna's room, Brunhart cast one final glance over his shoulder, finding Malklith staring after them with the seething gaze of a hunter who'd missed his mark.

Mianna rushed into her bedroom ahead of Brunhart, clearing away the extra pillows so that Albtraum could more easily be laid down. Servants hovered at the doorway curiously, peering after them.

"I'll need some bandages," Mianna instructed them sharply. "More blankets, and wine for the pain. Quickly!"

The girls scampered away quickly, hastened by her tone. She huffed as Brunhart crossed the room to set Albtraum down on the bed. Albtraum stirred and winced as he did so.

There was an ugly gash at the side of his forehead, bleeding freely. His breaths came ragged and labored, his right arm hanging limply at his side. He shivered again, letting out a hitched breath of pain as he did.

Mianna nodded to Brunhart. "First thing, we've got to get him out of these wet clothes. Help me."

Joaquin's designs were made to be layered, making them comfortable and versatile, but Mianna was cursing his fine work now as they struggled to get each layer off of Albtraum without causing him more pain. Brunhart mumbled encouragement to him as they went, but Mianna wasn't sure Albtraum was conscious enough to comprehend it, and Brunhart sounded too panicked and unsure of himself to be comforting.

Mianna's alarm only increased when they'd managed to strip Albtraum down to only his smallclothes – a massive, dark bruise had spread across almost all of his side, stretching down the full length of his ribcage.

Brunhart ran a hand through his hair, cursing at the sight. "He must have hit the crags on the way down—God, it was such a long way..."

Mianna took a breath, motioning for him to stand back as she helped Albtraum roll flat on his back. "Bad as this looks, it may have slowed his fall and saved his life." Gingerly, she felt along his sides for breaks. His skin felt damp and cold from the water, and she could feel the swelling of fractured bones already beginning under his skin. Albtraum writhed, vocally objecting as she touched him, and she breathed a curse.

It had been over a century since she'd worked as a healer – from time to time she would observe Aleksandra, or even go so far as to assist with her work, when she had the leisure time for it – she had thought perhaps her skills had faded, but it felt natural to settle back into the role of a healer. Her mild panic had sharpened her senses and added quick precision to her movements.

Brunhart watched her intently, fists clenched tightly. The servants had started to file in behind him.

"Is he going to be alright?" he asked, his voice tight with worry.

Mianna sighed, looking down at Albtraum as he tensed and shifted in agony.

"Well... It doesn't seem he has a single rib left unbroken, his injuries are certainly serious... But he is alive, and that I can work with."

Brunhart only stared back at her, looking more distressed than she'd ever seen him. He circled to the opposite side of the bed from where Mianna stood, carefully taking hold of Albtraum's hand. Albtraum seemed calmer, if only slightly, in Brunhart's presence, as his shallow, sharp breaths became more even and consistent. Mianna stood watching Brunhart look down at Albtraum, beside himself with concern.

One of the servants approached and handed her a cloth, and she accepted it and dabbed at the bleeding gash in Albtraum's forehead. The flow of blood had slowed, but not as much as she would have liked. There was little she could do to treat his broken ribs, so she turned her attention to his shoulder, feeling around the parts that were twisted and swollen. Albtraum gritted his teeth and groaned as she did.

Gently, she spoke up. "Brunhart, I don't believe there's anything more you can assist me with, and you are only going to worry yourself sick if you remain here. I have all I need to tend to Albtraum. Your efforts would be better spent attempting to track down the person who did this."

Brunhart looked immensely torn, holding tighter to Albtraum's hand. He finally looked back to Mianna and gave a single nod before returning his attention to Albtraum.

"I've got to take care of something," he muttered carefully, smoothing back the wet hair from Albtraum's face. "I'll return as soon as I'm able, pup. Mianna will be sure you're properly tended too."

Albtraum's eyes fluttered half-open, and he groaned.

"Brunhart... before... did you... mean what you said? Truly?"

Brunhart's brow knit in confusion for a brief moment before he seemed to understand. "...Of course. I am more than certain you are the child I was meant to have. Even more reason I need you to endure this."

Albtraum nodded weakly before slipping into unconsciousness again. Brunhart hesitantly let go of his hand, crossing the room to the doorway.

He turned tersely to Mianna. "Have someone notify me if he worsens in any way at all."

She nodded to him, starting to shut the door as he left. "Of course."

When Brunhart had gone, she turned back to Albtraum, sighing. She waved over the servant girl who held the decanter of wine.

"Would you pour me some?" she asked.

The girl nodded, and did so eagerly – her expression twisting in confusion as Mianna sipped from it herself. She allowed the taste to settle over her tongue – it was merely wine.

Gently, she sat Albtraum up, sliding one of the extra pillows under him to support him. She patted the side of his face to wake him.

"Albtraum, I've got some wine here for you to drink. It will help with your pain."

Albtraum mumbled something unintelligible as she brought the cup to his mouth, and he drank, clumsy, wine dripping over the cup's edge. He grew less clumsy as she gave him a second cup, and then a third, before taking hold of his arm and shoulder.

"This will be quite painful. I apologize."

Just as Mianna felt the slight pop that told her she'd moved his arm back into its socket, Albtraum cried out, tears forming in his eyes as the sounds of his pain died down to whimpers. His shoulder was set normally again, though a dark bruise had formed around it. Mianna gave him another drink of the wine, then bandaged the gash on his forehead.

Albtraum had settled back into shallow but steady breathing. Mianna looked over him once again, searching for any other injury she could treat, feeling his torso for other wounds. His skin was covered in freckles, so many they looked like stars scattered in the night sky. Her hand brushed across the faint scars of his old wounds, faded to barely visible pinkish lines. It seemed so long ago now that he'd been a wild beast come to their door.

Determining she had done all she could, she layered the blankets the servants had brought over him.

"He needs to rest," she said to the servants. "I will send for you all if I should require anything else. You are dismissed."

The girls all bowed and filed out of the room. As they were leaving, Mianna noticed a Nerean guard standing in the doorway, peering in.

"Your Majesty," the man started, "A rather large portion of your guard has gathered at the gate and are asking of the ward's condition. There is—"

The man started and backed away as Joaquin shoved past him, throwing up his hands, looking furious. "Honestly, the nerve of you people! One of our own gravely injured and I have to force my way in just to learn anything of his condition!" His expression softened as he entered the room and rushed straight to Albtraum's side, not even seeming to notice Mianna standing there.

"My boy, what's happened?" Joaquin asked gently, kneeling at the bedside, stroking Albtraum's head.

Albtraum groaned and stirred. "Fell... from the balcony," he mumbled, before seeming to slip back into half-sleep.

"Pushed," Mianna corrected as Joaquin looked back to her for clarification. "I believe he will be alright. He just needs to rest and heal now."

Joaquin stood again, frowning. "Have we any idea who's done this?"

She glanced over her shoulder at the Nerean guard still standing there. "We will discuss that later. Brunhart has gone to search for the assailant."

Joaquin looked out the window gravely. "I will search as well. More eyes will make faster work." He sighed. "Our men are all quite worried since they heard he was hurt."

"Well, you can tell them he is resting safely here with me," Mianna replied, sitting down at the end of the bed.

“Good. See to it that no harm comes to him here,” Joaquin said briefly, an edge of concern in his voice.

“I will,” Mianna responded with a solemn nod, watching as Joaquin stepped out of the room, shutting the door and leaving her alone with Albtraum.

The room was silent but for Albtraum’s labored breathing, and Mianna moved to sit closer to him, watching him as he rested fitfully, his brow furrowed with lingering pain. The blankets were rumpled over his tall, slender frame, tangled into a mess by his shifting.

Sympathy for him crept its way into the edges of her heart. Gently, she reached out to touch his face to rouse him again, and his eyes half-opened to look at her. She reached across him for the wine, bringing it up for him to drink once again.

“Thank you,” he mumbled once he’d finished drinking.

“Of course,” she answered quietly with a small smile. “Joaquin, Brunhart, and the guards are all quite concerned for you, you gave them quite a scare.”

He breathed out a rough sound that might have been a laugh. “I’m fine.”

“Not to mention you’ve frightened me as well...” She reached out to brush his hair from his forehead again, but found herself hesitating.

He blinked slowly at her. “Have I?”

Her hand hung in the air, and she cleared her throat and checked the bandage on his forehead to busy herself.

“Mianna, I need to tell you something,” Albtraum said quietly, and she looked up at him.

“Yes, what is it? Something more about who attacked you—“

“I love you,” he interrupted. His voice wavered, but his tone was stronger than it had been before.

Mianna blinked back at him, vaguely aware that she was gaping.

“Albtraum... You’ve hit your head quite hard, I don’t know that you know what you’re saying...”

“I do,” he said firmly. “I... I have for quite some time now. You were the first to show me any kindness. And I admire you deeply... I have learned much from you, and when I am with you, any doubts I have as to my humanity are gone. My family... and *you,* are what has made me wish to stand against Lucifurius.”

She stared at him, her mind racing into a blur, unsure of how to feel. When he winced again, she snapped out of her daze and brought her hand to touch his face again.

“Mianna...”

She gently pressed a finger to his lips. “Just rest, Albtraum. I will be here when you wake.”

He nodded at her sleepily, and was asleep again after a few moments.

His confession settled over her like a tidal wave, and she paced the room as he slept, turning it over and over in her mind.

This was far from the first time someone had confessed their love for her. Normally she found it flattering, but quickly dismissed the sentiment. She'd simply never had the desire to be with anyone else in such a way.

So why *now* did she stop to consider it?

Her chest was tight with confusion. She glanced back to Albtraum, her mind a haze of unfamiliar emotion. She watched him as he slept, carefully settling in beside him as the sound of his breathing soon lulled her to sleep herself.

Chapter XXIX

Ismaire had wandered out of the estate for the day, feeling suffocated by the walls and rattled by the events of the day prior. She pulled on a coat and boots to ward off the slight chill of the air and strapped a dagger to her belt in case she encountered any trouble, feeling much more at ease in her own clothes.

No one had stopped her from leaving, even Mianna – she'd seemed agreeable to it, even. Ismaire was glad she would not have to pretend to tolerate the treasurer's foul behavior – nor Malklith's apathetic endorsement of it.

It was somewhat livelier in the town, though the conditions she observed there were surprising. Most of the people *looked* underfed, leading her to wonder just how little they were left with after the nobility had drained away everything they made like a leech.

She glanced down the path to the port, squinting, as she realized she recognized Brunhart among a group of men standing at the gate to the port. He appeared to be questioning them.

He caught sight of her as she approached them. Looking alarmed, he shoved his way out of the cluster of townsfolk to meet her.

"What's happened? Is everything alright?" he all but demanded, looking down at her intently.

She raised an eyebrow back at him. “What do you mean? Why wouldn’t it be?”

Brunhart’s eyes narrowed. “Ah. You don’t know.”

Annoyed, she crossed her arms, following him as he continued up the road, looking through the crowds. “Don’t know what? What’s going on, Brunhart?”

“Albtraum was attacked,” he answered over his shoulder. “I told Mianna to send for me if his condition worsened, and I...” He shook his head.

“No one sent me,” Ismaire replied. “Do you really think Mia would send *me* for something like that?”

Brunhart looked back at her, rolling his eyes.

She huffed. “What happened to Bonehead, though?”

“He was thrown from the balcony of the guest house and nearly drowned,” Brunhart muttered.

“What? By who? Was it the assassin? The one who killed our guards?”

“What else would it have been?” he snapped in response, clearly irritated.

Ismaire recalled something from her girlhood, then. She’d gotten sick from eating fruit that had spoiled, and her father had paced outside their tent, tensed and upset, snapping at anyone who got near him. He was normally quite the jovial man, but the clan all later said it had been the most unfriendly they’d ever seen him, and that he did not so much as smile again until Ismaire had recovered.

Brunhart was nearly always unfriendly, and Ismaire couldn't say she'd ever seen him smile, but he was rarely this tense. It seemed he truly did care for Albtraum.

"Well, I'm sure he's fine. Gods know he's hard to get rid of."

He merely grunted at her.

They continued up the road a ways before Ismaire noticed Joaquin moving in their direction, people parting to let him pass as he picked his way through the crowds.

"Have you found anything?" He asked Brunhart, sparing only a quick glance at Ismaire.

Brunhart shook his head. "Nothing yet. I don't know how he's managed to elude us this far. He can't have left the city without going through the port."

Joaquin huffed and pulled his coat tighter around himself. "Well, I certainly have a *theory* as to why that is... And if we haven't found him by now, I doubt we are going to. We should focus our attention on Albtraum for the time being."

Brunhart considered his suggestion before nodding his approval. "Yes, especially after this has happened... We can't afford to let our guard down anymore."

"It's unfortunate Mianna no longer has the ability to Imbibe," Joaquin sighed. "Though, I suppose you, Ismaire, did seem more prone to danger at the time."

If only you knew the half of it.

She sighed. "I'll keep an eye out for the bastard," she said finally after a moment.

Joaquin seemed somewhat surprised, but he held up a hand and shook his head. "No need, we have enough men searching and the last thing we need is you getting into some kind of trouble as well."

Ismaire opened her mouth to object, but Joaquin had already turned to walk back up the road to the palace, imperiously motioning for her to follow.

Dull, deep pain was the only thing Albtraum was aware of for a time. Though he slept, he could feel the ache of every shallow breath, every unconscious movement.

Lucifurius spoke to him then.

My child, he crooned. *You yet live. I feared I had lost you in that fall... I nearly did.*

There was a strange, primal comfort in the voice enveloping his thoughts. It almost felt as things had been long ago, when Lucifurius guided his every move. For a moment... Albtraum almost forgot the new reality of the past months.

But uneasiness tainted it. He could never truly go back to the way things had been before.

Perhaps you will lose me still.

Surprisingly, *I know I have distanced you. I have pushed you away. But, please, my child... If we unite once more, such injuries as this need not concern you any longer.*

I have heard all of this before.

This time will be different. I swear it. Bind yourself to me once more, and I will protect you.

Albtraum mulled over the suggestion. Danger did not concern him. Pain was not a deterrent.

Lucifurius sensed his hesitation. Panic. *They cannot give you the power they claim you will have. What I can give you is more than an empty promise...*

Power was never what I desired. Not then, and not now.

He woke then, fully, and Lucifurius' frantic efforts to sway him quieted as his eyes opened to the dim light of the room. It was evening, and the sun was setting. He rolled over, pain stabbing into him as he did.

"Careful, Albtraum," Mianna's voice sounded beside him. Very close.

He froze as he came face-to-face with her. He was sure he'd dreamt her being there with him.

And yet here she was. She was dressed only in a vaporous nightgown, bringing his attention to his own state of near-complete undress. He blinked at her, startled and embarrassed.

"You were cold," she gently explained. "So I stayed here with you to lend my own warmth. How are you feeling?"

He swallowed. Even his throat ached. “Hurts,” he croaked. “Everything. It all hurts.”

She frowned sympathetically at him. “I am sure. We are fortunate you survived.”

“Thank you for looking after me,” he said to her. He rolled over again, and she gently caught his arm.

“What are you doing?”

“I’m going back to my room,” he explained. “You’ve done quite enough, and I don’t want to expose you to scandal—“

Mianna scoffed. “Please, Malklith and his nobles are the least of my concerns right now. It’s been a good while since I’ve had a proper scandal – I was just thinking it was about time for one. You should stay here and rest.” She sat up, gazing at him intently. “I’ve considered what you said to me earlier...”

“Earlier...?” Albtraum waded back through the fog of his memory. His dazed confession stood out – *I love you*. He grimaced.

“I... I apologize. I was not in my right mind, I should not have been so forward. I did not intend to put you in an uncomfortable position...”

She laughed softly. “Do not apologize, Albtraum. Though I can’t say yet whether I return the intensity of your feelings.”

He felt his heart clutch up, and a lump form in his throat. “Ah. I see.”

You see, nothing can ever match the bond between us. Return to me, my child.

"Hold on, now," she muttered, leaning closer to him. "What's that look of defeat for? Though your feelings may not match my own, I do relish the thought of courtship. Life becomes so dull when I only ever involve myself in politics."

He stared back at her. "Courtship?"

"We shall spend our days together and act as partners to see if the arrangement suits us. I haven't held someone's affections in quite some time, and it would do you well to practice these matters yourself."

Practice. It seemed she had already doomed anything between them. He fought to keep the disappointment from his face. "If that is what you wish."

"You need not be so businesslike about it!" she teased, twirling her finger around a strand of his hair. "Part of courtship is being able to share affections on a more intimate level... That we might feel more comfortable dispensing with formalities and being our true selves."

Though he was disappointed that she hadn't reciprocated his confession, he could not help but feel pleased to be closer to her, if only a minute amount more. "I know nothing of these matters, I'm afraid. What else is involved in this sort of arrangement?"

She did not answer him with words. Instead, he found her mouth pressed close against his.

He yelped in surprise and tensed, sending a wave of pain through his torso – but as she pulled him in deeper, his shoulders relaxed, and he melted back into the pillows. Lucifurius seemed to be numb. He said nothing. His very presence in Albtraum's mind seemed to turn icy.

He'd read stories of love and longing, usually finding them to be overblown and saccharine affairs he'd scoff and skim past, but this was worlds different. For a moment, he almost forgot about the many aches and pains that gripped his whole body.

He did not have anything to compare to, so he had no real way of knowing if all kisses were as soft and gentle and vaguely damp as this, but he liked the idea that they weren't. That Mianna had some sort of benign magic in her that made her this intoxicating.

Mianna smiled when she pulled back. Her chestnut hair fell over her shoulders in soft waves. "My, you look taken by surprise."

"I... have been," he replied, flustered. "I must confess, I was not expecting this outcome in the slightest."

She smoothed his hair away from his face, her hands dainty and gentle. "Romances between Order members are not traditionally allowed... but with the world in the state it is I believe we can afford to ignore some of the more... bothersome traditions."

Slowly, he reached for her hand, nervous and trembling. She laced her fingers through his.

"You have become a fine man, Albtraum. I will be glad to call you mine for a time." She settled in beside him, still holding his hand.

His eyelids grew heavy again. "Mianna..."

"You should sleep, darling."

He curled closer to her, hesitant to get too close, still feeling that all this was not quite real. "Will you still be here when I wake?"

She smiled, leaning in closer, touching the tips of their noses together. "Of course."

Albtraum weaved in and out of consciousness for the next several days. This seemed to be to stave off the pain of his injuries, though Lucifurius' uneasiness kept him from gaining any real rest. He talked with Mianna in his waking moments, and she remained at his side, reading to pass the time while he slept.

For the time, he was awake, and more alert than he'd been since before his fall.

"I thought that perhaps you might enjoy studying at the university in Sylva once we return," she said to him as she brushed out her hair to dress for the day.

"Will I have time to do that? It seems as though there will be many other things I will need to do once we return, if I am to take the throne of the dark world."

"We shall have to make time for it. A proper education will be crucial to your success." She shed her nightgown, and Albtraum heard her laughing to herself as he awkwardly averted his gaze. "Though you are already leaps and bounds ahead of many rulers already sitting on a throne. I've quite enjoyed your company these past months, you know. It's refreshing to have someone else to converse with who can keep pace with me intellectually."

He looked down at the duvet while she sat on the bed and pulled on her stockings. “I have been poor company of late, though.”

“I wouldn’t say that.” She looked over her shoulder at him, smirking. “Even when you weren’t available for conversation, looking at you has certainly been pleasant enough.

He cleared his throat to hide his embarrassment.

She sighed. “As much as I’d like to remain here with you today, I do need to converse with Malklith today if we have any hope of securing his support. Joaquin will be here soon to stay with you today, so you will not have to be alone.”

Albtraum nodded his acknowledgement.

“He and Brunhart did come by a few times to look in on you, but you were sleeping.” She stood, crossing the room to put on her dress, deftly lacing the bodice herself. “I will write to inform our other hosts that we will be delayed—“

“No,” Albtraum said quickly, sitting up with a wince. “No... There’s no need for delays. We’ll be travelling by sea again for a while, will we not? That will give me all the time I need to recover.”

She looked back at him in surprise, then sighed, crossing the room to smooth back his hair. “You should take care this youthful tenacity of yours does not lead to your undoing, darling.”

Her speech toward him had turned more affectionate since their agreement to court, and he enjoyed the way she addressed him now. Reciprocating her affection was still somewhat awkward – he felt as though the right did not belong to him, that she was still out of his reach, a thing he could only admire from afar.

"Well, I should be off. Joaquin will be here shortly, but the servants are just outside the door. Call for them if you need anything." Mianna stooped to kiss him, and he reached up to place a hand on her shoulder from his uninjured arm, attempting to draw out the gesture even a moment longer, enjoying the soft warmth of her face against his. She drew back, smirking. "You're a fast learner. Well on your way to being an excellent kisser."

"Th-thank you... I suppose."

She tapped the end of his nose before turning to leave. "You're blushing."

She shut the door behind her as she went, leaving him there. He leaned back into the pillows, tired of the dull ache that gripped his body. He looked to the nightstand and saw that someone had brought in a stack of books, along with the robe Joaquin had given him on the ship.

He'd changed clothes since Mianna and Brunhart had to strip him down, but all he was able to wear were soft velveteen trousers. His chest, sides, back, and arms had hurt too much to bother with any kind of shirt.

Albtraum carefully stood from the bed, groaning as his injuries protested, and carefully pulled the robe on around himself. He did not want to remain in bed as he'd done for the past few days, so he stretched carefully and paced the room, the stone floors cold under his bare feet.

A knock at the door came as he circled the bed over and over, and before he could answer, Joaquin entered. He'd barely gotten dressed, still in his sleeping clothes with a cloak hastily wrapped around himself. "My dear boy, you should be in bed!" he exclaimed, rushing over to take his arm and guide him back to lie down.

"The bed's the only place I've been for days," he complained in response, frowning.

"It wouldn't do for you to worsen your injuries," Joaquin told him firmly, patting his shoulder and pushing him back into the pillows as he sat down. "How are you feeling? The guards are all quite concerned for you, Glen most of all. He's been looking after Renegade... The poor thing won't stop crying and searching for you. And Brunhart's been pacing the perimeter of the estate, close as the Nerean guard will allow."

Albtraum frowned at the thought, wishing he could have his pet and his friends at his side again. "I'm alright, I think. I... I want to return to our business as soon as possible."

"Albtraum... do you not hold any interest in stopping the man who did this to you?"

Albtraum sighed. "Joaquin, his attempt failed, and he fled. Either he believes I'm dead, or he can live with the shame of failure. We have to keep going."

Joaquin raised an eyebrow, frowning at him. "Why all this rush?"

"I..." Albtraum looked to the window, drawing a shaky breath.

You know why. The line has begun to blur again. You think you survived that fall all on your own?

He swallowed hard. "I don't know."

"Well, we are still on schedule, so you can be at ease for the moment," Joaquin assured him. He turned to face Albtraum, leaning against the post at the foot of the bed. "Mianna has certainly been... behaving differently around you, I've noticed." He smirked, quirking up the white-streaked side of his moustache. "Have you two discussed anything?"

Albtraum groaned, throwing his head back into the pillows and squeezing his eyes shut in embarrassment. "When she was tending my injuries, I... I told her I loved her."

He heard Joaquin give a slight gasp. "Goodness, subtle, are you?"

Albtraum glared sharply at him, eliciting a teasing laugh.

"What did she say?"

"She isn't sure if she feels the same," Albtraum muttered. "But apparently we're courting, now."

Joaquin grinned, his face lighting up. "Wonderful news!"

"Is it? She may not return my feelings. I don't desire some casual courtship with her..." He thought back to words he'd heard Brunhart use, describing his wife. "I want to always be with her."

"Courtship is the first step, my dear. You've got to give her time. Mianna can be..." Joaquin sighed. "I've been her friend longer than anyone. She can be quite distant. It takes her time to truly sort out for herself how she feels about someone. It's a common problem among immortals, unfortunately – you see, there's no precedent for how we are meant to form relations with others outside the bounds of mortal time. Consequently, many of us become socially inept to some extent... Strange, since you'd think years would equal experience in these matters."

"That makes sense, I suppose," Albtraum sighed.

"So this courtship may serve some practical purposes, and allow her to finally hone her interpersonal skills."

Albtraum grumbled, looking out the window again. “Practical purposes. Of course.”

Joaquin patted his leg. “Give it time, my dear. Enjoy your courtship. All will be as it is meant to.”

Chapter XXX

Mianna considered knocking on the half-open door to Malklith's office, but decided against it, carefully pushing her way inside past the guards, who made no move to stop her. They, at least, seemed to respect her authority as a member of the Order.

Malklith was sitting at his desk, and Elemnestra sat across from him. Their conversation died off as they heard Mianna enter the room, both turning to look at her as she stepped in.

"Malklith, I apologize for my rudeness the last time we spoke. But you understand, surely, Albtraum is of vital importance to our cause and I could take no chances with his life." She did not like having to bow to the whims of him and his enabling wife, but she could not lie to herself. They had far greater chance of success with his support.

He sighed. "Yet another ugly display of behavior. Honestly, it is as though you seek to make yourself as unattractive as possible." Elemnestra looked coldly at her as her husband spoke, clearly relishing in his verbal lashing.

Mianna forced down the tingling of rage at the back of her neck. "I would ask you to forgive my outburst and lend more support to my men as they search for the assassin. They have felt unsupported by your guard – and if the assassin has not already escaped the city, they require more assistance to find him."

Elemnestra turned in her seat to face Mianna, shifting to find a comfortable position for her child-filled belly. "Malklith has decided against involving himself in this conflict," she informed Mianna curtly.

"He failed," Malklith agreed with a shrug. "Let the shame of his failure follow him back to whoever sent him, and they will surely deal with the man."

Mianna narrowed her eyes at him.

How had she not considered this sooner? Was she really so blind – and foolish, to leave Albtraum alone here, even for a moment?

"Ah, I suppose you would know that, considering he was yours."

Malklith glared at her. His eyes were ice. "I beg your pardon, Mianna?"

"You heard me. What was it you said – that you doubted this would come to war? Because by all your intents, Albtraum would be dead before we left Nerea." She huffed. "And I know *exactly* what you are thinking – with Albtraum dead, Lucifurius will cease to be a threat. But if he dies, Lucifurius finds another host – and the entire damned cycle starts over."

"You are going *mad,* Mianna." His expression had shifted from offended anger to concern – fear, almost. "Now I understand why corruption is of such importance to you – you are falling to it as we speak."

"I am the Oracle," she said in a low voice, standing and leaning against Malklith's desk. "Chronus entrusted me to see to the Order's interests. I should not need to convince you of this plan of mine, and in truth this journey should have been little more than a formality."

Elemnestra stood, her lips pursed angrily, her eyes wide with fury. "You have far less experience in these matters than Malklith does, yet you would presume to laud power over him and pretend that your title of Queen Regent means anything? The Order is far too fractured and broken to accomplish anything of use, so what good are you as its head?!"

"Am I not attempting to remedy that problem by placing new leaders in power?" Mianna snapped back, but Elemnestra did not step down. Mianna composed herself before continuing, "The Order is more than just a closed political circle. Our existence is vital to the state of our world. We hold great power, and it is our duty to use that power to shape the world well. You can stay here and lock yourself away from all things that frighten you and pretend that these gilded walls will hold back the darkness, but I promise you, when Z'xolkuloth decides to make Nerea his next mark, everything you've stolen from your people will do *nothing* to save you."

Malklith stood. He stared her down, but she stared back with the same fervor.

Finally, he scoffed, looking away. "Truly, Mianna, you should rest. You are unwell."

The last of the fire in her gaze faded, and she turned on her heel, hesitating for a single moment, before she swiftly exited the room and slammed the door behind her.

It had not been long when at last the guards' judgmental gazes has finally convinced Joaquin to leave, and Albtraum found himself feeling somewhat lonely now that the room was empty.

He was glad when a knock at the door came, calling "Come in," and hoping he would see Mianna walking through the door.

He frowned as he noticed it was a servant – the same servant who'd spilled the wine. He took care to straighten his expression as the boy brought over a decanter. His head hung low, his posture hunched and guarded.

"I've brought more wine, my lord," he said, holding it up, with a cup. "I will not... I will not spill it this time, I promise you."

"It's quite alright. It was only a mistake." He noticed the boy's hands still trembled. "You can leave that on the table. I will pour it myself."

He nodded. "As you wish, my lord. Do you need anything else of me?" Uncomfortably, he turned to face Albtraum – and at last he saw why the boy's posture had been so carefully turned away from him. His eye was bruised darkly, there was an ugly gash in his lip. As Albtraum looked at him in horror, he could make out the dusky imprint of fingers on the boy's throat.

"Are you... Are you alright? What happened to you?"

"Ah... Lord Ceallach." The boy's hand unconsciously moved to his throat. "He has quite a temper, I'm afraid. And my actions... well, you are aware what happened."

Albtraum's heart dropped. "He did this because I..." his voice trailed off – he bit his lip and shook his head. "I am so sorry. This was not at all what I intended, I..."

The boy looked even more uncomfortable. "May I go now, my lord?"

Albtraum nodded, and he briskly walked away.

Albtraum fell back on the pillows, feeling tears welling up in his eyes. He'd attacked Ceallach to save the servant further beating... but his efforts had only brought even more of it down upon the poor boy.

You thought your presence would ever bring anything but more destruction?

Albtraum scowled, rolling over to pour himself some of the wine. Wine made his thoughts hazy, and he disliked feeling so lethargic, but there was the benefit of it making Lucifurius' voice seem more far away.

The door opened once again, without a knock this time. Mianna stood there, looking flustered, her face flushed. "Albtraum," she said breathlessly, then gestured to the wine in his hand. "Did you drink that?"

"No, I—" He was interrupted as she rushed over, plucking it from his grasp and taking a somewhat undignified gulp from the cup.

"As I thought... poison."

"*Poison?!*" Albtraum jolted forward, panic tightening his chest, but Mianna gently pushed him back down to rest on the pillows.

"Please, Albtraum," she smirked, "you should know by now that poison has no effect on me. In fact, I find I've gotten quite fond of the taste in certain dishes. Seems I arrived just in time, though." She let out a long breath.

"What's happened?" he asked as she sat down on the bed.

"I... lost my temper with Malklith as I realized the assassin was his. This," she gestured to the wine, "just serves to further prove it. Even so, justified as I was, there is no hope of securing his support now. He believes

I've gone well and truly mad, and he denies responsibility for the assassin, of course."

Albtraum sat forward, hesitating before he reached out to take her hand. "I am sorry this has been so difficult... Is there anything I might do to help you?"

She smiled tiredly, laying back on the bed and closing her fingers around his. The sunlight filtering in through the tall windows shone on her chestnut hair, making it appear to be threaded with strands of gold.

He knew this was hostile territory – the poisoned decanter loomed in the corner of his vision, proof enough of that. But he wanted this quiet moment between them to last.

"It is nice... to have someone I can speak with about these matters. That truly helps more than I can say."

He watched as she sighed, releasing his hand and sitting up again, gazing out the window.

"Perhaps there is more I could do," he mused.

She turned again to face him. "And what is that?"

"I could speak with him. I know what kind of man he is – I have some ideas how to garner support from him by appealing to what he desires. As of right now, there's no benefit to him to supporting you – not in his eyes."

Mianna looked down, seeming worried. "I must admit I am nervous to allow such a thing... after he has now tried to have you killed *twice*—"

He sat up straighter, wincing slightly. "But I don't believe that had anything to do with me... it seems he simply wants to put *you* in your place."

She seemed to weigh his counterpoint. "It is still a risk I do not—"

At that moment, they were interrupted by a rapping at the door, and Mianna raised an eyebrow before crossing the room to open it.

"Ismaire!" Albtraum heard her exclaim. "What are you doing here?"

Ismaire rushed inside, shutting the door behind herself. "Berate me later, but I was listening at the door. And I... think I should go with Bonehead."

Mianna perhaps looked more surprised than Albtraum was. "You do?"

Ismaire grumbled, looking over to Albtraum and running a hand through her hair. "Look, for what it's worth, I'm... *ugh,* I don't know if *glad* is the word, but I guess it would have been pretty bad if you carked it."

He blinked at her. "*...What?*"

"Gods...It's good you're not dead, alright? And Malklith..." She scowled. "He doesn't respect Mia, and he *won't,* but you're right, if the two of us can show some kind of unity and tell him what he wants to hear, then... perhaps we can convince him."

Albtraum stared at her for a while, and she shifted nervously. He was glad for the change in her attitude toward him, but he could not deny it was somewhat jarring.

As if she could see what he was thinking, she scoffed. “I’m not doing this for *you,* Bonehead. Mia is being exceedingly kind to you, going so far as to let you have the bed? Don’t get used to this sort of treatment.”

“Not to worry, I wouldn’t make the mistake of thinking this was for my benefit. It is politics, after all.” He grunted as he stood from the bed, Mianna catching his arm to steady him.

“Are you certain you’ll be alright?” she asked him, looking up with concern as he wavered on unsteady legs.

“Yes, I’m well enough.” He looked over to Ismaire. “I assume you’ll at least try to stop the assassin if he decides to present himself at our meeting.”

She rolled her eyes. “Yes, yes. I’ll at least be a decent shield if nothing else. We should go now. Strike while the iron is hot, so to speak.”

He merely looked at her blankly.

“Gods, have you *never* heard an idiom? Lord of all Daemons couldn’t even teach you that.”

He turned to glance back at Mianna. “I know this is not the safest venture, but I must start to fend for myself politically at some point. Regardless of the outcome, I might at least learn something from it.”

Ismaire looked down. “Yeah, and... I know a thing or two about convincing people, and giving them the lies they want to hear.”

Mianna’s brow furrowed. “Yes... you do. Still... be careful, both of you. I will be waiting.”

"Come on, then, Bonehead, Malklith won't convince himself." Ismaire turned on her heel to head for the door, and, casting one more glance to Mianna, Albtraum followed.

How much lower am I going to stoop?

Ismaire watched as Albtraum drew himself up before the servants in the hall. He still stood awkwardly – clearly in pain from his injuries, though he didn't let it show on his face and he kept his voice steady. She had seen the crags below the window he'd fallen from... It was nearly an impossibility that he had survived at all.

"We would like an audience with the king," he said to the servant. His voice was soft, agreeable. She was beginning to understand how he had won over so many.

The servant merely nodded, and ran off to the office – Malklith emerged a moment later, looking surprised and confused to see them.

"Good afternoon," he said in greeting. "Albtraum, you should still be resting. You wished to speak with me?"

"Yes," Albtraum confirmed. "Regarding Mianna."

Malklith's eyebrows raised. In a fluid motion he dismissed the servant with a wave, motioned them to follow him and turned to step back into his office, shutting the door behind them as they followed him in. "Please, sit."

Albtraum thanked him, and sat. Ismaire sat beside him, silent, keeping her posture straight and her hands folded in her lap.

The office was spacious, lacking the lived-in comfort of Mianna's in Sylva. The cushions on the chairs were stiff and uncomfortable, everything polished to blinding perfection. The window hardly let in any light, the colors of the stained glass were so deep – necessitating many candles throughout the room.

"Simply put," Albtraum sighed, "we are concerned. Mianna has become paranoid – in fact, she blames *you* for the attempt on my life, even though there is no basis for this and nor would you have anything to gain from my death."

The relief that unfurrowed Malklith's brow was almost palpable. *Got him.* "Ah, I am glad you feel the same... In truth, I am worried the ideas Chronus keeps putting into her head may well have driven her mad by this point."

"Before we discuss any of this further, though, I... I must apologize for what happened yesterday evening after dinner."

Ismaire watched him as he spoke. He did not seem to her to be a particularly good liar – his tone was flatly ingenuine, but it seemed Malklith did not notice as he was drawn in even further.

"No need for apology. I could see on your face – Lucifurius had taken hold of you as he had before, had he not?"

Albtraum nodded, without hesitation. "Yes... Unfortunately the spilled wine conjured some... unpleasant memories, and allowed him to cross that threshold once more."

"I should be the one apologizing – for the incompetence of Ceallach's fool servants. Though you'll be glad to know he properly punished the boy."

"That is good," Ismaire interjected. She had to appear supportive – although she could not speak up too much, lest she reach a level unbecoming for a woman. "It was an unacceptable error."

"Albtraum, I could tell you bore some pity for the fool boy, but you must keep in mind your station," Malklith stated. "They are here to serve you, regardless of what drivel they tried to feed you in Sylva."

Albtraum nodded slowly. "Yes... Sylva has been my only real exposure to human culture, and I will admit I had no idea the proper treatment for the nobility – well, some idea from books, I do enjoy Machiavelli. But seeing it enacted is far different to reading it in a theoretical text. And it's precisely that that's led me to the proposition I bring to you now."

Malklith leaned back in his seat. "Do go on." Albtraum was playing him like – well, much better than he played the violin.

"You lend your support to Mianna. But knowing that she believes Chronus chose the both of us, Ismaire and I should encounter no trouble in influencing how those resources are used. Ismaire is much cleverer than most give her credit for, I believe the two of us could accomplish much."

Malklith's eyebrows raised even further. "My, that is certainly a bold proposition... and a clever one. It would mollify Mianna, and given she's no sense for how things must be run, the two of you would encounter little trouble in influencing her- perhaps even taking over altogether. I must admit, she does wield a great deal of power in the form of the Order archives, and Sylva's connections to the nobility of the world – Sylva could have been a great kingdom, greater than even my own. But ah, I suppose that is what happens when a peasant born to a whore is allowed to rule. I will construct some excuse to change my mind – and I trust you will keep in touch to inform me how this goes. Perhaps it is time Sylva had another king."

Ismaire imagined smashing his smug face into the desk. She smiled pleasantly.

"Yes, B—Albtraum *would* make a good king, I agree." She wanted to vomit on the pristine carpet beneath her feet.

"Seems we are all in agreement, then. I thank you for your time – and I look forward to working with you." Malklith reached out for Albtraum's hand.

The twinge of disgust on his face as he clasped Malklith's hand was barely perceptible – but Ismaire saw it.

"I thank you for your support. We should go now – it would not do for Mianna to become suspicious."

"Yes, yes, of course. You need your rest, as well. I assure you, my men are hard at work scouring the city for any sign of the man who attacked you."

Malklith was not a particularly good liar himself.

Ismaire quietly followed Albtraum as he hobbled out of the room, and they rounded the corner.

The halls were silent as they walked, but Ismaire could see something ahead as they drew closer – Mianna, standing at the head of the hall to the guest quarters, grinning widely.

"Were you *listening?*" Ismaire asked in a harsh whisper, dumbfounded as to how she'd scampered all the way back here. She looked around for anyone who could be listening, finding the halls empty.

"We have all been doing our fair share of eavesdropping, and to be completely honest, I was beginning to feel left out." Mianna let out a giddy laugh. "Masterfully done! Malklith was putty in your hands... You two are certainly a force to be reckoned with."

Ismaire could not help but share in Mianna's joy. She smiled. "We did pull it off, didn't we, Bonehead?"

Albtraum nodded. "Thank you, for... putting aside our differences and saying what you did. I appreciate it."

Ismaire looked up at him. "Yes, well... Thank you for saying what you did, too. Seems I misjudged you after all."

Mianna beamed at the two of them. "I am proud of the both of you. Albtraum, darling, you're doing better than I ever could have expected from you."

Ismaire frowned, taken aback by Mianna's affectionate tone with him. *Darling?* What was she calling him that for?

She got her answer, then, when Mianna stepped forward to kiss him. Much to her dismay, it was far from a friendly peck.

Ismaire staggered back, numb. The pride she'd felt at their triumph was snuffed like a feeble flame.

By the time Mianna broke away from Albtraum to address her, she'd already taken off running down the hallway.

Chapter XXXI

It was not with a little rushing that they left Nerea soon after that – by the time Mianna had explained to Joaquin and Brunhart what she had managed to determine, that it was indeed Malklith who had sent the assassin, everyone had been hurried to leave.

Albtraum sat at the center of it all, the anti-sacrificial victim. Mianna tasted every bit of food or drink he was given for the next several days as they prepared to leave, Brunhart and the guards continued to scour the area for sign of the assassin, but it seemed that in Albtraum's agreement to partner with Malklith, the attempts on his life had ceased.

There had been meetings with Malklith, during which he insincerely apologized to Mianna, stating that Albtraum had convinced him of the dangers Lucifurius posed and that he had indeed decided to offer Mianna his monetary support after all. He did this with such sidelong, knowing glances in Albtraum's direction that he had been surprised the man had not *winked* at him, but Albtraum was relieved that his ruse had accomplished what they had set out to do.

Mianna was careful to keep her displays of affection away from where Malklith could see – Albtraum understood, of course. If he suspected the relationship between them, he might have re-examined Albtraum's admittedly novice-level lying and seen through his true intentions.

This, of course, meant Albtraum was all the more eager to conclude business for the day, when they returned to Mianna's quarters, curled up in bed together and whispering excitedly about their next moves.

Strangest, though, was Ismaire – she had disappeared after they had returned from meeting with Malklith, and Albtraum had scarcely seen her since. She had conversed a few times with Mianna – in short, clipped sentences before disappearing once more into her own quarters.

Mianna merely sighed, seeming to understand her odd behavior, but seemed unwilling to explain it to Albtraum.

Albtraum had never thought he'd be happy to be back on the ship – but Nerea's overbearing opulence and Malklith's presence were near to sickening, and he missed being in the presence of his friends.

"Do keep me posted on how everything is progressing," Malklith said to Mianna in parting as they stood at the docks, but he looked at Albtraum.

Mianna cast Albtraum a smirk as they turned to board the ship.

She wasted no time returning to her affectionate behavior with him – linking her arm through his and kissing him on the cheek as the ship departed from the port. The guards were quick to take notice, and Albtraum could see some of them snickering – though it seemed to be more playful than mocking.

As Mianna left Albtraum to direct the servants, Edmund appeared, giving him a hearty slap on the back which quickly drew a wince. "Oh, sorry, Al! Forgot you're still banged up. Seems you managed to get more than just King Malklith's support while you were in Nerea..."

"Yes, a tremendous distaste for nobility and aristocracy," Albtraum joked in reply.

"And a *queen.*"

"Al!" Glen shouted, running up beside him, looking overjoyed to see him. Renegade followed, barking happily, jumping up on Albtraum's hip to greet him with a huge smile and a furiously wagging tail. "Why didn't you tell me you had feelings for Her Majesty?!"

"Well, I... Truthfully, I never thought anything would come of it." he stammered as he greeted Renegade. He could feel his face flushing with embarrassment.

Glen grinned in response. "I'm happy for you."

Do not presume to think this witch's affection has given you any more value. You are as worthless now as you ever were.

"Ah, Ismaire!" Edmund called out as he saw her approaching them. She looked his way at the sound of her name, but merely scowled and rushed past, stomping below deck.

Glen frowned in her direction, raising an eyebrow.

"She's been acting oddly for a while now..." Albtraum attempted to explain, but Edmund sighed.

"Yes, think I know why."

Before Albtraum could question him as to what he knew, Brunhart joined them, gently placing a hand on Albtraum's shoulder in greeting. "You shouldn't be on your feet so much just yet, pup."

"I am fine," Albtraum assured him, though he did not seem convinced. "Truly. I could not take another moment lying in bed right now."

"Not even with me?" he heard Mianna's voice asking behind him. Edmund chuckled at her, Brunhart merely seemed to be slightly exasperated. "Joaquin's given me some documents to look over, I thought perhaps you might help me."

"...Well, I think I will go lie down, then," Albtraum said to Brunhart, to which he gave a satisfied nod as they left.

"We can all share a meal together tonight, and you and Glen can tell us more about *Canterbury Tales,*" Mianna told him as they descended the steps. Renegade followed along beside them, looking up to Mianna for attention, which she gave in the form of lightly scratching his ears.

Being with her still felt to be an impossibility. He had restrained himself from vocalizing his true feelings, though he returned her "darling"s and affectionate touches – she had made it clear she did not *love* him, not in the same way he felt toward her, but her new openness with him was still enough to send him to dizzying emotional highs. He tried to keep his mind from wandering to how it might feel once she grew bored of him.

They settled in to Mianna's room – Albtraum's belongings had been brought there as well, though they took up next to no room compared to Mianna's. They sat on the bed together, and Mianna checked his healing wounds.

"Please tell me this is not as painful as it looks..." She grimaced.

"It's... improving." He tried to sound reassuring. In truth, the pain was still quite terrible, every breath, every tiny movement hurt. But he was enjoying conversing with her. He fidgeted in bed and sighed. "I'd give anything for a dance with you," he murmured.

"Soon," she assured him. "As soon as I can hold you without hurting you. And perhaps we can show off our dancing skills in Raazenia."

He could not help but feel glad at the fact that she had pride in him enough to show him off.

That is all *she wants to do with you. You are nothing more than a cheap trophy to her.*

“Albtraum, darling? What’s the matter?” Mianna asked him. He noted that his brow had furrowed in a frown.

“Oh... just Lucifurius,” he answered quietly.

Mianna sighed. “I can’t imagine how awful it must be, to not even have your own thoughts to yourself.”

“I can quiet him if I concentrate hard enough... But he’s still able to cause me pain at times. He wants me to merge with him again... I believe since I came so close to death the separation between us has weakened.”

“Just as it did when you fell in Sylva, only that time it allowed you an advantage over him,” Mianna mused.

“His presence feels stronger in my mind than it has since then,” Albtraum said. “Enough on that, though... Tell me more of Raazenia. The final kingdom we are to visit, yes?”

She nodded. “Yes, though we have much time to prepare. This will be the longest stretch of the journey... Additionally, we will be visiting Ismaire’s family before we go to Raazenia. They have already agreed to lend their support, so it will be mostly a visit for leisure... which, I imagine, will be a nice change of pace.”

Albtraum nodded. “And perhaps it might cure Ismaire of her foul mood, whatever the reason for that might be.”

Mianna gave a single laugh. “Perhaps it will.”

He laid back on the bed. The cabin they were in was modest, but it felt worlds more comfortable than anything in Nerea had. Renegade settled in to sleep on the spare duvet that was folded on the floor. “Who rules Raazenia, then?”

“Her name is Zyrashana. I wish I could give you details to prepare you for our visit... But I am afraid I have never actually been to Raazenia, and my dealings with Zyrashana have been kept short. Arion never knew her well either – something about her made him quite nervous, and he never spent much time around her during our Order symposiums...”

“Do you have any idea as to what you can expect from her?”

Mianna sighed. Her expression fell, she looked almost upset. “None, I am afraid. In truth, I... rather expected things to go at least *somewhat* better than they did with Camlion and Malklith... I suppose I underestimated how little respect they have for me.”

Albtraum frowned. He was unsure what to do, but the sight of her mood suddenly saddening pained him. He moved closer to her, pulling her into a hesitant embrace which she was quick to return, nuzzling into his chest.

“This journey hasn’t been easy...” he muttered. “I know it must be particularly difficult for you, having to fight so hard for the respect of people who should be your allies.”

“It is, but...” She sighed, leaning into him. “The fault is partly my own. I’ve never fallen in step with what they wanted me to be. And it is awfully charitable of you to worry about me when you are the one who nearly *died.*”

"Still, that felt... oddly less personal than watching your allies brush you aside repeatedly."

"Mmh. Well, I shall not hold my breath for what happens in Raazenia. It would be nothing short of miraculous if Zyrashana agreed to give us the might of her military forces, but I will save myself the disappointment and prepare for failure. If nothing else... at least I now have company for the journey." She turned and reached up to his face to kiss him before they both melted back into the pillows.

"Well, I can happily provide that," he mumbled as she broke away.

"You know, for once in my life I have no desire to talk of anything political. I would like to hear more about the books you've read – it's been so long since I've had time to properly read one myself. Hmm, something romantic you've read, perhaps?" She twirled a finger around his hair, as she'd seemed to have grown fond of doing lately.

"I'm afraid I don't much care for written romance."

"Really? This from the man whose first thought when he returned from the brink of death was to abruptly confess his love?" She laughed.

He looked away, embarrassed. "I will never cease being reminded of that, will I..."

"Not so long as you still turn such an amusing shade of pink."

The journey progressed uneventfully, but Ismaire stewed, pacing the bottom decks, forgetting to even eat until her hunger made her so dizzy she had to get something from the ship's kitchen.

That Albtraum and Mianna could be together... The thought was more than she could bear. What gave him the right? Mianna had Imbibed *her,* she thought that had to mean *something*. And Albtraum got to swoop in from gods-knew-where and steal Mianna right out from under her?

Ismaire sank to the floor, her back against the wall, and let out a cry of frustration. Who the hell did he think he was?

Mianna had no subtlety, either. As the party took their meals together, or lounged together talking on the deck, she always sat beside him, head on his shoulder or their fingers laced together. It was so sickening to watch, Ismaire had to eat from the leftovers once everyone had gone to bed for the night just to avoid having to see them. Edmund and a few of the guards had attempted to talk with her, but her foul mood had been quick to scare them off.

She heard someone descending the stairs and turned to face them—It felt as though ice was crawling up the back of her neck as she saw Albtraum.

He seemed surprised to see her as well. "Ah, Ismaire. I haven't spoken to you since you ran off after our meeting with Malklith."

"What the hell are you doing down here?" She spat back, summoning all her ire to her mouth.

He looked confused. "I came to stretch my legs and practice a bit with my dagger... Joaquin and Brunhart aren't letting me do anything. Is... something the matter?"

“Oh, like you don’t know.” Ismaire stood, scowling fiercely. “I won’t lay hands on you because I don’t want to upset *her,* but if we were in any other position I’d drag you above deck and hurl you into the sea without a second thought.”

“This is... because I’m with Mianna?”

“Of course it is, are you really that empty-headed, or are you just playing dumb?! What did you say to her to manipulate her into this?!” she demanded.

Albtraum took a step back. “I only... told her I loved her. She told me she wasn’t yet sure if she felt the same, but that she wanted to court me.”

Ismaire’s tensed shoulders lowered, if only slightly. There was still a spot of hope, then.

“Don’t get any ideas about this,” she warned, pointing at him. “She does not love you, and she never will. No one ever could!”

He frowned as he looked back at her, and for an instant, a pang of regret shot through her at the genuine, deep hurt in his expression.

But it was gone in a flash, and he was stony-faced again. “Sorry to have bothered you,” he muttered, turning and walking back up the steps again.

Ismaire’s scalp prickled with rage and anxiety as he went. She slumped back against the wall, gritting her teeth and holding her head in her hands. She was no less upset at his relationship with Mianna... but she knew he didn’t deserve her harsh words.

Why did this happen? She was always losing her temper. Hurling scathing insults. Hurting those around her.

But Mianna was the one person who saw good in her. And he had taken that from her. They were on course to visit Ismaire's family, and she feared after what she'd done that they would not welcome her back. But Mianna had been there in the back of her mind, that even if her family turned her away, Mianna would accept her.

And now that Albtraum had her... Ismaire had no one.

She stood, starting to go after Albtraum, but her knees weakened, and she stumbled to a stop at the steps, unable to go further.

CHAPTER XXXII

Ismaire had not been seasick in years, but by the time they reached the port she felt so ill she could hardly stand, even though the weather was pleasantly hot and she enjoyed the feeling of the sun beating down on her face again.

She looked over the ship railing at the desert port, the hot, dry air welcoming her back in like an embrace from an old friend.

She looked back at the rest of the party as they prepared to leave the ship, leaving most of their belongings and a few of the guards and servants to stay on the ship while the rest of them went to meet with Ismaire's clan.

The guards had all changed out of their heavy woolen uniforms and into lighter, looser clothing – Even Mianna had exchanged a dress for loose trousers and a silken shirt. Joaquin had thrown a thin cloak around Albtraum's shoulders and over his head to keep him shaded from the sun. Renegade circled him, panting heavily. Albtraum stooped to give him water from his canteen from time to time.

Mianna stood expectantly behind Ismaire, Albtraum close behind her. "Well, this is your territory," she teased with a smirk. "Lead the way, Ismaire."

Ismaire led the group into the port city, looking around for anyone she recognized. The clan spend most of their time wandering the desert from one oasis to the next, but occasionally made their way to the port city to send letters and get supplies. They'd written ahead to inform the clan of their impending arrival and had received a confirmation from them, so someone was supposed to be waiting in the city for them.

She squinted through the crowds, eyes widening when she finally saw someone she knew. “Roma!” she cried out, rushing over to greet him.

Roma was as she remembered him, with another scar or two on his face. He had long, dark hair and warm brown eyes. He pulled her into a hug as she rushed up to him, ruffling her hair. He laughed. “That was easier before, you’ve gotten taller, Izzy.” He grunted as she hugged him. “And stronger.” He looked at the rest of the group. “These are your friends?”

“The Sylvan embassy,” Mianna introduced. “This is Albtraum, our other ward, Joaquin, my seneschal, Brunhart, captain of the guard, and our guard force.”

Roma nodded in greeting to them. “It’s only about an hour’s walk to the current settlement, and the sun will be setting soon, so it will get cooler.”

Ismaire could not keep herself from laughing, though nerves were gnawing at her still. “Good for those not suited to the desert heat, like these mountain dwellers.”

The trek to the encampment was pleasant enough at first. Ismaire tried not to glance back too often, so she wouldn’t see Mianna walking hand in hand with Albtraum.

The heat did seem to wear on the party as they went. Ismaire at one point heard Noman, lagging at the back of the group, groaning up a storm about the heat and the sand.

“It’s like the devil’s armpit,” he groaned. “The devil’s *sandy* armpit.”

"Oh, come now, Noman," she heard Glen, panting. "It's not... so bad." He was sweating so much it looked as if someone had doused him with a bucket.

Ismaire felt more energetic than she had in a long time. The heat awakened something in her... she was most at home here in the desert.

Albtraum stooped to Renegade's level when the dog seemed to be lagging in the heat. He dribbled some water from the canteen into his mouth, then let him hop up atop his shoulders. He threw his cloak over him to protect him from the sun, then continued on walking.

"Are you alright to do that?" Mianna asked with concern. "Your injuries aren't yet fully healed."

"It's fine," Albtraum grunted as Renegade shifted on his shoulders.

Ismaire couldn't help but find it amusing, though her feelings toward Albtraum were still somewhat prickly.

The sun had just begun to dip when they crested a dune and Roma pointed downhill to a small sea of tents near an oasis. There was a grove of trees surrounding a large pond. The heat distorted the sight from afar.

Ismaire's heart beat faster as she realized how close she was to reuniting with her family. She wasn't yet sure if she was prepared, but she was out of time now. Steeling herself, she took a deep breath and descended the dune, the group trailing behind her to the encampment.

Roma called out to announce their arrival, and the people came out of their tents, looking half-awake. Ismaire had been gone so long she'd almost forgotten – her people were generally more accustomed to sleeping during the day hours to avoid the most intense spikes of heat.

The wave of familiar faces that came to greet her were overwhelming at first, but Ismaire found herself soon lost in the familiarity of home. It was soon as though she had never left.

But her breath caught in her chest as she turned, coming face-to-face with them.

"Mama," she breathed. "Papa. It's been..."

"Six years," her mother said sternly. She was a very short woman, but stocky, even if her age had softened some of the hard muscles and added a few wrinkles to her face. Her dark hair was loosely tied back, and Ismaire noted that the graying strands had grown in number since she'd left home.

"We've missed you so," her father chuckled. Ismaire had forgotten just how hulking of a man he was – towering over even Brunhart, the tallest member of their group, by several inches. His heavily scarred face was the same as she'd always remembered it, and he'd let his thick black hair grow long. Unlike her mother, grayness had not yet touched her father but for a few hairs in his beard.

Ismaire had so many things she wanted to say to them. She wanted to throw herself into their arms and sob for hours about how sorry she was, but she swallowed hard, taking a breath. "I'd like to introduce you to my friends. This is Mianna..."

Ismaire's mother stepped forward, her hardened expression fading into a welcoming smile. "Ah, how wonderful to finally meet you! You are truly the vision of Wadjet... Thank you for caring for our daughter. I am Ketshaka."

"Salman," Ismaire's father greeted, nodding to Mianna. "I cannot tell you how much good it does my heart to see our girl well looked after."

Mianna smiled at the both of them. "It is good to finally meet you both. Ismaire has become a dear friend of mine, and she's spoken much about the two of you."

Ismaire looked at her feet before continuing. "This is Albtraum. He is Mia's other ward."

Albtraum let Renegade down from his shoulders and nodded in greeting to them.

Ketshaka laughed. "Goodness, what an unusual dog! I'm sure he'll like playing with ours."

"They're quite common where we're from," Albtraum replied, holding Renegade back from jumping at them. "I'd certainly be interested to see what your dogs look like."

Ketshaka smiled warmly at him. "The love of a dog is considered by some to be the sign of the gods' favor."

Ismaire let out a brief, quiet huff. It seemed Albtraum held sway even over her own family.

"Good to see Ismaire has made friends in her time in Sylva," Salman commented with a chuckle.

Albtraum fell quiet at that, seeming unsure how to respond - *Well, Bonehead, I suppose friends don't really talk to each other the way I've talked to you after all.*

Ketshaka nodded. "Indeed. Well, you all look quite parched, let's get you all some water." Ketshaka motioned them all into the largest of the tents, where the group sat down on the rugs that covered the sandy floor.

"Mama," Ismaire started as Ketshaka handed out bowls and poured water from a large skin into them. "We have something important to discuss with you."

Ketshaka watched as the group gratefully drank. "Do you have need of our forces for a war?"

Mianna shook her head. "Not just yet, no. But..." She looked to Ismaire to continue.

"Mama, I have told you of the Order in my letters," Ismaire explained.

"Yes," Ketshaka confirmed, sitting beside Salman. "They follow the same roles as our own gods."

Ismaire nodded. "They need me... to become one of them," she said, almost too quiet to hear.

"Our leader, in fact," Mianna added. "She was chosen by one of the most powerful among us."

Ketshaka did not seem shocked, but seemed to take a moment to process what had been said to her, responding with only a reserved nod. "We have always known our girl was sent here by the gods, and was to one day return to them..." She sighed. "Though I cannot say we will not miss her. How much time do we have before she must go?"

"Ketshaka, Ismaire may travel from the other world as often as she likes, provided her duties are being met," Mianna assured her. "In fact, I encourage it. It will help her perform to the best of her abilities to maintain a connection to her family."

"That is most wonderful news!" Salman exclaimed. "We feared our time with her might be limited by her duties to the gods."

"It won't be at all, Mama, Papa." Ismaire sighed. "You see, I've already been... made immortal."

"An action I took to protect her," Mianna explained.

Ketshaka's eyes did widen in surprise then. "Already a goddess among us, then. Ismaire, your friend truly is Wadjet on this earth. I hope you have expressed proper gratitude for what she has done for you."

"She has," Mianna answered before Ismaire could admit that her expressions of gratitude left much to be desired.

Ketshaka and Salman stood again. "There are many tents near the water's edge we have set up for your group. Please, make yourselves at home, and feel free to ask one of the children for help if you should need it. We have some catching up to do with our daughter."

Ismaire's joy sank to the pit of her stomach and dissolved there. The moment she'd dreaded. She sighed, following them out of the tent, looking over her shoulder as the Sylvan embassy finished drinking the water they'd been given.

She caught Albtraum's eye. The look he gave her was encouraging... perhaps sympathetic, even.

Something about it dampened her nerves.

Ketshaka opened the tent flap, gesturing for Ismaire and Salman to step inside. This was something she'd always done, as long as Ismaire could remember, when they had something important to discuss as a family.

"Have a seat," Ketshaka said sharply, motioning to Ismaire's bedroll in the tent. It was the same one she'd slept on as a child.

Ismaire quickly did so, fearful and tense. Salman stood off to the side of the tent.

“Slave trading,” Ketshaka started. “Whatever might have possessed you to do so is beyond me. We taught you to behave in such a way as to please the gods of our clan, and our gods do not condone such evil behavior.”

“I am sorry,” Ismaire muttered, staring down at the worn pattern of her bedroll.

“As you should be. You are only lucky the people who took you in after that happened to be benevolent and spare you the punishment you deserved.”

Ismaire clenched her fists and tightened her jaw, shame enveloping her.

“That being said,” Ketshaka continued, tone softening. “You cannot know how happy we are to see you again.” She knelt to pull Ismaire into an embrace. “Gods, those two years when we received no word from you, we feared you were gone. But we waited every day for a sign from the gods... and we’ve waited every day since to see you again.”

Ismaire blinked back tears, wrapping her arms around her mother’s stout frame. “I was so afraid you wouldn’t want me anymore.”

“Ismaire,” Salman said softly, placing a hand on her back. “From the moment we found you in the dunes, we knew you were a gift from the gods, and that you were ours. That will never change.”

She nodded. “Thank you, Mama, Papa.”

Ismaire slept deeply for the first time in years.

The feel of her bedroll in the soft sand was heavenly, and she curled into it, breathing in the scents of the sand and smoke from the fire and listening to her parents' soft breathing from across the tent.

She could hear movement outside, and she slowly sat up, looking around. The light had dimmed – the sun was setting, meaning everyone would be waking up.

Quietly as she could, she stood and exited the tent, careful not to wake her sleeping family, finding the majority of the Sylvan embassy gathered around the camp's main fire, being served dried meat and fruit. Albtraum was peering suspiciously at the food, while Mianna seemed to be explaining to him what it was, exactly.

Ismaire sighed as she watched them. Jealousy still stung at the insides of her heart, but she could not seem to sustain her hateful feelings toward Albtraum any longer.

She looked around the camp. It was odd, seeing her friends from Sylva mingling in the camp with the people she'd grown up with. She didn't want to leave, though she knew this destination would be their shortest stop of all. Her family did not need to be swayed. They'd promised Mianna their support from the beginning.

She stepped over to join the circle around the camp, sitting close to Albtraum, hoping to open a conversation between the two of them in which she could begin to work at repairing the damage she'd done. Mianna was deeply absorbed in telling Albtraum a story, and didn't notice Ismaire sit down a short distance from Albtraum.

Albtraum did, though. He glanced at her out of the corner of his eye, then moved ever so slightly closer to Mianna, turning to face her and leaving his back to Ismaire.

She blinked at the back of his head, somewhat surprised that he seemed to plan to just ignore her. She took a breath, ready to spit an insult, but it died before it reached her tongue. She could not be angry. He had every reason in the world to be wary of her, and the last time she'd spoken to him directly, what she'd said to him...

Downtrodden, she got up from the circle and left to stand near her family's tent again.

She turned around when she heard footsteps crunching in the sand behind her, surprised to find herself facing her father.

He rubbed the sleep from his eyes and put an arm around her shoulders. "Your friends seem to be settling in well."

She leaned into him, feeling like a young girl again. "Papa, I'm sorry for being gone so long... Truly, I am."

He rubbed her arm. "I know, Izzy. Your mother and I are proud of the woman you've become. The people you've found... They are good people. I believe you've found the path the gods meant for you."

She watched the gathering around the fire, noticing that Brunhart and Joaquin had made their way over to sit beside Albtraum, embracing him in greeting and staying close to him as they talked with him and Mianna.

She frowned. “Papa… I know I’m not your child, not really. What made you and Mama take me in? How did you decide?”

“Decide?” he asked, looking confused. “There was nothing to decide. You were our child and we knew it from the moment we found you. That isn’t the sort of thing that requires thought or consideration.”

She nodded, wondering if Joaquin and Brunhart felt the same towards Albtraum. They certainly seemed to.

She had always feared that her parents did not truly consider her their child. They’d given her no reason to believe this, but it ate at her, especially after her time as a slaver. She realized that she had not simply been envious of Mianna’s attention to Albtraum, but Brunhart’s and Joaquin’s as well. He never had to doubt their love, it seemed.

She sighed again. “I’ve been awful to Albtraum. He never did anything to me… I just…”

Salman looked at her knowingly. “You’ve often let envy create rifts in your life. You will be working with him. You should work on mending your relationship.”

She nodded absently, watching the gathering at the fire. Another arm wrapped around her, and she looked to her other side to see her mother had joined them.

“I should imagine by now you’re quite used to needing to make amends. Should be no trouble for you.”

Ismaire scowled. “Mama, how long have you been listening in?”

“I hear everything, sweet one.” She pulled Ismaire down to kiss her cheek.

Ismaire stood with the two of them in silence for a long while, listening to the sounds of the camp around them. She felt tears burn in her eyes. All of this would return to the sand and be gone, she would outlive everyone she knew. She'd once thought she'd stay in this place forever, but now she'd rapidly come to the realization that it would be gone before she knew it.

"What's the matter, Ismaire?" Ketshaka asked with concern as she noticed the tears in Ismaire's eyes.

"Mama, I... I was so sure I wanted to do this, but knowing I'll have to go on without everyone... I'm scared to be alone."

Ketshaka took her hand. "You aren't going to be alone, Ismaire... There are many people here and in the future who will be there with you. You couldn't expect that you weren't going to outlive us anyway... And we never meant for you to stay here in this desert for your whole life. There are greater things ahead for you."

Ismaire wasn't sure she believed it yet, but her mother had a way of making all her words comforting when she wanted to. She closed her eyes and enjoyed the presence of her parents, the road ahead seeming less daunting, if only for the moment.

"Oh, Ismaire!" She heard Mianna call out, and opened her eyes to see her friend waving her over. Albtraum was eyeing her uneasily, a slight frown written across his features.

Ismaire and her parents joined the circle next to Mianna. Ketshaka sat closest next to Mianna, taking her finished fruit rind to toss into the fire.

Ismaire found it very strange that Ketshaka's natural mothering tendencies extended to Mianna, a woman almost three times her age. Then again, Ismaire had often felt as a child that her mother was parenting her and Salman at times.

"I was planning to explain to you more what the Order's plans are, but I believe I'll allow Ismaire to do that," Mianna said to them. "It is her duty as an ambassador of the Order, anyhow. And I'd like to give her more time with you all, I know she's been looking forward to this visit for a very long time."

Ismaire looked down at her hands, scoffing. "Yeah... drove you half to madness asking about it every week."

Salman gave a low, rumbling chuckle. "You've no idea how comforting that is for us to hear."

It was the early morning, meaning everyone in the camp would be settling into sleep soon. The sun had just reached over the dunes to where the camp was. Albtraum was lazing under a tree near the water's edge with a book, and Brunhart sat not far from him, carving finishing details into something he'd been working on during their sea voyage.

"What are you reading?" he asked Albtraum.

"*The Prince,*" Albtraum answered, almost in a sigh.

Brunhart chuckled. "Again? You've read that one a few times before, haven't you?"

“I notice more details every time I read. Or I view things from another perspective, gaining more insight.” Albtraum looked up as Renegade trotted up to him, panting hard from exertion. He’d been playing with the children in the camp while Albtraum read, but it seemed he missed his master’s company. He walked to the water, greedily drinking from it before returning to lay at Albtraum’s side.

There were three children were not far behind him, none older than three or four. They called to Renegade, but he did not move from Albtraum’s side.

As soon as they realized that Renegade would not be coming without Albtraum, the boy of the group toddled over to them.

“Can the doggie come play?” he asked, reaching down to pat Renegade’s head. Renegade stayed where he was.

Albtraum looked frozen in place for a moment before setting aside his book. “I-I think you’ve tired him out.”

The boy grabbed his hand. “You come play then!”

Albtraum hesitantly stood and followed the children around the water’s edge, Renegade slinking slowly behind them. Albtraum looked like a giant next to them, awkward and gangly, bent over so they could lead him by the hand. He seemed uneasy around them, but abided their child-games all the same.

Brunhart watched them carefully as the children led Albtraum into the water, splashing at him and tugging at his hands to pull him in deeper.

“They’re adorable, aren’t they?” a voice sounded behind him.

Brunhart turned to the source of the voice, finding himself looking up at Salman.

Salman chuckled as he watched the children coax Albtraum into the water while he sat in the shallows, laughing as one of the girls tugged at his hair.

"Makes me miss when Izzy was that age," he mused. "What of you, sir? Do you have any children?"

Brunhart turned again to watch Albtraum over his shoulder. The children were splashing and pestering him, but he was longsuffering and patient, and perhaps even seemed to be enjoying himself.

"Yes," Brunhart answered quietly. "A son."

He noticed Mianna approaching from the edge of the camp, carrying a canteen.

"Albtraum left this," she explained, handing it over to Brunhart. She nodded in greeting to Salman before noticing Albtraum with the children, playing in the water. "He seems to have gotten quite good at making friends," she observed with a wry smile.

"Ismaire was quite like that before she left. Always a gaggle of little ones following her wherever she went." He stepped back, turning back toward the camp. "I've got to go get the men organized for the day's watch, but Ketshaka is in the camp if any of you should need anything."

"Thank you, Salman," Mianna said with a smile.

Brunhart waited until Salman was out of earshot to speak up again. "You and Albtraum seem to be getting on well," he commented gruffly.

“We have been,” Mianna answered. “I think he has been enjoying our courtship. I know I have been. It’s been quite nice to—“

“I think you should take care that he is not taking this more seriously than you are,” Brunhart interrupted, looking up at her from where he sat.

She frowned. “What do you mean?”

Brunhart grumbled. “I’ve seen how you are with the people you court. Everything a political play or a business transaction. He does not deserve to have his heart broken because he does not view every relation he forms through the lens of politics.”

Mianna fell silent for a long while, watching Albtraum in the distance. Finally, she answered softly, “I understand your concern, Brunhart, but you needn’t worry about that.”

He looked up at her again, then back to his carving, adding the last details. “Good. I’ve enough to worry about already.”

Chapter XXXIII

As the group was preparing to leave the encampment, Ketshaka was loading down each of their packs with different fruits for them to take along on their journey. Albtraum was thanking her and informing her that he had more than enough, but she only laughed at him as she gave him more.

Brunhart watched them prepare from where he stood in the shade of the trees. Ismaire was watching her parents wistfully, sitting against a tree and leaning heavily on her arm. She looked up at Mianna, who was standing beside her.

"I don't want to go yet," she sighed. "Do I have to go to Raazenia? Can't I just stay here till you've finished all the business you have there?"

Mianna raised an eyebrow at her. "Raazenia is perhaps the most important leg of our journey, you cannot be absent for it."

Ismaire sulked.

"However, I might allow you to return for a brief visit *after* we have gone to Raazenia, provided you can convince a few of the guards to escort you."

Ismaire squinted as she looked around at the guards, seeming to be trying to discern who was the least unhappy here in the desert.

Brunhart left them to join Albtraum where he stood. Ketshaka approached them with a smile, handing Brunhart a small melon.

“For the road,” she said to him.

He nodded his thanks. “I see you’ve given Albtraum enough to feed an army.”

“He seemed to like the melon. And if he’s going to get anywhere near as big as his father, he’ll need to eat thrice as much.”

Albtraum and Brunhart glanced at each other as they heard Ketshaka’s observation. Albtraum looked pleased with what she’d said.

Brunhart patted his shoulder as Mianna joined them, Ismaire trailing close behind.

“Thank you for hosting all of us,” Mianna said to Ketshaka. “It was a welcome reprieve from all the business we’ve had of late.”

“It was the least we could do to thank you for taking care of our girl,” Salman said with a good-natured chuckle.

“Hopefully I’ll be able to return for another short visit before I have to go back to Sylva,” Ismaire said to them, stepping forward as they both pulled her into an embrace.

“Only once your work is done,” Ketshaka said sharply to her, grabbing her face with her hand before smirking and kissing her cheek. “Listen to Mianna, and be kind. Don’t forget to write us.”

Ismaire shifted uncomfortably. “I won’t, Mama.”

Once all goodbyes had been said, the party set out again, Ismaire leading the way back to the port. There was a light wind, making the heat more bearable. Brunhart hovered at the back of the group, watching Albtraum and Glen converse, Albtraum carrying Renegade on his shoulders.

"I'm telling you, Glen," he heard Albtraum say, though the wind snatched most of the volume of his voice, "Nothing that large could survive under the sands. Nor would anything want to. Sand such as this is a terrible place to burrow into, it all just collapses as soon as you dig into it."

Glen was grinning. "But doesn't it just *look* so much like a giant or some other massive creature could be buried underneath these dunes?"

Albtraum sighed and shook his head, but he was smiling. "All that reading seems to have given you a rather unusual imagination."

It was midday by the time they reached the port, just before the sun grew hottest, and Brunhart was glad for the chance to rest in the shade below the deck of the ship. They boarded again, the process being much easier this time, as their belongings were already loaded aboard the ship and they were ready to set off.

Albtraum was eating a piece of melon as he waited against the mast next to Glen and Mianna for the ship to set off. He rushed over when he saw Brunhart.

He first offered Brunhart a slice of melon he'd cut off, which Brunhart accepted. "Can we go below deck to spar?" Albtraum asked eagerly. It was as if he had been waiting to ask since they'd first left the ship. Mianna followed behind him, taking his hand.

Brunhart frowned at him. "Your injuries aren't fully healed yet, are they?"

"No, but I can't be stopped by every bump and bruise I ever get. I'll need to fight injured at times."

Brunhart's frown deepened as he realized Albtraum had a rather valid point. Still, he didn't like the thought of causing him needless pain and exhaustion, even if it would someday be inevitable. "Why don't we just take this time to rest? We've only just gotten back on the ship, we've walked a long way already..."

Mianna looked up at him earnestly. "Brunhart has a point, darling."

Albtraum shook his head at her. "I can't afford to fall behind in my learning just because of a small injury..."

"How about a compromise," Joaquin's voice sounded behind Brunhart, startling him. "We start teaching you the intricacies of war and battle tactics. Just as important as combat, but no risk of further injuring yourself."

Brunhart smirked. "Debatable. I have seen tactical discussions end in blows."

Joaquin huffed, crossing his arms. "Well, I should like to think that would not be a risk among reasonable men such as ourselves."

Albtraum raised an eyebrow, pushing his hair away from his sweat-hazed face. "You know something of battle tactics, Joaquin? That is somewhat surprising."

"You learn many things in six hundred years of experience, my dear."

"Also allows plenty of time for your knowledge to become stale and outdated," Brunhart muttered.

Joaquin looked sharply at him.

"Joaquin actually admitting his age," Mianna gasped with a wicked grin. "Now *that* is surprising."

Joaquin shot her a warning look, eyes narrowed. "Information, of course, I trust you to keep to yourself..."

Mianna loosely pulled Albtraum into an embrace. "Well, I'm afraid I don't have much to contribute to the discussion that Brunhart can't explain better than I. I will take care of my own business, writing letters to contact the allies Malklith has put us in touch with, and informing Zyrashana of our pending arrival. That way we can spend our time to our liking this evening."

He smiled softly at her. "I'll miss having you, though..."

She pulled back, her hands moving to grip his. "I've kept you all to myself for quite a while now, I'm sure Brunhart and Joaquin are missing their time with you. And as you said... It would not do to fall behind in your education."

"I can't believe you're using my own words against me," Albtraum sighed.

Joaquin cleared his throat. "Enough flirting, you two. We've much work to do." He led Albtraum below deck, Brunhart following close behind them.

They went right to Joaquin's room, which was perhaps the biggest on the ship to hold all of his belongings. Brunhart looked around, mildly amazed.

"Did you have to bring *everything* along with you?"

"Of course," Joaquin scoffed. "You never know what you may need, or when. For instance, Brunhart," he grunted as he moved his trunks to reach one near the bottom of the stack, "you did not bring along a chessboard, did you?"

Brunhart sighed. "No. Can't say I did." He was annoyed. Chess was a good way to introduce beginners to the concept of battle tactics, and it was fortunate Joaquin had brought the necessary materials with him. He was not about to let Joaquin know that, though.

Albtraum sat on the bed, waiting patiently as Joaquin dug out a finely carved wooden box from the trunk. Brunhart vaguely recognized it as his own work, done years ago. This was not their usual chessboard – it was one Joaquin used only during travel, and he had asked Brunhart to craft him a box that would be easy to transport.

Joaquin brought the box to the bed, opening it and beginning to set up the pieces as Albtraum watched intently. Brunhart had to resist the temptation to sigh at the board – which was, in his opinion, needlessly opulent. Inlaid with gold foil, the pieces carved from marble. When Brunhart had learned, he played with pinecones and pebbles, and drew a board into the earth.

"There are many different types of pieces in the game, just as there are different types of warriors on the battlefield," Brunhart began. "This is the king, the queen, the bishops, the rooks, the knights, and the pawns. Each one can move and attack differently." He demonstrated with each piece type on the board, and Albtraum repeated his moves to demonstrate his understanding.

They played a few games. Brunhart won each one easily, and Albtraum stared at the board between each round with his brow furrowed in frustration and concentration.

Brunhart reached out to pat his clenched hand as he knocked over his own king in surrender for the fourth time. "A word of advice... You seem to become too focused on one or two pieces, mostly your knights."

"Brunhart is also wickedly skilled at chess," Joaquin sighed from where he sat across the room from them. "In fifty years' worth of matches, I've beaten him only six times. And I'm rather sure three of those were handed to me out of pity."

"I've never pitied you," Brunhart shot back.

"Knights are made for combat, makes sense they should be the ones waging it most often," Albtraum explained, setting up the pieces again. Brunhart corrected a few he'd put into incorrect positions.

"True, but every piece on the board can win or lose the battle on either side. Just as one man holds the potential to turn the tide of battle, no matter his position. Focus more on the army as a whole, what each piece can do alone, what they can all do together. If you use them all as a unit, you'll see a better chance of success."

"Quite a bit to keep track of," Albtraum muttered.

"Here," Joaquin said, shooing him away. "Watch a few matches between Brunhart and I."

Brunhart was fairly certain he did not see Albtraum blink as he intensely studied their every move for the next hour or so as they played. By their third game, he was suggesting moves to Joaquin, muttering into his ear... moves that earned him a win.

"Hah!" Joaquin laughed, grinning. "And there we have seven."

Brunhart was unfazed. He was still hundreds of wins ahead of Joaquin. "That is a good introduction to the mindset of commanding an army," he said to Albtraum. "Of course, with real men, on a real battlefield, there is more to consider."

Albtraum seemed to perk up. "Oh, I've got a book by Machiavelli about battle tactics, perhaps that might help as well."

"If we ever want our boy to take an interest in something, pray it's a subject Machiavelli has written about," Joaquin chuckled to Brunhart.

Brunhart could not keep a smile from his face as Albtraum carefully put away the board and pieces, fiddling with a few of them in his hands before placing them gently in the box.

Watching him play with the pieces reminded Brunhart of something. "Ah, almost forgot." He reached into his pocket, withdrawing the wood carving he'd finished at the encampment. "I made this for you."

Albtraum accepted the wood piece from him, smiling as he examined it. "It's a dog," he observed. "That's the second time you've given me a dog as a gift."

"Albtraum..." Joaquin started, taking the chess box from him to put away. "I believe I can speak for both Brunhart and myself when I tell you how happy we both are to have been able to meet you and help shape you into the person you've become. I think the both of us have come to consider you like our own son."

Albtraum blinked at them, looking caught off guard, and Brunhart cleared his throat. "Yes, pup. We're proud of you."

Albtraum looked down shyly at his hands, fidgeting with the small wooden dog. "That's part of why I want to serve the Order. I want to repay you for what you've done for me... I owe everything I am to you."

Brunhart stepped over to rest a hand on his shoulder. "Albtraum, Order duties or no, we love you. You don't need to repay us for anything."

"Not a thing," Joaquin agreed.

Albtraum nodded, standing to pull Brunhart into a hug, Joaquin moving over to join them. "I love you both," he murmured.

Brunhart was happy to have such a moment to connect with Albtraum the way he'd wanted to, to officially take him in as his own. He felt more content than he had in a very long time.

He started to pull back from the embrace when Albtraum moved as though he was uncomfortable. Concern struck him when he noticed Albtraum was holding the sides of his head, grimacing in pain. He stepped back from them and sat back on the bed.

"Albtraum, are you alright?" Brunhart asked him, alarmed.

Albtraum only groaned in response, his breath hitching as he doubled over. "It's just... Lucifurius..."

"What is he doing?" Joaquin asked, rushing forward to look Albtraum over, though other than his expression, there were no outward signs of his pain.

Albtraum whimpered, hands moving to press against his eyes. "Not again, not again, not again," he whispered.

Brunhart and Joaquin looked at each other, at a loss. Brunhart paced back and forth in front of the bed as Joaquin tried to comfort Albtraum, stroking his back, though Albtraum seemed oblivious to his presence.

He was struck by the realization that he was powerless. This was a threat to his son that he could not see and could not protect him from. His gut tightened as he realized that all he could do was watch and wait as Albtraum suffered.

Finally, the pain seemed to subside, and Albtraum blinked back to alertness, sitting himself up slowly. "I'm sorry..." he muttered. "Lucifurius was angry. I—"

"Are you quite alright?" Joaquin all but demanded, taking Albtraum's face in his hands.

"It's fine," Albtraum sighed. "I'll be rid of him soon enough."

Joaquin reached down, squeezing his hand. "You have carried that monster bravely. Ridding you of him will be our first priority once we return home."

As Brunhart watched Joaquin stroke Albtraum's hair, trying to be soothing, he realized that he had not lent much thought to the threat Lucifurius posed – Albtraum didn't speak of him much, and consequently, Brunhart hadn't considered him.

But he was always there in Albtraum's mind. The biggest threat his son faced, locked in a battle of wills with him, clinging on desperately to what control he once held. Albtraum had suffered in silence all this time.

Brunhart was not sure if he hated Lucifurius or himself more for that fact.

Chapter XXXIV

Raazenia, their final destination on their journey, was about a day's walk from the port. They had rented steeds and carriages to see them there, but even removing the added exertion of walking did little to help the heat.

This land was less arid than the desert sands had been, some of the hills bursting into lush patches of green from the dark, heavy soil. Yet still the heat seemed worse than it had been in the sands, as though it radiated from the very earth.

Albtraum was uncomfortable and anxious from the feeling of sweat sticking his clothes and his hair to his skin. Renegade sat across his lap, adding to the unbearable heat as the late afternoon sun beat down on them. Even tying back his hair hadn't kept it from clinging to his neck. He looked over to Glen, who seemed to be worse off than even he was.

He rode his horse closer to Glen's, reaching out as he had many times before that day to pour some water from his canteen over Glen's head to cool him off.

Glen had been in a daze from the heat. He yelped in surprise as the water ran over his head.

"Al!" He laughed, shaking the water from his hair as it dripped into his eyes. "You should save that for drinking."

Albtraum poured some over his own head before giving some to Renegade to drink. “It’s the only thing that makes the heat bearable.”

Mianna was riding a short distance ahead of him, and looked back over her shoulder. “Take care not to waste all your water, darling.”

He smiled slightly in acknowledgement, looking ahead over the crest of the hill. He could see the city in the distance – a great fortress surrounded by smaller stone buildings. The city in comparison to the structure in the middle was small, smaller than Sylva, though the disparity between them was not so great as it had been in Nerea.

The city itself, as they moved through it, was unassuming – the people watched the group move through curiously, but otherwise seemed unbothered.

Albtraum was staggered by the size of the fortress as they approached – the walls constructed of great slabs of dark stone, so high they blocked the sun from where he stood. Heavily armored guards ringed the walls, even their faces obscured by hoods and helmets – Albtraum wondered how they bore the heat, dressed as they were, but they seemed unbothered.

They had dismounted their horses and stood at the gate to await their escort, and Albtraum could hear Mianna let out a tense sigh from where she stood beside him.

He reached out to put an arm around her shoulders. “We can succeed in this regardless of whether we win support here, Mia, I’m sure of it.”

She shot him a wry look, but reached over to touch his hand where it rested on her arm. “I would tell you I am not concerned, but it seems you’ve seen through that ruse already... but you are right. Zyrashana’s support would be a great boon, but it is not paramount.”

He pulled away from her as he could see the royal escort had arrived, and he assumed the woman at their head was Zyrashana.

She was tall – as tall as the men that guarded her, dark-skinned with black hair and eyes of a deep amber. She wore a dark, loose-fitting dress that was much more unassuming than anything he might have expected a queen to wear, but the light, flowing material managed to look elegant all the same. Mianna seemed notably more tense as she approached than she had at any of the other rulers they'd met with – and he understood why. Something about her seemed intimidating, in a way he could not place.

He expected that perhaps Lucifurius might level a snide remark, as he always did, but he was oddly silent.

"Mianna, it has certainly been a while," the woman said. Her tone was oddly good-natured, her voice higher than her appearance had led Albtraum to expect.

Mianna cleared her throat. "It certainly has, Zyrashana."

She motioned them inside. "We can make our introductions over dinner. I can see you are all tired from the road, and the sun is particularly hot this day. Come."

Albtraum stayed close behind Mianna, and he noticed that Ismaire had also fallen in step beside them. She no longer looked at him with such a withering glare, but the two of them had been awkwardly avoiding each other ever since her outburst.

He felt foolish that he hadn't managed to ascertain Ismaire's feelings for Mianna – it was obvious, when they'd last spoken, that her harsh words were out of envy. When he thought back to all the time they'd spent together on the road, Ismaire's vying for Mianna's attention was clear. He understood the pain she surely felt at Mianna's rejection, and wondered if perhaps he was truly worthy of her affections himself... but it did not stop Ismaire's words from stinging.

It certainly had not made him particularly eager to speak with her again.

Albtraum looked around as the group made their way inside the fortress. It was a beautiful structure – all made from dark volcanic stone, the air inside much cooler despite the many flames illuminating their path. Tapestries lined the walls and floors, and the hallways bustled with activity, much like in Sylva. He felt his shoulders relax somewhat at the atmosphere of the place as they were led to the dining hall, where a small feast waited. Renegade trotted alongside him as they walked, his tail wagging as he sensed his master's increased comfort.

Mianna hesitantly took his hand as they stepped into the hall, and he wrapped his fingers through hers, trying to be comforting. It seemed to have the intended effect, as her posture, too, grew somewhat more confident as they took their seats at the table.

Mianna looked at the spread of foods before them as they sat to eat. She was unsure of Zyrashana's past, though she suspected it to be something like her own – she often seemed to opt for practicality, and the cuisine she'd had served was closer to the food of commoners. A variety of roasted vegetables, herbed cheeses, and smoked meats – it had been so long since she'd had a proper meal, her mouth watered at the sight of it.

"I am sure the journey must have been somewhat unpleasant, unaccustomed to the heat as you all are," Zyrashana said as she began to eat from her own plate. Some part of Mianna had long been envious of her – Mianna herself was slight and short-statured, and her features had always been soft and rounded, almost girlish, even once she'd come of age. Zyrashana was hard and sharp and imposing, her raven-black hair neatly tied and falling almost to her waist.

"I did not find it terribly so," Mianna answered, carefully spreading a soft cheese over a slice of bread.

"You are burned from the sun," Zyrashana pointed out with a light smirk. "Though not quite so badly as... Albtraum, was it?"

He nodded. "Yes, I did not fare so well, it seems. Though I did enjoy the sights as we walked. Raazenia has quite an interesting landscape." He reached under the table to feed scraps to Renegade.

"I am told by the scholars that is due to the volcano we sit atop. Evidently the molten rock that runs beneath the earth enriches the soil," Zyrashana explained.

Albtraum seemed fascinated. "I suppose that explains the level of heat we felt. It seemed as though it came from the earth itself... I suppose because it did." He chuckled, and Zyrashana seemed to at least mildly return his amusement.

Mianna let out her tension in a breath, her carefully neutral expression giving way to an easygoing smile. After Nerea, she had expected to be met with coldness, if not outright attack... it set her at ease to see Zyrashana be genuinely welcoming to them.

"You seem quite suited to the heat, Ismaire," Zyrashana continued, and Ismaire seemed surprised. "You are Ismaire, yes?"

"Y-yes," she answered, flustered.

"Given your appearance, you must hail from somewhere in this part of the world."

"Yes, across the Levantine Sea, to the south," Ismaire answered.

"Egypt, then. I've long found that pantheon to be quite interesting. And what god do your people worship?" Zyrashana asked with genuine curiosity.

"All of them, of course," Ismaire replied, seeming to open up as they conversed. "But Ra above all."

"God of the Sun, I see. I have never followed gods myself, but I find the concept interesting, to be sure."

The group ate together for a while, chatting together with ease, before Zyrashana turned her attention back to Mianna. "I suppose we have business to discuss, then. Would your people care for a tour of our gardens? The volcanic soil mentioned earlier allows us to grow a collection of magnificent blooms."

"That does sound lovely," Joaquin cut in, turning to Brunhart beside him. "Especially for Brunhart. I've not seen your brow unfurrow in days. Mianna, you've no need of our assistance, have you?"

Mianna looked over to him. "Ah, no, I do not believe—"

"Your seneschal and captain are more than welcome to join us, if you would prefer it," Zyrashana offered.

“Thank you, Zyrashana,” she replied with a smile. “But I believe you’ll find Albtraum and Ismaire are more than capable of following discussions of business.”

“Good. My servants shall see yours to their accommodations, then, and offer a tour of the gardens.” The servants nodded at their orders, and led the Sylvans away from the dining hall, leaving the rest of them in sudden silence.

“You should know I’ve had quite some correspondence with Malklith,” Zyrashana began, and Mianna felt her heart sink. Of course, this could not be so easy – “And as such, I’ve been eager to meet with you.”

“You *have?*” Mianna replied, stunned. Noticing she was gaping, she snapped her mouth shut. “Given how things went in Nerea, I… assumed anything you heard from Malklith would be…”

“Demeaning? Discrediting? It was. He called you a madwoman, he said you would come to me raving of rifts and corruption, that I should be cautious. And yet I see a woman of apparently perfectly sound mind before me.”

Mianna allowed herself a sigh of relief. “Yes, I will admit I grew rather temperamental with him…”

“Such anger is understandable with such grave matters in question.” Zyrashana folded her arms and leaned forward on the table, her eyes downcast. “I have been a part of this Order for many centuries… I have seen firsthand the harm that corruption brings, as well as the effects of rifts. They are not to be taken lightly. Malklith forgets that.”

Mianna could have wept. Trying to convince Malklith and Camlion of the seriousness of these matters had felt something akin to beating her head against a stone for years, and she had grown to believe that

Zyrashana might have dismissed her outright. Her acceptance nearly made the frustrations of the rest of the journey feel worthwhile.

"It gladdens me that you see reason. Removing Lucifurius from power will be no easy feat – and it is likely a long war awaits us," Mianna explained. "As such... the might of your forces would be a welcome help. Malklith's support, unfortunately, remains tenuous at best."

"Well, I will spare you the long discussions, as I am sure you've had more than your fill of them – I will lend you my armies when the time comes." Zyrashana sat back in her seat, and Mianna beamed gratefully.

"Truly, Zyrashana... I cannot thank you enough."

Zyrashana nodded, but her attention turned elsewhere. "Albtraum, you look troubled."

"Ah, I am sorry," he answered softly. Mianna glanced over at him. "It is just... Lucifurius has been quiet. Unusually so."

"Perhaps he is trying to unsettle you," Zyrashana suggested. "Since we've gotten the business discussions out of the way, perhaps we might join the others in the gardens."

Mianna reached out to touch Albtraum's hand – Zyrashana seemed unfazed at her action. "Yes, darling, perhaps that might put your mind at ease."

They left the dining hall then, guided by the servants, as Albtraum looked around the hallways, asking Zyrashana questions about the city and her people, listening intently as she answered.

Mianna fell in step beside Ismaire, speaking to her in a low voice so as not to disturb them. "You've been quiet lately," she observed.

"Yes, I know. I've been an arse and I'm not sure what to do about it. I'm sure Bonehead's already told you about it."

"Actually, he's been rather dodgy when asked about what's happened between the two of you. I assumed you both must have quarreled over something somewhere between here and Nerea."

Ismaire sighed as they neared the garden. "Less of a quarrel and more just... Me hurling insults while he remained irritatingly composed. I wish he'd at least snapped back, so I wouldn't have to feel so rotten about the whole thing. Now every time I try to apologize, he's avoiding me."

"I am certain you'll be able to corner him one way or another. Do not give up hope just yet."

The gardens were lush, not only with flowers but with people, milling about, talking with the Sylvans. The flowers grew in wild, uncontrolled patterns, some on vines over the walls and creeping over the walkways, bringing a decidedly relaxed feel to the geometric stone walls surrounding them.

Mianna found herself once again awash with relief, watching her people finally feel fully at ease. She stood at the edge of the garden, observing as Joaquin and Brunhart conversed animatedly about something. Ismaire sat sullenly on a stone bench, but Edmund and Piotr soon made their way over to speak with her, and before long, she was chuckling with them over something.

Mianna joined Albtraum again at the edge of the garden, and Zyrashana approached them. She had hardly spent time with Zyrashana before this, but her camaraderie already made her feel like an old friend.

"I noticed a book in your satchel when the servants took it from you in the dining hall," she commented to Albtraum. "*The Prince,* was it?"

Albtraum's expression brightened. "Yes, it was! I quite enjoy Machiavelli, and that is perhaps my favorite among his work."

"I have quite the fondness for his writing myself," Zyrashana said with a nod. "It was certainly revolutionary, what he did... making the knowledge of the inner workings of a tyrant's court accessible to the average man. People can say what they like about his advocacy for cruelty in governance – his work was meant for peasants, that much is clear as day."

"I've often said just the same," Albtraum agreed with a wry smile. He leaned closer to Mianna, about to take her hand again, but she could see him stop himself, pulling away again.

Zyrashana must have taken notice. "I see you and Mianna have perhaps developed more than simply professional feelings toward one another..."

Albtraum stammered, beginning to object, but Mianna spoke first with a light laugh. "Yes, we seem to have simply fallen into it as we were forced into close quarters in Nerea. I trust you'll not object."

"Not so long at it does not cloud your judgement... but the two of you strike me as practical and clearheaded. We have far greater concerns at the moment, anyhow."

With Zyrashana's voiced approval, Albtraum again stood closer to Mianna, draping an arm around her shoulder. He still felt overly warm from his time in the sun, and they both smelled of sweat and dust from the road. She wanted nothing more than to sink into a cool bath with him at the day's end.

Mianna and Zyrashana chatted more about the state of the Order kingdoms, Mianna recounting what had happened in detail along their travels as Zyrashana listened intently. Somewhere along the conversation,

Albtraum pulled away from Mianna, informing her he was going to speak with Brunhart. Renegade trailed dutifully after him.

Zyrashana watched him go before turning her attention back to Mianna. “I assume we do have more business to speak of, but I did not wish to overwhelm Albtraum or Ismaire. It seems they have had much to endure of late.”

Mianna sighed. “Yes... I am not sure what Malklith told you in his letters, but he did an exceptionally poor job of hiding the fact that he attempted to have Albtraum killed. Not a few moments after he denied the assassin, I walked in to find Albtraum being served poisoned wine. I can only imagine what might have happened if I had not arrived sooner.”

“I suppose he thought his ruse would hold once you found Albtraum dead? ...He is a fool, there is no doubt on that.” Zyrashana crossed her arms, watching the garden with a slight smile. “I have fond memories of Arion and I snickering at him behind his back at the Symposiums we attended. Your father, too, before...” She trailed off.

“You do not need to spare me talk of my father, Zyrashana. I never knew him – my only knowledge comes from what others have told me.”

“So much of what is said is about what he became once addled by corruption, but... I remember your father. He had a horrifying temper, and a hideous sense of humor. He amused me to no end. Though we’ve not spent much time together yet, I sense you must be quite like him, at his best.”

“And I fear that has done me no favors in Malklith or Camlion’s courts.”

“Camlion?” Zyrashana scoffed. “He is nothing but a fool boy. How disappointed Arion would be to see how spineless he’s become.”

Mianna frowned. "Yes... He would be."

"On the subject of Arion, Mianna..." Zyrashana turned to face her. "I feel I should tell you – we met briefly before his disappearance."

"Oh?" Mianna's heart clutched at the mention of him – it had not been long ago, in the greater scheme of things, that she'd last seen him. Some days it felt like an eternity.

"He was..." Zyrashana hesitated. "He was not well. Corruption had taken root – he was half raving mad, but above all... He asked that I look after you."

Mianna's chest grew tight, a hard lump forming in her throat. "I see."

"I thought you might like to know that... even in that state, he thought of you. He wished the best for you," her voice trailed off to a murmur. "And he believed you were the Order's best chance."

Mianna smiled sadly. "I suppose I truly have no choice now, then."

Zyrashana hummed her agreement. "It is growing dark," she commented. "And you are all very tired, I am sure. I will have the servants see you to your rooms."

Mianna thanked her, and reunited with Albtraum as they were led to a sparsely furnished, but comfortable room with large open arches that looked out over the land, a light breeze blowing pleasantly through the room. Soap and two washbasins had been left for them, and Albtraum was quick to strip away his shirt to wash himself. The ugly bruises from his fall had at last mostly faded, though Mianna could still make them out if she looked hard enough at his pale freckled skin. Renegade had curled up in front of the pile of Albtraum's belongings in the corner.

The door of the room latched heavily as Mianna pushed it shut, and the instant it did, she could feel tears welling in her eyes. She tried to wipe them away, irritated to find they only flowed more freely.

And Albtraum was quick to take notice as he finished washing. "Are you alright, Mia?" he asked, his voice raised in concern, quickly crossing the room to her.

"Yes," she answered, her voice thick and strained. "Zyrashana spoke briefly of Arion, and... it caught me more off guard than I would have liked."

He swallowed hard, clearly unsure of what to do, but he did pull her into an embrace. His bare chest was still damp, and he smelled of soap. "Would it help you to speak about it?"

"Perhaps." She sighed, wrapping her arms about his waist. "Zyrashana only confirmed what I had suspected – Arion had succumbed to corruption, and he was leaving to die before it destroyed him utterly. I knew – I *knew* this was the case, and yet... Having it spoken aloud, having it confirmed..."

"Now there is no hope." Albtraum frowned.

"Precisely... and it just... it is simply very sad." She wiped the last of her tears away. "But I should not be crying. We have had a great success today, and I am here with you, and tonight we can sleep safely in the company of friends."

She washed herself from the basin as well, laughing lightly to herself as Albtraum still took great pains to avert his eyes, looking at her again only once she'd dressed in a thin nightgown and settled in to sleep beside him.

"I am glad in a way though, I suppose," she mused as she snuffed the candle and curled up against Albtraum's back, gently reaching around him to rest her hand on his chest. His scarlet hair was soft against her cheek.

"What for?" he asked, his voice a sleepy haze.

"Even addled as he was, Arion believed I could do this... and I will."

"He was right. Pity anyone who gets in your way," Albtraum mumbled as he held her hand where she'd rested it.

Her exhaustion stole away any further words, but she felt herself smile once more before drifting off to sleep.

It was still dark when Albtraum next found himself awake – he could still feel Mianna curled up at his back, but only the faintest moonlight filtered in from the windows. Carefully, so as not to disturb Mianna, he slid from the bed and crossed the floor, searching for what had woken him up. Perhaps nothing.

This is simply the darkness you were meant to exist in.

Albtraum was not sure whether to be startled or relieved that Lucifurius had spoken again after such a prolonged period of silence. He settled for ignoring him as he moved closer to the door and heard something – footsteps. Somewhat rushed? Renegade lifted his head at hearing Albtraum stir, but Albtraum motioned for him to stay where he was.

Carefully, he pulled on his shoes and a tunic that had been hastily folded and stuffed into the top of his trunk before quietly slipping through the door and shutting it behind him, heading in the direction he heard movement.

The hallways were silent – eerily so, Albtraum encountering not even guards as he moved at a brisk pace to catch up to the footsteps.

He thought perhaps he'd simply been hearing things as the sounds led him down several flights of stairs and outside – he squinted at the lack of light, even further compounded by the black sands he stepped out onto, but his eyes were quick to adjust. He made out a figure in the distance, calling out as he realized what he saw.

"Ismaire?"

She whipped around to face him. "Bonehead!" Her voice was a harsh whisper.

"What are you doing?" he asked her, lowering the volume of his voice to match hers as he drew closer to her.

"I couldn't sleep, so I was walking around the halls – I saw someone else but the instant they laid eyes on me, they *bolted*. Don't you think that's odd?"

"Perhaps they were startled to see you."

Ismaire huffed at him. "Yeah, well... Past that, I haven't felt right since we've been here. Something about all this, it just... it feels *wrong*. Now, I know what you'll say, but listen—"

He looked at her, exasperated, as her voice increased in volume. "Ismaire..."

"Listen, I said! This has all been just a bit too easy for my liking – and I know that because... Because I used to do this exact thing. I lured people in by being exactly what they wanted, by saying what they wanted to hear, by—"

"Ismaire."

Annoyed, she snapped up her head to look at him. "*What?!*"

"You... you do not need to convince me. I've felt somewhat unsettled myself."

Her surprise was so great she nearly stepped back. "You... you have?"

"Yes, I cannot place it, exactly, but I..."

He was interrupted by a sudden clamor of sound behind them as a large group of guards rushed around the side of the fortress – many of them heavily armored, faces covered, as Albtraum had seen when they first arrived.

Albtraum took a breath to call out, to explain themselves, but he'd scarcely made a sound before a crossbow bolt whizzed through the air, grazing his side and leaving a shallow wound. In an instant, the guards had charged.

He heard Ismaire shouting in pain and rage, and looked back to find a bleeding wound in her shoulder – she'd been shot as well.

The reality of the situation struck him – the guards were attacking intentionally. They'd shouted no warnings, they'd made no efforts to identify Albtraum or Ismaire – though it was not so dark at this distance that they could not clearly see who they were.

Albtraum was snapped out of his distraction when two guards rushed at him, swords drawn – he cast a glance back to Ismaire, ripping the bolt from her flesh and lunging at the guard who'd just injured her, though the wound had healed already. She grabbed the man by the neck, bringing her knee to his face. Albtraum dropped to one knee and grabbed the short sword from the belt of the now-unconscious guard, freeing it from the sheath after some difficulty.

Ismaire drew a knife from her boot and charged forward.

As if by instinct Albtraum stood, striking out at a guard who was fast approaching him – and the blade of the sword sunk into his gut in the gap between his breastplate and fauld.

Albtraum shuddered as blood gushed from the wound, making the hilt of the sword slick in his hands. He stood frozen as the man staggered back, gasping, before falling to the ground. The sword slid from the man's flesh.

The memories of battles and slaughter had seemed distant since the Sylvan people had taken him in, drifting back to him on occasion, but in this moment they were suddenly as close as they'd ever been. He remembered the smell of years of blood and rust caked on his armor as though it had just clung to him. The feel of blades tearing through flesh itched in his limbs.

Lucifurius raged as Albtraum turned and faced the next guard, circling him with surprising ease in his movements, his grip tightening on the blood-slick sword in his hand.

You will not harm my child – you will not—

The guard did not move to attack, but Albtraum leapt forward as if by instinct, swinging the sword at the man's head. The blade sliced through his throat. He collapsed, gagging on his own blood.

The last guard facing Ismaire had retreated. Albtraum stood with the sword still gripped in his hand.

The threat had passed. He tried to release his grip.

His hand would not move.

He locked eyes with Ismaire in a panic, and she looked back with confusion.

We are one again...

Albtraum fought. To take a step forward. A breath. Anything.

His body did not obey.

He tried to call out to Ismaire, but his voice never made it past a faint stutter in his throat. He felt himself turn around as more guards charged in to replace the ones they'd felled.

My child, this is what I've longed for! I am close now, closer than I have ever been, the time is near for us, soon our power will be enough!

Albtraum was frantic, a prisoner in his own body. *Oh no, no, no, no.* He fought, but he could only watch as his arms wielded the sword against the approaching guards.

He turned, and his blade struck flesh again – though this time, the man he'd struck did not fall, but stood fast. His eyes widened as recognition flooded him – The man who'd approached him at the port. Who'd pushed him from the balcony.

As he was distracted, a stampede of guards grabbed him, forcing him to his knees. He tried to comply, tried to let himself be subdued. But his body thrashed and he snarled like a wild animal.

The guards responded in kind, forcing him down, metal boots kicking his still-tender ribs as he was forced face down on the ground. He felt tears well in his eyes from the pain.

It took four men to pin him down, and from where he lay pressed against the ground, his head turned to the side, he could see that Ismaire had been forced down as well.

He tried again to struggle against the grip of the guards, but he felt something heavy clobber the back of his head, and his vision went black.

Sleep, child.

We will be rising again soon enough.

CHAPTER XXXV

It was late morning when Mianna awoke, blinking hazily before her eyes focused to take in the emptiness of the bed beside her.

She frowned, reflexively reaching over the spot where Albtraum had been. She'd hoped he might still be there when she awakened... But then, the sun was high in the sky, and Albtraum was often restless.

What struck her as odd, though, was Renegade's head popping up over the edge of the bed, his tail wagging furiously as he crawled up to greet her. She scratched his head and sat up, looking around – Albtraum's boots were gone, and his trunk had been opened – clear signs he'd dressed and left. She wondered why he hadn't taken Renegade with him.

Mianna quickly dressed herself and made her way to the dining hall, Renegade trailing after her. The hallways bustled with activity, servants and guards moving about with purpose, most paying her no mind except to nod in greeting. When she entered the hall she found the Sylvans gathered together, eating and talking contentedly. Just as there had been for dinner the previous night, there was a magnificent spread of food – but no sign of Albtraum.

Her frown deepened as she crossed the room to where Joaquin sat, finding him confused at the sight of her alone.

"Good morning, Mianna. Where is Albtraum?" he asked.

"I thought to ask you the same question. He had already left when I woke this morning."

Joaquin looked across the table. "Glen, any sign of Albtraum this morning?" he asked.

Glen looked across the table at Joaquin on hearing his name. "Ah, I haven't seen him yet, but Edmund said Brunhart had his breakfast early and was walking the grounds... Perhaps Al went with him? Strange he left Ren, though..."

"No sign of Ismaire this morning either, Your Majesty," Noman informed Mianna with a frown.

Mianna stood. "I will find Brunhart, then."

She swiftly made her way to the grounds, her footsteps increasing in urgency, the people in the hallways beginning to cast her odd looks as she ran. Eventually she found herself outside, the heat of the sun uncomfortable as she searched for any sign of either Brunhart or Albtraum. She was certain she'd find them walking together, that her worry would be for nothing, but—

When she crossed Brunhart's path, he was alone.

He caught sight of her quickly, shooting a questioning look as his eyes flitted from her to Renegade, then back to her.

"Have you seen Albtraum yet this morning?" she asked breathlessly, coming to a stop before him.

"I assumed he was with you," Brunhart answered tersely, his mouth forming a deep frown.

“He was, but… He wandered off some time this morning… There is no sign of Ismaire either.”

Brunhart was quick to rush past her. “We should inform Zyrashana, then.”

“Yes,” Mianna agreed, and together they made their way back inside Raazenia’s fortress.

Her mind raced as she rushed through the long hallways, following closely behind Brunhart, Renegade easily matching her pace. This was unlike them – either of them, particularly Albtraum. She struggled to conjure possibilities – any possibilities – the only ones that surfaced she quickly pushed away.

It was not long before they encountered Zyrashana, standing in the hallway near her office – But Joaquin had found her first, and Mianna could tell even from a distance that he was speaking to her in panicked tones, his body language tense and his hands worrying at the hem of his tunic.

Zyrashana looked over to Mianna and Brunhart as she saw them, her brow furrowed and her mouth in a hard line. “You’ve not found either of them, I assume?” she asked.

Mianna shook her head. “No… And we’ve walked across a good deal of the grounds, and neither have my men seen either of them.”

Zyrashana waved over a guard. “Have all the men not otherwise engaged search for Ismaire and Albtraum. It is important they’re both found.”

The man gave a brief nod, and rushed off to do as he was told. Joaquin looked more upset than Mianna had seen him in years, his hair in messy disarray as he nervously ran his hands through it over and over. “The assassin in Nerea was never intercepted,” he said pointedly, his voice quivering slightly.

Mianna felt her stomach twist itself into anxious knots. She’d considered it, of course. Far in the back of her mind, hardly a conscious thought, but hearing it spoken aloud...

“I will gather our men to search as well,” Brunhart stated abruptly before rushing off.

Zyrashana turned back to Mianna, her expression dark and serious. “You do not think Malklith would have sent his assassin all the way here?”

“Honestly, I—” Mianna’s words caught in her throat. “I... would hope not but... There were two attempts in Nerea alone, and he followed us from Sylva all the way there. He would be capable of following from Nerea to Raazenia...”

Joaquin blanched, leaning heavily against the wall.

“We will find them,” Zyrashana said to Mianna. “No one rests until we do.”

Albtraum sat silently against the wall of the cell as Ismaire paced, swearing and huffing and kicking at the ground.

There was only a single small window far above their heads, casting dim light through the cell as the sun was beginning to set outside. The cell itself was pristinely kept, no cracks in the walls and no dust or dirt gathered on the floor.

"I wonder why they locked us in a cell together," Albtraum mumbled. The shallow wound in his side stung, but it had stopped bleeding, at least. He leaned against the wall and shut his eyes, the stagnant heat of the cell doing nothing to help the throbbing ache in his head.

"Look, Bonehead, I..." Ismaire sighed. "I'm sorry for getting us into this mess."

Albtraum's eyes opened again and he sat forward in surprise. "You are?"

She huffed again. "I mean, I was *right,* about all this... It felt rotten from the beginning, and now I know. But I am sorry I dragged you into it."

Albtraum leaned back against the cell wall. "I suppose it was stupid to think anything could be easy..."

Ismaire paced for a while longer, examining the frame of the door and the walls around them. She knocked the heel of her hand against the door, frowning as the impact made little sound. The metal of the door was thick.

"We've got to find some way to get out of here."

Albtraum looked over at her with a tired sigh. "We don't fully understand what's going on yet... Perhaps this is a misunderstanding. Perhaps we should wait to see what happens."

Ismaire snorted. "Would you stop that? You're supposed to be the *bad* one, remember?"

He frowned at her, raising an eyebrow.

"Yes, yes, you're a changed man, I know." Ismaire ran a hand through her hair. "Doesn't feel much like a misunderstanding to me. Especially not since the assassin showed his face, apparently. You're sure it was him?"

"That's not the sort of thing one forgets."

"We could lure the guards in somehow..." Ismaire mused. "They can't kill me, after all, so it would be easy to overpower them."

"But I haven't seen a guard come near the cell since we were thrown in."

Ismaire stepped over to sit beside him against the wall. "They'll have to come for us some time."

Albtraum scratched at his nose. "Or they'll leave us in here until we starve."

"L-look, it's like you said...let's just wait and see what comes of this," Ismaire said, clearly trying to be reassuring. "I'm sure Mia's working at this from the other end. She clearly cares a lot about you."

Albtraum shifted, finding it impossible to get comfortable on the hard stone floors and walls. "She cares about you also. More than she does for me, considering you're the one she Imbibed."

Ismaire felt a frown tugging down the corners of her mouth. "I'm sure she wishes she'd waited for you."

"You don't need to spare my feelings, Ismaire."

She huffed. "*Truly,* you idiot. She only Imbibed me because Chronus asked her to, and..." As she trailed off, her gaze sunk to the floor. "You want to know what happened, really? How I ended up in Sylva and why she had to Imbibe me?"

"I suppose I can't refuse," Albtraum sighed.

"Gods, Bonehead, I'm actually trying to open up for once."

"Let's hear it, then."

"Alright. Well... You've heard about the whole... slaver business, I'm sure. And you've met my family, so you know I don't have some sob story to excuse it. I knew better... I did. When I met those men in the city, I thought it would be fun and dangerous, that we'd be like pirates in the stories, maybe rough up some sailors and make off with some loot. But it was nothing like that. The first time I saw the 'cargo' we were moving... Well, honestly, I tried to run."

Albtraum shifted to face her, listening intently as she spoke.

"The leader's name was Serrano. I saw the chained-up children below deck on his ship, and I just... Turned and ran. He caught me up, he said he'd kill me or throw me in with them. I should have spat in his face and let him, but I didn't. I was terrified. I said I'd do whatever he wanted if he let me live."

"And for years... I did just that. I got really good at convincing street children to follow me, to listen to Serrano... right up until they were sold. I tried not to think about it. All I focused on was my own fear. And then finally, one day... I woke up. I don't know how or why. But staring at the back of Serrano's head, across a gaggle of stolen children, I realized I was tired of following him, tired of him making me be the hands that did his dirty work. So... I stole a sword from the belt of a guard – later found out it was Piotr – and attacked him. I was shit at fighting then, and he just about gutted me – but I got him in the throat, and that was that. Mia got to me right before I died, and the next thing I knew I was invincible. Well, almost, as she explained it to me later. She could still kill me if I went too far out of line."

Albtraum let out a soft sigh. "You did the right thing in standing up to him."

She scoffed. "Yeah, years too gods-damned late."

"You could argue the same of me," he muttered. "You have, in fact."

Ismaire frowned, then shook her head. "No... it was different. You didn't know better. I did. My parents raised me to be good, to be strong... and I was weak, and a coward."

"If it's any great consolation, 'weak' and 'cowardly' aren't the first words that come to mind when asked to describe you."

"Bonehead, if you keep this friendly shit up, I *will* vomit."

"I have a *name,* you know."

"Fine, *Albtraum.* Your name doesn't exactly roll off the tongue, you know—"

"Just shorten it like the others do," he grumbled, rubbing his forehead with the heel of his hand.

She settled back against the wall. "You know... back there, when you looked at me... I've never seen you look so terrified."

Albtraum looked down at his feet.

You need not be afraid, my child. We will be one again... and then nothing need ever cause you fear again.

He saw no need to be dishonest with Ismaire. “Lucifurius took control of my body once again. I believe killing that guard may have given him a burst of energy he needed to overpower me again.”

Her expression darkened, a grave frown. “But he can’t hold that control, can he?”

“In truth, I am not sure. Every moment that goes by, he could take over again, if I do not actively resist him. It has always been this way.” Albtraum rubbed his eyes, then dug through his pockets, relieved as his fingers closed around the small dog carving Brunhart had given him. He had left it there after Brunhart had given it to him, and thankfully, it hadn’t been confiscated when the guards captured him.

Ismaire blinked at him, and seemed to be struggling with a response. “Well. Must be exhausting.”

He considered that. “It’s the only thing I’ve ever known. But... Yes, I am eager for it to be over with.”

“I’m sorry I’ve been so harsh with you. I suppose I just... Well, you’ve seemed to fit in so well in Sylva. I’m envious... Even after the four years I’ve spent there, it’s not as much my home as you’ve made it yours. And the family you’ve made for yourself... I also envied that you seemed so secure in the fact that they love you. I’ve always doubted that my family cared for me... even though they’ve given me no reason to, as you’ve seen.”

Ismaire’s confession stunned him, and he stared at her for a long moment before taking in a sharp breath to respond. “Ismaire, I don’t—I have doubts every moment that my family truly cares for me, just as you do.”

She blinked back at him before letting out a scoff. “Yeah, well...they do, clearly.”

"And so does yours."

A pang of loneliness shot through him at the mention of his family. Though he hadn't been apart from them long, he wasn't sure how he was going to get to see them again, or when.

Albtraum shoved the wooden dog back into his pocket as the sharp sound of the metal door of the cell bursting open startled him from his musing, and he backed against the wall, his bruises protesting as his back thumped flat against the stone.

A whole cadre of masked guards filed in, pinning Ismaire to the wall before she could resist, hauling Albtraum up by the arms. He was dragged from the cell, not resisting, but struggling to get his feet under him.

He wasn't sure where they were taking him – the hallways were empty as they wound through them and up the stairs, out of the prison section of the fortress and back into the main halls.

He was pulled inside an open door that was quickly shut behind him, and he stumbled to his knees, hands splayed out over a thick rug, before drawing himself up to look around. Books, a desk, papers, lit lanterns – an office. He finally turned to see who had followed behind the guards into the room, and found himself face to face with Zyrashana. Her expression was oddly... cheerful? He found it impossible to properly read.

Albtraum narrowed his eyes at her, drawing a breath to demand what was going on before it was abruptly knocked from his lungs – as she rushed forward, pulling him into an embrace.

Albtraum simply stood tense and unblinking as he struggled to conjure an explanation.

"I am sorry my men were so rough with you," she said breathlessly as she pulled back, patting his face. "I could not think of any other way to get you away from them..."

Albtraum pulled back abruptly, knocking into the desk and sending an inkwell clattering to the floor as Zyrashana's joyful expression turned confused.

"Away? From who?" he asked, bristling and withdrawing, wrapping his arms close to himself and leaning into the desk as she moved toward him again.

"From them, of course, you--!" Her expression fell. "Do not tell me... Did Father not..."

I am sorry, Zyrashana. I could not save him from their grasp. He believes he is one of them now.

Albtraum felt his heartbeat quicken, his eyes widen as Zyrashana's did too – though their respective horror was hardly from the same source.

"You—"

Almost reflexively, unsure of what he was doing, Albtraum's hand shot forward – Zyrashana started to dart away, but not before his fingers closed around something solid at the side of her head –

And what had once been empty air revealed itself to be a dark, gnarled horn, twisted forward into a point – and another, broken, on the other side.

Albtraum drew back as if burned. "You... you're..."

Do not tell me you intend to scorn your sister as you have scorned me, when she has waited so long to finally meet you.

"A daemon, like you. But my birth killed my mother, so she had no chance to take my horns as yours did." She sighed, turning away from him. "I see now why father warned me not to expect a happy reunion – you truly do consider yourself one of them, don't you?"

Albtraum stayed where he was, one hand gripping the edge of the desk behind him as he leaned into it. "You... carry the other half of him."

"Yes, brother. Yours is Lucifurius, mine is Skulthur – but they are both fragments of Z'xolkuloth."

She paced near the door – Albtraum remembered what he had been when Lucifurius controlled him utterly. He could not stand against that as he was now. The shadows under the door gave away the presence of guards – he was trapped.

He swallowed hard, his mind a muddled tangle of half-formed thoughts. "You hid your horns," he murmured, trying desperately to keep her talking so he could formulate some sort of plan. "How?"

"Father gave us many gifts –" Her horns once again vanished, though Albtraum could see more clearly now what he'd seen before – a slight distortion near her head, barely perceptible. "Illusion, strength." An inky darkness covered the lower half of her arms as she turned back to Albtraum, a smoldering flame bursting forth in her palm. "His gift to us... can take on any form we choose."

His breath hitched in his throat as he kept talking. "Th-the assassin," he stammered in a rush. "Malklith truly had no knowledge of him, and he fought alongside your guards. He was yours, you sent him. Why?"

"He was first a warning to Mianna that she was treading dangerous ground, keeping you from your birthright. But you, he was never meant to kill – never. Father promised he would keep you alive, no matter what my assassin did. I thought the only way to take you from them was to make them believe you were dead... But I underestimated how far they would go to keep you in their fold."

He stayed silent as she stared at him, eyeing him up and down with abject pity. "How weak you've grown," she murmured, grimacing. "Barely a year with them, and this is what you've become. Indistinguishable from a human... hardly a trace of your daemon blood."

Albtraum stayed silent, allowing her to go on, as his eyes darted around the room for anything he could use to escape. Predictably, there was nothing he could handily use as a weapon – and after that display of whatever power Zyrashana had, he doubted that would have been effective anyway – as well as the fact that Lucifurius would broadcast any plans he made directly to her.

He waited as she went on.

"You could have power like mine. Father is infinitely forgiving – if you only step away from them and return to us. He will accept you again without question."

"Do you know what our siblings do, in the dark world? They gather armies... they kill each other for a chance at Father's throne. And you—" she drew in a sharp breath, her eyes meeting his, boring into him. "You've seen what the humans do to daemon children, you know what monsters they are. The Sylvans have convinced you this world is yours, that you share it with them, and that you must protect it – for *them!* You are here with me now, and we have the chance at being a family... and making a place in this world for more of our brothers and sisters."

That is all I have ever wanted, my children.

"We could finally take this world from the humans who have killed and mutilated us for years... and all of us might live in peace."

Albtraum's gaze fell to the floor, and a long silence hung between them.

"We can both hear him," He observed finally, prompting Zyrashana to look at him with confusion. "He speaks the same words to us both."

"Yes," she answered. "He spoke to us independently when you were far from here, but as we draw nearer to one another, his two halves speak as one."

"Ah. That does explain why he has been so quiet since we arrived here."

"Yes, he did not wish to confuse me as he spoke to you, before you were aware of who I truly was." Zyrashana's tone had softened, her posture relaxed as, seemingly, she believed he was open to hearing what she had to say.

He squeezed his eyes shut and shook his head. "No, Zyrashana. That is not why."

Albtraum at last took a step forward from the desk he'd pressed himself against, drawing his posture up as he faced her. "Do you know how he speaks to me? Do you know what he does? Some days, it is every moment. Some days it is so incessant it drowns out anything else until my head is nothing but a sea of his cruelty. And that is to say nothing of the actual pains he gives me, like he is trying to split my skull from the inside out. Even before I had anything to do with humanity, he nearly drained me completely, and I realize now that my doubt began long before I ever set foot in Sylva's walls!"

His voice increased in volume until he was shouting, and he could feel tears forming at the corner of his eyes as his tone dropped to a whisper. "Perhaps he is your father. He is not mine. I was nothing but a vessel to carry him. Do you know, other than the day he gave it to me..." A harsh, mirthless laugh escaped him, and he raked a hand through his hair as his tears blurred his vision. "He has never called me by my name?"

Lucifurius was infuriatingly silent. Of course, he would not stoop to the way he'd always spoken to Albtraum – not with another observing. But the blooming ache at the base of his skull was confirmation enough. Zyrashana only watched him, her mouth in a hard, silent line.

"The people of Sylva were kind to me," he rasped, humiliated that he could not stop himself from crying but at once too impassioned to care. "I arrived on their doorstep a monster, fully intent on killing them to the last – and they treated my wounds, fed me, taught me how to be more than what I was. They gave me a chance, and they showed me what love is – *real* love, not Lucifurius' false blandishment that lasted only so long as my every move served and pleased him."

A long silence again passed before Zyrashana hummed a short, contemplative sound. "Yes, I know about the love you believe you've found in Sylva. Father told me about your feelings for Mianna – and that she does not feel the same way you do."

Albtraum scoffed at that. "You think... that matters? That I have not already made my peace with it? Yes, perhaps she will quickly move on from me. But we were dear friends before we were lovers, and we still are, and she..." He breathed in sharply. "...was the first person who ever showed me kindness, and treated me as an equal. And whether she returns my feelings or not, that will not change. I will always have what she gave me – a chance to be who I am now."

Zyrashana's expression went flat, emotionless. "I see. Their lies have seeped into you deeper than I could have imagined. Then I must keep you here until you see reason, and forget them." She turned to the door, shouting a word in a language he did not understand, and he heard the guards turn to open the door.

While her back was turned, he quickly reached into his pocket, withdrawing Brunhart's carving and dropping it to the floor, nudging it under the desk with his foot as the guards burst forth into the room, grabbing him again by the arms and dragging him back down into the depths of the prison.

His heart thudded in his ears as he stumbled to keep up with their rushed pace.

Child... you haven't the barest inkling what your insolence has wrought.

Albtraum thought perhaps they had made it to the door of the cell – but his consciousness was engulfed in agony so great that the world around him turned to a shattered cacophony of darkness, and he was aware of nothing else for a time.

Chapter XXXVI

Renegade whined as Mianna scoured the bedroom for the fifth time, desperately searching for any clues as to where Albtraum could have gone.

He'd taken nothing with him – just boots and a tunic. His books remained neatly packed in the trunk, his clothes were still messily folded inside. With a frustrated huff, she sat back on the floor, her skirts in a tangled pile around her.

Her head snapped up as someone passed by the door. "Edmund," she called. "Anything in Ismaire's room?"

He shook his head. "Afraid not, Your Majesty. Me and the lads are going to the village to look around again."

She stood. "I will come with you, then. Clearly I am doing no one any good here."

Renegade followed closely behind her, his gait anxious as she rushed to keep up with Edmund. They had searched all of the previous day, most of the night, and were now well into the late morning – and there was not so much as a trace of either Ismaire or Albtraum. She'd tried to keep the darker possibilities from rising to the surface of her mind, but they loomed there like a great black cloud over her thoughts as she struggled to maintain her composure.

When they arrived in the village she was glad to see that Zyrashana was among the search party, questioning a group of men that stood on the street.

"Mianna," she called. "I have every man I can spare searching. We will find them both and return them safely, you have my word."

Mianna sighed as she stopped before Zyrashana. "Thank you," she said breathlessly. "I have grown very worried. I thought we might find them yesterday... And with Malklith's assassin still at large..."

"I feel very strongly they are both alive, Mianna. And they will be returned safely to you, I swear it."

Mianna followed Edmund past them, nodding in farewell to Zyrashana as she did the same. The sun shone, and it was as hot as it had ever been, many of the townspeople seeking shade and watching curiously as the Sylvans and Raazenians alike scoured the area.

Edmund asked those they crossed on the street, some seeming impatient as they'd clearly been asked before, others listening attentively as he and Mianna described Albtraum and Ismaire in as much detail as they could.

"Yes, I know who you're talking about," one man confirmed with a nod, and Mianna's spirits lifted slightly – "I saw them when you lot arrived, but I've not since. My apologies."

Edmund breathed a curse as the man walked away.

It was not long before they found Joaquin, sat in the shadow of a merchant's stand, looking exhausted. Someone had given him a skin of water, and Noman stood beside him, patting his shoulder.

They were both dressed lightly, and Joaquin looked far more disheveled than Mianna had perhaps ever seen him, his hair a ruffled mess and his clothes plain and covered in black dust from the sand around them. He clearly had not rested since the night before.

"No one's found anything still," Noman said lowly, his tone encouraging.

Joaquin frowned. "That is not comforting in the least. The longer this goes on, the more possibility there is... that..." He bit his lip.

"No sense making yourself sick worrying about it until we've found out more," Noman sighed at him.

Joaquin jumped to his feet as he saw Mianna. "Have you found anything else?"

"Nothing yet. It is... truly baffling. There isn't the slightest trace of them."

"We'll keep searching, Your Majesty," Edmund said as he began to walk off with Noman. "You and Lord Harlan should rest for now."

Mianna nodded to them as they left, looking out past the boundaries of the village to the sands. The heat of the sun made the lines of the horizon dance in her vision as if reflected on water.

Joaquin pulled her aside to an empty line of merchant stands then, his voice lowered to a whisper. "I believe it is time we began questioning Zyrashana's involvement in this."

Mianna blinked. "Surely you're not serious... we've no reason to suspect her."

“Have we? Or are you feeling more concerned with playing politics again?” Joaquin shot back.

“Joaquin...” She frowned. “No, I... It is only that we should be careful before wildly levelling accusations... Zyrashana’s support is important, and we should take care to retain it.”

“By putting Albtraum’s *life* at stake? Mianna, the two of you are courting! I had thought that perhaps after so many years of treating everyone you courted as a piece in some game, you might see what a wonderful young man he is and allow yourself to have some scrap of genuine affection for him.”

Mianna gaped at him. “Joaquin, I...”

He huffed. “You are my dearest friend, Mianna, but Albtraum is my son. I won’t allow you to put politics over him. Involve him with the Order if you must, but do *not* lead him around by the heartstrings only to scorn him later on. He deserves *love* after what he’s had to go through, not some lukewarm dalliance.”

Mianna and Joaquin had often argued over the many years they had been friends, and normally she would have shot back with as much ferocity as he did, but she felt silenced by his words as she considered them.

She had never treated courting as a serious business. It had always been for amusement, or to eke out political favors – in fact, very often she found she did not even care for the people she courted.

“And for goodness sake, Mianna,” Joaquin breathed, his anger seeming to leave him. “You deserve that too. Finally you’ve found someone who ignites a spark in you, you cannot continue to cut yourself off and act as if you are no longer suited for human connection just because you are immortal.”

All of Joaquin's ire had not weighed as much on her as this one insight did now. She frowned, turning away from him, holding her arms close to herself as she considered what he'd said.

She had held others at arms' length, she knew. Of all the people she'd ever known, she could count those she'd been truly close with on one hand. Her position required a great deal of responsibility on her part... and at times, it required action that she herself viewed as inhuman.

"That is not the reason," Mianna sighed. "Joaquin, I... I do not see *myself* as the sort of woman Albtraum should be with. Your pride in him is well-deserved... I only... I suppose after all I've had to do for the sake of my duties, I do not feel I have enough love to give, or that it's been... Tainted, somehow." She scoffed bitterly. "If you are right – and you well could be – then I've failed yet again, every step along this journey has ended in failure, and Albtraum... deserves better."

"Mianna," Joaquin sighed. "Albtraum adores you. He sees the world in you. Your past regrets do not matter to him, and he's found a kindred spirit in you."

Mianna opened her mouth to respond, but closed it again as Glen came rushing over to them from the street, sweaty and panting hard. It seemed he'd run a long way.

"Your Majesty, I found someone who says they saw something," he reported, winded. Renegade sniffed at him as he heaved to catch his breath. "A man says he thinks he saw Al – and perhaps someone who looked like Ismaire walking around the fortress very early in the morning yesterday, before sunrise... and a large group of guards went that same direction not long after."

Mianna and Joaquin looked at each other – and Mianna's heart sank.

She was not naïve. Zyrashana being involved was indeed one of the first possibilities to cross her mind when it had become apparent Albtraum was missing... But she had been so exhausted by everything she had seen on the journey thus far – Terce, *Arion's* Terce, succumbing to the infectious rot of a rift, Malklith's utter and complete disdain for her and her kingdom, the ever-increasing knowledge that war would be an uphill battle. Zyrashana's apparent support was such a welcome relief, Mianna did not wish to consider what lay behind it...

But now it appeared she must.

She muttered to Joaquin. "I will... I will speak with her. Please try to inform the others – we need to be ready to move quickly."

Joaquin gripped her shoulder. "We will win this, Mianna, whether the rest of the Order stands with or against us. Now let us get them back."

It was already late in the afternoon by the time Mianna made her way to Zyrashana's office, inquiring directions from guards who were eager to helpfully point her the right way.

Zyrashana was in the hallway, directing more men to the search. She rushed over when she saw Mianna approaching her. She, like all the others, was in a state of general dishevelment – though she'd tied her hair back and seemingly at least made attempts to brush the dust from her clothes.

“Mianna, is everything alright?” She asked as she slowed to a stop before her, gently placing a hand on her shoulder.

Mianna nodded. “Yes, I... I am just finding it difficult to keep myself from growing too worried. Have you found anything else?”

“No, nothing yet, but... you should come sit down in my office for a moment, perhaps I can help calm your nerves.”

Mianna let out a breath. It was not difficult to feign anxiety – most of it was certainly genuine. “Yes, thank you... I suppose I have not so much as sat down in quite a while.”

“Come, I’ll pour you some wine.”

Mianna stepped inside the office and collapsed into the armchair across from Zyrashana’s desk – once again finding that her exhaustion was more genuine than she’d perhaps believed – as Zyrashana poured her a glass of wine from the decanter on the small table in the corner of the room. Mianna gratefully accepted it, taking a somewhat undignified gulp from the glass – the wine was rich and sweet, and she had been parched. She held the glass in her lap, looking down at it as Zyrashana took her seat at the desk across from her.

“Mianna, I don’t wish to alarm you, but...” She sighed. “Given the lack of any evidence we have found thus far, do you believe it is possible they left of their own accord? They are facing down a nigh-insurmountable task, becoming the new heads of the Order... And given the assassination attempts, they must be intimidated.”

Mianna looked up from the wine in her hands. “No,” she said simply, with a bit more force than she intended, before lowering her voice again. “No. They would not – neither of them. Albtraum did have doubts before, yes, but... he was quite open about them. Ismaire is confident in her abilities to a fault. And here, with your promise of support... They both felt more sure of themselves than ever."

Zyrashana nodded slowly. "It is only that... nothing else seems to make sense. No one has seen them, they left no trace behind." She stood and turned to examine something on the shelves behind the desk.

As Mianna looked down again, something caught her eye – a piece of wood on the floor? She reached down to pick it up, her eyes widening as she realized what it was.

Brunhart's carving – she had seen Albtraum fiddling with it often.

Albtraum had been here.

She was quick to tuck the carving into the pocket of her skirt as Zyrashana turned around again. "Another thing, Mianna... My guards informed me that a number of your servants were seen leaving the city with quite a lot of cargo. It appeared to be your party's belongings... Even the dog. Were you aware of this?"

The edge in her voice was clear as day, but Mianna replied with a lie readily. "Yes, I asked them to go. If Albtraum and Ismaire somehow make their way back to the port, someone should be there to meet them. And I did not wish for the servants to have to make their way all the way back here simply to retrieve our trunks – since I am holding out hope we will soon find them and return to Sylva."

Zyrashana seemed to weigh whether to believe her. "I think you should be careful, Mianna," she murmured. "Such paranoia is a heralding of immortal corruption. Your father was much the same near the end of his life."

"I am not paranoid at all, Zyrashana... I simply know Ismaire and Albtraum well. I cannot believe they'd have left on their own."

Zyrashana stared at her for so long she shifted uncomfortably. "Perhaps you should get some rest, Mianna. There are plenty to continue the search in your stead."

Mianna thought to argue, but something told her that she had been given a chance to step away and should take it. The stark change in Zyrashana's demeanor was chilling – they had been so at ease around one another before, but suddenly Mianna was deeply unsettled.

She nodded once, setting her wine glass on the desk, standing, and walking out of the office back to her room without a word.

There was a rhythm that came with waking up two mornings in a row from unconsciousness, and Albtraum groaned as his eyes slowly opened once again to the dim light of the prison cell.

He was – surprisingly – not as uncomfortable as he expected to be, and he noticed as he moved to sit up that a jacket had been folded up and placed under his head.

He turned his gaze to the corner, where Ismaire sat. "You're awake," she observed, her eyes widening. "Thought you'd be out a lot longer after that..."

He brought a hand to his forehead, rubbing along the ridge of his brow. His head felt like a vase that had been shattered and pieced back together several times. "Perhaps I should have been," he muttered groggily.

"You, uh, alright though? You were in fits and crying out for... hours."

"I'm fine now. Seems Lucifurius exhausted himself." He let out a breath, reaching back to hand her the jacket back. "Thank you."

"Yeah. Glad you're alright. What happened?"

He shut his eyes tightly as he struggled to recall what had happened before the tidal wave of pain Lucifurius had unleashed upon him. Slowly, bits of it came to the surface, until his recollection was complete.

"Zyrashana is—"

The moment he opened his mouth to speak, the cell door burst open again, and he and Ismaire jumped, turning to face the door.

The assassin stood in the doorway, leaving the heavy metal door hanging open behind him.

All three of them froze, before finally Albtraum and Ismaire looked at each other. Albtraum tensed, pressing his back to the wall. In this state, he knew he could not move fast enough to rush past the man.

"Come to finish the job?" Ismaire asked snidely, prompting Albtraum to shoot her a sharp look. "What?"

The man stepped inside. His posture was oddly careful – like a hunter presenting itself to an animal, attempting to appear as though he presented no threat. "I understand the two of you have no reason to trust what I say, but please, hear me out anyway." His voice was rough, gravelly.

"My name is Almar. Ismaire, you were captured at my behest – Zyrashana promised she would not harm you if I brought her Albtraum as well."

Ismaire's eyes narrowed. "And what do *you* want with *me?*"

"That, I must explain when we next meet – this is not our time." He knelt, unfastening something at his belt, presenting Ismaire and Albtraum each with a sheathed blade. "I took these from the guard barracks – you will need them when we leave here."

"What is this?" Albtraum asked.

The man, now introduced as Almar, raised an eyebrow. "I did not think you would need it explained to you what a *blade* is, after—"

"No," Albtraum snapped, the lingering pain in his head thinning his patience. "Why are you *helping* us?"

The man looked over at Ismaire. "I... It would seem I have misjudged many things. But there is not time to discuss this – your Sylvans have already begun their fight to free you. They are on their way here now."

Zyrashana! Your fool assassin has released them!

Albtraum snatched up the blade, jumping to his feet. "Lucifurius – he's telling Zyrashana—"

Ismaire was already bolting for the door. "Then let's *go!*"

They ran from the cell, Almar following close behind – Albtraum tried to remember where he'd been led when the guards had taken him to Zyrashana, but his head was still in a fog. He drew the blade he'd been given, tossing the scabbard aside.

They ran for a long time – surprisingly long, Almar leading them through the hallways, steps echoing sharply on the stone. Albtraum could feel himself lagging – he was beaten down, exhausted. The unconsciousness he'd spent much of the past two days in was not truly sleep.

Finally, they encountered a group of Raazenian soldiers – some barely dressed for battle, one with a hood covering his face. Almar rushed forward first, felling several of them easily – one managed to skewer him with a spear, but he ripped it out and kept going. Albtraum slowed as they ran past the felled men – some of the blood pooling in the hallway appeared black as ink.

As Almar stopped at the head of the hallway, allowing his wounds to heal and watching for more enemies, Albtraum knelt, pulling the hood from the head of the man bleeding black onto the stones – silvery hair spilled out, long ears twitching as he turned his large golden eyes up to Albtraum with the last of his strength. A Shadran.

Albtraum backed away with a sharp gasp, his attention turned back to moving forward as Ismaire shouted to him. "Al, come on!"

He ran with them, again – he could hear shouts sounding in nearly every hallway they passed as more soldiers pursued them. He gritted his teeth, gripping the hilt of the sword tighter in his fist.

Somewhere along the way, he noticed Almar was no longer running alongside them.

"Ismaire..." he called, his gait slowing again. "He's—"

"No time for that!" She grabbed him by the arm, dragging him forward. "Keep moving, come on!"

They had nearly reached the massive gates of the fortress when Albtraum heard a great commotion up ahead – his knees nearly buckling with relief as he saw the Sylvans engaging with the Raazenian guards up ahead.

Brunhart – and Mianna, even – were at the head of the fight, swords drawn and many felled soldiers at their feet. Brunhart had taken the brunt of the attacks, that much was clear from the remnants of his shirt, nearly slashed to tatters but all the wounds beneath having quickly healed. Mianna's hair was tied up messily, her skirts mostly stripped away to allow easier movement, and what remained clearly having caught a blade or two, but she looked every bit their queen all the same.

The Raazenians seemed hesitant to engage them again, standing at a slight distance, poised defensively. The rest of the Sylvan guards stood behind Mianna and Brunhart, some sporting minor wounds, but ready to push forward – then Mianna glanced to the side as she heard the clamor of Albtraum and Ismaire's footsteps, and she shouted to them.

The Raazenians – some among them Shadrans, Albtraum could now tell by their obscured faces – sharply changed targets, rushing to Albtraum and Ismaire. Ismaire poised her blade to strike, and cried out – but abruptly, everything came to a halt as a voice sounded behind them.

"Albtraum!"

He whirled in place – Zyrashana strode toward him from the direction they'd come from. He expected she might be leading nothing short of a small army, but she was alone.

"Stop this," she called, staggering to a stop in front of him. "Leave them. They are not your family, they are not your people. They never will be. They will lie to you and tell you that you can be one of them – you *cannot.*"

"Nothing has changed, Zyrashana," he shot back. "You know my answer."

Her mouth formed a hard line again, and the shape of a blade formed in her hand from a cloud of black nothingness. "Then they all must die – so that you might see the truth."

Chaos erupted at the juncture of the two halls.

The Raazenian soldiers charged the Sylvans, and Albtraum rushed Zyrashana – the blade she defended with was hard and translucent, almost like glass, glistening in the light of the torches in the halls.

She drew back – avoiding attacking him, but he pressed on, with everything he had. He circled her, lashing out again and again, the metal of his blade making sickening screeches against hers. The dark substance covered her other hand, formed into any shape it needed to be to defend against his strikes.

He would not be able to defeat her – he knew as much, but he could hold her back until the Sylvans fought their way through.

Abruptly, her stance changed, and she charged him, shoving forward with a shape like a shield and knocking him flat on his back. She pressed a knee into his chest and her hand gripped his throat.

Bodies lay on the floor, blood pooling around them, and Albtraum felt his stomach turn as some of it seeped its way beneath him.

"You must stop this," Zyrashana pleaded, her voice a hoarse rasp. "You will destroy everything our father has sought to build. He has been fighting to make this world ours for centuries, and you would undo it all for a kingdom built on nothing but lies!"

Her hand was closed around his throat just enough to keep him from speaking, but he struggled against her – and suddenly, she let go, leaping to her feet.

The sound of blades connecting with flesh reached his ears. Albtraum turned over, pushing himself up on his elbows – to see it was Brunhart facing her down. A long gash ran across his shoulder, and Albtraum leapt to his feet to rush over to him.

Brunhart had managed to injure Zyrashana, too – a hideous wound cut across her neck and down into her chest. She drew back, choking on blood that rose in her throat, as the wound started to heal.

"Brunhart, are you—"

He shook his head, gripping Albtraum by the arm and rushing for the gates. "Later, Albtraum – we have to move—"

Albtraum followed him as they all ran, fast as they could, to the gates – a path had at last been cleared. More soldiers were coming, the sound of their booted feet on the stones quickening and increasing in volume before dampening as they reached the soft sand outside.

They ran through the town, the villagers shouting in alarm at the sight of them charging through with the soliders not far behind. Everything was a blur around Albtraum, his lungs aching as his legs struggled to keep up the pace.

They did not slow or stop as they passed the bounds of the city, and kept running – their steps becoming more labored in the sand, with the heat of the sun beating down.

At last, as they drew to the crest of a dune, they slowed – everyone in the group letting out a collective sigh as they saw that the soldiers – and

Zyrashana – had gathered at the edge of the city, and were no longer pursuing them.

The two groups stared across the sand at one another for a long time, the heat distorting the sight in the distance. Then, finally, Zyrashana turned slowly on her heel, back to the fortress – and disappeared into the city streets, the soldiers following close behind.

CHAPTER XXXVII

The Sylvans had a brief and breathless reunion on the dunes before they kept running – pace slower, but still hurried. It was not long before they were met by Glen and Noman, who'd arrived with a group of horses from the town for them – a welcome relief from their over-exertion.

They rode in exhausted silence back to the port town, piling into a small inn the servants had scoped out. They'd scarcely spoken on the journey, but once within the safety of the inn's walls, an eruption of grateful joy broke out over the group. They embraced one another, tended their wounds, and settled in to finally rest in the main hall of the inn, eating and drinking gratefully as the workers served them. Renegade had happily returned to Albtraum's side, gazing up at him with all the love in the world.

They were dirty, roughed up, bloodied, and dead tired – but they'd all survived.

Albtraum stood with Joaquin amidst the commotion. He had not left his side since they'd arrived, keeping one hand on his shoulder, and both spoke to Brunhart as Piotr helped tend the injury he'd sustained in the fight.

"It looks painful," Albtraum said with a grimace, unable to look away from the faint bloodstain beneath the bandages. "Are you certain you're alright?"

Brunhart grunted in response. "It'll have to heal slow, but not to worry, pup – Pain's not a thing I've been troubled by in a great many years."

It felt as though a stone had formed in his gut as he considered what might have happened if Zyrashana had gone any further.

My sweet child, the thought terrifies you now... But just you wait until they all lie dead at your feet. You will never have felt such freedom, such release.

"Albtraum," he heard Mianna said in greeting, and Joaquin finally released his hold on him as he turned to greet her, the sight of her instantly soothing his frazzled nerves. She embraced him, holding tightly for a long time. "I am so glad you are alright."

"You too," he murmured in response before gently pulling away, instantly feeling the pain in his head lessen. "I... there is much we need to discuss."

She sighed, smiling tiredly at him. "Yes, clearly there is... come, they've brought a roast to the table. We can talk while we eat."

Piotr tied off the bandages around Brunhart's shoulder, and he pulled on a shirt Joaquin handed him before they all made their way to the table together, where Ismaire already sat with Edmund, Glen and Noman.

They settled into a hush as they ate, waiting to hear what Albtraum had to say as Mianna ran a hand across his shoulders, trying to be comforting.

"Well, credit due first to Ismaire," he began awkwardly, gesturing to her across the table. "She felt something was wrong, and on investigating... she encountered the assassin who attacked me in Nerea. She went after him, I heard her, and followed."

He went on to explain their imprisonment after clashing with the guards, and the group listened carefully. "Then... Zyrashana had me brought to her office, and revealed to me that... she is a daemon as well.

She carries the other half of Z'xolkuloth... Skulthur, she said he calls himself. The assassin was hers all along, and he was meant to deliver me to her, not to kill me."

Mianna's eyes widened in shock at this, and she seemed to struggle to respond. "Z'xolkuloth has infiltrated the Order for... that long? I... That certainly does explain much of what I have seen, but..." She let out a breath. "This is going to be a far more difficult conflict than we anticipated.

Joaquin frowned at him. "I am so sorry, dear boy. That must have been painful..."

Albtraum slowly shook his head. "It... It does hurt... to know that she will not see reason, that she is fully in thrall to his whims. But... She is not my family, and neither is he. I have found that already with all of you."

"Sylva is happy to have you, kid," Noman chuckled. "Always has been."

Albtraum smiled back at him. "Further, though... The assassin."

Ismaire's eyebrows raised. "Oh, right! Mia, apparently this assassin made a deal with Zyrashana to get Al – but he wanted something to do with *me?* Got all cryptic about it before we escaped, and then just... disappeared. But yes... that was certainly strange."

"That is definitely something we must look into when we return home..." Mianna muttered. She looked back to Albtraum. "I did think – I mean, it did seem somewhat odd, Malklith had no reason to kill you, but if the assassin belonged to Zyrashana, that does explain it. But the poisoned wine..."

"The servant," Albtraum said finally, after a long moment of thought, and Mianna looked at him with confusion. "The one I defended from the treasurer. He was harshly punished for my interference... he was the one who..."

He let out a sigh before mumbling, "I only wished to help him. But the beating he suffered because of me was tenfold. Of course in his own mind he had every reason to hate me..."

Ismaire frowned. "It's difficult, trapped under someone's thumb like that. Hard to see where the real source of your problems lies."

Albtraum nodded. "Yes... Seems that's something both of us understand."

Mianna looked between them. "Regardless of all of this, I am very glad to see the two of you safe, and getting along so well. You did very well escaping together."

Ismaire smirked at Albtraum. "We did, didn't we?"

Albtraum felt his distrust and uneasiness around her had finally eased. "We did."

"Well enough I believe you deserve some time back home with your family," Mianna said to Ismaire.

Her eyes widened. "Really? Truly?"

Mianna nodded. "Piotr and Edmund have agreed to escort you. You can stay with them for a few weeks... I don't believe we'll be needing you for anything for a time. You should spend time with your family while you have the chance to, before the real work begins."

"Ah, just as Al and I started getting along? Damn shame," Ismaire sighed, but she was grinning. "I won't stay too long, I promise. I'm eager to get to work."

Mianna caught herself in a yawn. "We should all get some rest... I'd like to leave bright and early tomorrow." She gently took Albtraum's hand. "And you need a warm bath, I think."

The idea was quite appealing, and the feeling of Mianna's hand clasped around his made all the tension and hardship of the past days melt away.

Joaquin stepped by, patting his head. "Get some rest, dear boy, I will see you tomorrow."

Brunhart chimed in as well. "Yes, good night, pup."

Albtraum said his good-nights and stood to follow Mianna up the stairs to the bedrooms, Renegade trotting behind him. The windows were open, allowing the cool night air to blow through the hallways. The soft smell of the sea in the distance filled the rooms.

Mianna led him into her bedroom and shut the door behind her, leaving Renegade slipping inside and curling up at the foot of the bed to sleep. Mianna collapsed onto the bed with a heavy sigh and motioned for Albtraum to sit beside her.

Albtraum did so, leaning back on his hands, looking around at the room. He'd been staying in Mianna's room ever since they'd departed Nerea, but being here with her still felt surreal, like moving through a dream.

He frowned slightly as he considered his feelings for her again. He'd been trying not to lend any thought to them ever since they'd agreed to court, hoping they would lessen, that he would be satisfied with Mianna's casual arrangement. Though the more time passed, he realized his feelings had grown beyond his control. There were times she was the only thing his mind allowed any thought for.

Oh, my child. I will free you from this witch's curse, I swear it.

Albtraum rubbed his eyes. Of course, no matter how much of his thoughts Mianna occupied, Lucifurius was ever-present.

He longed for the day he would be able to have his own thoughts in peace.

Mianna drew him from his thoughts with a tap on the shoulder, and when her turned to her, he saw she was holding out Brunhart's carving.

"You found it," he muttered with a soft laugh as he accepted it. "I... I can't believe that worked."

"Joaquin suspected Zyrashana from the start, and... admittedly, I did as well. But seeing this confirmed it for me, and that is when I decided we would fight through to save you both. Of course, little did I know, you two had already handled that part." She smiled.

"I had to get back to you."

Mianna wrapped her arms around him. "You are quite the gem, Albtraum. You've done so much for our cause, you have fought so valiantly..." She looked up at him. "To that end, I have something I'd like to discuss with you."

"What is it?"

"When you went missing, and we could not find you... I realized that I was not concerned for the impact that would have on our cause. That I was not considering your role in our plans... It was no longer of any importance to me." She placed a gentle arm around his waist.

"Have I given you cause to reconsider my involvement with the order?" he asked, concerned at what she was implying.

"No," she replied with a slight laugh. "Nothing like that. Albtraum... The cause was no longer of any concern to me because *you* were all I was concerned with."

He scanned her expression carefully, but found nothing he could derive any meaning from. "What do you mean?"

"Goodness, you really are going to make me come right out and say it, aren't you?" She laid back against the bed, pulling him back with her. She looked into his eyes, and he stared back, feeling something tighten in his chest.

"Albtraum..." she laced her fingers through his. "I have not allowed myself to delve into my feelings for you, because, quite frankly... They are unfamiliar to me. In all my years I have never felt for someone as I have for you, and I suppose... It alarmed me."

Albtraum could hardly believe her words, but he stayed where he was, captivated as he watched her speak.

She sat up to look down at him. "I love you, Albtraum. You are the first I ever have. And... I hope you will continue to love me in return—"

"I do," he said quickly, sitting up to face her. "I... I will. Always. I..."

Mianna watched him expectantly, and he looked back at her, his words caught in his throat as he let the realization of the moment settle over him.

"Sylva is my home. And no matter where I hold power... You hold my heart."

She looked stunned for a moment before smiling at him. "For someone who claims to dislike cloying romance stories, you certainly sound just like one."

Albtraum sighed. "Perhaps I decided to give some of them another chance."

Mianna raised an eyebrow. "And?"

"I still detest them. They are inferior to real love."

Mianna pulled him into a deep kiss, and he relaxed under her touch, his heart beating hard in his chest, unable to contain his joy.

Why do you turn your back on me?! Why do you scorn me so?!

She can give you nothing that I can! The power she offers you is but a mirage, an empty promise...

You say she is the one who holds your heart?

Just you wait... She will be the one who crushes it.

He winced, and Mianna broke away from him, seeming to understand what was happening as he looked back at her apologetically.

"We will rid you of him soon, darling, I promise."

"It's odd," Albtraum sighed. "I... there seems to be more separation between us now – he did not realize it when I dropped the carving – and I can obscure some of my thoughts from him, but..." He bit his lip, his voice lowering to a whisper. "He is growing more aggressive, and the pains are growing worse."

"When we arrive back home, separating you will be our first priority." Mianna smoothed his hair back from his face. "Now... Shall I draw us a bath?"

He nodded, nuzzling into her hand as she stroked his face. "Yes... I should like nothing better right now."

Albtraum awoke early in the morning – very early, the sun had not yet risen.

Mianna slept soundly beside him, and he curled up against her, appreciating the soft warmth of her body beside his.

The events of the previous day were a haze. In just that short time, he'd gone from being locked in a cell in Raazenia, to running from the kingdom with Zyrashana and her forces on their tail... to coming here, and having Mia confess that she returned the feelings he held for her.

He could hardly believe he had her love. At times it felt there was too much love for him to hold, between Mianna and his family and the friends he'd made. But love was a pleasant thing to be overwhelmed by.

He buried his face into her hair, freezing as he heard her give a sleepy, muffled laugh.

"Sorry," he muttered. "I didn't mean to wake you."

She sat up and rubbed her eyes, then looked out the window. “The sun’s peeking out from the horizon. We’ll need to be leaving soon.”

Indeed, as Albtraum listened he could hear the movement of the party downstairs as they readied themselves for departure. He groaned.

“Can’t we stay here for a while longer? Ismaire is going home to her family, surely Sylva can do without us for a while as well.”

She smoothed back his hair, smirking down at him. “My bed in Sylva is far more comfortable than this. Come to think of it, even the guest bed we put you up in was far superior.”

Albtraum sighed, standing from the bed, stretching. “Can you tell me more stories of your political ventures, then?” he asked, looking eagerly at her.

“You’ve asked for so many!” she exclaimed as she rose to change from her nightgown into her travelling clothes. “I’m going to run out at this rate.”

“Then you can tell them over again.” He turned around to give her privacy.

“I’ll only bore you,” she sighed, stepping around him. He shut his eyes, eliciting a hushed giggle from her.

“You could never bore me,” he assured her, opening his eyes again as he felt her pull him down by the shirt collar to kiss him. He leaned forward, expecting another deep kiss, but she only pecked the end of his nose.

“Go on and ready yourself. We’ll have plenty of time to lounge about on the ship.”

Begrudgingly, he did so, changing into his travelling clothes. He packed his books and closed the trunk before opening the door, sending Renegade trotting along down the stairs to where the group waited, his tail wagging.

He headed down the stairs to find Ismaire and her escorts fully prepared to depart. Their packs were full and laden down with supplies, and Ismaire seemed unusually chipper for the early hour.

"Glad I caught you," she called out as she saw Albtraum heading down the stairs. She awkwardly cleared her throat. "Just, ah... Wanted to say sorry, again. For how much of an arse I was."

Albtraum shook his head, smiling slightly. "It's alright. Thank you for helping me escape."

He turned when Mianna approached behind him. She was dressed plainly in a loose-fitting, light blue dress with simple embroidery at the hems, her hair braided back loosely. She put her arm around Albtraum's waist and nodded in greeting to Ismaire.

"You're prepared to leave, then?" she asked.

"Yes. When would you like me back?"

Mianna's brow furrowed as she considered it. "You should be boarding to return to Sylva in no more than a month. That will place you back with us a few weeks after we return – and we will need to get to work soon after that."

Ismaire nodded. "Thank you once again, Mianna... for everything you've done for me. Look, Bonehead—*Al,* sorry— you take care of her, alright?"

He opened his mouth to answer her, but Mianna beat him to it. "If anyone needs to be taken care of, it isn't me," she chuckled.

"Ah, well." Ismaire smirked. "Can't help but feel that way. I'll see you all at the end of autumn. I hope the journey back is pleasant for you all."

"You as well, Ismaire," Mianna replied. "Send a letter when you're on your way back to Sylva."

Ismaire nodded, and turned to the door to leave, waving over her shoulder. "Goodbye, all. Safe travels."

Albtraum watched her go, then turned his attention to the guards who remained, still preparing to leave. Glen approached them when he noticed Albtraum.

"Good morning, Your Majesty, good morning, Al!" he chirped. "I'm quite excited to see our horses again once we get back into the port where we last left them."

"Yes, it will be good to finally be headed home," Albtraum agreed.

Glen beamed. "It will, won't it? Especially now that you know it's home. And I know things will be difficult for a while, with the Order..." He turned his attention to Mianna. "But you should know, all the men are ready to fight for Sylva. No matter what happens."

"Sylva has always made me proud to be its queen," Mianna replied. She looked up at Albtraum. "And perhaps it's time it had a prince consort?"

Albtraum stammered at the suggestion, but Glen laughed. "Yes, I think the people would love him. I was a bit worried perhaps you'd move on from us, Al, once everything with the Order began... but it seems you'll be staying forever, won't you?"

Albtraum turned the word over in his head. *Forever.* He found the permanence comforting... the thought of having a place to return to, people waiting for him, no matter where his responsibilities took him.

He nodded. “Yes.”

Glen grinned and embraced him. Mianna stood watching them, smiling warmly.

Albtraum was so enveloped in the joy that surrounded him, he hardly noticed the burning pain that shot through his nerves until it nearly overpowered him.

And his happiness slowly soured into fear as they headed to the port to at last journey home.

After their escape from Raazenia, the idle time spent aboard the ship seemed to be even duller at by comparison, but Mianna dared not complain. She knew that the moment she set foot back in Sylva, more work would already be waiting for her. She had to take care to utilize this time, lest it slip from her fingers.

Mianna had taken to passing time by observing Albtraum. He was an interesting creature, of far more interest to her than anyone she had courted before.

His affections had been far less restrained since she'd confessed to returning his feelings for her, and she relished his attention. He would take her hand whenever he approached her, pull her into an embrace unprompted, nuzzle into her hair when they stood close.

Even the sight of him now was enough to instantly lift her spirits.

They had been at sea for a weeks' time before stopping at a port, and Albtraum looked confusedly over the ship's railing as the vessel was maneuvered into the docks.

"We're stopping?" he asked with a frown, turning around to face Mianna.

"Yes," she replied, walking up beside him and taking his hand, looking out at the dock as they approached. She smirked up at him. "Eager to be back home, are you?"

He leaned against the railing, regarding her with a tired smile. "Well, I haven't been there since I've decided it was home. I imagine that will be different... and I wonder how the people of Sylva will take me now. I am hardly the same person I was then..."

"Well, seeing as you are on quite good terms with the queen, I believe you will have no trouble winning over the rest of them." She smiled, wrapping her arms around him and leaning into his shoulder.

"I suppose I am hoping we do not have any more business to attend to here. I've become accustomed to having you to myself."

"Well, you are in luck. We are only stopping here for supplies, and I fully intend on passing the time with you," she assured him. "What do you say we walk down to the shore?"

He nodded his agreement, and they waited for the ramp to be placed on the ship's edge before walking down to the docks. The air was growing cooler as they travelled further and further from the heat of the desert areas and autumn was fast approaching.

Mianna's footsteps crunched on the gravel as they stepped off the dock onto the shore. It was a lovely afternoon, the sky was just overcast enough to keep the sun from beating down, and a cool breeze amplified the scent of the salty water washing up against the rocks.

She turned her attention to Albtraum as they walked. He was often quiet and contemplative, but he seemed tired and distracted now, his gaze distant and unfocused. There were dark shadows forming under his eyes, and his face looked wan in the washed-out light cast over the shore.

"I quite look forward to seeing how you take court politics, when the time comes," she mused, hoping to engage him in conversation. "I usually have enough success on my own, but with you there to charm them, I imagine we will be a force to be reckoned with."

"*Charm* them? And how do you suppose I might do that, being as I am?"

"You've been improving quite rapidly at the violin," she pointed out. "A noble who hones a skill or craft is quite impressive at court. But even without that, you are well-spoken, observant, and kind. Those are qualities sorely lacking in any frame of the political stage."

His laugh turned to a grimace. "I may be the most charmless individual on this earth. You are the only one who sees any such quality in me, I'm afraid."

She laughed. "I have interacted with a great many charmless individuals, Albtraum, you are not among them. Also, I believe Joaquin might box you about the ears if he heard you speak of yourself this way." Her smile faded as she watched him look out at the horizon, exhaustion written clear across his features. “Are you alright? Your sleep has been fitful, and you’ve been rather quiet since we left Raazenia.”

He looked back over his shoulder at her. “Why, have I woken you in the night?”

“Well, yes, but that was not my concern. Is it Lucifurius?”

Albtraum brought the heel of his hand against his forehead. “He’s been quite active and talkative since Raazenia... And more and more I find his activity causes me to feel poorly.”

Mianna felt her gut twist, and her fair mood darkened as she was reminded of the reality that faced them. “I am sorry, sometimes I do forget just how taxing he must be to you...”

Albtraum was quick to shake his head. “No, no... It... You need not concern yourself with me, truly. I should not have burdened you with this.”

“To love is to share in all things, darling, burdens among them.” She closed the distance between them once again to embrace him. “Please... do not withhold things from me for fear of burdening me. Or from the others, for that matter.”

His silence of late concerned her. Albtraum had never been forthcoming about his troubles, but he’d been even more withdrawn, and she worried what Lucifurius might be saying to him.

Albtraum looked down at her for a moment before pulling her closer against him. He smelled faintly of cedarwood, and the loose layers of his clothes made for a comfortable embrace. Even through her fears and worries, her affection for him, and his in return, was a great comfort.

"Let's not talk any further of Lucifurius," he muttered, pulling away slightly.

"Alright, then. Sharp as you are, I thought perhaps you might like to receive an education at the university in Sylva, once all this is over. You will need it to rule effectively, as well. Would you consider it?" She asked him.

"University?"

"Yes, you can attend there to be educated in more sophisticated matters, such as the nuances of politics and ruling. And a host of other subjects, as well. We have many distinguished scholars who have made Sylva their home, I believe you could learn a great deal there."

Albtraum's eyebrows raised slightly with intrigue. "I should be very interested in attending, yes."

"Good. And with your education as an excuse, you can stay longer in Sylva, by my side." She frowned and sighed as she broke away from him, continuing to walk along the water's edge. "I must say, I am not looking forward to us being king and queen of kingdoms an entire world apart."

Albtraum followed quietly after her, peering thoughtfully at the rocks below his feet. "Surely I won't need to spend my every moment there. Besides, we have all of eternity ahead, what's a few months or years spent working when I can periodically see you? Although..." He glanced sidelong at her. "You will not be in service to the Order forever, surely?"

Mianna shook her head. "No, and neither should you be. When I feel my rule has run its course, I will abdicate my throne. You can do the same, though I hope that will be a great many hundreds of years from now. After that, we will remain immortal, but reduced to the status of Wanderers."

Mianna had pretended for many years that she was not bothered by the lack of true romance in her life, that she was content to use courtship and affection as tools to accomplish her goals. The years when she'd been a girl dreaming of the perfect partner to come and sweep her off her feet were long past, but she could not help be feel pangs of disappointment from time to time, feeling she was slated to live without a lover for all her many years.

Albtraum had been a surprising relief. Someone she shared common goals with, who would be able to truly understand her goals and aspirations, who could work towards them alongside her. Someone who would be a part of the society that had long been the backbone of who she was.

Albtraum looked forward. His eyes looked like a sunset in the overcast light. "It's overwhelming. That much time ahead of us."

"I find it rather exciting. I for one cannot wait to see what the future holds... I've seen many great advances of humanity in my time, and I hope to see many more." The end of Mianna's Order term, once a far-off event she'd dreaded, was now something she looked forward to, knowing she would have someone to share in the future.

"I suppose that will be interesting to see," Albtraum agreed, his voice soft with contemplation.

Mianna watched him for a moment and then took his hand again, pulling him back towards the road. "Let's see what the merchants are selling in town, shall we? We may find another book for you for the way home. You cannot simply read *The Prince* for... What is it now, the *fifth* time?"

"I can," Albtraum said with the barest hint of a smirk. "And I *will.*"

The port was quiet as they walked through, Mianna noticing with a frown that most of the people seemed leery, watching from around corners and quickly looking away. There was a sparse supply stand at which Joaquin stood, attempting to purchase what they needed.

"It seems there is not much here. Further down the path, perhaps?" Mianna suggested, leading Albtraum that way with his hand in hers.

"Not that way!" Mianna heard someone shout after them, and she turned around to the source of the voice, finding a man running up to them on the path. He was dressed warmly – they were well into autumn by now, and the man's breath clouded in the air as he rushed after them.

"May I inquire as to why?" Mianna asked carefully, raising an eyebrow and releasing Albtraum's hand as she turned, though he still stayed close at her side.

"Land's cursed. Won't be long before it comes this way too. We're all getting ready to leave this place – if you came to this port a week later you may not have found us here."

She looked at Albtraum, and his brow furrowed as he turned back to look up the path.

"Thank you for the warning," Mianna said to the man. "But we will see for ourselves."

The man stared after them as they continued up the path, but eventually, he turned away.

Albtraum's mood had darkened again as they walked, he looked around in reserved silence at his surroundings as they moved further and further along the path. The bright autumn colors faded to browns and grays, before they were gone entirely, the trees stripped bare to dark skeletons.

The landscape faded to ashen nothingness as they finally came upon the remnants of a village.

Most of it had been burned some time ago, by the looks of it – desiccated weeds grew up through the charred beams of the skeletal buildings, slowly collapsing as time passed.

Mianna could see as she looked closer – the ground was black not just with ash, but with the moldering of corruption that heralded a rift. Long-decayed remains of the village's former inhabitants were scattered within the fading outlines of the houses they'd once occupied, picked clean by animals and bleached by the sun.

Her heart sank as she looked around – would this be what became of the rift-tainted village near Sylva?

There was a burned pile of something at the center of what had once been the city, in front of what she now could see was the rift itself. Albtraum had wandered closer to it, and she broke into a run to catch up to him as he knelt to touch something.

"Albtraum!" she called, remembering Terce – the thought briefly occurred that he might attack her if she drew closer, but she only wished to keep him safe. She reached out to touch him, but he remained in place, shoulders slumped, before finally turning to face her, showing what was in his hand.

It was clearly a child's skull – missing a few teeth, a gouge in the brow that had likely been an old wound. On each side, three bony nubs. A daemon boy.

Mianna dropped down beside Albtraum, wrapping her arms around him. "We will rid you of him soon, darling."

Gingerly, he set the skull back where he'd picked it up from. There was a pile of bones – several other child-daemons among them.

"He paints humanity as the enemy," Albtraum murmured, his voice low and breaking. "Forcing us – his children – unwillingly upon them, and leaving us to suffer the consequences of what he's done." He stood, Mianna rising with him, keeping a hand at the small of his back, hoping it would be of some comfort. "He claims to care so much for us that he would unmake this world to give it to us... but he allows this to go on and on."

Mianna looked up at him, her free hand moving to hold his.

"No more," he said absently, and she was no longer certain if he was speaking to her. "There will be... no more."

They stood silently for a long time before Mianna tugged Albtraum back in the direction they came. "Let's get back to the ship, darling. You should rest."

He nodded once, and followed her lead.

Mianna found, suddenly, that she was anticipating Lucifurius' release more than ever before. That he would finally have a physical form – that he could suffer as he deserved.

Chapter XXXVIII

There was a sharp chill in the air and the mountainside was awash with warm colors as the leaves had begun to turn. The early afternoon sun had already begun to dip behind the mountains, leaving a bright halo of gold along their edge. From this distance, especially with the changing of the leaves, it almost made the mountain appear to be consumed with fire.

Albtraum was restless, shifting in the saddle of his horse as they rode forward down the road. He was happy to be returning to Sylva, but his excitement was dampened by his uncertainty as to what Lucifurius would do. He had gained strength at the last rift they had found, and ever since then he had grown more distant – but far more vicious. Albtraum could hardly sense his presence at all, most times – but when he lashed out it was with more force than ever before.

One instance had been so bad that Albtraum had fallen into fits for hours, woken up in the dark and surrounded by everyone who could fit into the small cabin he and Mianna were staying in. Joaquin especially had hovered around him for days after.

The silence should have been a relief. He should have been able to enjoy having his thoughts to himself, and in a way Lucifurius' withdrawal felt very much like being able to walk out in the open after being trapped in a small room for a great deal of time. But the fear of the eventual resurfacing darkened everything.

The more Lucifurius pulled away, the less Albtraum would be able to anticipate his actions. He had to be prepared. He could not allow himself to be caught off guard and taken over when Lucifurius was this powerful.

Albtraum kept himself vigilant by incessant worry. If he never ceased thinking about it, he thought, he would be ready if anything should happen.

"Al!" he heard Glen call up ahead, and Renegade's ears perked up at the sound of his exclamation. It was strange to see him in this place again. When they had left Sylva, Renegade was small enough to fit curled up into the saddlebags. Now, upon their return, he was nearly fully grown, and energetic enough to keep pace with the horses.

Albtraum rode his horse forward, noting that he'd fallen behind the rest of the group. "What is it, Glen?"

Glen was grinning. "I can read the road sign!" He pointed to the carved wooden trail marker. *Sylva.*

Albtraum blinked at him a few times, unsure of what he meant, before smiling in return. "Oh... That's wonderful. There are even more books at the estate for you to read, too."

"I suppose that skill will serve you well as our new cavalry captain," Brunhart said over his shoulder, looking back at them from where he rode just ahead on the path, Joaquin riding next to him.

"Cavalry captain?" Glen echoed, brow furrowed in confusion. "What do you mean?"

"Before we left on our journey, Captain Bashkir informed me he wished to retire soon and asked that I consider you as his replacement," Brunhart explained as Glen and Albtraum caught up with him. "And given what I've seen from you on our journey, I am inclined to agree with his recommendation."

Albtraum watched Glen as he processed Brunhart's words. He gasped. "You mean I'm going to be—?"

"Hold on, now," Brunhart grunted. "We'll need to wait until Bashkir's retirement is official, and you have a few things to learn before you take over."

Albtraum chuckled at him. "Looks like you can finally ask for Aleksandra's hand," he said.

Glen looked overjoyed as they rode, he could not keep the grin from his face as he moved to the front of the group.

Brunhart watched him go before turning back to Albtraum. "You seem to be pursuing romance further yourself," he commented.

Joaquin smirked. "Indeed. It's been difficult to have you to ourselves for all the time you've been spending with Mianna, and you haven't told us a thing about how you two are getting on."

Brunhart smiled, but the expression quickly fell, just slightly. "Is everything going well with the two of you?"

Albtraum nodded. "Yes, in fact... It's gone very well. After Raazenia, she said that she loves me as well."

Joaquin's eyes widened in surprise and he steered his horse over, the beast whinnying as it was led to nearly collide with Brunhart's steed. "My goodness, why have you kept this from us, my boy?! You've sat on this all this time?"

Albtraum was startled at Joaquin's exclamation. "W-well, I... We had so many other things going on, what with Mianna preparing for our return, and you assisting her..."

Brunhart sighed. "You do talk so much it's difficult for anyone else to get a word in edgewise, Joaquin."

Joaquin gaped and stammered, offended, but shook his head and returned to the subject at hand. "I am glad she has finally seen reason."

Albtraum shifted in his saddle again, looking ahead to where Mianna rode, conversing with a few servants who rode alongside her, no doubt still planning upcoming events with them. Even dressed plainly as she was in a simple green cloak and ivory dress, she still looked regal, almost otherworldly. He wondered how she managed it.

"I only hope I can prove myself deserving of her."

Joaquin looked at him with an expression he found difficult to read. "I wish you could see yourself as we do, my dear."

The steep climb up the mountainside took the better part of an hour, especially with the caravan wagons. Renegade ran circles around the horses, barking from time to time, but the larger animals ignored him but for the occasional annoyed flick of their tails.

When they finally crested the mountain, the sun had nearly fully set, and darkness had begun settle over the city.

Sylva was quiet as they rode through it, but as more of the people spilled into the streets to welcome their returning queen, shouts and cheers filled the cold afternoon air. They were dressed in wools and furs, their cheeks and noses pink in the chill that surrounded them.

The stable guards called out cheerfully as they saw the returning party. They greeted everyone as they helped them down from the horses and began to unpack the caravans. Albtraum stretched and looked up the road at the estate with a renewed appreciation. *Home.*

Tiredness weighed heavy on him. He stood watching everyone converse as the party readied themselves to head inside, shaking out the stiffness of their limbs and wrapping their cloaks more tightly about themselves in the chill of the evening air.

Mianna startled him when she approached from behind to link her arm through his, but he soon relaxed again at her presence. “I’ve neglected you these past few days, I’m afraid.”

“You’ve had business to attend to. It’s alright.” Albtraum looked up towards the gates as they neared them. A large gathering of guards and servants were there to greet them.

“Welcome home, Your Majesty!” he heard one of the servants call out. “We thought we’d have a banquet and a celebration prepared for you tonight, if you’d like.”

Mianna held tighter to Albtraum’s arm. “Oh, yes, that sounds wonderful.”

Albtraum noted the servants peering curiously at them, and he could feel the questions burning in their gazes. A faint smirk lingered in Mianna’s expression – she seemed to be reveling in their reactions, though no one had ventured any inquiries yet as to why she currently had her ward on her arm.

They made their way inside the estate, and Albtraum was glad for the warmth within the walls, the bustling of activity he could count on to be friendly.

Oh, yes. They will be all the easier to slaughter.

Albtraum bit down hard on his tongue, trying to distract himself as he felt Lucifurius' presence seep into him like blood into water.

"Can't wait to be sleeping in my own bed again," Noman groaned as he trudged past them, rubbing his neck. Glen followed after him, looking much cheerier.

"We shall meet in the banquet hall in two hours' time, I trust that will be enough time to have everything ready?" Mianna asked one of the servants as they lifted the cloak from her shoulders. She pulled away from Albtraum.

"Of course, Your Majesty."

Albtraum was startled to find his own cloak taken, and he turned around to find Joaquin, who chuckled and smoothed down the flyaway strands of hair that had escaped his braid. "I believe you're going to find yourself rather popular with the servants now that Mianna has claimed you and marked you as desirable," he muttered softly.

"Joaquin," Albtraum shot back with a withering glare, his voice a low rasp.

Let them come... Humans are fools, easily attracted by a pretty face. It will be their undoing.

Brunhart approached his other side, mussing up his hair and undoing the work Joaquin had just done. Joaquin scowled at him.

Brunhart raised an eyebrow at Albtraum. "Have you gotten taller?" he asked. He stood back a single pace, then gave a slight chuckle. "You have, haven't you? The top of your head was just at my line of sight when we left here, but now you're looking me in the eye."

"Well, you've always been taller than I, so I paid no notice, I'm afraid," Joaquin sighed. He looked over towards the doorway of the foyer, where Mianna had been swept away by the welcoming party. "Go on with you, then! You'd best run along after Mianna if you don't want to lose her to the people."

Brunhart nodded in farewell. "We'll see you at the banquet."

Albtraum carefully maneuvered his way through the dense gathering to reach Mianna where she waited at the doorway. "Oh, what a journey that was," she sighed. "I shall be very glad for a bath when we get back to my bedchamber."

Mianna took him by the hand once more and led him up the winding steps of the castle to her chambers. It was a well-worn path after years and years of footsteps traveling it, the stones had been worn until they dipped slightly in the center. It was a section of the estate he'd never been to before they had left on their journey. They reached a large wooden door, and Mianna pushed her way inside.

The room was large, easily three or four times the size of the room they'd put him up in before. The ceilings were high, and there were great tall windows looking out over the city and the forests beyond it. It was a beautiful sight, illuminated by the soft golden light of the setting evening sun.

The bed was large and made up in a fine velvet duvet, with a tall canopy and heavy curtains surrounding its perimeter. There was a fire already roaring in Mianna's fireplace, lighting the room and making the stone floors around it comfortably warm. Two servant girls followed them in, helping Mianna out of her travelling clothes.

There was a large lowered pit of stone in the floor, and Albtraum wondered what it was until he saw that it was filled with steaming water. A bath, and the servants had already filled it.

He sat, feeling tense and awkward as the servants helped Mianna undress, chatting with her about the journey and looking over their shoulders at him from time to time.

"Albtraum and I are courting," she finally explained to the servants. "So I would like you to tend to him just as you do me for as long as he is here."

They chuckled at that, looking at one another before turning their attention back to Albtraum and nodding. "Of course, Your Majesty."

"My lord?" one of the girls asked, standing attentively before him, waiting for him to stand.

"Oh, I..." He shook his head. "It's alright. I'd rather do it myself."

"Might we take the dog for some scraps from the kitchen?" another one of the girls chirped, grinning widely at Renegade as he wagged his tail.

"Yes, he'd like that very much."

Both girls nodded and bowed quickly before leaving the room with Renegade in tow, smirking at one another.

Albtraum gazed at the closed door as he shed the layers of his clothes, folding them neatly and setting them on top of the chest of drawers at the end of Mianna's bed. "What was *that* about?"

Mianna laughed softly as she sat in the bath. “They have had a wager as to when I would fall for you,” she muttered, watching him with a smile as he made his way over to the bath, somewhat embarrassed at his own nakedness. He eased into the water next to her, finding its heat soothed the aches that travelling had brought on. “I thought it silly at the time, but it seems I have stood quite corrected.”

The bath was quite roomy, and allowed him to stretch out his legs. Mianna did the same, leaning back against the edge of the bath with a contented sigh. She rested her head against Albtraum’s shoulder, and he was happy for the closeness.

“I am sorry I have been so preoccupied,” she muttered.

“I don’t mind, darling,” Albtraum replied. In their weeks together on the ship he’d grown more comfortable being affectionate with her. “Truly. But you did promise me stories, and I must confess I have been awaiting them rather eagerly.”

She laughed. “Yes, of course. What interests you most?”

“Your time with the Borgias,” he answered quickly. “And Machiavelli.”

“You have been waiting to ask me more about this since I first mentioned it, haven’t you? Alright, well... It is one of my most interesting stories. Considering that is where Joaquin and I met.”

“Is it?”

“And Brunhart.”

“Well, now you must tell me.”

Mianna stretched out further into the bath. "I was in Vatican City on business, of course. My stay ended up being longer than I wanted as Cesare Borgia and I considered the possibility of marriage—"

"Marriage?" he asked, feeling his brow furrow at the very thought.

"Albtraum, I thought we discussed this before? Marriage seldom has anything to do with love."

You are just another one of her playthings. How foolish you are to believe she actually cares for you.

But you can still have your revenge... we can still kill her.

Albtraum flinched, and moved away from Mianna quickly enough that water splashed out of the bath.

She blinked at him, startled. "Albtraum?"

He stared back at her, then shook his head. "Nothing... It... The water is quite hot."

She did not seem to believe him, but she closed the distance between them and wrapped her arms around his waist. "As I was saying... I was staying in Vatican City... Cesare Borgia was... *aware* of my immortality, so Imbibing was part of our negotiations as we tried to glean some mutual benefit from a marriage between the two of us."

"If there is one thing Cesare excelled at, it was idle chatter. Rumors spread that I was immortal, and most dismissed them as superstitious tales. Except, of course, for Joaquin, who is immortal himself. He was also in Vatican City on business... He has quite a talent for organization, and he'd spent his years wandering from monarch to monarch, working for them until he could no longer justify his lack of aging."

"I can't imagine Joaquin ever working anywhere but Sylva," Albtraum mused.

Mianna smiled. "Neither can I. And I believe he had grown weary of having to find a new place to make his home every decade or so... He sought me out, and offered me his services. I was relatively new to ruling, and in dire need of a seneschal, so I accepted his offer. Of course... That was not all he wanted."

"He had a price on his head, a king who he'd slipped out on who was paranoid that Joaquin might sell his secrets. So the king hired—"

"Brunhart," Albtraum interjected.

"Have you heard this story before?" Mianna asked wryly, reaching for the soap.

"Brunhart explained his part in it. Though he isn't as good a storyteller as you are."

"Joaquin had learned Brunhart was immortal himself... and feared he might actually be able to kill him. He could not have, of course, Wanderers can only be killed by immortals of higher rank than themselves. When Brunhart tracked Joaquin down, I offered him the option of dying, or entering my service. Obviously, he chose the latter."

"I'm glad for that." Albtraum relaxed against the edge of the bath. "For all of you."

Mianna looked into his eyes with a loving smile. "As are we for you. Now, would you like to hear more of Machiavelli?"

Albtraum nodded. "Yes. So long as you are the one to tell it."

After they'd bathed and dressed again, Mianna and Albtraum made their way back down to the banquet hall. Much of the guard force had been in attendance, as well as the party they'd travelled with – and a large number of the townsfolk. Albtraum had sat quietly at Mianna's side through much of the meal. He'd tried many different foods on their travels, but pierogies were still his favorite, and they had been plentiful at the banquet.

There was much to inform the people about with all that had transpired on their travels, and they had listened with a willing ear as Mianna told them of all they'd done – and what was surely to come.

"This means, unfortunately, as you have already been informed..." she sighed as she drew to the end of the tale, "War with Raazenia looms on the horizon. We must begin to prepare ourselves for that. And I swear to you all – I will protect this place. I will never let Sylva fall."

"Raazenia'll be sorry they ever tried," one of the guards at the back of the room hollered, and he was met with scattered shouts of agreement around him, which seemed to at least slightly dampen some of the worried expressions of the townsfolk.

"On a happier announcement..." She took Albtraum's hand, looking at him with a smile. "Albtraum and I are now courting. And I... well, Sylva will be welcoming him as a Prince Consort very soon—"

Gasps broke out across the table, and Albtraum was sure he could pick out Joaquin's over all of them.

Mianna's voice lowered as she leaned closer to Albtraum, though the room had gone so quiet he was sure they all could hear her still. "That is, of course, if he'll have me."

"Do you have to ask, Mia?" he murmured in response. "Of course."

He was surprised at the happy shouts that followed, the guards he'd travelled with shouting loudest of all. Some rushed to congratulate Mianna, and the table fell back into excited chatter.

It was surreal, especially after the hostile and treacherous environments they'd travelled through, to be so genuinely well-liked... to be surrounded by friends. He could scarcely believe it.

Because you are not loved by these people at all. You are an interesting bauble they are infatuated with. They will soon see how worthless you are. Prove them wrong. Kill them.

"Albtraum?"

All of them. Let it be only us. Nothing will ever need trouble you, nothing will ever stand in our way.

Only we will remain.

"Albtraum..."

His gaze snapped over to Mianna. "Yes, darling?"

"Since we've finished eating, I thought some music and dancing may be a good way to end the evening. Would you be so kind as to show off your musical inclinations to our guests?"

"That sounds lovely," an older woman chimed in from the edge of the group.

Feeling expectant eyes on him, Albtraum stammered out a response. "I... ah... Yes, alright." He noted, with a small sigh of exasperation, that Joaquin had produced a violin seemingly from nowhere.

He nervously made his way over to the edge of the room and settled into position to play. He'd had a great deal of time to practice aboard the ship, and playing had become quite fluid and effortless – but he'd never done so in front of anyone but Mianna or Joaquin.

Trying to ignore the crowds around him, he brought the bow to the strings and began to play a simple, somewhat jaunty melody Joaquin had taught him.

To his surprise, after a few minutes of his playing, some of the people began to dance. He watched them wistfully as he remembered how Mianna had taught him, and he wished to join her in a dance once more. She watched him play with a smile.

After a while longer, Joaquin gently took the bow from him. "I can take over from here, if you would like to join them."

Albtraum nodded as Joaquin picked up the melody where Albtraum had left it, although he played with far more skill. Mianna took Albtraum by the hand and led him to where the other people had started an impromptu dance floor.

"I was right about you being a charmer, darling. All eyes seem to be on you," she teased as they began their dance.

"I wish they'd be elsewhere," he muttered, pressing closer to her.

She rested her head against his chest. “We will retire for the night soon. I know you are tired. But when we are married you will need to get used to the people of Sylva looking to you,” she teased.

And I will be sure to whittle you away until you have no choice but to kill every last one of them.

Or... you could kill the villagers, now. All of them unarmed, all of the guards allied to you... It would be so simple, my child...

“Darling?”

“Mmh?”

“You’ve got that faraway look in your eyes again.”

Albtraum blinked and shook his head to clear the haze. “Forgive me, Mia. I’ve a lot on my mind.”

Her smile faded as she looked up at him. “I am sure. Why don’t you go and rest on one of the sofas for now? I need to speak with a few of my organizers before we turn in, anyhow.” She stood on her tiptoes to kiss him, gently, before pulling away and weaving her way through the crowd.

Albtraum walked to the edge of the room and slumped down into one of the sofas there. He leaned back into the soft cushions, shutting his eyes to try to quell the aching behind them.

How many others has she kissed that way, do you suppose? How many other men has she danced with and called ‘darling’?

You are nothing to her. You are just another thing to gain her favor with her flock. Like flies to rotting meat.

Albtraum clenched his jaw. *Be. Quiet.*

Lucifurius' presence oozed smug amusement, but he quieted for the time being.

Albtraum scarcely noticed that he had dozed off, free of Lucifurius' ceaseless taunting. He jolted awake when someone laid a gentle hand on his arm, and found himself facing Mianna.

"Sorry to have awakened you," she said softly. "But the guests are beginning to clear out for the night."

Albtraum looked around. Joaquin had been replaced by a whole group of impromptu musicians, gently playing but clearly winding down for the night. A few people still danced, but most were standing along the edges of the room, deep in conversation. The candles had all been snuffed by now, meaning he had to have been asleep for hours. He grimaced.

"I am sorry... I hope I did not embarrass you by sleeping through most of our welcome celebration."

She smiled gently. "No, in fact, when anyone inquired about it I told them you were simply exhausted from all the work we've done of late, which is no lie. They were rather impressed."

"Still, I... I should have represented you better."

"Hush, darling," Mianna said, placing one finger on his lips and a hand on his shoulder. With a gentle tug, she began to lead him backwards out of the banquet hall and into the cooler, darker, quieter stone hallways. The music and rumble of people could still be heard lights still spilled out of the doorways they had left behind, but the sounds faded as they moved further down the hallway.

“Let’s go up to our room,” Mianna said. She held up a few papers that she had been clutching. “I have some things to review before we begin working tomorrow, and I could use some company while I look over them.”

Albtraum liked the way she phrased it. *Our room.* “You don’t suppose you might tell me more tales while you work?”

“Of course, darling.”

The darker parts of the castle had started to cool as night fell. The stones did not hold much warmth, and though it was not quite winter yet, the feel of it hung in the air like an ever-present reminder that this day would not last. It was comforting when they stepped into the bedroom to find a fire had been lit in their absence and still burned large and strong in its hearth. Renegade waited for them at the foot of the bed, stretching sleepily as he saw them.

Albtraum was glad to change into his sleeping clothes, standing beside Mianna as she did the same. He wished he could remain in these moments with her forever, everything simple and quiet and sweet.

How many others have there been? Don’t act as if you haven’t been asking yourself over and over again.

If you kill her now, before she tells you any more, you can pretend you are the only one there has ever been. And you will have been her last.

You want this moment to last forever? Then make it so, and kill her where she stands.

Albtraum hastily made his way over to the bed, burying himself under the duvet, trying to drown out Lucifurius. But his voice came from within, and his efforts were for naught. He could not hide from something that existed inside him.

“Albtraum? Are you alright?”

He pulled the duvet back, shaking his head to clear it. “Yes... Let’s get back to your stories, shall we? Th-that might help.”

She smoothed back his hair as she sat beside him. “Of course.”

“So what was *that* like?”

Mianna looked up from the contracts she was reading over. She normally made a rule of not bringing business into the bedroom, but she needed to read over all her contracts quickly in order to continue negotiations, and her bed was a great deal more comfortable than the rigid desk chair in her office.

“What was what like?” She'd been absentmindedly conversing with Albtraum for a while, and some time had passed since either of them had spoken. He had been asking her of the men she’d courted and dealt with over the years.

She frowned on looking at him, it was clear from how intently he studied her actions from where he sat at the end of the bed that he had been far more invested in their conversation than she had.

She sighed and set aside the papers, noting that the candles lighting her work had burned down to stubs. She'd been at this all night.

“Cesare Borgia,” Albtraum clarified, looking almost hurt.

Mianna sighed again. "Oh, Albtraum... Cesare Borgia has been dead for more than fifty years, you have nothing to worry about." She'd never thought him to be the jealous type.

"I'm not sure how I can be expected to compete with the expectation he left you," Albtraum continued, seeming to have ignored what she said. She grimaced slightly, realizing that she had been talking at great length about Cesare and her time spent in the Vatican. In truth, she just found the entire ordeal to be a very amusing story, but to Albtraum it had quite obviously come off as a lingering infatuation with the cardinal-turned-general.

"Albtraum, he left me no expectations." She smirked. "Expectations for something better, perhaps, yes, but he was *entirely* unfulfilling. He masqueraded as an intelligent man, but he *bored* me. He talked far too much about nothing at all."

Albtraum did not look to have taken any comfort in that. "I know I must be... unexciting by comparison, and I have nothing so great to offer you as Cesare or any of the others did. You've been with so many men."

She laughed. "*And* women." When he did not return her amusement, she crawled over to him, tugging his sleeve until he joined her in the pile of pillows at the head of the bed. "Darling, you're worrying over nothing. I am with *you* now, and however many people I've bedded, I've only ever loved one."

He looked astonished, and not in a good way. "What? Who?"

She laughed again, sitting up next to him. "Albtraum."

She saw the flicker in his expression as he realized what she meant, and he looked embarrassed. "Oh... I..."

"Why wouldn't you assume yourself to be the subject of that statement?"

He scowled. "You have your choice of anyone, why me?"

"Why not you?" She asked.

"I'm hardly someone you can properly show off to your noble connections--"

She huffed. "Albtraum, I don't *care* what some puffed-up nobles think of me, or you. I don't *want* someone I can show off," she assured him. "I want you. I want the way you look at me, your kind heart, your biting wit, your hunger for knowledge. I have no desire for a marriage that brings me political power – I can sort that part out on my own just fine."

He finally relented, at least somewhat. "So I'm better than Cesare Borgia, then?"

She smiled. "Far better."

Satisfied, he retrieved his book from the nightstand – *Discourses on Livy,* again – so that she could get back to her work.

She looked up from her papers again. "Of course, there was Lucrezia..."

Chapter XXXIX

Albtraum was awakened by a knock at the door of Mianna's bedroom the next morning – she herself had awakened absurdly early, but he'd drifted in and out of sleep beside her for some time.

He groggily opened his eyes as Mianna leapt from the bed to answer the door, finding her fully dressed for the day – a servant greeted her and handed her a parchment.

"Ismaire has written to inform you she has set off on her way home."

She accepted the parchment from the young man with a nod of acknowledgement. "Thank you for notifying me... Seems this was dated quite some time ago, so she should be home any day now." She dismissed the servant and shut the door.

Albtraum was stirred as she turned around, squinting in the bright morning light. Renegade was sleeping at the foot of the bed, but he stood and moved to see Albtraum as he heard him waking.

"Word from Ismaire?" Albtraum finally managed to ask coherently as he sat up, rubbing his eyes. He brushed his hair out of his face – it was stuck out every which way, and he must have looked like a wild beast with a tangled mane. Mianna laughed softly at the sight of him.

"Yes. But her letter has arrived much later after the date than I would have expected..."

Albtraum frowned, looking outside and remembering the heavy, freezing rains they had encountered on the journey home. "Well, the weather has been quite foul. Perhaps that has something to do with it?"

Mianna sighed. "Perhaps. I suppose we will know once she arrives. I must be off for the day, darling, but I may have need of you later." She kissed his cheek before leaving the room, the door slightly ajar, allowing Renegade to slip out after her.

Albtraum grumbled sleepily to himself as he stood from the bed, stretching. The room was empty and lonely now that Mianna had gone, the stone floors were cold beneath his bare feet – and Renegade was sure to find trouble if Albtraum did not soon join him.

He dressed in one of the new outfits Joaquin had made that he had not yet had the chance to wear – a soft silk shirt and a black velvet doublet threaded with embroidery that Albtraum thought may have been real gold. He pulled on his canvas trousers and soft leather boots, loosely tied his hair back and threw a heavy velvet cloak over his shoulders.

He left the room and shut the door behind him, making his way downstairs. He could hear someone speaking, tone terse and annoyed - Joaquin. Renegade stood before him, looking up at him with a smiling face and clearly no understanding of the consternation he had caused.

"From the look on your face, Joaquin, I'd say Renegade's caused you some trouble?" Albtraum asked with a chuckle as he walked over to scratch Renegade's ears in greeting.

Joaquin huffed. "As soon as he saw me, he jumped – and look! Shed fur! Everywhere! I know you love that dog, my boy, but he is a nuisance, and it is going to take me ages to get the fur off of everything, for how it clings."

I wonder how he would care to have his precious clothes stained with his blood.

"In any case... Mianna and I are making our preparations for what is to come. Our first priority is you – and separating you from Lucifurius. I imagine we might need to discuss some of our plans with you soon, so don't stray too far today, alright?"

Distracted by Lucifurius' taunting, Albtraum nodded. "Yes, I will see you later."

Albtraum took a moment to compose himself before he set off in the same direction, Renegade following at his side. It had been quite some time since he'd last navigated the halls of Sylva – but he found it as easy as if he'd been here his whole life. He remembered that before they'd set off on their travels, he often walked along Brunhart's guard route with him, and set off to find him.

The halls were abuzz with flurries of activity, and Albtraum tried to maneuver through them without drawing attention to himself. He made his way toward the main gate, where he knew Brunhart usually started his morning routine.

Sure enough, Brunhart was there, dressed somewhat lightly, directing more of the guards as they began their patrols for the day.

Weaker armor. Easier death. You could take the sword from his belt and run him right through, and I doubt he would even lift a hand to stop you.

Brunhart smiled as he saw Albtraum approaching with Renegade. "Good morning, pup."

"Good morning," Albtraum replied with a short nod. "Mianna has work to do, so I thought I'd come and spend the morning with you."

"I am glad to hear it. Are you feeling alright? You look rather worn."

Distressingly aware of the ever-worsening ache in his head, Albtraum sighed. "Just a bit tired from the journey, I think," he lied. "I'll be alright."

"Well, since we're all still recovering from the journey, I'm mostly here for show today." Brunhart motioned for Albtraum to follow him back into the estate. "Given that you're not usually awake at this hour, I'd venture to say you haven't had any breakfast yet?"

"Not yet."

"Here, then." He handed something to Albtraum – a biscuit. Albtraum bit into it gratefully, enjoying the slight crisp of the outside and the soft warmth in the center.

He walked with Brunhart out to the courtyard. It was cold out in the open air, nipping and foggy from the previous few hours, but not yet nearing cold enough for snow or ice. It was a damp sort of chill that blew through the dimness of the early morning and threw everything into sharp relief.

The town itself was quiet. Albtraum found it pleasant to escape the bustling in the estate, trading it for the tranquility of the Sylvan streets.

Brunhart reached over to pull up the hood of his cloak. "You should wrap up, it's much colder here in the mountains than it was in the other places we travelled through, especially with winter on the way."

"I'm alright," Albtraum assured him, muffled by a mouthful of biscuit. He swallowed and wiped his mouth on his sleeve. "Brunhart, do you think we could spar later?"

Brunhart raised an eyebrow at him, peering around the edge of his hood to look him in the eye. "We could, yes... But you've done excellently when we practiced on the voyage home. You've gotten much stronger... Surely you've earned a day of rest."

"Practicing sparring clears my head." That much was true – the act of sparring made him feel more in control of himself, even if it did increase the intensity of Lucifurius' taunting.

"Perhaps after you've had more to eat, then."

Just then, Albtraum heard a shout across the courtyard, and turned on his heel—

"Captain!"

Glen sprinted across the stone path, people darting away to let him pass, his expression wide-eyed and nervous.

"Th-there's..." He stammered as he skidded to a stop in front of them. "It's – there was an ambush... the guards on the lower roads – an enemy army! It's Raazenia!"

It has begun, child.

Albtraum could almost feel the color drain from his face as he looked to Brunhart, who was stone-faced, expression betraying nothing.

He was already leaving the courtyard by the time Albtraum finally processed what Glen had said. "Get Albtraum inside, then rally as many men as you can. Quickly!"

Glen nodded, grabbing Albtraum by the arm and running as fast as his feet would carry him into the estate as Albtraum struggled to keep up without tripping. He could scarcely focus on anything for the ringing in his ears, but he noted Renegade running alongside them.

"Glen – what happened?"

Glen's breaths were ragged as they ran. He shook his head. "Dozens of them, just – they came from nowhere, out of the forests... Captain Bashkir and all the guards on the lower road were killed, they were overwhelmed..."

Albtraum felt ill. Lucifurius spoke not in words now, but visions - Blood, endless blood. All of Sylva reduced to a sea of blood and a pile of corpses.

Finally, they came to Mianna's office – she sat at her desk, Joaquin across from her, the scene peaceful until Glen charged in with Albtraum in tow.

"Your Majesty! There's been an ambush – Raazenia is attacking!"

Mianna stood from the desk, eyes widening, and Joaquin turned around, gaping, as Glen stammered and struggled to say anything more.

Mianna's expression settled into a hard blankness that was at once enraged and fearful. "Calm down, Glen," she said gently. "We expected this would happen – it is only happening much sooner than we could have predicted. You know what to do – go, gather the rest of the men."

He took a few breaths to steady himself, then nodded, running from the room again, leaving Albtraum to stand in stunned silence.

"*Fuck,*" Mianna spat, collapsing back into her chair with a huff, a hand pressed to her forehead.

Joaquin rushed for the door. "I will gather the citizens – we can shelter quite a few here in the estate if the city walls are breached. We will bring the battle to them."

"Thank you, Joaquin," Mianna breathed. "I will ready myself and join the men at the front lines."

Albtraum had only just realized he was trembling as Joaquin vanished from the doorway – he clenched his fists to try to quell it, but that only seemed to worsen it.

"Darling," he heard Mianna say to him as she stepped over, gently touching his arm. "You must stay here. Zyrashana no doubt targets you – you must stay within these walls as we fight her off."

He looked down at her, trying to answer. His head felt as though it were filled with thick sludge, his thoughts grinding to a halt – and his vision suddenly going black.

No!

We are long past the point of objections! Lucifurius' voice boomed throughout his consciousness, the only thing that cut through the endless void. *You have reached the end of my patience and the end of my leniency.*

The guard captain, choking to death on his blood, despairing as he knows anything he loved in you is gone... The seneschal, hands shaking too much to grip a blade, knowing nothing of you remains behind your eyes, but he cannot raise a hand to harm you... The witch, welcoming death as a release from her own failure. And all the rest of them dying like insects at your hand.

This is what you have wrought! I have had more than enough of your foolish dalliances with this place! It is time we made it our last hunting ground!

Albtraum was frantic. *I'll go with you!* If he had spoken with his own voice, he would have screamed. *I will! Let go – let me go! Please!*

The silence was so heavy, it nearly crushed him. It might have gone on for a second or an hour – Albtraum had no way of knowing.

Finally, his vision returned.

He gasped, blinking as he stared ahead – Mianna, pinned against the bookshelf, his hand at her throat, books scattered around them. He heard a low whine from Renegade – Albtraum's sleeve was pinned in his teeth.

Horrified, he drew back, releasing Mianna and falling backwards as he scrambled to get away.

"Mia... I-I..."

She did not appear fearful, or even upset as she rubbed at her neck where his hand had been – only concerned. She stepped forward, kneeling beside him. "Albtraum, I know he is growing stronger – please, please try to bear it a little longer. Stay here – I will come back to you as soon as I am able."

He tried to stammer out an apology, but she merely pressed a hurried kiss to his forehead before rushing from the office, shutting the door behind herself, leaving Albtraum alone. Renegade nudged at him with his nose, whimpering quietly.

He bent forward, face buried in his hands. *I will go... I will go to the rift.*

On your feet, then.

Gulping down a few more shaky breaths, Albtraum placed a hand on Renegade's head, somewhat calmed by his presence. He ordered him to stay, and hesitantly, he laid down next to Mianna's desk, though as Albtraum left the office and shut the door behind him, he could hear Renegade stand and sniff underneath it after him.

He wandered through the halls for a long time before finding his way again – he was disoriented, sick to his stomach, but he eventually stumbled his way into the guard barracks, grabbing a sword without thinking.

He took care to avoid being apprehended in the hallways, but it seemed most of the servants were too preoccupied with panic to pay much mind to him.

He shivered as he left the estate, stepping out into the open air. He could hear the clamor of soldiers rushing to the battle, and that of the townsfolk fleeing deeper into the city toward the estate. It had started to snow – a light dusting covered the stones, disturbed by the frantic footsteps of those who ran across the courtyard.

He ran to the stables, the frigid air stinging in his lungs – the stalls were empty but for a few horses. He hurriedly saddled and mounted once, taking off into the streets at a gallop, further down the mountain, fast as he could go.

Abject pandemonium had besieged Sylva – he saw Shadrans and men alike in dark armor, bearing the insignia of Raazenia, charging into the streets, clashing violently with the Sylvans. Blood flowed across the stones – he caught sight of Aleksandra in the chaos, face set in determination as she treated a badly injured Sylvan soldier, and he thought of Glen.

He drew almost to a complete stop as he could see the front lines of the battle – and Mianna. She was armored just as the men who surrounded her, wielding a spear and running through her Raazenian opponents with a ferocity he'd only seen glimmers of before - If not for her waves of chestnut hair, which were beginning to escape from the braid she'd hastily put it in, he might not have recognized her at all.

He knew it was undignified, but he begged. *Please, if you must have this world... Please let this place be the one you leave.*

Lucifurius' laughter was low and roiling. *To the rift first. Then I will decide if you grovel well enough.*

He ran the horse until it was wheezing, stopping for short periods of rest as he skirted the edge of the city, avoiding the battle. The snow grew heavier as he put Sylva behind him, the sounds of the battle growing distant as he rode deeper into the forest until he could no longer hear them at all. His cloak eventually soaked through from the heavy, wet snow of early winter, and he shivered as the forest grew darker and colder.

Finally, the horse stumbled to a stop at the steps of the temple, Albtraum all but falling off its back as he scrambled to get inside.

It was as he'd seen it last – unassuming, but teeming with familiar power. The stones were almost entirely grown over with moss, browning and covered with a layer of frost.

He could not help but gape, eyes wide, as he took in the sight of the inside of the temple. The walls and floors were marred with moss from age, but beneath that they were glossy and black, with glittering flecks that made them look like a night sky filled with stars. A pattern of symbols adorned the top of the ceilings, and they glowed faintly, a soft bluish color, dimly illuminating wide, dark hallway. It was beautiful in its ancient, looming foreboding.

Albtraum shed his cloak and left it in a wet, crumpled pile beside the doorway. The air was damp and cold inside, and Albtraum tried to rub the chill out of his arms as he proceeded.

The hallway descended into more stairs, such that they seemed to go on forever. After a while, the light from outside that filtered in the doorway no longer spilled after him, and the only light that remained was the faint glow of the symbols on the walls.

We are so close. The dark world lies right before us... home... We are so close to being home...

The steps finally came to an end, opening up into a large room. There was a great pit in the center of the room, like the bathhouse in Sylva. Rather than any liquid, however, it was filled with unnaturally dark shadows that almost seemed to suck in the light around them – like the darkness Zyrashana had wielded, forming into a blade. The shadows shifted mercurially, and Albtraum found it hurt his eyes to stare too long at them.

This is it... the raw power from which I will be reborn. Enter the rift, child... Become one with the dark again.

Albtraum took a deep breath and stepped toward the pool of shadows. He hesitated at the edge, a prickle of doubt holding him there a moment—

Rest assured, child, if you turn your back now whatever returns to that city will not be you. And I will raze Sylva to the ground, and all your precious fools and weaklings with it.

Pain unlike anything he had yet experienced liquefied his mind. His vision blurred to nothing, and he felt as if acid had hollowed him out. He felt a scream well up in him, then melt, blended with everything else. Every thought, every sensation became a muddied, corrupted blur.

Lucifurius' voice was the only thing that came through, hard and clear and sharp.

Do we have an understanding?

Albtraum stood frozen in place. He could not even crumple to his knees. Then, just as soon as it had come on, the pain eased, the fog in his head cleared. He gasped softly as the bizarre sensation eased, and he returned to himself.

He clenched his fists and stepped forward, into the pitch blackness that lay before him. His footing felt uneven beneath him, and he nearly tumbled over. It was as though he were trying to walk on a stretched-out cloth.

He stood steady, for a moment, letting the shadows envelop him. The nebulous darkness was cool and soft, the air around him felt clean and crisp. He was almost enjoying the sensation, particularly after the pain Lucifurius had put him through.

It seeped into him. It caressed his bones, filled his mouth and his nose and his lungs.

And then it tore away, taking all the air and the warmth in him with it.

Albtraum sputtered and gasped, desperately scrambling for the edge of the pool. His flailing hands finally found purchase on the pool's stone edge, and he held fast, hauling himself over the edge and collapsing onto the cold stone floor.

He panted, his breaths hard and ragged. His skin felt as though it had been frozen atop the rest of him. Slowly, as the chill in him eased and he regained his breath, he pushed himself up to sitting.

Albtraum came face-to-face with Lucifurius, standing on the other side of the pool.

He was at once exactly as Albtraum has imagined him, and entirely alien.

Lucifurius was tall and thin, like Albtraum himself, with the same pale skin and wildfire eyes. Night-black hair fell to his waist, parting in several places on his head to reveal horns – two long, straight sets behind his ears, and one short curved pair at the top of his forehead. His face bore strong resemblance to Albtraum's sharply angular features, though Lucifurius' were oddly softer, almost feminine.

The darkness had wrapped around him like a robe. He strode towards Albtraum slowly, his eyes wide with wonder, easily holding his posture as he walked across the uneven surface at the base of the pool. He climbed up and knelt before Albtraum, long, reaching fingers taking delicate hold of his face.

"My child," Lucifurius whispered, his fingertips dancing over Albtraum's face like crawling insects, sending shivers of revulsion down his spine. His voice was exactly as it had been in Albtraum's mind, though oddly more invasive now that he physically spoke. "This is the first time I have looked upon you with my own eyes..."

They remained there for an uncomfortably long time, Lucifurius gazing into Albtraum's eyes, Albtraum too afraid to break away. Mercifully, Lucifurius finally pulled back, a contented smile breaking across his face.

"Come, then," he said softly, reaching a hand back in Albtraum's direction. "It is time for us to return home."

Albtraum stood, looking down at Lucifurius.

His mind was finally quiet. His thoughts were his own. He was free.

"No."

Lucifurius recoiled as if he'd been bitten. "*...No?*"

Albtraum only stared back, letting the weight of the word hang between them.

Lucifurius stared back at him, rage beginning to come to life in his eyes. "You... disappoint me. I created you... I gifted you with life. I guided you this far, loved you... and this is how you intend to repay me. With scorn and rejection."

Albtraum only shook his head. The glare he shot Lucifurius was withering.

"You have never once shown me anything close to *love*."

Before Albtraum could answer him, a dark shape resembling a blade formed in his hand. Though it was ever-shifting and ill-defined at first, eventually it solidified in to a hard, sharp form, slightly translucent, like volcanic glass.

"This will not stand."

Albtraum was only barely quick enough to draw the sword at his belt as Lucifurius rushed at him. He deflected the first strike and darted back, his heart catching in a skipped beat as the blade snapped at the first strike, leaving him with nothing but a hilt and a few inches of blade. The broken sword clattered to the ground as Albtraum tossed what remained of it aside, lunging out of the way as Lucifurius brought down the blade with such force it broke through the stone tiles as it hit them.

Lucifurius' movements were erratic, yet oddly predictable. After all... he had moved Albtraum in this way for years, a marionette. Albtraum had with him the advantage of planning and... oh, *finally,* a mind of his own. Even as he paced around Lucifurius in the dance of battle, a joyful laugh escaped him.

The sound only served to enrage Lucifurius, and he whirled on his heel as Albtraum stumbled, nearly falling into the pit of the rift, catching himself on the stone edge.

The shadows swirled around Albtraum's arms, as if drawn to him – he remembered Lucifurius and Zyrashana.

He scrambled to his feet to dodge again, but Lucifurius was faster, kicking him down with such force Albtraum could hear his own ribs cracking as he hit the hard stone floor. He cried out sharply, rolling out of the way as Lucifurius brought his foot down where Albtraum's head had been a second prior.

His vision swam with pain, but looking down at his hands as he pushed himself up, he saw they were still enveloped by the same ink-black shadows he'd seen in Zyrashana's hands, and now Lucifurius' – his mind struggled to conjure the same response they had—

And as he did, the shape of a blade formed in his hand.

He marveled at it, a glistening night-black glass the same shape as the blade he'd held a moment prior, and he swung it around to parry another strike from Lucifurius.

The blade held against the collision this time, but the sharp pain that shot through his arms told him the delicate bones of his wrists had not. Struggling to stay focused, he backed away, adrenaline numbing him to the pain of his broken body as he heaved to catch his breath, feeling his ribs protest every tiny movement.

Lucifurius stood back, his posture relaxing slightly. "Ah... You've finally accepted my gift to you. You might have had this all along – such a wonderful feeling, isn't it? Yours to form to whatever you wish."

Albtraum stared at the blade he held before him – and, as Lucifurius watched him curiously, he exploited the momentary distraction.

He ducked low and rushed forward. His own blade caught Lucifurius across the leg.

Lucifurius wailed in pain as dark blood oozed from the wound and he retreated back, breathing hard.

"You were my only companion in the solitude of my conquest, and now, even you turn against me," he spat. "After all we conquered, all we accomplished together, you have turned your back on me, you have chosen to give in to their lies, when you could have had them all at your feet!"

Albtraum gritted his teeth and tried to force back the dimming at the corners of his vision. "You think I wanted that – power? All I wanted... was to be loved. You never..."

Lucifurius grinned, dark humor beneath the expression. "What you want does not exist. Not for a thing so worthless as yourself."

They whirled around eachother again, blades clashing and scraping against eachother in a cacophony of sound.

Taking advantage of his closeness, Albtraum drew back and slashed up.

There was a sound he was distantly but intimately familiar with as his blade tore through flesh, scraped over hard bone.

Lucifurius let out a sound that was more animal than human, and Albtraum quickly broke away from him as Lucifurius crumpled to the ground.

The wound was wide and ugly, starting at his jaw and continuing up diagonally across his face. The end of his nose dangled loosely, and the white of his slashed eye quickly filled with blood.

Albtraum felt his shoulders loosen slightly. He skidded on his heel to reel back again—

He saw the blade slice through him in an instant long before he felt it.

From his hip to his shoulder, Lucifurius' blade had cut cleanly across his torso, scraping along his broken ribs, shattering his collarbone.

He gasped, his breath hitching, as everything went silent, he was vaguely aware of the sound of his blood dripping on the stones before he staggered back, and fell.

Lucifurius stepped forward, peering down at him as he pressed his heel into Albtraum's throat. He choked, trying to reach up to push him away – his left arm remained uselessly limp on the ground beside him, but he thought he saw his right hand feebly move to push the foot on his throat away.

Lucifurius panted raggedly, blood dripping from the wound across his face onto Albtraum's. It felt hot as fire. "When you are ready to join me in your proper place, I will be waiting."

He stepped away, out of Albtraum's view as he could do nothing but stare unfocused at the ceiling, desperately trying to move, unable to do anything but lie in his blood as it pooled around him.

He thought he heard something – a voice? – call out before his senses began to blur, and his consciousness faded.

Chapter XL

"Albtraum!"

Brunhart knew that the figure that turned to face him, eyes wide, half its face a mangled mess, could be none other than Lucifurius – but in that moment, he did not care, rushing across the temple floor to where Albtraum lay, struggling for breath.

Lucifurius, strangely, seemed equally disinterested in Brunhart himself, stepping away and retreating into the pool of darkness in the room's center. He vanished, as if he had been nothing but a mirage.

"Albtraum," Brunhart called again, his voice strained and strangled. He fell to his knees beside him, reeling, carefully sliding an arm beneath him to lift him up.

The wound was terrible. It had cut so deep Brunhart could see the hard forms of broken bones in Albtraum's chest, blood bubbling as he fought to breathe.

Relief washed over him as Albtraum gave a faint moan and his eyes fluttered open, reflecting the faint light and glinting as his gaze settled in Brunhart's direction. "Brun..hart..."

Quickly, but gingerly, Brunhart gathered Albtraum against himself. "I'm here, pup. It's alright, I'm going to get you home."

Albtraum weakly clung to him, his breaths ragged and shallow. “I-I tried… to st-stop him…”

“Hush, my son, it’s alright. You did well. We will get you home.” Brunhart could *feel* the broken bones as he held him, and his stomach turned. Blood had drenched his clothes, and was quickly seeping to Brunhart’s woolen coat. Tears streamed from Albtraum’s eyes and he whimpered, weak and breathless. Brunhart knew he had not a moment to spare.

He undid the fastening of his cloak and pulled it off to wrap around Albtraum, pulled the hood over his head, then hefted him up into his arms, carefully and swiftly as he could.

“He escaped… into… th-the Rift…”

Brunhart clutched him tighter as they scaled the steps. “Don’t worry yourself about Lucifurius, pup,” he replied softly. His legs ached with exertion as he climbed, but he could not afford to slow down.

When Brunhart finally caught sight of light from outside filtering down, relief flooded him, spurring him into a sprint. He scaled the last of the steps and stepped back outside.

“Captain!” he heard a shout as he emerged back into the daylight, and he saw Glen rushing over to him. Snow was falling heavily now, melting as it fell and running rivulets through the gore splattered across Glen’s armor.

Glen had run from the battlefield, following Brunhart, after he’d returned to the estate to check on Albtraum and found him missing – and his eyes widened in shock as he took in the sight before him now.

He rushed to help Brunhart get Albtraum onto the horse, paying no mind to the animal’s objections to the sharp scent of blood as he lifted

Albtraum into the front of the saddle. Albtraum sat, wavering unsteadily, and Brunhart had to stop to right him several times as Glen wrapped a saddlebag strap around his waist, fastening it to the other side to secure him there.

When he'd finished with it, Brunhart quickly mounted the horse behind Albtraum and held him tightly. His head rested heavily on Brunhart's shoulder.

Brunhart spurred the horse forward into a gallop. Without his cloak, the heavy snow quickly soaked through his clothes, but in this state he could hardly feel the chill in his bones as they rode forward, up the path.

The pace was excruciating. Fast as the horse ran, it was not fast enough.

"Just a bit longer, pup, we're almost home," he murmured breathlessly, shifting Albtraum to hold him closer.

Albtraum whimpered softly in response, curling closer to Brunhart as they rode up the mountain.

They rode the horses as hard as they could up the mountain, around the edge of the city, far from where the battle raged. Brunhart dared not look that direction, dared not lend the battle a passing thought – Albtraum was all that mattered now.

A side street led them into the city, the hooves of the horses thundering noisily on the stones, great clouds of breath bursting from their noses in the freezing air. The fickle weather of late autumn had melted into rain, but it was no less frigid around them.

They eventually came to the courtyard, and Glen leapt from the back of his horse with a spectacular lack of grace, nearly tripping as he rushed over to steady Brunhart's horse as it came to a stumbling stop, its sides heaving with effort.

"Help me with him," Brunhart grunted, undoing the straps that had held Albtraum securely in the saddle and shuffling him over to Glen. Glen seemed to struggle under Albtraum's weight in his arms, but steadied himself and carefully lowered Albtraum to the ground so as not to drop him.

The horse would not hold steady enough that Brunhart could dismount, and his increasing frustration with the animal's anxiety only served to make matters worse.

As he struggled to calm his mount, he heard Glen address him, his voice high and panicked. "Captain?"

Brunhart looked down to where Glen knelt beside Albtraum. Glen's eyes were wide and his mouth hung half-open, as though he'd been about to say something and the words had left him. Brunhart's gaze shifted to Albtraum.

He was frighteningly still, and paler than Brunhart had ever seen him. The cloak wrapped around him was soaked through with blood, and Brunhart looked down at himself – his own coat was drenched with dark blood.

He felt as if the world had been turned on his side, and he stared forward at the horse's ears and they swiveled and pinned back. Glen was speaking to him, but his voice sounded far away.

"Captain... He's not breathing..."

It might have been an eternity before Brunhart slowly looked back down at them.

He stammered, unable to get a word out. "For God's sake, Glen," he finally managed, his voice a sharp rasp. "Get him out of the rain."

Brunhart shook as he slid down from the horse's back, falling to his knees, stumbling into the estate's foyer where Glen had dragged Albtraum.

He knelt at Albtraum's side, gently placing a hand on his forehead, then carefully bringing it to his still-tearstained face. Even through Brunhart's leather gloves, he felt cold.

"Albtraum," he called gently, moving his hand to Albtraum's shoulder to shake him. He pressed his ear to Albtraum's gashed chest, and—

Heard no heartbeat beneath the grisly wound.

He pulled away, dizzy, leaning back on his arm to keep himself from falling.

"Captain," Glen's voice sounded behind him, "What do we do?"

Brunhart paid him no mind. "Albtraum, please," he begged, gripping his shoulders as he searched his ashen face for any sign of life. "We're home. I won't let him hurt you, you're safe here..."

The moments grew longer, but Brunhart's strangled pleas received no response.

He sat back on his knees. He felt tears burn at the corner of his eyes, blurring his vision, and he tried to blink them back, only finding them replaced by more.

He waited in stunned silence until despair finally doubled him over, sobbing, as he reached forward to pull Albtraum against him, feeling the need to anchor himself to something as the world fell away around him. Albtraum was cold all through. He'd been holding him just moments ago, he'd held him all the way home – how had he not noticed the warmth leave him?

Brunhart held tightly to him and cried, until everything in him ached, every breath like an edge rattling through him. The pain was so sharp and persistent he could hardly stand it, but each passing moment saw it sinking deeper and deeper.

Brunhart found himself in an endless cycle, struck over and over by the feeling that if he could only just turn back time a few moments, somehow, this would be different. He wailed and pleaded to nothing – to everything – to let this be some terrible unreality, that he would soon awaken to find his son alive and well. He would keep him at his side, refuse to let him out of his sight. He would keep him safe. Perhaps if he simply waited here long enough Albtraum would wake up, everything would be alright.

But the skies held no angels for him this day.

Glen was doubled forward, wracked with sobs. His body shook, his shoulders hunched forward. He lifted his head to look up at Brunhart, then to Albtraum in his arms, and he crawled forward and took gentle hold of Albtraum's hand.

Brunhart inhaled sharply, his instincts urging him to pull Albtraum away – but Glen was his dearest friend. Brunhart could only think that he would not want to be taken from him.

The two of them sat there, unmoving, as the freezing rain continued to pour over the stone streets, ignorant and unfeeling to their despair.

Brunhart felt drained of everything in him. After a time, he was no longer even able to weep.

"I have to get him home," he finally stated, though he was not sure whether he spoke to Glen or himself.

Glen's tears had not stopped since they'd begun. He gave Albtraum's lifeless hand a hesitant squeeze before letting go and drawing back, curling into a ball and burying his face in his knees. "I'm sorry," he choked. "I'm so sorry..."

Brunhart said nothing and stood, gathering Albtraum's limp, broken frame against him.

He moved forward slowly and deliberately, as if controlled by an outside force, through the foyer and into the estate.

Home. He had to get Albtraum home.

A distant part of him bitterly thought that this was no longer possible. Home no longer existed.

"Has anyone found them yet?"

Mianna's demand was met with scattered denials, and her mouth pressed into a hard frown as she looked around the main hall at the guards who had followed her.

They were turning the tide of the battle, and Mianna had retreated to delegate, and catch her breath. It hadn't been long before she was informed that Brunhart had vanished from the battlefield – and on her return to her office, she'd found Albtraum gone as well, only Renegade whimpering for company in his absence.

"Back to it, then! Go!" she shouted, and the men were quick to do as they were told.

Her eyes darted downward as she saw Joaquin had handed her a tankard – she drank it down greedily, too exhausted to taste or care what it was. A warm ale, perhaps.

"You should stay back and rest," he murmured, his face drawn with worry. "I fear in this state you are no use to anyone. The sight of you frazzled as you are would hardly raise the morale of our men."

She huffed as she finished the ale and handed the tankard back to him, and he set it on the tray behind him. "I cannot leave them alone to face this."

There had been no sight of Zyrashana yet – only seemingly endless waves of Shadrans and Raazenian men that had only just started to wane. Mianna thought, perhaps, she might not have come at all – but what sort of ruler sent an army out alone? She knew she had to return – she could not leave her people to face this threat without her.

"Still, I—" Joaquin stopped abruptly as he heard the departing guards shouting something – and as Mianna looked the same way, she felt her heart drop like a stone.

Joaquin was first to rush forward as she froze, petrified where she stood. "Brunhart!" He shouted. "What's happened?!"

She took in the sight in pieces - Brunhart. He looked alarmingly ragged – soaked to the bone from the rain, his expression drawn and exhausted. He held something in his arms, his shoulders hunched forward with effort.

Albtraum.

"Brunhart..." Joaquin staggered back.

Mianna watched as Joaquin gasped and backed away, allowing her full view of Brunhart standing there.

Details kept making their way to her slowly – Everything bloodstained. Rainwater dripping onto the stone floors. Brunhart's face pained, Albtraum's ashen and blank.

She could not move as she watched Joaquin anxiously circle around Brunhart. "What's happened?" he demanded again, carefully bringing a hand to Albtraum's head, turning it to get a better look at him.

Mianna felt as if she were watching from afar as Brunhart looked down at Albtraum, his expression so tired he almost looked his two hundred years. "He went to the temple, alone, to release Lucifurius. I was too late. He died on the road." His voice was barely audible, the words strained as if he'd had to rehearse them.

“No,” Mianna heard herself interject. She staggered, clumsy, nearly falling forward as she rushed to him. “There has to be something we can do. How can you be sure, Brunhart? We have to take him to Aleksandra.”

Brunhart stood still as a statue as she rushed over, all but shoving Joaquin out of her way. Hesitant, fearful, she gingerly reached out to touch Albtraum’s face. He was pallid and cold.

“Mianna,” Brunhart choked out weakly, his shoulders sagging the barest amount. “He’s gone.”

She could hear Joaquin behind her, heavy breaths beginning to form sobs. “He’s right *here,”* Mianna said more firmly, and Brunhart only seemed to wither further as he looked back at her.

“He’s right here,” she repeated, gripping the cloak wrapped around his body. “Albtraum – darling – *please—”*

There was nothing.

She sank to her knees, a sob catching in her throat. Carefully, Brunhart knelt in front of her, gently lowering Albtraum to the floor – she reached forward without thinking to hold him, reality finally breaking her denial, and a strangled wail escaped her, so cracked and breathless as to be almost inaudible.

She held him, stroking his wet hair as Joaquin, too, collapsed to his knees beside her.

Her lungs ached against her ribcage as she choked out a few strangled sobs, but she felt desperate, unsure of what to do, crying did not seem enough but she had little will in her to do anything else. She pulled back to unwrap the cloak from around Albtraum's shoulders, examining his wounds carefully and finding her vision further flooded with tears as she did.

The gash was wide and deep, and the blood that soaked through his clothes was dark as it had begun to dry. He was cold, broken, bent awkwardly in her arms.

She was not sure how long they stayed there – Joaquin's sobs eventually grew raspy, then silent. Brunhart never moved nor uttered a word.

Finally, someone approached them. "Your Majesty," the young guard called timidly, clearly painfully aware of what he was interrupting. "Raazenia... They've called a retreat. They have withdrawn. We've won."

She hardly heard his words. It no longer mattered.

Brunhart finally spoke up, his voice a broken whisper.

"Come then," he uttered, taking Albtraum in his arms once again, Mianna feeling hers fall heavily at her sides as she let him go. "We can't stay here."

She was vaguely aware of following him as he left the hall, Joaquin in tow, but everything faded out for a time, her awareness of her surroundings sunk into despair, and she walked a revenant as the halls went dark around her.

Chapter XLI

"Quite a lot of traffic on the road, hasn't there been?" Piotr asked absentmindedly as they scaled the last escarpment on the path.

"Lots in the inns too."

Ismaire frowned bitterly as they rode through the cold fog. "And it's already practically winter. Seems unusual, doesn't it?"

Even wrapped in a heavy cloak, the bitter, damp chill of the air still cut through her. Edmund and Piotr, by contrast, had stayed huddled under the tents out of the heat the entire time they'd spent with her family, and seemed much cheerier now that they were back in the mountains.

They rode on without incident for a long time before Edmund cut the path of his horse across hers. "Ismaire," he warned.

She looked ahead – stifling a gasp of horror as she took in the sight before her. It was the clear aftermath of a battle – the ground was stamped with the imprint of thousands of boots, dark with old blood that seeped into the soil. Discarded weapons and pieces of armor littered the roadside.

She rushed around Edmund, onto Sylva's main road. Her heart quickened as she ran – wondering if she should be relieved when they made their way to the city and found citizens exhaustedly going about their daily activites.

"Ismaire!" Edmund called after her as they finally reached the courtyard.

She ran up to the first guard she saw at the main gate. He seemed alarmed at the sight of her.

"What happened?!" she demanded, gesturing the direction of the battle scene behind her.

"Raazenia attacked," he answered quickly. "We fought them off. Lady Ismaire, you should—"

She shoved past him inside, Edmund and Piotr running after her as she tore through the halls, her heart thudding in her ears. She whirled in place, looking around frantically before they finally ran across Glen and Noman walking up the corridor towards them. Noman had a hand on Glen's shoulder, and Glen was dressed in the same uniform as him – a captain's uniform. His shoulders were hunched forward, and he looked at the ground.

"Looks like they've been made captains," Piotr commented. "So then..."

Ismaire quickened her pace to meet them. "Glen, Noman! Where's Mia?!"

Glen only looked back at her miserably, his eyes ringed red as though he'd been crying. Noman looked equally upset – he was normally in a foul mood about something, but this was different.

"Gods, what's with the two of you?" she asked without thinking, her tone more flippant than she had meant in her nervousness.

She'd always been bad about that—

The words had scarcely left her mouth before a fist connected with the side of her face with such force she was sent stumbling back to the ground. She stayed there, dazed, for a few moments as her likely broken jaw quickly healed. As she looked up, Glen stared down at her with a haze of tears in his eyes before rushing past them.

"Glen?!" She heard Piotr call. "Where are you running off to?"

Edmund helped Ismaire back to her feet, frowning at Noman. "What's gotten into him?"

He started to answer them, but sighed. "Queen's in the east hall. You should probably go alone, Ismaire."

Ismaire's panic reached its peak, and she rushed past Noman to the east hall, leaving her belongings where she'd dropped them. As she turned the corner of the hall, she glanced over her shoulder. Noman was conversing with Edmund and Piotr, but she couldn't hear what he was saying from here. Just before she passed around the corner, Edmund caught her eye, frowning, his brow furrowed.

Her alarm only grew as she passed more guards and servants nearer to the east hall, all looking decidedly more somber than usual. Her mind raced over the possibilities, and she nearly tripped over her feet as she arrived at the most obvious conclusion – *Mia. Something's happened to Mia.*

She pushed her way past the people exiting the east hall, too afraid to stop anyone to ask what had happened. There had been a gathering there, but it was beginning to dissipate.

Through what remained of the crowd, her gaze fell upon Mianna, conversing with someone from the town – and her knees weakened with relief.

But as she drew closer, she noted that Mianna had almost certainly been in tears. She'd never seen her friend cry in the years she'd known her, but her eyes were red and she looked drawn and tired, more so than Ismaire had ever seen. Her clothes were black and plain.

It was then that she looked closer to the head of the room – and realized she had stumbled her way into a funeral.

Perhaps it's no one I know, she thought desperately, but she'd already realized who it was.

Albtraum.

She staggered to a stop a ways away from where Joaquin and Brunhart were standing at the side of the altar he'd been laid out on, feeling unsteady. She did not notice that Mianna had approached her until she spoke.

"Ismaire." Her voice was thick from crying.

Ismaire turned to face her, aghast. "What happened...?" She asked, feeling suddenly out of breath.

"He went to the rift," Mianna answered flatly. "Lucifurius separated himself – and killed him."

"I don't understand," Ismaire blurted before she could stop herself, the words spilling out of her faster than she could stop them. "You all made it home. You were going to be able to stop him. Everything was supposed to be... fine..."

Mianna said nothing, looking down at the ground.

Ismaire turned back to face her. "Who are we going to place in power now?"

Mianna sighed. "I do not know. Daemons are not exactly plentiful or easy to find, nor can we hope to find any as well suited to the position as Albtraum was."

Her tone was curt, and Ismaire immediately regretted the question. "Gods, Mia, I... I'm sorry, that's not what—"

"I know," Mianna replied softly. "I know. Please, Ismaire... Leave us be. I believe we all wish to be left alone."

Ismaire shrank back. Of course, she hadn't earned the right to really call herself his friend, not after how she'd treated him. She had planned on making her reparations upon her return, but the chance was forever gone now.

She walked blank-eyed until she reached the staircase that lead up to her loft.

She could hardly fathom that he was gone. How many times had she wished for this, even for the chance to do it herself? When he'd first come to Sylva, getting rid of him was all she could think of.

Childishly, she placed the blame on her own shoulders, as if wishing him dead all those months must have made it so. This was not true, she knew as much... but she could not help thinking that somehow, perhaps if she had been kinder to him, events might have progressed differently.

Servants had tidied her things and made her bed when she reached her loft, but she could hardly appreciate it in this state. She sank into her bed, buried her face into the pillows, and wept until sleep dragged her under.

Brunhart had not left Albtraum's side since he'd been brought to the hall, nor had Joaquin. Renegade had sat beside the altar, unmoving, for as long as they'd been here. Mianna approached them after the last of those in attendance had offered their condolences and left the hall, leaving them alone.

They'd done their best to set the broken bones to right him, to hide the horrific wound. Annette, who ran the tavern, had tried to gently tell Brunhart he looked peaceful – but to Brunhart, there was no peace in this. He only looked dead.

"I see Ismaire has returned," Joaquin commented disinterestedly, fidgeting with his sleeves.

Mianna nodded. "I haven't even the beginning of an idea how to proceed from here." She bit her lip, and her eyes misted over.

Brunhart sighed, watching as she tried to keep herself from breaking into weeping again, though he felt long drained of the energy to do so. "We should tend to Albtraum first. You've decided on the grave?"

"The estate gardens," Joaquin answered, his voice tight and strained. "I won't have him any further from us than there."

Mianna nodded her agreement. "I could not have him brought all the way to the city graves. I..."

Brunhart looked back at her and said nothing, agreeing with their reasoning.

It seemed wrong that they had to bury him at all when he should have been there walking the estate halls still, preparing for the revolution, stealing free moments with Mianna and his friends when he could. He'd likely have spent all his time in the library, poring over military texts. He would have attended the university to get a proper noble's education. He'd work himself too hard, of course, but Brunhart would be there to send him to bed when he'd fall asleep over a desk. Joaquin would bring him plates of food from the kitchens when he'd forget to eat. He would have married Mianna. He would have been happy here.

Instead, they stood over him discussing where to have his grave. In all his two centuries, Brunhart had never witnessed a greater injustice.

"I... I'll take care of it," he said softly. He felt himself choke up again. "I... do not want anyone else to..."

Mianna merely nodded. She stared down at Albtraum for a long time before bending to kiss his forehead, whispering something Brunhart could not hear. After another long moment, Joaquin did the same.

No one wanted to move for a long time, but finally, Brunhart lifted Albtraum from the altar. Joaquin had made a soft shroud of a material Albtraum had liked, draped over him like a blanket – and Brunhart wrapped it closer around him as he held him. Renegade rose to his feet to follow – but Mianna motioned him to stay. His ears drooped, and he sank to the floor like a dog ten years older.

He said nothing to them as he turned for the gardens, but he could hear them both restrain their sobs as he left the hall.

The gardens were withering with the approaching winter, and Brunhart distantly thought to himself it was a small mercy to be doing this before frost hardened the ground. He hated himself for thinking it. What he wouldn't have given to have Albtraum there with them even a moment longer.

He carefully laid him on one of the stone benches at the garden's edge and crossed to where the tools were kept, finding a large spade – and a place to dig.

The pace was agonizing. Brunhart, in his despair, had not eaten or slept, and his body refused to let him forget it. His arms ached and protested with each spadeful of earth – but Brunhart gritted his teeth and continued.

After what might have been hours, the spade clanged against stone. He'd dug down as far as he could, reaching the estate's stone foundation. The smell of the upturned earth was sharp in the damp cold. He hauled himself up out of the grave, looking over to Albtraum dolefully.

He stood, stepping over to carry him to the grave – but he stopped halfway there, sat at the grave's edge, still holding tightly to Albtraum. His body ached of despair, but he could not let him go, not now.

He wept, hard, dry sobs. "I am sorry, Albtraum," he whispered. "I should have protected you. I should never have left you..."

Brunhart carefully placed him in the grave, hesitating before reaching into his coat pocket, where he'd put the dog carving. They'd found it sitting atop the stack of books in Mianna's room, and she had given it back to Brunhart without a word.

He pressed it into Albtraum's hand and covered him with the shroud. "I hope you know how loved you are, my son. Always will be." He crawled back out again, and haltingly began to fill in the hollow in the earth again.

"You'll be with Anya now," he muttered. "I know she'll love you just as I do. She will take care of you."

Even that thought did not bring him any comfort.

It was dark by the time he'd finished, and his breath clouded in the air before him. His hands were numb and blistered.

Brunhart lingered there for another moment before trudging back inside the estate. He heard commotion from the kitchens, no doubt preparing the evening meal for the guards and servants. Bitterness filled him at the thought that anything existed outside the sphere of his grief, that anything could continue to be normal amid all this.

When he'd returned to his quarters, he sat at the edge of his bed in the dark, staring ahead at nothing. He did not sleep.

It was days later before Mianna emerged from her room.

No one was sure how to treat her, how to act. The servants hovered about her anxiously, attempting to anticipate her needs as she did not speak them. Renegade followed after her everywhere she went.

She sat in her office, staring at blank beginnings of letters that had to be written. Such was the way of things for nearly a week. Joaquin would come in from time to time, and neither of them spoke.

For the most part, she did not weep. When she did, it caught her unexpectedly. Eating porridge for breakfast, suddenly unable to swallow, overwhelmed by breathless, painful sobs. In the morning, she found herself curled into a tight ball, awakened by the sound of her own wailing. Sitting at the side of the grave, which was long covered over with snow, silent rivulets of tears streaming down her cheeks.

Other than minor daily activities, Sylva was in suspended animation. With the revolution all but called off and nervousness in the air following Raazenia's attack, no one was sure how to proceed. They were effectively right back where they had been before Albtraum had ever set foot in Sylva – but those who'd cared for him sported new holes in their hearts.

She largely ignored her business until Joaquin brought it to her attention. He had buried himself in work, but it seemed to provide only a small distraction to him.

"Mianna," he said as he delivered the stack of letters she'd received. "I'm afraid you're going to make some kind of decision on these matters, or at least call off all of your contracts for funds and supplies for the time being. I've written Malklith and Camlion to inform them of what happened, but I'm afraid the other matters require your attention specifically."

Mianna accepted them. "There's so many," she commented flatly.

"I'll help you," Joaquin said decidedly, and sat across from her at the desk, reading through each of the letters.

They discussed how to respond to each of them, and for a while Mianna was almost able to forget her pain, drifting in peaceful apathy as she dictated to Joaquin what to write and where to send it.

A soft knock at the door caught her attention, and she looked up. "Come in," she said flatly.

Glen opened the door. No longer was he the cheerful young man who'd bounded into her office to deliver the day's news – he seldom smiled anymore, his brow near always a furrowed line. "Your Majesty," he greeted carefully. "A messenger – from Raazenia."

Her heart leapt into her throat. Joaquin stared at her, awash with worry.

"...Bring them in," she ordered, and Glen nodded.

Her eyes widened slightly as a Shadran stepped into the room. His sleek, silvery hair was severely braided back, his eyes an icy blue. He was dressed as a messenger, and carried no weapons – not that she could see, anyhow.

He bowed deeply. "Your Majesty."

"Speak quickly. I find I am short on patience these days."

He seemed taken aback – as much as he could, with a face devoid of any feature but eyes. "As you wish. I bring a treaty of peace from Her Majesty, Queen Zyrashana – she is eager to begin a discussion with you as to how the Order will move forward from here."

"Is she, now?" Mianna stood and snatched the parchment he held out to her, and looked it over. Her eyes danced over the words – *alliance – since the death of my brother – let this lie in the past.*

Joaquin looked to her expectantly. The Shadran stood like a statue before her.

She gave one last cursory glance over the parchment, scoffed – and tossed it into the fire.

She leaned forward over the desk, her gaze hard as a blade and the Shadran withering under it despite his attempts to stay stoic.

“Tell Her Majesty, Queen Zyrashana,” she murmured, low and dangerous, “that the war has only just begun.”

Made in the USA
Columbia, SC
21 February 2021

32864993R00371